Our Song

Memento Mori

OTHER BOOKS BY PG LENGSFELDER

FICTION
Beautiful to the Bone

NONFICTION
Filthy Rich and Other Non-Profit Fantasies (co-author)
Non-Profit Piggy Goes to Market

Our Song

Memento Mori

A NOVEL

PG LENGSFELDER

WOODSMOKE PUBLISHING

Boulder, Colorado

Woodsmoke Publishing
Colorado, United States

www.WoodsmokePublishing.com

Publisher's Note: This is a work of fiction. Names, characters, places,
and incidents are a product of the author's imagination. Locales and
public names are sometimes used for atmospheric purposes. Any resemblance to actual people, living or dead, or to businesses, companies,
events, institutions, or locales is completely coincidental.

Cover and interior design by BookDesigners.com

Our Song, Memento Mori/ PG Lengsfelder. – 1st edition
ISBN 978-0-9972513-3-3 (Paperback edition)
ISBN 978-0-9972513-4-0 (eBook edition)

This book is dedicated to men and women firefighters
who put their lives on the line for us daily.

And to Brooke & John, who shine through all the smoke.

TABLE OF CONTENTS

"Bound by wild desire
I fell into a ring of fire.
I went down, down, down
And the flames went higher"
Johnny Cash

CHAPTER I

Father Blu

From an early age, my twin brother Jory and I believed we were as much a part of nature as the mountains, the wind, the snakes and our dog Ataraxy. Jory named her. Ironic, considering how her face bent when a thunderstorm was on its way.

She was a rescue dog, a Husky mix with a creamy coat and sad, Harry Dean Stanton eyes. She foretold storms. And when she did, her face twisted and her teeth chattered. I held her tight to me as the darkness skulked over Dracut all the way north to the New Hampshire border. Then the sky turned evil—there was no other way to describe it. The wind rattled the screen door in the back, and dust devils clawed at the ground. And when lightening cracked the sky, stripping our backyard of color, Ataraxy became as electric as the storm, lost in the light, even though I still had hold of her. Jory spoke softly to her, reassuring her that everything would be alright.

. . .

Father Toll had summoned me once again, and despite the shaft of November light that scratched across his desk, decay hung in the room. Cold oozed from the furniture, walls, the carpet. Our Lady of Sorrows was like that.

"Ask yourself again why you stay in the priesthood." Father Toll slicked back his silver hair, still the leading man. He'd played his role long enough to simply sleepwalk through his lines. And as the leader of his nest, he cornered me with serpentine eyes.

"What else would I do?" I asked.

He placed his left hand on the desktop, then idly, crept to his favorite solid glass paperweight, the one with Saint Florian etched into it. "That wasn't the question, Father Bluterre. Do I need to repeat myself?"

"No, no," I said. "I understand the question." *His mornings started late; preening so time consuming.*

"I had hoped this Ducotty thing might be of benefit to you *and* his family," he continued. "An errand for God . . . 'Speak up for those who cannot speak for themselves, for the rights of all who are destitute.'" Father Toll's words of service and compassion often had the ring of a man striding to war rather than cultivating kindness. What was better, to say something I'd regret or say nothing, and wish I had? It was getting like that.

"Of course," I said.

"Well, then . . .?"

"I'm not doing enough. I lean on Him; I give everything over to Him. But still. . ."

"Have you learned more about this Ducotty fellow?" Father Toll rapped his finger against the desk. "Any signs of recovery?"

"I'm afraid not."

"I was told he was showing signs of coming out of it."

"No, sir."

His head canted; his condemnation palpable, even before he spoke. "Then you're probably right, you're not doing enough."

"It's not that I don't welcome saying Mass, hearing confessions, working in the chancery offices, but . . . "

"But what?" He lowered his head in challenge.

"I should be doing more," I said. "But I don't know what."

His lips curled, implying satisfaction. "Do you have too many responsibilities here? Maybe you should stop fussing around with the garden. We have others who can manage the heleniums and monkshood."

"No. No." *He was going to throw me out.* "I have faith my prayers are heard, Father. He'll see me through."

"He will. But in the meantime, maybe you'd be better off in another vocation—an insurance salesman, a mechanic, a funeral director. Whatever will bring you peace."

"Father Toll—"

"I'm not endeavoring to be cruel," he said. "But for a spiritual man, you've always seemed to lack faith."

"Father—"

"No, I mean it. Your travels within the church are becoming legendary. How long have you theoretically been in service to God, nine years?"

He knew full well.

"Eleven," I admitted.

"Eleven. Still, suffering is all around us. Perhaps you should be more concerned with the eschatological ramifications, for yourself and the planet. Men, women, children are drinking and drugging themselves out of awareness, or shopping to forget. Or relying on godless psychology. I stuck my neck out for you, Father, bringing you to New York, to this parish."

How surprised he would be, were I to lunge across his desk, knock him out of his high perch. "Yes, sir."

"Might be your last chance."

"Yes, sir."

"Don't squander it."

"No, sir."

He lay his palms on the desktop. "We'll all suffer until this city is cleansed. Until then, we must pray, we must tend to the congregation with love, humility, kindness, to moderate the suffering. Nothing more. And if you're not up to it—to accepting the suffering—then you're not made out for this parish, maybe not for the clergy at all. Many aren't."

"But we shouldn't judge," I offered. "Francis says so."

He didn't blink. He leaned toward me. "Just pray, follow canon."

"Strict guidelines." My mouth ahead of my brain.

His eyes narrowed. "You're on thin ice. Read Matthew again; we have permission to judge so long as it's done rightly."

Rightly? Mom rarely met my eyes after the accident.

"I need to do more than busy work and prayer!" I lowered my voice. "Not that I don't appreciate the opportunities here."

His jaw loosened. "What do you have in mind?"

"What?"

"You heard me. What about Sean Ducotty? Can't you do more for him? For his family?"

As always, his pursuit made so little sense. "You want me to spend so much time with him . . ."

"I do."

Why could he not see what was so obvious? "But he's . . ."

He leveled his supreme piety at me. "A child of God."

"Vegetated. Prayer seems . . ."

"What?"

"I need to do more than pray for him," I said. "Under the circumstances."

He smoothed back his hair again, contemplative and with the kind of satisfaction that begs for a mirror. "More than pray."

"Yes," I said.

"Good, it's about time. Okay. Then do that, get to it." He didn't ask me what that might entail. "I'll expect you to continue to visit him twice daily. I want reports."

I'll ready the obituary.

"Pray for his soul," Father Toll continued. "Don't let this Ducotty fellow die in sin. Hear his confession, if possible. Bring me in, if possible. And if not, lighten the family's burden by finding out *why* he put himself in this state. You understand?"

"Yes, sir."

"But be respectful. Do things quietly." He shifted gears. "You've got this other thing—your intemperance—under control?" He hoped to sanitize everything.

"Yes, Father."

"Then we're done. I have plenty of my own responsibilities ahead of me. Think about what I've said. And keep me apprised of Ducotty's condition."

A fool's errand.

• • •

"Excuse me, Father Bluterre," said the nurse." I need to feed Mr. Ducotty."

"Yes, of course."

She brushed by me, the scent of hand disinfectant following her. She hung over Sean Ducotty, changing his drip bag, cooing to him as if he could hear. "You comfortable, Duke?"

My collar pinched.

She fluffed his pillow; her attempt at compassion, I suspect. But tangible support or true comfort impossible for "Duke" Ducotty. She checked the dozens of tiny electrodes and tubes that bore into his face and scalp, feeding the shiny unidentifiable machines marshaled around him. Whether bound for heaven or hell, Ducotty's body would soon be food for worms, whatever she, or any of us, did.

CHAPTER 2

Duke

"Too bad." The woman's voice came from a distance, a blue and shifting shadow, checking a clipboard somewhere in space. "Only fifty-five," she said. "And his eyes, locked open like that, like a freakin' cadaver. . . spooky. He's alive but dead."

"He'll hear you." Another distant voice.

"Yeah, right. He's been here longer than I have. He's long gone. Like I said, a breathing cadaver."

Oh fuck, I'm alive.

"What do the doctors think?"

"Guillain-Barré. Akinetic mutism. Something like that, they're not sure."

"Brain dead."

"Yeah."

Hey, no, I'm here. I'm here!

The fluorescent light spread over me. The two interns, or whoever they were, disappeared into the white light, places I couldn't see.

I'd botched my suicide.

I tried to raise myself, but there was nothing to command my touch and nothing to launch my voice. Nothing . . .except Valerie's eyes, questioning. Locking me in. Marking my days. Valerie full of deceit. I loved her. I wanted it to work with us, more than anything. *More than anything.* Is love so impossible? But she was gone and I was there, wherever there was.

And then they started to file in, a line of doctors streaming in two-three times a day. My hospital room a kind of factory lab, the doctors probing for "neuronal firing," waiting for some revelatory pattern, lobbing guesses over my bed.

They fed me through a tube; a token exercise because several suggested death was imminent.

Did I still want to die? Shouldn't I, more than ever?

They checked my ventilator.

Had they found out what I'd done?

They medicated me to sleep, four hours a pop. In those drugged hours, Val came, half woman half moth; great ochre wings challenging the emptiness, with the grace of a flame and the will of a raptor, dragging me back into the light, into the fluorescent hospital room with the bleached shapes, that once again became doctors circling me.

A three-hour pause before the next dose could be administered.

She did this. No, I did this. But she had it coming.

They dripped medications into my cardiovascular system. They kept my heart pumping, not that it was *my* rhythm anymore. They jabbed the bottom of my feet, scraped my cheeks, abraded every pain and sensory receptor.

I didn't feel shit.

Everyone agreed with that assessment. They also agreed that my renal system functioned normally, piss poor consolation. They glanced at readouts above my head and sighed.

And the priest prayed at a distance, as if he could catch what I had: the bullet lodged in my brain. His were tedious visits, twice a day, day after day. He prayed clinging to his wooden cross. His hands mismatched, his eyes carrying defeat.

What was he doing there, bolstered by the gurney in the corner, and why? Well, *why* was apparent. I was a sinner. How would he save me given my condition? With the things I'd done?

The Father retreated from the doctors' discussions. I, of course, could not. They stood around my bed and one shot a beam of blinding light into my frozen eye.

"Nothing." The Korean doctor shrugged. He smelled of fish in the morning and sour coffee when he arrived in the late afternoon. He backed off my face—but only for a second—before leaning in again and lasering the other eye.

Except for those extreme moments, my senses seemed keener. I could smell Val. I could see the room without turning my head. Or perhaps it was all in my mind, what was left of it.

The Korean doctor pursed his lips. "Except for the occasional blip on the EEG, I see nothing more than we've seen these last six months. There's no brain function."

Six months!

"Hmm," said Doctor Kirschner, she of the magnificent chest. "And the tests?" She turned to an eager, curly-haired intern, a bulk of a kid. Yellow and red stains dotted his white tunic. Despite his Godzilla mouth, condiments must have routinely missed it.

He examined his clipboard. "Nothin', *nada*." He shook his head. "The cortical and subcortical areas lack activity of any sort."

Their expressions grim.

As the weeks progressed, I sensed that the doctors were irritated with me; their tongues pressing the inside of their teeth. Was it my confounding condition that pissed them off—was I gonna die any moment or remain static and vegetated—taking up their precious bed and their daily rounds?

"Worth removing the bullet?" The Bulk pulled an Almond Joy

from his pocket and tore at the wrapper with his teeth.

Dr. Kirschner viewed him with disfavor.

The Korean drummed his fingers on my IV stand. "Still too risky."

Kirschner studied my unresponsive face. "There's the outside chance it's Locked-In Syndrome."

Dr. Pak shook his head. "I think we'd know by now."

"Okay, then." She typed something on her electronic tablet.

"About that drink?" asked the Korean.

Kirschner lifted her head and sniffed. "That's it," she said, dismissing The Bulk. She turned to the Korean. "Dr. Pak, I told you. It's over." She snapped closed the tablet and left the room, waving Father Bluterre out of the hallway back into my well-lit crypt.

The Father shuffled wearily in, the Korean making a huffing sound as he walked out; his rejection all too recognizable.

Women!

Father Blu assumed his usual spot in the corner strangling the crucifix. A man in his sixties, I'd guess. Hair rough and turning gray. He bent his head. He began to pray.

I thought, *Give a man a match and he'll be warm for a day. Teach a man to build a fire and he'll be warm for a lifetime. Introduce man to religion and he'll die praying for warmth.*

But the Father stopped. He glanced at the clock, at its slow turning arc. I suspect he was questioning *how much longer?* How many more weeks? How many more days? How many more seconds . . . until his vigil would end?

He put on a pair of glasses. He crept close to me.

The flat, monotonous line of my EEG reflected in the lenses. I wondered, given my second chance, *Would I die—or worse, live?—* tubes keeping my doubt alive, never knowing for sure what I'd done to earn my heroism? Or what I'd done to warrant the eight twisted months of Valerie.

Her spoor hung in the air, haunting me still. The nurses and the doctors and Father Blu couldn't smell it. To them, the room was habitually caustic. But she was there, pointing at my sin. Watching my hell on earth. Commending my penance. Just me and Valerie, and the unanswered questions. With no way to answer them.

Father Blu would say my bullet was my sin. We both thought I was a sinner, but for different reasons.

CHAPTER 3

Father Blu

The electroencephalogram above Duke Ducotty's bed barely wavered; his eyes lacked horizon, his silence persisting. Each day a memento. Sometimes it's just too late, you need to move on. Enjoy what you can. Not likely I could ease his family's suffering, or deliver Father Toll's salvation. William James had it right: In spite of all our earthy fabrications, ultimately "The skull will grin at the banquet."

Behind me, someone cleared her throat. A chubby young black child, perhaps six, stood dwarfed by her elegant mother, a small bouquet of apricot carnations tightly gripped in the little girl's fingers.

"Father," asked the mother, palms on her daughter's shoulders, "would it be okay for Makayla to give Fireman Ducotty these flowers?"

"I'm sorry." I moved aside. "I'm sure it's okay."

"He saved my life," said the little girl. She stepped by me, walking uncertainly toward Duke. An ugly ridge of burned flesh scarred the nape of her neck, snaking down to her shoulder, disappearing beneath her sweater.

She stopped. Her sweet face contorted. She was overloaded by the sight of all those wires, hoses and tubes—especially those worming from Duke's mouth, nose, ears and manmade incisions. She looked back to her mother and me.

"It's okay," I said. She still didn't move, so I came forward and knelt next to her. I offered my hand. "Okay?"

She nodded and took it, and we walked the rest of the way together.

She placed the bouquet across Duke's lifeless hands. She looked at her mother, who assented. She gave Duke a small peck on his cheek before scampering back to her mom.

"We pray for him," said the mother. "He'll always be a hero to our family." She choked on the words. She kissed the top of Makayla's head. "How'd this happen?"

"We don't know," I said.

They stood there for a minute or two, watching Duke stare into space.

"We pray for him," the mother repeated as she directed her daughter out of the room.

With nothing but time to kill, I sipped my raspberry cough medicine, felt my shoulders dissolve, and prayed for Duke. If I didn't know better, I'd say Duke's eyes fixed on me. "So you're a hero," I said aloud, surprising myself. "Is there really such a thing? Well then, you have to come out of this." *Or what?*

Einstein would say I was exhibiting insanity. Nothing in Duke or in the room moved, except the clock. I wanted to slap him, to see his eyes blink. I needed a whiskey.

"You know what?" I said gathering myself for my nightly march back to Our Lady of Sorrows. *No one had come to pull his plug yet.* "God wants you here, I guess. I need a drink, I need to get Father Toll off my back; I need to do more than talk to myself and God. I need answers. Of the three, even with your sin, you may be the furthest from hell."

"Really." A doctor had wandered into the room. A redhead. She blenched at the sight of me, she made straight for Duke's bedside.

How much had she heard?

She wore her pressed, snow white lab coat with distinction, but it was completely overmatched by her freckles, her copper curls and luminescent green eyes.

I backed off to give her space. "No movement, as usual," I snorted.

"He'll rally." She patted his arm. "We have to have patience."

"Patience? It's been more than six months."

She turned briefly and gave me a puzzled expression. "Resolve," she added.

"You mean faith."

"No, I mean what I said."

"You think he can be saved?" I asked.

"*Saved?*"

"I don't mean because he's sinned, although . . . Life *is* sacred." I shrugged. "But what I mean is, you think he can come out of it? After all this time?"

Her face pinched and darkened. "You believe that? That he sinned? What are you doing here anyway? I didn't ask for you."

I'd been awake but asleep. "You're Duke's sister."

"And you're old school." Her cheeks grew taught. "Fifth Commandment. 'We're only stewards of our lives.' I've heard it before. But my brother's not going to hell, not the way he lived his life, is *still* living his life."

"I'm sorry. I heard you'd be coming. From out of state, right? The nurses wouldn't give me your number."

"Just go away."

"Perhaps he wasn't completely culpable—morally, I mean. Something was pressing on him."

"Father . . . ?"

"Bluterre. Jamie Bluterre." I waved at Duke. "It's a shame. Wouldn't he want to ask for forgiveness?"

"Who are you to provide a pardon?"

"I'd like to be of some comfort."

A bitter laugh. Her face corkscrewed. "God will decide—if in fact there is one—or my brother's own will. But not you, not The Church. What do you know about my brother?" She didn't wait for my response. "You can leave. My brother doesn't need your salvation. Go on, get out of here." She turned her back on me.

More than anything, I wanted to follow her demand, find a cozy place and a glass of something stiff. It might salvage the day. "He must have been suffering. That can diminish his responsibility."

"Just go."

"You're Charlene, right? Ducotty-Ryan."

She turned back to me. "*Really?*"

I spread my hands. *When did all this bargaining start?*

"Fine," she said. "It's Charli."

"Charli, I've been praying over your brother all week, and I—"

"What?"

"If any of the parishioners knew him I could ask them, but so far no one—."

"There's your answer. You can't do your job—God's work—and nothing divine is coming your way."

"You have mighty tough standards," I said.

"Do I? Well that's me."

"At some point your brother must have believed; he joined the congregation."

"He was mourning a dead friend, that's all."

"Tell me about Duke."

"Just go." She wouldn't look at me.

"I'd think you'd want to know." *Yet I'd become no better than Father Toll, unable to shake scripture: 'They promise freedom, but they themselves are slaves of corruption.'* "His nickname, Duke, for Ducotty, I suppose?"

She kissed his forehead. "Duke, for The Duke of Doo-Wop; a name given him at the firehouse."

"Was he a good fireman? Was he happy being a fireman?"

"My brother had—has—two loves, being a firefighter and music. He's a helluva fireman, a hero."

That again. "And the music?"

She gazed at him. "He's encyclopedic about music."

"How so?"

She never took her eyes off him. "You really want to know?"

"I do."

She dropped her chin; traveled inward for a moment. "Okay, all right. It started as a child with fifties doo-wop and rhythm and blues music; Mom and Dad listening to it." She paused to catch herself, as if her story was rooted in melancholy. "Anyway, he knows music, he loves it. Everything since the fifties and sixties. Even today, if it's music, he knows it. What does that have to do with anything?"

My mom was a clinical woman. Not tight, just precise. A scientist. "What does that have to do with anything?" she'd frequently ask. Not dismissively, but rather challenging my brother Jory and me to make a connection, one piece of information to another. Perhaps as a foil to our great grandfather's Mohawk legends.

"She just wants to keep you breathing in the present," Dad would say.

"What does that have to do with anything?" Charli repeated, eyes moist. I recognized her desolation. Despite Duke's shadow presence, her brother was kindred, and that without him another strand of her would vanish.

She heaved her exhaustion at me. "I've lived more than eight hundred miles from my brother for almost twenty years. Without my lab transferring me here last week, I'd still be miles from him. *I* had to call him—every three months."

"I'm sorry. But this isn't your fault."

She cradled her head in her hands, rubbed her eyes, and faced him again.

"Was Duke unhappy—the last time you spoke to him? Did he leave a note?"

"No."

"Why do you think he did it?"

Her whole body clenched again, all the way to her teeth. "Because you hope to qualify it, give him an out?"

"Not exactly," I said.

"Oh, I get it, you're going to earn your eternal place; you're hoping to be a hero like my brother." Her fingers dragged along the bed's railing, her nails bitten to the quick.

"Did he ever talk to you about the fires he fought?" I asked.

"No."

"Never?"

"No."

"Does that seem strange to you?"

She huffed. "No, my brother keeps most everything inside."

"How about a therapist?"

A chortle. "My brother? Not likely."

"His captain at the firehouse?"

"Said he never saw it coming." She faced me square. "Just leave us alone."

"Maybe you have other family in the area? He had friends?"

"He and I are the only family. And friends? I'm not familiar with any." Some small recognition passed over her eyes. "Maybe Winston."

"Winston?"

"Chuck Winston, his mentor from the fire department."

"Would that be okay with you, if I were to talk to this Chuck Winston?"

She closed her eyes, as if she was dealing with a child. "He was the first person I called."

"And?"

"He had no idea why Duke would do this."

"Can I talk to him?"

"I'm not in charge of your soul. If you're aching to find a loophole, go find it yourself. I just want my brother back. Now leave us alone."

CHAPTER 4

Duke

Valerie. Damn Valerie. We were on a plane from Miami. I was returning from a fire protection clinic, the latest applied research the NFPA puts on twice a year. The drinks and the carousing only went so far for me at those things. By the second evening I hid out in my hotel room watching *Rescue Me* reruns, ready to go home.

I'd barely closed my eyes when we hit turbulence. The first jolt opened them. The middle-aged woman next to me grabbed my forearm. Her face, bloodless. Her knuckles too, locked around the armrest. Then the crunch—a gruesome sound, like a large beer can crushed under boot—and the plane dropped. Passengers shrieked. Her eyes began swimming, ready to be sucked down a drain.

The captain came on to tell us (overly composed) that we had to return to the terminal and to stay buckled in. Whimpering broke out. You didn't have to be a genius to recognize death was near.

The woman groaned and began to tremble. She turned to me, deep fissures snaking from the corners of her eyes. *But those eyes:* a staggering mocha color, edged in waves of charcoal hair.

"Take my hand," I said. "Pretend we're old friends." I'd used the line once before with an elderly woman in one of the subway fires.

"No." She clutched my palm anyway, and held it tight. "We're lovers. New. I mean we've just begun."

What do you say to that?

"Okay?" Her eyes frantic. "Say you won't leave me. Tell me I'll still have time to be me."

The plane took another precipitous drop and our stomachs launched into our throats. We hurtled downward.

"I won't leave you," I said.

. . .

When we landed back in Miami they handed us overnight hotel vouchers. She clung to me as if we were still airborne. As I hailed a cab, she pressed her lips to my cheek. "Did we land or were we shot down?" She ran her fingers nervously up and down my arms. Her smell gathered around me, sharp and hazardous, very foreign, and disabling. I hadn't noticed it before.

I'd never had much success with the ladies, unless you count the librarian in Staten Island; she was smart, she was appropriate. I took photos of her, like the others. We spent most weekends together before she disappeared with the trucker.

But Val, she had me off balance. Or maybe it was my vertigo surfacing again. She had her arms around my neck and her odor overcame me, she insisted we have a drink together. *To celebrate,* she purred.

I was tired. I should have followed my instinct, but she was in my nose and on my tongue. "Just one," I said, her smell indisputable, tempting me to roll around in it like a dog rubbing profligately and uninhibitedly over a dead carcass.

"Isn't this lovely?" She sipped from her orange Tropical Sunset, a sweet rum concoction. Over its rim, her eyes, like polished chestnuts, promised more. My feet dug into the sand, a warm breeze rippled the tiki torches and swelled the palms. Fire and wind, never a good combo.

I gazed past them to the stars.

"Are you with me?" She reached for my hand, eyebrows knitted in worry and self-preservation.

Or she may have seen my fear.

A tiki halo backlit her hair. Merriment broke out of the darkness, a table closer to the shore, people comfortable with each other. The flames danced across her cheeks, the fire's light bobbing restlessly to the band's rhythm. "Are you with me?" she repeated.

"Yeah, sure."

"I love this song." She took another sip of her marigold liquid.

"'Jet Airliner.' The Steve Miller Band," I said.

She laughed. One of the few I ever heard from her. "Yes, I guess. Appropriate, don't you think? This could be our song."

Our song?! "So . . . what brought you to Miami?"

"I'm thinking it's you." Her lips, full and painted coral, parted into a small, ungraceful grin.

"No, really." I stretched my neck left and right.

"I don't mean to embarrass you." She reached again for me but I lifted my scotch. "Don't you believe in fate?" she asked. "Don't you think some things are meant to be?"

I mumbled something into my drink. The ice cubes cascaded down the glass onto my face. I tipped them back and wiped my sleeve across my wet cheek.

She inclined conspiratorially across the table. "You'll appreciate this: when a friend tries to fix me up with a date, I have a secret code with them."

"We're not on a date."

She sat up, poked at her grilled Mahi Mahi. "If I don't like the guy, I order steak, coleslaw, maybe a baked potato, dessert and at least a couple of drinks to get me through the evening."

"Hmm." The waitress passed by and I lifted my glass to indicate another.

"Me too," Valerie called to her, then went on. "But if I like the guy, I order light—fish, coleslaw, vegetables, that sort of thing. And I stick with one drink. No dessert. Oh, but don't get the wrong idea because I ordered another Sunset. I really like you."

"Well, I'm glad." I started to rise. "I'll get the check."

She looked hurt. "We just ordered another drink." She motioned for me to sit down. "Do you find me attractive?" She ran her fingers through her abundant hair. Soft lines gathered around her eyes, character I'm sure hadn't been there ten years earlier.

"I do." I dropped back down. The cut-glass tumbler gave me something to hold on to. I pressed my lips to it.

"But . . . ?"

"No buts, you're a very attractive woman," I said.

"But there's something, isn't there?" Her face instantly aged, as if she'd fallen from the forty or forty-five that I'd guessed, to ten years older.

"No, not at all. I'm just . . . " I sighed. "I'm not used to fast relationships."

"Well then . . ." She receded from me. "I'll prove myself to you."

With what appeared to be absentmindedness, she unfastened the second button on her blouse. I couldn't help exploring her cleavage and tan skin—only for an instant. But even in that moment I thought it was a strange thing for her to say. Later, I simply wanted the memory of that first date, of that firelight on her, to go away.

CHAPTER 5

Father Blu

After my busywork at the chancery, I spent a few hours online, reading archived accounts of firefighter bravery—an unusual number of them involving Duke and Duke's firehouse. The articles painted a grim portrait of death and near-death. Also of great heroism.

My brother Jory was the courageous one. His fearlessness propelled us everywhere. Like the time he and I snuck out to the Long Pond wetlands even though Mom forbid us to do so. We wanted to catch pike. We padded calf deep into the marsh, and while we're moving like wolves through the tall reeds, Jory sees it first, moving fast for my leg. A large copperhead. In one motion, his hand swung down, caught the snake by its tail and threw it high into the air, twisting and turning above the bulrushes until it landed breaking stalks about twenty feet away. It was that heavy.

If you believed the accounts, Duke had courage. And yet he'd lost it all. Over what? Are we only a blink away from vulnerability? A small refraction of light aligning our benefit or dragging us into darkness? That we never saw coming? Changing everything we knew, everything we believed?

The answers weren't going to come from my daily visits to

Duke's hospital room, no matter how insistent Father Toll was. I branched out.

"Thank you for seeing me, Chief Winston."

"Chuck. And I'm retired. I'm nobody's chief." He glanced at my attire. A quick inventory, I suppose; speculating how dogmatic I might be, something of which I wasn't entirely sure myself.

"Please sit, Father. Some water?"

"Thank you, no." The room had a comfy air, dark except for a light hung over his desk. The shelves and walls were cluttered with memorabilia—statues, awards, an oversized magnifying glass; a banjo, a collection of small handguns, and an autographed photo of Chief Winston standing with Hall of Fame football coach John Madden, next to Madden's famous motor coach, The Madden Cruiser.

He waved an unlit cigarette. "I'm trying to quit." An ashtray half full of smoked butts lay to his left, alongside an open pack of Camels. "Sometimes you win," he said acknowledging the butts. "Sometimes you lose."

"Yes," I said.

"You sound unsure. You recently been on the lower end of the seesaw, Father?"

"Did it sound that way? Sorry, no, not really. But I'd take that water after all."

He grabbed the pitcher and a glass. He filled it and handed it to me.

"Thanks."

"So . . . The Duke." He eased into his chair, light bouncing off his shiny pate, white tufts ringing his dome, reminiscent of a friar's tonsure. He played with the cigarette but didn't light it. He bent his head. "Apparently he got an even worse result than he'd hoped for." He must have seen the surprise and conflict on my face. "I'm sorry, Father. I'm sure you don't see it that way."

"Well, I understand."

"Yes, well, it makes little sense." He rested the Camel on the ashtray, then fidgeted with a paperclip, unbending it, re-forming it, throwing it back down onto his desk. His eyes gravitated back to the cigarette. A coffin nail, my dad called it.

"You were his only friend?" I asked.

"Friend, perhaps. More of an advisor. I was his battalion chief before my years as a fire marshal. It may sound egotistical, but I think he saw me as something of a father figure. You're aware that he lost his father early. And *only friend?* No."

I put the water glass down. "He has other friends in the department?"

"I'm not aware of any after Steiny."

"Steiny?"

"Yeah," Winston said. "Benny Stein."

"He's a firefighter too?"

"Was." The chief inspected his khakis and patted off the wrinkles.

"Retired?"

"Dead. Lost in the Harlem subway fire. Maybe you read about it."

I shook my head.

"A fearless man. A great firefighter. Could be funny too, when he wanted to be. Duke's only friend . . . that I'm conscious of." Winston closed his eyes and they stayed shut; I wasn't sure he'd open them again. As if he were changing locales and his body followed. When he finally reopened them, they radiated violence. "Some torcher started it; there's real scum out there. They need to be taken out." He picked up the cigarette, so tightly that it snapped in half. He tossed it back into the ashtray. He let go his vision. "Whether it was for money or ya-yas or to hide a crime, we never caught the sonuvabitch. It devastated The Duke."

"How long ago?"

"Two-three years. So hot it bent steel girders. Steiny was trapped when the street above collapsed on him. Ironic."

"How so?"

"Duke almost lost his life not far from the same spot—above ground, but not far."

I persisted. "When was this?"

"Nine months, a year ago. I told him then, time for you to get out. They're gonna push you out soon anyway."

"Who's going to push him?"

"He's fifty-five, right? Old for a firefighter. He was gonna get forced out. Maybe a desk job, but that would never suit Duke. It's his one love."

"His job."

"It's more than a job to The Duke. It's his life. That's number one. It's his reason for being. And his music. He didn't make much time for anything else. In fact, made *no* time for anything *or* anybody else, as far I could tell. Maybe that changed. But last time I saw him he seemed happy the way he'd set it all up."

"Until now."

"Apparently, yeah."

"You said, 'It's more than a job to Duke.' What do you mean?"

"He had a strange relationship with fire. I guess we all do, us firefighters."

"But?"

"In some ways it consumed him. It's what he dedicated himself to."

"I've heard."

"He'd say, 'There's a rhythm to it'—to the fire. He could be poetic like that, some of the things he said. I once found him reading Kierkegaard. Stuff like that. But he was practical. His life was essentially about two things. He kept it *real* simple.

"I tried to convince him to go my route, to transition to fire marshal or the AIU—the Arson Investigation Unit. He certainly had the aptitude for it. He had no interest. I tried to get him out. He had no interest. He kept stuff to himself. And Steiny's death ate at him."

"How about women?" Definitely a Father Toll question. I rephrased. "Any partners in his life?"

"Never had time. Or hadn't much luck. Kinda shy with the ladies. But I don't think he was gay, if that's what you're thinking—I know that kinda thing can be touchy for you, Father. But I'd bet my pension on it."

"I don't know what to think," I said. "But I'm *not* real touchy about *those kind of things*, actually."

"Then why the interest?"

Father Toll's hounding. "I'm looking for anything."

"I got that, but why?"

"'Suicide is contrary to love for the living God.' It's a sin." That was no answer at all. "I want to understand—the church wants to understand—if he was fully responsible or even responsible at all for his action. What was his state of mind when he did this?"

Over the chief's shoulder, on the wall, the photo of Coach Madden and The Madden Cruiser pressed down on me. Not unlike the motor coach that veered into my brother Jory's car, killing him.

Chuck Winston gave me a long look before speaking. He rose and extended his hand. "Okay. If I can be of more help, give me a call. Because I'd like to understand too. But don't be too—excuse me for saying this, Father—inflexible in your thinking. We all have our weak points, don't you think?"

He tried to pick up a piece of the unlit cigarette, then let it go. There was something else Chief Winston wasn't telling me, just as I wasn't telling him, about my motive.

I remained seated. "What was Duke's weak point?"

He tarried, losing himself first in the unlit pieces of Camel then in the large magnifying glass hung on his wall.

"Chief?" I asked again.

"Maybe loneliness."

Yes. "That was Duke's provocation?"

"I didn't say he was angry."

"No? Then his incentive? What was he living for?"

"I told you," Winston said, "he loved his work."

"But not enough to fend off loneliness."

"Look, I don't know. I could be completely wrong." Winston opened his office door and ushered me out.

· · ·

From the moment I laid eyes on Cantor Jean Stein, her superior intellect shone through. Eyes clear, narrow streamlined face, beautiful but not in a traditional way; she exuded a bright, curious and sympathetic aura. No more than five foot, but very much alive in her late sixties.

"I appreciate you seeing me on such short notice, Cantor."

"I'm always happy to meet a man of God." She offered me a chair.

"I'm not sure I'm here on an ecclesiastical mission."

"Well, you're here." All of her was an invitation to live. For a woman eight years or so older than myself, she retained the sensuality of a younger woman.

"I-I came here to talk about Duke Ducotty."

"Oh." She caved just a little, as if I'd cuffed her.

"Sorry, is that okay?"

She took a breath. "Absolutely." She reorganized herself. "What can I tell you?"

"Your husband, Benny—"

"Benjamin."

"Yes, Benjamin. He and Duke Ducotty were very close."

"They were. Two firewalkers on their own bed of coals. I'm lucky I had tits."

I swallowed a laugh. "I'm sorry, I . . . "

"No, don't apologize for laughter; we need more of it. I wouldn't have said it if I hadn't meant it. They were like mismatched brothers."

"Well, ah, I'm sorry for your loss."

She nodded. "What are we to do? It's life." Her hands fanned around the office and out to the empty synagogue, then returned to her lap.

"Yes." Her office had the supple corners of a home. "I don't know if you've heard about Duke?"

"Yes, Chuck Winston called me at the time. You mentioned that you know Chuck."

"Only this afternoon for the first time," I conceded.

"So, what can I tell you?"

Where to begin? "I'm hoping to determine Duke's motivation for trying to kill himself."

"Not an easy thing to determine, a man's heart. Or his mind."

"No." I settled into the chair. "Were you acquainted with Duke personally or only through Benny—Benjamin?"

"Both."

"Why do you think he did this?"

"Duke and I haven't spoken in years. I think we talked once after Benjamin's death, maybe four months after the fire. It was probably me that called, probably out of some loyalty."

"To Benjamin?"

"To both. Ben wouldn't have survived as long as he did without Duke. I could probably say the same about Duke. Anyway, Duke didn't know what to say to me. What could he say?"

"Duke survived the fire and Benjamin didn't," I said.

"Yes." She glanced at her hands, open in her lap, as if willing herself to stay accessible.

"What can you tell me regarding Duke, something that only a close friend would know?"

She considered then said, "He's an odd man, Sean Ducotty. With strange habits and a narrow view of things."

"What kind of habits?"

"He read a lot of philosophers, but I'm not sure he ever found one that truly resonated for him. He played certain records over and over again. As if he was trying to embed them into his psyche. Not just into his head, into his whole body. "He came here for dinner once and pressed Ben and me to listen to *Outcast* three hundred times in succession. Right through dinner. The whole night."

"Don't know the song. Is that a group?"

"An obscure R&B tune; sixties, I think. Eddie and Ernie."

"Three hundred times."

"I can remember the lyrics to this day—well, the first verse and chorus: *Oh, what have I done, to be abused this way? I'm left out of everything, each and every day. I'm just an outcast, I don't know how long I'm gonna last. When will this all be over? Baby, come on and help me discover.*" She punctuated the thought with an assured dip of her head. "I think that says a lot about Duke."

"Despondent?" I said.

"Sort of." She sat back, a slightly muddled look, not at all consistent with the woman with whom I'd been sitting. She placed her arm across the top of her chair, grounding herself. "But he had a sense of humor that went with it."

"Told jokes?"

"No, kind of a trickster." Her eyes cleared and she was, once again, an unusually captivating woman.

"For instance?"

She searched her memory. Something shot into her head,

something she instantly rejected, frowning and shaking it off. "I can't think of one now. Ben didn't often share them with me. In fact, rarely. But I know Duke pulled them."

A moth trailed through the room and out.

"You said he had a narrow view."

"Yes," she continued. "He could show some compassion once he got to know you. It was his way of offering affection, but it was detached. Does that make any sense? Otherwise he didn't have much time for people. And if you got on the wrong side of him . . ."

"What?"

"Not pleasant. Which is why he and I had obstacles in our relationship after Ben died." Her jaw moved back and forth. "He and Ben had a terrible fight just before the subway fire that killed Ben."

"Over what?"

"I never knew. I asked Ben, but he just hung his head and said 'You don't want to know.'"

"Did Duke drink a lot? Do drugs? Anything like that?"

"Not that I'm aware. But there are so many mistakes available to us as humans. Anyway, Benjamin was his friend, not me. I just came along, occasionally, for the ride. I think Ben felt I should know the guy. I'm not sure I ever did."

"And Duke didn't call you after Ben died?"

"No. I had to pick up the phone."

"That seems strange, considering how close they were," I said. "What was it that connected Ben and Duke?"

"I can't speak for Duke, but for Ben it was their shared preoccupation with flame. There were times when I think they forgot I was at the table, they got so engrossed in dissecting fire. I don't get that wrapped up talking opera with my closest friends.

"Anyhow, Benjamin rarely shared much with respect to Duke or his relationship with him, except he clearly liked him. I mean, he was his best friend—not only in the department but out."

"Would Ben have had any friends who might have known Duke?"

"If there were, I don't know them."

"Did Duke have any girlfriends?"

"Don't know, but I doubt it. Anything else I can help you with regarding Duke?"

"No, thank you. For now," I said. "If you think of anything else . . . " But I couldn't help myself. "Would you like to have dinner with me sometime?"

"Well," she said, a wry smile crossing her lips, "I'd welcome that."

. . .

An hour later, my evening walk was blessed by a pre-Thanksgiving warm spell. I luxuriated in it until I descended into the basement of the Church of the Resurrection. Built in the mid-1800's and appropriately named for some, the church offered minimally more warmth than my parish. And privacy: a closed meeting where the questions were not about my garment, but about my addiction, the one I'd admitted to.

The meeting came to order, as it always did, promptly at 7:30 PM. We observed a moment of silence, followed by the Serenity Prayer. Next, excerpts from the Big Book and an oral history from a fifty-something Hispanic woman, Teresa, who had greeted me eleven months earlier when I'd first started coming, at the behest of Father Toll.

"Do you ever grieve?" she'd asked me at the time; a strange way to open a conversation. I'd dodged it, I don't remember how. But generally, she was a voluble woman, wide and cheery until she started talking about her sobriety. Despite her early introduction to me, she rarely spoke with me. Nor did most of the others, I assumed, because of my collar, though I did nothing myself to encourage conversation.

But Father Toll demanded I maintain my collar. "When you

strip yourself of your garments you manifest a weak sense of your identity as a priest." As if my collar kept me upright in my faith. More than ever I counted on God and my black raspberry tonic to prop up my determination.

Most of the meeting I drifted, not really wanting to be there but thinking I should, taking control of *something*. Notions and opinions of Duke and Charli, and now Chuck Winston and Jean Stein, interspersed with Teresa's soliloquy.

" . . . I needed to go beyond myself, to a higher power," Teresa said.

And this was where even Father Toll was at odds with my rehabilitation. In my attempt to reform myself, I was also—according to him—denying the validity of Revelation. Revelation with its vindictive language and calls for vengeance.

"The Supreme Power must be God, not some blind force," he said. "Not some intellectual trick." His conviction clear, pupils slit. "You understand this, of course." He wrapped his boney grip around my triceps and gave me a hard, admonitory squeeze.

"Yes," I said. Like a parrot.

"You and a higher power," Teresa continued, "whatever that is for you, are the only forces that can restore your sanity. Alcohol is a spiritual disorder. Until I fully understood that and declared that unequivocally, I was lost." She paused and made eye contact with those of us in the last rows. "And that is what we're talking about here, day after day, every day: yielding to the present. I fully understand my need to escape. I can't ever forget that. It's my admission every day for thirteen years, two weeks and three days." The group responded affirmatively, calling out to her in support.

I'd acknowledge long ago that I, too, wanted to escape. That I'd come repeatedly to God for that very purpose, thinking that by putting faith in Him would release me. And yet, it hadn't.

CHAPTER 6

Duke

Shirley, the matronly nurse with the butch cut and teeny tiny ears, scribbled down data from the blinking mechanical gods keeping me alive. Apparently no new answers there because she never bothered to look at me, not even a glance. Then left.

Not like Valerie . . . She kept an eye on me, and when she did . . . particles in me vibrated. It often felt like she was studying me, like the nurse, taking measurements. Aiming to get me into bed? Keep me out of bed? Testing me? She asked too many questions.

"When you were a boy, did you play a lot of sports? Did you get down in the mud with trucks? Play war games?"

"Sure," I said. "I did all those things." I thought on it. "Not a lot of sports."

It was our second date, back in New York, late October, the honey locust trees dripping with gold, fall on its way. She'd insisted. No woman had ever *insisted*, so I said yes. And there was her smell. Tangy, but somehow it fit me. Another sample couldn't hurt.

Sitting in Ripley's Tavern as it filled up, she peppered me. "Why not?"

"I didn't have that many friends—you know, to have teams."

She raised the glass, balanced it on her lower lip, peering over the table's candle. Her Scarlett Johansson teeth didn't match the rest of her face, maybe her eyes. But with all that hair she commanded a lot of space. The candle sparked. "But you obviously like teams, you like being on them. You're on a team in the firehouse, aren't you? That's important to you, isn't it?"

"Well. . ." It seemed a safe question. ". . . I do. I do like teams."

"You seem surprised."

"Probably, a little," I admitted.

"Why?"

"It's kind of an intuitive observation."

"And that surprises you?"

"Yeah."

Her lips opened, her tongue glistening in the light. "You liked playing with matches." She didn't smirk, she wasn't trying to be clever.

"You think because I'm a fireman . . . ?"

"Is it true?"

"Lots of kids play with matches when they're young," I said.

"It wasn't an accusation."

I think that was the first time I really scrutinized her.

She reached across the able and brushed my face with the back of her hand. "Teams. They're about trusting someone in a pinch, that has to feel . . . gratifying, just to know you're not alone." Her eyes were soft, her voice genuine. She reminded me of Miss Levine, the school psychologist.

I relaxed. "I never thought of it like that, but yeah, sure."

"It's a pretty macho thing to be, a fireman." She undressed me with her eyes, no longer any similarity to Miss Levine.

"Well, I don't think of it that way, *macho*." But coming from her, it warmed my chest, a long-forgotten warmth.

She put her elbows on the table and leaned toward me. "Well,

I do."

A Dinah Washington song sliced through the steady din of the tavern. The candle quivered.

Out of the blue, Tim appeared above us. "You ready for a—? Oh, hey . . . it's Sean freakin' Ducotty."

Talk about a buzzkill. "Tim, what're you doin' here?"

"What does it look like?" His mouth tight. He ran his hand over his waist apron and raised his note pad. "We can't all be firemen, can we?" He peered down at us. A wretched smile, yellow and blackened teeth; some dissolving at the gums. He twitched.

Valerie constricted.

"Well," I said tapping the menu, "this must be a good place to work, eh? Good tips, I mean."

"You gonna give me a good tip, Ducotty? Like the last time?" He had all the charm of a timber rattler.

"Sure, if you get us another drink." I patted my empty glass. I forced a smile.

"Oh, for a superhero like you, why the fuck not." He leered at Val.

I took her hand. "Valerie, another?"

"Yeah, Valerie," he said. "Ya gonna have another?"

She pulled away, nodded uneasily.

"Another mojito for the lady, and Johnnie Walker for me, Tim. Thanks."

"Yeah, thanks, thanks to you, Ducotty." He didn't move.

After several seconds, seconds that felt like hours, I said, "Well, we sure could use those drinks."

"Right, drinks for the white knight." He nodded and slithered off.

Valerie asked, "You gonna explain that?"

"Long story. Guy wasn't firefighter material; probably thinks some of us voted him down."

She pulled her jacket from the back of her chair. "I want to get out of here."

"Sorry about that," I said. "But we did order another round."

Her head dangled, unconvinced.

"He won't bother us, really."

The moment, so promising only minutes earlier, had been fractured. We rearranged ourselves in our seats several times before an older waitress brought us our drinks. Tim was nowhere to be seen, Valerie still uncertain. She finished off her first drink and started on the second. She kept glancing around.

"Where were we before we were so rudely interrupted?" I said, hoping to reset the mood.

She rubbed her forehead. "I don't remember."

"Well, I do." I'd somehow taken the lead.

"Can't we just leave?" she asked again.

"Ah, you okay if I go to the men's room first?"

"Can I come too?"

"Ah . . ."

"It was a joke." She sat back. "Sure, go ahead, I'll be alright."

I remember getting up, passing the kitchen, and heading for the can. Nothing else. Another blackout.

On my return, she looked slightly annoyed. "That was some piss, mister."

"What do you mean?"

She checked her cell phone. "Twenty minutes. Was there a line or were you setting up a late date?"

"No, of course not." I began to sit down.

"Get out!" A scream from the kitchen. "Everybody, get out!" Two sous chefs, our waitress and another, blasted through the swinging kitchen doors, dragging an inky black smudge with them.

"Fire!" Yelled our waitress. The half-packed room turned to her in unison. Some patrons jumped to their feet, knocking over chairs.

"Everyone," I called out, "stay calm. Walk slowly to the door. There's plenty of time and no reason to panic. Just be sure you've picked up all your things. Wait outside. It may be nothing." I grabbed our waitress as she rushed by. "What kind of fire?"

"The kind with flames." She wriggled free and headed for the door.

"Who's still in there?"

"Chef and Andy, the manager."

The shrill blitz of the fire alarm filled the restaurant. I pushed aside my chair, then an onrushing couple in business suits. I made my way to the kitchen, past the swinging doors, through the cloud of smoke and into the line, where the food meets the waiters. The chef and manager stood back surveying the flames leaping off the large stove top.

I yelled. "I'm a firefighter. What's the source of the fire?"

They looked at me. "Grease, we think. But the damn baking soda's over there." The manager pointed to the other side of the flames to a long, stainless steel shelf crammed with assorted jars, boxes, bags and a warped, jumbo-sized plastic bottle of olive oil.

The blaze already too large for baking soda. No fire extinguisher in sight. Sprinklers not responding. *You know this drill.* "Your biggest pots?" Hollering barely cut through the siren and the crackle of flames.

"What?"

"Where are your biggest pots?" I asked.

"Down there." The chef coughed. He waved again, to the other side of the fire. He pulled off his toque. "Shit."

In another minute the flames would be licking the ceiling. "What the fuck's wrong with your sprinklers?"

The two men shared a look.

"What?" I asked.

"I told you." Chef castigating the manager.

The manager sheepish. "We've been meaning to get to it. It's only been a day, maybe two."

"Jesus. You two, call nine-eleven and get out of here. And get me the fire extinguisher."

"Already called. You need to get out of here," said the manager. "You're not authorized."

"But he's right." The chef moved toward me.

"Stay back." I jumped the line and dove below the bonfire stove, slapping open the oversized cabinets. Needles of spitting grease showered the walls and floor.

"Geezus!" Any worse and I wouldn't be able to handle it.

I pulled the largest iron pots and a wok to the floor. Their impact hardly pierced the screeching alarm. Or the deafening roar of the flames. Chef tossed me a large glove pot holder. I reached for the burner control knobs. The heat rocketed, scathing my right arm. I quickly withdrew it. My arm hair completely seared off it, my skin a rose color. *Spreading too fast.* I stepped back. "How many burners are on?"

"Four of the six—the ones on the right."

"Large tongs? And where's the fucking extinguisher?" *I'd expected they'd have an extinguisher.*

"Tongs are there." Chef pointed to a set of hanging tools. "Extinguisher . . .?" He looked lost.

"I'm going to make sure everyone's out," said the manager. "And you two should get out of here. You're fucking crazy. Fire engines'll be here soon."

I threaded the long tongs through the flames and twisted off the first of the burners. Then the second. The tongs started to blister, the heat traveling through the glove, roasting my hands, then igniting the glove as I peeled it off. I grabbed my hand. I hadn't planned on that kind of pain. "Shit!" The glowing tongs hit the rubber matting below, sticking upright, glued to it, like a sinister Francis Bacon sculpture.

"We oughta get out of here," called the chef.

The shelf above the stove began to bow. Everything on it, including the remaining olive oil, crashed into the heart of the flames. The inferno bloomed higher, voracious. Seedling flares scattered along the floor. The chef stomped on them. *It was getting out of control.*

And fuck, my hand! I dumped the largest pot upside down on the first stove top, hoping to smother its oxygen. Chef handed me a second large pot. I took it in both hands. My right was numb. I fumbled the pot, then dropped it onto the second stove top. Around its edges, flames still climbed upwards, flattening horizontally along the ceiling. *This wasn't a good idea.*

"You better get out," I said. The room's temperature frenzied above a hundred—getting harder to breathe.

Chef took the wok cover, came up beside me and tossed it onto the third stove top. Then tried to pull me away.

"One more," I said. "Where's your fire extinguisher?"

"That'll contaminate everything."

"You'll still have a kitchen."

"But . . ."

"Where is it?" I screamed.

"Behind." He waved at the serving line. "Behind the pass."

"Where?"

"Turn around, behind you, in the corner."

I ran to it, pulled it off its bracket. Flames strafed across the room, knocking Chef down. I yelled at him. "Get out." He was dazed. I checked the extinguisher. It could handle Class B. "Get out."

"No."

"Then stand back. Cover your mouth and eyes." I sprayed. I sprayed again. Till the pale, yellow powder set off small surges of vapor then suffocated the remaining fire.

· · ·

After I packed my hand in ice and the fire truck arrived, I exchanged pleasantries with a couple of the crew. The tavern's manager thanked me, and I waved off the paramedics. Valerie slipped her arm around mine and we walked into Washington Square.

"You're sure your hands are okay?"

"I've had much worse. I'm fine."

"You're as advertised." She'd regained her admiring stare.

"Excuse me?"

"You *are* macho." She snuggled closer.

"Just doing what I do best."

A small jazz combo had set up in the square. A few people were dancing to it. The top of a trashcan had been removed and several people were warming their hands over the small fire that had been set in it. Sparks capered above it. I thought about interceding, but it really wasn't a threat. Besides, she tugged me down onto a bench, then brooded. "What happened in that kitchen?"

"Don't know. Looked like someone left olive oil too close to the heat."

"You'd think the kitchen staff would be smarter than that."

"Well, it happens," I said.

She saw me drift away for a second. "What?"

"Just wondering . . ."

"About?"

"Tim. He's an angry guy. Maybe when I was in the bathroom . . . Someone who's conversant with that kitchen could get in and out very fast and set up the olive oil."

"Yeah, well I don't think it was him." She shifted, ill at ease.

"Why not?"

"Because the whole time you were away, he watched me from the other side of the room. Creepy. He wasn't out of my sight more than two minutes, and only when he went to the bar, not toward the kitchen. But you think someone might have planned it?"

"I don't know, maybe not."

"Hmm. Well," she turned to look at the combo. "I was asking

about your favorite things growing up."

Here come the questions again. "Oh, I don't know." My clothes still reeked of smoke. I scratched at the bench. "No, of course I do. . . Music."

She turned back to me. "Music. Why?"

No one had ever asked me *why*. But a fair question. "It kept me company."

"Company." She lay her arm over the back of the bench, dropped her head to it and looked at me, sweet, almost innocent. "Company, yes; it comforted you."

"I think that's true."

She pressed her hand to my heart; I took it as a measure of solidarity. "Um," I said, "have you listened to Miles Davis? *Kind of Blue? Sketches of Spain?*"

"I don't think so."

"But you've heard his name: composer, played the trumpet?"

"Maybe."

Smoke wafted from the nearby fire, merging with my clothes, choosing me again. "Listen to his music sometime. Listen to every tune, the way he finds his own voice and offers a landscape for the other musicians in his band to find their voices. Every cut. Sometimes it works, sometimes it doesn't. But it's authentic and very present. Very precise."

"And comforting?"

"Yes, very comforting. And almost every one of the musicians that played with him ventured out with clearer, more personal voices in their own music. He never stopped searching for his true voice in any note; it kept changing, his music an exploration." Her big brown eyes were all mine. "It's a beautiful thing, that pure voice, that precision, that Miles gave us, note by note."

"Mmm, quite the poet."

"Me? Nah, I don't think so."

"Maybe, someday, you'll play Miles Davis for me," she said.

"Of course." The smoky air caught my throat, I coughed. *You committed before thinking*, asshole.

Her eyes and mouth softened. She tapped the bench. "Come closer. Was your dad a fireman? Come." She tilted her head. "Please."

Again, she had me at a disadvantage. I wanted to sit closer, parts of my body telling me so. But I was paralyzed—not the way it would come to pass in the hospital room—but suspicious, unsure of what I'd gotten myself into; it had been a while. But it felt encouraging.

"Duke? Tell me about your dad."

My dad. He wasn't a big man, but Mom said he'd been strong, before the tumor got him. "Acoustic neuroma" they called it, fast growing, she said. Pressed on his brain; the nerve from his inner ear to his brain, until he couldn't stand up. Until the last thing he cared about was Miles Davis or Fats Domino or The Beatles. Before it killed him. I was six.

"No, my dad was a cop," I said.

"Oh." Valerie cooed, sounding impressed, color flushing her cheeks. She patted the bench once more. "Please come here. You want to, don't you?" Her lips went crooked, and inviting.

Yes. No. Yes. I didn't want to think about my dad. Not at that moment. A good guy, but unlucky. Forced to retire. I didn't want that. Didn't want to think about his sickness—the dizziness, how he kept falling. They thought he was drunk, and they treated him that way. Later he'd black out completely, couldn't remember hours at a time.

She tugged me closer. She petted my arm. "Tell me about him."

"I'd rather not."

She laid her hand on mine, showing concern.

I removed it. The comparisons with my dad unnerving. The dizziness. The blacking out. Often runs in families. "Let's talk about something else."

"I'm sorry." She kissed my ear, fussed my hair; her scent as provocative as her touch. I let her massage my shoulders.

My arms snaked around her. I bent to where her neck met her collar bone. I settled into her, inhaling her, and the smoke. . .

Beyond the smoke, nothing more than a contour: Makayla, the little girl in the three-alarm East Village fire. Her weeping and then her wails seemed to come up through the floor and through her, till they burst into screams. Her parents prayed outside on the street with the rest of the crowd, counting on me to do my job, while my crew held everyone at bay. Flames consumed the sofa, snapping through the walls, crackling the tenement timber, engulfing the space. Me on my knees reaching out to the child. And then it disappeared, all of it. I blacked out.

That was the first time. Until the smoke filled my lungs and I began hacking. The cough woke me, sprawled less than six feet from the child, her braids on fire. No longer screaming. Eyes vacant. Paralyzed in fear. After that, I heard my partner calling from down the hall. I must have smothered her flames, and we were on the street, her burns, thank god, nasty but survivable, considering. But it was a warning. My first. And I said nothing. I did nothing.

"Duke? *Duke?*" Valerie stopped rubbing my shoulders.

I let go of her. "Yeah?" I sat up.

"What drove you to be a fireman?"

I reset. I took a deep, welcoming breath, filling my lungs with the fire's nectar, reawakening to its essence. "Best job in the world."

"How's that?"

I closed my eyes. I envisioned Makayla's parents, relief and tears in their eyes as I exited the building with their daughter clinging to my neck; the odd Swiss woman with the glass eye and her gentleman friend still addled from the subway fire, stiffly but earnestly hugging me as best they could; Dad and Mom and Charli and I, gathered around the fire pit upstate telling stories. My breathing steadied. "I'm completely at service."

"But aren't you afraid of fire?"

"I respect it. It can be dangerous. It can also be a place of safety, warmth, light, energy, rhythm."

She gave no visible indication that she'd digested what I'd said. "Of course, but what you have to do, *that's* dangerous. It's brave. You go into a space you know nothing about—like tonight—not knowing if you'll come out of it the same way you came in—or if you'll come out of it at all."

"You're embarrassing me," I said.

"No, I just think you're courageous."

"Okay, well look, I treat fire as an acquaintance, not an enemy."

She angled away from me. "Are you addicted to it?"

"No, that's a strange question. Listen, I understand fire, so no, I'm not afraid of it. And yes, I respect it, of course. But I'm here to help people, out of tough situations. Sometimes life-threatening ones. I'm very lucky, I'm not just selling them another *thing* that goes on a shelf in a closet and gathers dust."

Just above a whisper she said, "Okay, yes." Her eyes turned from mine, drew in, and to the dancing couples in the square.

I leaned forward to see her face. "So, you understand?"

"Uh hum."

"Great. So what do you do? Your job?"

She offered a tepid smile, she tapped the back of the bench. "I ask a lot of questions. I'm sorry." She gazed at the combo. They were playing King Pleasure's "Little Boy, Don't Get Scared."

"No, no, it's fine." I deliberated before I rested my fingers on her shoulder. She turned to me. I swallowed. I heard myself say, "Would you like to dance? I'm not very good but—"

"Yes, I'd like that. I'm not very good either. I tend to lead." She took my arm.

We zigzagged our way toward the music. But instead of luxuriating in her aroma as she hugged me closer, the question of danger and responsibility returned. Questions about me were circulating around the firehouse. My upcoming physical presented serious problems. Could I reliably pull people out of flames? Was I a liability to my fellow firefighters? I walked a thin line between maintaining my self-esteem and my alleged honorable dedication to service. A very thin line.

CHAPTER 7

Father Blu

Firehouse EO27 is an austere place, and in some ways as cold as Father Toll's office, but without the artifice, without the clutter. The cavernous stone two-story structure had been in service since the 1930s and carried the weight of all those years without reclamation. Korean War era canned rations were stacked along a wall next to three Geiger counters because, as Captain Hoyle explained, "We're about utility. I'm pretty sure even our coffee cups are the originals. C'mon with me."

He showed me up the stairs to the dormitory, a vast open room with some thirty beds, most not occupied, and a small corner room where five men were dealing cards.

"Oops, no, I guess we can't meet in here."

Four of the five men glanced up from their cards, apparent surprise or displeasure at seeing me, though I'd never seen any of them before. They quickly returned to their game, one with a frustrated expression as he slapped down his cards.

"Let's try this," the captain said, pointing me down the hallway. We passed several crew photos dating back to the 1930s and a photo of someone who looked very familiar.

I pointed to the photo trying to pin a name to it. "That's . . ."

"Steve Buscemi, the actor," said the captain. "He started here as a fireman. We're very proud of him."

"Wow."

Continuing down the poorly lit hall was another recognizable face, a yellowed, water-stained photo of Duke, much younger, propped against a fire truck. A small "Donations for Duke" box on the wall next to it. I stopped and pointed to that photo. "He's got a funny expression on his face."

"What does it look like to you?" Hoyle crossed his arms, rubbed his chin.

I pulled closer to the photo. "Well, he's standing by a fire truck—"

"A hook and ladder."

"A hook and ladder. And the look on his face . . .? I don't know . . ."

"Take a guess."

Despite his obvious youth, Duke's face had the twist of a gnarled tree. "Mortified?" I ventured.

Hoyle took a step toward me, a hint of cigar followed. "Very close. I'd say humiliated, but close enough."

"Why humiliated?"

"You notice where the ladder is located?"

"Appears to be downtown Manhattan," I said.

He nodded. "Anything else? I get that it's not a very wide shot." Hoyle rubbed his arms up and down, like a fly stroking himself.

"Appears like the truck—the hook and ladder—is parked *across* the street, on both curbs."

"Uh huh. He was a rookie, just coming off probie—probation—trying to impress everyone that he was ready to handle big man duties." Hoyle shook his head, reproachful, but smiling. "The captain that day, I'm told, decided Duke could drive the apparatus downtown, a great show of confidence. Duke, all puffed up, started to drive it out of the firehouse, then apparently realized he hadn't checked the past night's journal to see if the truck and tools were properly updated, loaded and ready to go. So he jumped out of the apparatus and ran into the station.

"When he got upstairs to the journal, his captain was hanging up the phone. 'Okay," said the captain into the phone, 'I'll look into that.' The captain turned to Duke and said something like, 'You're driving today aren't you?'

"'Yeah,' said Duke.

"And the captain said, 'You're in charge of the apparatus, aren't you?'

"'Yeah,' said Duke.

"Captain said, 'You might want to go check it. Dispatch got a call that it's rolling down Broadway.'"

Hoyle clicked his tongue and snickered. "He'd forgotten to fasten the brake." Again, the captain shook his head. "Fifty to sixty feet of rolling tonnage."

"Whoa," I said. "Did anyone get hurt?"

"Luckily not." Hoyle pondered it a moment then waved me forward. "Come on."

He ushered me into a tiny office, more like a large closet without windows. He asked me to step in, moved the chair in front of his desk to allow us entry, shut the door, replaced the chair and offered me the seat as he squeezed behind his desk.

"Okay, now, what else would you like to know, Father?" He added, "Any improvement with Duke?"

"I'm afraid not."

"Sorry to hear that. He was a good firefighter. How can I help you?"

The room became palpably more claustrophobic. Who was I to

poke at a hero? "Did he screw up a lot?"

The captain examined the empty desktop, pinched at his mustache which appeared to be dyed. He was rationing his response. I thought, *Ah ha, maybe Duke's not so immaculate.*

"Not really, no. Like I said, he was a good fireman. A damn fine firefighter."

"Oh . . . So he was a hero?"

Rifts branched out across the captain's large forehead. "Everyone here is a hero."

If I was looking for a fellow imposter, it didn't appear to be Duke. "Of course. Did he have any friends here in the station, people he might have confided in?"

"You're still searching for clues to his suicide."

"His attempt, yes."

"Why? The cops and the parish priest came around shortly after Duke's attempt."

"Hopefully to ease his family's confusion," I said. "There're still so many questions."

"Might make it worse."

"Why do you say that?"

He waved me off. "Nothing."

"You had something in mind."

He clicked his teeth. "He kept to himself."

"Why might it make matters worse?"

"I don't know, people have secrets. I shouldn't have said anything."

"But you did."

He checked his watch, he folded his arms. "I'm running out of time."

"Tell me something exceptional about Duke."

"I don't know about *exceptional*." His mouth softened, an appreciative grin took over. "Okay. He had an odd sense of humor for such a quiet guy. Kind of wicked in a way, like he bottled up his emotions and it came out different. You can kind of see it in that photo back there."

"Different?"

"Well, you're aware that he worked a lot in the subways. And those fires, at least to me, can be the most oppressive. It takes a certain kind of mindset."

"I can imagine."

"Well, actually you can't. But the point, Father, is that in a fire-house, if there's something embarrassing about you, you can be sure the rest of the guys will remind you of that—regularly. Just like they reminded Duke, almost every day, about letting a fifty-foot long hook and ladder roll into a busy downtown street. But Duke, being a quiet guy, retaliated at others a different way . . . Like he processed his emotions into something else. 'State of the art suppression techniques.'" He laughed. "Sorry, insider joke, firefighter's jargon."

"How do you mean?"

"We had this guy in the station—I won't say who, but he was the same guy who took the photo of Duke after his rookie screwup. The guy's all puffed up being one of the first to buy one of those energy-efficient tin can hybrids that were coming out fifteen-twenty years ago.

"The guy struts around the station, all holier-than-thou, spouting off mile per gallon figures. And Duke gets this idea and vets it with his old buddy, Steiny. And while Steiny plays lookout for roughly two-three weeks, Duke sneaks out to that hybrid and keeps filling it with gas.

"And every day the guy with the car comes in more astonished and more stuffed with bluster. He says, 'I still haven't had to put even a gallon into my tank. This car is the most amazing car I've ever owned.' He pushes hard on the rest of us to buy one, every day, all the time. The guy never shuts up about his damn energy-efficient car or what losers we are for owning our gas-guzzlers. A real pain in the ass."

I hooted. "Kind of ingenious."

"Yeah, I think so. But there's more. After the third week, Duke starts syphoning gas *out* of the guy's car. Every day. The guy's filling his tank, sometimes two times a day. Once, it was three times. Duke was on it."

Captain Hoyle hugged his arms to his chest. "We kept asking the guy, 'How's the new car? Great mileage?' And the guy shut the fuck up—sorry, Father. The guy was miserable for weeks, until Duke decided to let it be."

"Was the guy mad when Duke told him?"

"Duke didn't tell him. Nobody told him. Some things you just let drift into the past." Captain Hoyle skipped his fingers over the desktop. "I should be getting back to work." He pushed away from his desk.

"Of course. But who was the guy with the car?"

Hoyle wagged his finger. "Uh-uh."

"Did Duke punk anyone else?"

"Sure."

"Want to tell me who?"

"No."

"Did he have enemies?"

"Maybe. I guess he could irritate some people, but I'm not aware of them." He stood up. "I hope I've been helpful. He didn't deserve this."

I squeezed away from the desk and into the hallway, Hoyle following me. "Is it worth looking at his locker?"

"It's been cleaned out for months. Wasn't much in there—shaving stuff, a clean shirt. Sent it all to his sister. No one's taken it over yet, superstition maybe. But I've always got a key, if you ever need to take a look."

"Did the cops test for traces of gunpowder in it?"

Captain Hoyle seemed surprised by the question. "Don't know, don't think so. I think they would have told me."

"Was Duke into guns?"

"Guns?" Hoyle lengthened his neck, beginning to find me a nuisance. "You mean handguns? Not that I'm aware. I'm into rifles, a few of us are. But I don't remember Duke showing any interest."

"Well, thanks, I appreciate your time. Okay if I talked to some of the other firemen?"

"Not anymore today, we're pretty busy. Another time. And, of course, it's up to the individual if he or she wants to talk to you."

"Naturally."

I stopped at Duke's donation box. "Is he getting a lot of donations?"

Hoyle cleared his throat. "No, he's not. And Father . . .?"

"Yes?"

"We're kind of a private society here in the firehouse. Keep that in mind."

CHAPTER 8

Duke

I'd made some lame excuse about the exam, about my sister coming into town; the second time I'd put the department doctor off. I was pretty sure it would be the last time he'd allow it. On the other hand, I could easily forget to mention the dizziness, or if he were to ask, simply deny it. But I could feel the department closing in, looking for excuses to retire me.

Tony S had mentioned that there was this young kid—*six-two and strong as an ox*—that the department was trying to slot in. "He can play second base, too." Tony S waited for me to say I was ready to step down. When I didn't, and the silence became unwieldy for both of us, Tony S changed the subject. "Ya heard about the City Hall Metro fire?"

"Heard something about it. Why?" I said.

"Dunno. I heard Conroy say it was another one of those suspect fires. Just wondered if you'd heard anything?"

"No, not really."

"Sure seems like somebody's gettin' their rocks off." He studied me. A big guy, dark Italian good looks, Tony S let his hair go longer than procedural. But no one called him on it, which pissed me off, and I'm sure he knew it. An ass, but a good fireman.

"I'll bet Arson's working on it," I said.

"Yeah, I guess." Mostly Tony S talked about the women he'd bedded. And he was graphic. The other guys ate it up. At first, it kind of intrigued me, but after a while it made me uncomfortable . . . and deprived. I often walked away from his literal blow-by-blow encounters; he must have noticed. He liked prodding me. "You ever see the woman on TV who set her bush on fire?"

"No. That's a real thing?"

"People do the dumbest shit for fame." He waited to see my reaction. I just shook my head in disbelief.

"Can I ask you something?" Tony S rested against the shelf of hose packs. "When you were in that East Village blaze, the one with the little girl grab—Makayla was it . . . ?"

"Yeah?"

"You were in there a long time."

"Yeah?" I feigned disinterest.

"I dunno, it seemed long for you to be in there. I thought you'd be out sooner."

"What's your point?" I said.

"Nothin', I was only wonderin'."

"Yeah, well, there were flashovers in the next apartment and hallway."

"Sure." He nodded. "O' course."

He turned and called to three guys settling around the poker table. "Hold a chair, I'm in." I returned to my headphones, to thoughts of Valerie, and to The Passions' 1959 hit:

There is nothing I wouldn't do,
Just to be with you.

. . .

Valerie, Date Number Three. She'd been steadfast on taking me to New Jersey to "Have some fun. One of the last races of the season." She was late picking me up, irritating the hell out of me. She dressed in a train engineer's stripped bib overalls, an engineer's cap, and no shirt, which seemed odd and inadvisable given the chill in the air, but which offered me an even greater view of her cleavage. She had her hair pulled to the side and looked even better than I'd remembered.

On arrival at the racetrack, through the ten-foot-high wire fencing, the last racecar, "Canned Heat," move into position. Its flaming orange lettering promised speed. The speakers around the racetrack came to life; barbed-wire dissonance flooded the stands. The announcer implored the crowd to trigger the race. In unison the horde began its count down. "Three, two, one."

The announcer bellowed, "Drivers start your engines."

The Camrys, Fords and Chevys roared, vibrating through the bottle of water I'd raised to my lips, and spiked into my heart. Even with foam rubber plugged into my ears, the sound was intolerable. Valerie's idea of fun.

"Geezus!" Valerie pushed away from the fence and me. She ran to a little boy, maybe four, who stood transfixed a few feet away. "What kind of mother are you?" Valerie cupped her palms around the child's ears and bared her teeth to the ostensible parent standing by the child. "Didn't you bring ear plugs for him?"

The young mother, a tall blonde in stripped Capri pants, grabbed her son. "Ain't none your business, lady."

"The fuck it isn't," yelled Val. "You want me to report you to Child Protective Services?"

"What the fuck?" Blondie looked ready to fight.

"Get out of here or I'll call the cops. And don't fucking come back here with your child unless his ears are protected. Unless, of course, you want to lose custody or have him go deaf at an early age."

"Fuck you," said the mother.

Valerie rose up demonic. "Get the fuck out of here, now." Val clinched her fist.

The mother, seeing it in Val's eyes, took a couple steps back.

"Now," Valerie repeated.

The blonde wavered, but only for a moment, before retreating to the exit, dragging her little boy and watching over her shoulder to make sure Valerie wasn't following. When she was far enough away, she gave Val the finger. I do believe Val had been ready to seriously kick ass, possibly more. It impressed and frightened me.

Valerie returned to my side. With the cars at the far end of the track I asked her," What was that about?"

"I'll tell you later." She looked once more to see that the mother and child were outside the gates heading for their car or truck. She swung her head in disgust. The roar of the racecars came around again obliterating any chance for further discussion.

"So?" I asked, when the race was over and we trooped back to the car, her face still flush from the excitement, the crowd moving as one in a steady stream to the parking lot. "You going to tell me what happened back there?"

"It was nothing." She could see I wasn't buying it, yet persisted in playing it down. "Really, no big deal."

"How come you never talk about yourself? Like when I ask what you do for a living."

"Is it important?"

"Well," I said, "if I'm going to get to know you, yeah."

She seemed to mull this over. "Okay, what would you like to know? But," she quickly added, "I think a little mystery is good for a relationship."

"What was that about?"

"I'm a counselor," she said.

"At a camp?"

"No." She chuckled. "A child counselor, a therapist."

"Really?" I never would have guessed.

"Is that so strange?"

My doubt, as little as it was, had twisted her face, made her irritable.

"No . . .I'm just uninformed about things like that. You're a psychiatrist?"

"Psychologist."

A psychologist. "In the city?"

Before she could answer, we ran almost head on into a man going in the opposite direction, struggling against the tide. Both the man and Valerie stood straight up upon seeing each other. He was tall, unusually thin with tortoise shell glasses. Stringy straw-colored hair fell in front of his dark green turtleneck and he wore a western bolo, silver and etched with a Native American symbol of some sort, which dangled from his neck.

The crowd continued around us, like water around a rock.

"Well, hi," he said, an awkward smile on his face. He squinted at me, questioning, then back to Valerie. "Who would've thought . . .?"

She'd turned white, tightened up. She gulped. "What're you doing here?"

His shoulders dropped and he smiled. "Nothing says I have to *stay* in Miami."

"Of course not."

He glanced at me as if she would introduce us but she did nothing of the sort. Instead, she took a half step in front of me, as if what she really hoped was that I'd disappear. An old boyfriend, I assumed.

She continued, "Didn't realize you were a stock car fan."

"Didn't realize you were one either." The skinny guy got bumped from behind.

She shifted from one foot to the other. She wasn't going to introduce me. I began to extend a hand to him, but she quickly ended the encounter. "Good to see you."

He peeked once more at me then faced her. "You too." He delayed for a moment, then slapped his hips. "Well, I've got to get back inside; left my jacket." And he was off doing his best to part the oncoming current with his gangly body.

"Let's go," she said, pulling at my arm. "I'm tired, I want to go home."

We drove back to the city in the red Nissan 370Z she'd rented, swerving in and out of traffic, at seventy MPH.

"How bout you slow down," I said and started to roll up the window.

"No, I want them open," she demanded. The cold night air swept over us, assaulting our eyes so we both were struggling through tears. She came up within a couple feet of a United Parcel truck. She put her weight on the pedal and yanked to the left.

"You angry about something?" I asked.

"You afraid of a little speed?" She hurtled toward a white van.

"I'd appreciate if you'd slow down."

She sniffed, tears running down her cheeks, and gunned it, blind to what was ahead in the right lane.

Neither of us said a word after that. I had no idea what she was thinking. All the way home she challenged every vehicle in front of us, her eyes clouded. It gave me pause. Plus, she hadn't introduced me to the skinny guy.

When we arrived at my apartment, I said, "Bye," and opened the car door, just thankful we hadn't become a statistic.

She wiped her eyes. "That's it?" She sulked.

Somewhat reluctantly, I bent closer and began to kiss her on the cheek. She put her palm against my chest, stopping me. "What's going on here? Do we have an attraction or not?"

I didn't want to make a big deal about her driving, or react jealously; it was a little early for that. Still, there was a warning there. Her scent drifted over me. "Definitely, yes," I said.

"Then mean it." She turned full face to me, lips parting, as if she were sucking me in, those mocha eyes half shut but locked on me. Her pungency tugged at me. I found her mouth, warm, almost sweet. Her tongue, large, pushed deep into mine, probing every corner until I was out of breath. As I pulled away, she grabbed the nape of my neck and drew me back in while at the same time running her hands along my thigh to my crotch. Her fingers idled there, rubbing me slowly, up and down. I grew; I moaned.

She let go abruptly and aligned herself behind the steering wheel.

A series of deep breaths later, I opened my eyes.

She pursed her lips. "Good," she said, her chestnut browns focused on the street ahead. "Till the next time."

I stepped out, feeling excruciatingly hard and massively manipulated. Too familiar.

She drove off.

CHAPTER 9

Father Blu

Captain Hoyle's admonition to be cautious with the firehouse fraternity—however insular it might be—seemed odd considering I was trying to help one of their own. Tip-toeing around my best (and possibly only) source of information would be downright wasteful. With a little raspberry medicine to calm me, I decided to test my chances.

Around 11PM I made my way back to the firehouse, suspecting there'd be little activity at that hour, most of the firemen and women asleep or at home. Those few awake and on duty would feel freer to talk to me with no one around.

Above the buildings, electricity whitewashed the night sky into day, promising *The Thunders*. To the Mohawk, the powerful storm spirits were to be respected and feared, something Jory and I understood intuitively from an early age.

The front vestibule of the firehouse opened into several dim truck bays. I wandered toward the bright station office. Its blinding blue light forced me to blink twice as I stepped in.

No one there. But the glass-enclosed space, with its outdated desk, chair and scattering of papers, resembled a dog-eared cockpit. Not a spot you'd want to hang out in all night. No place to hide.

"Can I help you?" Without seeing her behind me, the woman's physical presence drove me into the small office.

"I'm Father—"

"Yeah, I know." She was, maybe, twenty-four. Smooth, flawless skin. But a hard face, a stony temperament.

"I hoped I could ask you a question or two? About Sean Ducotty."

"See the captain."

"He said that it was up to the individual."

"Of course he did."

I reached out to her. "I'm Father Blu—"

"Look, you gonna push me for answers? That why you're here?"

"Well, I'd like—"

She snorted, she put her hands on her hips. "Okay. You see that hook and ladder?"

"Sure," I said. I was going to get another lesson in firefighter protocol.

"I'm gonna have you climb in that bucket."

"I don't understand."

She slapped her knee. "Exactly." She took my hand and directed me. "Now step into the bucket. You want to ask me a question, don't ya?"

"I'm not—what is this all about?" I said.

"Heckuva question. But until you get in . . ." At best, two firefighters could squeeze along the low railing. I thought she'd join me. "Go on," she insisted.

I stepped into the tight rectangular cage, feeling hemmed in, as if I was on trial.

"I want you to understand—we all want you to understand— what it's like, even in a small way. Give ya some experience. Maybe you'll leave us alone."

"I just have some questions," I repeated.

She secured the bucket gate. "You'll find a latch in there too." She pointed.

The large corrugated door on the fire station bay rattled open, chains scrapping along the walls. The hook and ladder rumbled to life. I hadn't noticed anyone in the cab. "Hey?" I said.

She walked along side as the truck pulled into the night, not far, and stopped. The firehouse door clanged closed behind us, and the bucket and I began to climb along the face of an empty office building. Distant car horns barked at each other. Lightning continued to illuminate the sky. An ambulance siren gave way to the truck's hydraulics, or whatever was lifting the ladder.

"Hey!"

The ladder groaned, its tremor surrounded me. Office windows started passing and sinking quickly below me. The cold night attacked the back of my neck. I pulled my jacket tighter.

She called to me from down below. "See that yellow strap? Put that on, grab a hold of something and don't move."

A wind slapped the side of my head and shoulders. Below, the few trees got smaller and the wind bent them, even where they were mostly protected. The basket hit a gust—almost knocked me off my feet. Wolves gathered in the wind, howling. Lightning tore open miles of sky.

"Wolf relies on control of his environment," Great Grandfather said. *"He appreciates the high vantage point."* But not me . . .

The yellow strap lay close enough. But when I tried to wrap it around my waist, I fumbled it. I reached again, bracing against the side, the thrum of the basket running up my arm. I grabbed the strap, stayed low and secured it with a click that I could barely hear as the wind became more vengeful. I looked up.

"Oh no!"

I'd passed the first rooftop, quickly climbing past floors of high-rise buildings. The wind grew ever-more malicious, plowing through the city canyons, bending the basket and the ladder, wailing as it jammed through the ladder's steel struts.

Despite the gale's force, I must have rocketed past eight-ten stories, rising rapidly, swaying more violently than ever. The sky flared. My stomach lost anchor and curdled. "I'm gonna be sick." The firefighter could no longer hear me.

"It's a TL, a turntable ladder. You're telescoping. Imagine if you're surrounded by flames, and they go up another hundred feet *above* you." Her voice came filtered and cracked through a small speaker. "What do you think so far?"

A headset! I fell to the floor reaching for it. I scrambled to put it on.

"Get me down."

Windows blurred, buildings flew by. Rocking to-and-fro, I clutched my stomach, but there was no stopping its attack. I must have been more than 100-feet in the air, with nothing more than the crossbar between me and a plunge into oblivion. The Thunders laughed.

"Please take me down." Yet, somehow, I knew I had it coming.

No response. Could they even hear me? I wouldn't look over the rail. Sludge burrowed up my chest into my mouth, burning it. I spit it out. I spit it again.

The basket stuttered and jolted to a stop. It wobbled side-to-side, the wind high and indifferent. We'd break in half. I closed my eyes. We circled several times. I pulled up to peer over the edge. I couldn't do it. I waited for breath. I looked up and over. The sky exploded with pure pearl light.

The motor coach struck me with a force that splintered me in millions of pieces.

And then I was back, the bucket swinging and staggering.

Fragments of me drifting in the air. On the street below, two specks looked up at me—one the young firefighter.

The wind shifted. Out of The Thunders' opaline blindness, a gargantuan moth appeared below and ascended swiftly toward me. Immense hazel wings passed over my shoulder, and disappeared beyond my head. My stomach spasmed. Liquid chunks exited my body. The wind blew them back in my face.

Down into the bucket, trembling, pooled in my own uncleanliness, I closed my eyes and prayed. The ladder revolved elliptically to the wind's whim.

Then cranked... and began to descend. "Oh, Lord, thank You."

Still, the basket and I shook in the squall. I clutched my knees in a fetal position. We dropped past steel and glass and brick. Blood rushed to my head. My body spasmed.

When I got to the ground, still shaking, the young firefighter said "Pretty cool, huh?" She opened the latched door. I groped my way down. I bent over, panting, my heart still palpitating. *I deserved this.*

"You seem a little wobbly. You don't smell so good either."

I held my stomach. "What were you thinking?"

"Is that your one question? Cause that's all you'll get from me. And then you better get the hell out of here—I'm being nice because of your religiosity."

I looked up at her. "One, why only one?"

"Because I say so. And like the captain said, it's up to me." She veered away. "Pee-yew, what'd you have for supper?"

"Okay." I spit the remaining vomit onto the concrete slab. "Let me catch my breath."

She pointed. "Out!"

"Okay, okay. You knew Duke?"

"I won't count that either. Yeah, of course. Start walking." She pointed to the exit.

"What can you tell me about him? Something that might explain his attempted suicide."

I slowed to hear her answer. She kept pointing to keep me moving.

"I tried once to connect with him," she said. "Told him I was going upstate for a camping trip and did he have any suggestions. I'd heard he'd spent time up there as a child. You know what he said?"

"What?"

"He said, 'Don't touch a dead timber rattler. They'll still bite you, their nervous systems remain active for some time after death.' That's the last time I tried to engage him; the guy was just weird. Now get out of here before I call the cops."

"Oh, come on."

"Out."

Somehow, I got several blocks. With my feet on the pavement, I began to readjust. I'm not sure if I ever felt so grateful to return to my undercroft. When I did, all I could muster was to wash the puke off myself, take a sip of my cough medicine, and go directly to bed. I tossed and turned for several hours before finally succumbing to my exhaustion. My dreams churned, one after another, harrowing flames licking at me. I was drawn to them, unable to pull away, unable to save myself.

. . .

I woke early, pasted in perspiration, scarcely able to move. Finally, at 8AM, feet firmly on the ground, my stomach memory still a gray green, I hiked three flights up to Margaret Stott's apartment.

By the second landing, the musty, once-grand building had overpowered the sweet fragrance of the tomato soup I'd brought her. Sealed tight since its inception in 1932 (a tarnished bronze plaque reminded me), the building suffered its history in the damp smell of its walls, staircases and worn marble steps. In its stillness, not unlike Duke's hospital room, hiding stories. I thought I might be sick again.

A dreary place, day or night, but its ashen-yellow light all she could afford, and barely that. It shared the dictum and drone of the seminary. What was it that Hemingway said? "The priest was good but dull. The wine was bad but not dull." A drink would settle my turgid stomach and ease my quaking body. But no.

Breathing heavily, I let myself in. The pong of her apartment even more oppressive than the hallway. It too promised the cold hand of death. And except for my footsteps, a startling lack of sound.

"Margaret," I called out, "I brought you some soup, your favorite."

A door banged in a nearby apartment; it echoed down the stairwell.

"Margaret?" *This is the day she's gone to the Mother of God. Perhaps merciful at 97.*

In the desolate living room there she was, slumped in her wheel-chair facing the window. "Margaret?"

She didn't turn around. "Would you like to live like this, Father?" Her chest clanged like trash cans set against each other, she coughed.

I put the soup on a side table and moved to face her. "You doing any better today?"

She didn't look up. "Would you, Father?"

"We've talked about this," I said. "I know it's hard. I'm hoping to find you someone—"

"What would you know about it, hour after hour, day after day? Someone? It can never be like it was. I had family; I had friends. I was once . . .desirable." She worked for the next breath. "I made good money at the Green Door." Her coughs intensified, a thick slimy sound that she eventually expressed into her hand, then reached out to me with it, a green-yellow mucous. Some of it still hanging from her chin.

"Hold on," I said reaching for my handkerchief, and strangling my repulsion. I wiped the glop into it and dried her hand and chin. "How 'bout some soup?"

I stepped into the small kitchen and opened the trash. The odor of soggy, mustard-colored diapers overtook the room. I dropped my handkerchief into the receptacle. Streaks of her effluent still stuck to my fingers. I turned on the faucet and, after a few seconds of clanking and spitting, oily water trickled out and I rinsed my hands.

Back in the living room, she began again. "I'm washed every third day, clothes changed for me every second day, wiped once a day. And thanks to you and Mrs. Kranepool, I get food most every day. But why're you making me live like this when every day you can walk away, and I never will?"

She was asking *that* question again. "I can't."

"No, you *won't*. And neither will that damn Mrs. Kranepool."

"It's against God's will. It's a sin." Auto responses that had out-lived their usefulness.

"You've become comfortable with small sins, haven't you, Father?"

"Margaret."

"I'm begging you to die."

'For all is vanity.' "How 'bout I take you outside today. It's brisk, but if we wrap you up good . . . "

"Won't change a thing."

"Fresh air. C'mon now, Margaret, have some soup. Then we'll wheel around the block, we can talk. You can tell me your stories." I opened the container and offered her a spoon.

"God doesn't know I'm here. My stories don't matter now. Damn you." She struck the container and spoon from my hand, showering the crimson soup over the wooden floor.

Ezekiel's 'Blood will be spilled in your streets.'

She began to sob uncontrollably. I kneaded her boney shoulders, wary of bruising her brittle frame. I bent my head to hers and held her like that for ten minutes or so, until her convulsions stopped and she fell asleep. I was of no use to her. Would Duke be any different?

...

Nothing had changed. I was hiding out in the open, just like I did in Madagascar, stopping for a few playful words with the children scavenging the trash bins, the flies congregating on the meat, the mud and raw sewage flowing through the streets. Meanwhile, I plied my trade with the white, entitled, tank-topped tourists safe behind their dark glasses, ogling my lustrous stones.

I waved cheerfully at the black, impoverished Malagasy-descended slaves—all the while bargaining with their French colonist masters. Then came Jory's death and the priesthood.

The cross and chain dangled from my fist, the crucifix above me. I bowed my head. Even with my voice low, the chapel reverberated with my words. I prayed for a censer's smoldering incense to lift my prayers to Heaven.

"Dear God, enlighten what's dark in me, mend what's broken in me, revive whatever peace and love has died in me. I cry out for all whose spirits feel broken. But if it's not your will, let it slip from my grasp and give me peace so I can release this burden."

Father Toll injected, "'For all those who exalt themselves will be humbled, and those who humble themselves will be exalted.'"

The cross slipped through my fingers clattering to the floor and skidding under the pew.

"I didn't mean to startle you." Father Toll rested against the stone wall partially obscured in shadow. He came into the light, walking toward me. "Devine guidance; I too was moved to pray in this moment. I'm so pleased to see you here, but I apologize for the interruption. I thought it proper for you to be aware that not only God was hearing your prayers. Shall I leave or can we pray together in silence?"

"I was just leaving." I reached for my cross but Father Toll, in the pew behind me, did the same and came up with it.

He ran his finger along the chain and scrutinized the cross in his palm. "I know things have been hard for you, and I apologize if I seem to make things harder. I'm not a man of much patience. And it's true that your past indiscretions rub me the wrong way. But I'm hoping to help you heal, and for you to help heal others." After more than a few interminable seconds, he handed the cross back to me.

"Thank you," I said.

He sat and bent his head as if to pray. But as I slid out, his head still down, he spoke to me, his tone, once again, characteristically uncompromising. "Mrs. Kranepool called."

He waited for me to respond.

I stopped in the aisle.

"She says you upset Mrs. Stott this morning. So much so, that Mrs. Stott doesn't want you coming around anymore."

"Father—"

"Mrs. Kranepool says she's never seen her so distraught. She agrees with Margaret Stott that your visits aren't productive. She asked if I could send someone else to pray with Mrs. Stott."

"Father—"

"It will happen sometimes, people at the end of their tether, though I trust you are always appropriate."

"She wants to die," I said.

"Then you must pray for her."

"I do."

"And taking her outside, that seems unusually risky given Mrs. Stott's shaky condition—pleurisy isn't it, among other things?"

"Yes, but—"

"Don't play God," he said.

"I was hoping to brighten her day."

"And possibly kill her."

Take a breath. "That wasn't my intention."

"Yet certainly a potential outcome."

When you know that your words mean nothing, and that, at best, you'll be struck down, you say nothing.

Father Toll recomposed himself. "There are others for whom you can do more. We can't know what God intends, but you can do more. Have you made progress with your inquiries into Mr. Ducotty's suicide attempt?"

"No, Father, I haven't."

"Sean Ducotty's sister must be suffering."

"Yes. I think she is."

"Perhaps you can do more. And then perhaps you can both find some peace in that resolution."

"I will try," I said. Peace, more and more elusive.

. . .

After work, it could have been a pleasant walk from the church to the little gem shop eight blocks away.

Considering my queasy ride the night before, the December evening settled in with an unlikely temperate breeze and the arrival of a large brown moth circling my head. Everything reminiscent of that improbable September evening in Madagascar, more than twelve years earlier, when out of the blue the humidity broke and the sky filled with thousands of sepia-tinted moths.

Only months before Jory's death.

I hadn't yet put on the collar; emeralds and tourmaline and other gems consumed my time, along with women. Always women. But those moths, that night, were unforgettable.

She was a funny young woman, with a face akin to the revered Madagascan lemur, extinct everywhere in the wild world, everywhere but Madagascar. Tiny, wide-eyed and curious, she watched the moths with alarm and surrender. She said, "Mr. Jamie, do you think it's angatra?

Her fear of the moths, phantoms left ignored.

We stopped everything we were doing in that little tanning shed. We'd just unwrapped our bodies, taken our hands and mouths off each other.

"Miss Lili, we won't ignore them. We'll give them our full attention." She put her arm against my neck and rubbed it. She was willing to be consumed by their power if that was their will. They were the exalted: the recently dead, those between life and death, "Gods on earth," souls searching and struggling for peace, homesick for old surroundings, looking for someone to pray for them.

Traditional Malagasy see God differently from Christians. Their dead are God's emissaries, intermediaries to the living with potent powers to affect their fortunes—for good or evil. More celebrated than the living, these dead are easily offended if neglected. You want to avoid the trouble these phantom emissaries can cause. The Malagasy conviction firm regarding that, mine not so much. At least, back then.

We watched for an hour until the last moth and its spectre departed.

"I have something for you and you must promise with it." She held her gift in a small elegant weaving of burnt umber, black and orange. When I reached for it, she pulled her hand back and repeated, "You must promise."

When I did, she unwrapped the Black Phantom quartz, placed it in my palm and curled my fingers around it. "You see its spirit?" she asked.

"Purportedly induces awareness of one's addictions."

"What is purportedly?"

"Believed to be."

"You must believe." She was as close to animal as I could wish for in a partner and she already knew that she would destroy me. Before I heard

the voices of her Masikoro *neighbors, she had kissed me and was gone. I never saw her again.*

It was also the first time I thought about serving, which—following Jory's death—led me to the priesthood.

And once more, phantoms were inhabiting my life.

The large copper-colored moth continued flittering above my head. Swiping at it didn't deter it from darting inches from my face or alter its persistence to follow me down the block. Margaret Stott or Duke already emissaries?

When I arrived at Pete's Gems, a sign posted on the door announced:

"Closed for family emergency.
Expect to return in a week.
Sorry for the inconvenience."

The moth hovered just out of reach then took off when a man with a long, disheveled, alabaster beard and white flyaway hair to his waist, intersected me as I drew closer to The Alibi saloon. He curtseyed majestically, evocative of a cloud-riding Christian God, or Father Time, or a drug dealer I once knew. With great deference, as a doorman to a palace might do, he welcomed me in.

I vacillated.

A chunky young woman, pretty with a nose ring, grinned at us and accepted his invitation. She stepped in front of me and with a wink, entered. Father Time stooped once more beckoning me in. The Alibi's subdued light held out hope, the salve of simple, anonymous, unambiguous conversations about nothing. That's what I was most thirsty for.

"Father. We haven't seen you in months." Buffalo the bartender—all 300 pounds of him—toweled off a mug. "What'll it be?"

I slid onto the stool. "Ginger beer."

The guy next to me sniggered.

Buffalo waited. "That's it, Father?"

"That's it," I said, determined to hold back my lust. Buffalo moved to his refrigerator to uncap the bottle. He placed it and a frosty mug in front of me.

"A little tame for this time o night," said the guy next to me, already well past his first libation. He swayed on the edge of his stool like a slowly orbiting satellite. A wiry guy in a cowboy shirt—one of those shirts with an embroidered yoke, this one black—and a scruffy mullet halfway down his neck. A bright yellow and black-stripped pizza delivery hat dangled from his back pocket. "How bout I buy you somethin' with more bite, Father? That's okay isn't it?"

My chest tensed. I could taste his offer on my tongue, but no. "Thanks, I'm good." I tapped the mug.

He stuck out his knobby hand and introduced himself. "Lyle Kind." He clinked my glass with his, and the aroma of his bourbon passed my nose.

"Kind?"

"Yes sir. Have ya heard my name before?"

"No, no I haven't . . ." His smile shifted gears, as if he'd *hoped* but wasn't surprised that I hadn't. "Should I?"

"No, not really." He regarded his bourbon. The pizza hat and the lines mapping his face gave him away. Short on cash and opportunities.

"You from around here?" I asked.

"These days, yeah. Hopin' to get a recordin' contract."

"You're a singer?"

"That's me." He took another belt and motioned for Buffalo to bring another.

"Country music?"

He laughed. "I guess it's pretty obvious." He pumped up a bit.

"Texas?"

"No. Minnesota. You should come see me play while I'm in town. Bring the rest of your congregation."

We both laughed. I couldn't imagine most of my congregation being able to make it to a music venue, least of all a country one. I pictured Duke, wondered if his tastes ran to country. I refrained thinking about the bourbon idling in the stranger's hand. "Where are you playing?"

Buffalo delivered the next tumbler of bourbon and Lyle finished what remained of his first drink. "Workin' on it. But if you give me your address, I'll make sure ya know when and where. Ya sure you don't want a real drink?"

"Sure."

"Ya like music, Father?"

"Some."

"To me it's everythin'. Don't know what I'd do without it." His rheumy eyes blinked several times; he tried to focus on me. "Kinda like you with religion, I'd guess."

"I guess."

"No disrespect meant, but those ceremonies in church—not just yours o course, mine was Lutheran all about powerlessness and death—they seem . . . kinda depressing and removed."

"Removed?"

He rocked forward and almost lost his balance, at the last minute grabbing the bar to steady himself. He coughed. He wiped his mouth.

"I dunno, there's somethin' about music that's closer to the source, ya know. At least to me, Father. Like it hits home; it keeps me alive." He thumped his fist to his chest. "It keeps me alive."

Apparently, Duke had that kind of passion for music.

"Father!" A crisply bearded young man crossed the room toward me, a knitted scarf slung loosely around his neck, his inflection dire. I'd seen him in the bar two or three times before, his slavishly bleached hair combed to the side and the under-sized bowler badging his arrogance. A loudmouth, and to my mind conspicuously antagonistic to anyone with a uniform.

"Father, come quick." He waved to me, urgent. Heads turned.

I swiveled away from the bar and followed him. "What is it?"

"Just come with me . . ." His voice cracked, he bordered on tears. "It's Esperanta. She's out of her mind, she's speaking in tongues."

I followed him through a doorway past a couple of pubescent girls murmuring and absently smoking cigarettes. I lost my breath struggling up the second flight of stairs.

"Come!"

He motioned me through a metal door into a vacant loft lit only by the enormous digital billboard on the building across the street, a giant revolving roulette wheel hawking a Las Vegas casino.

"There." He pointed to a large open window, almost floor-to-ceiling. The unseasonably warm air had begun to give way to the night. He pointed again. "Please!"

"On the fire escape?" I poked my head through the window, left then right. *Not* a fire escape. The pretty young women with the nose ring stood on the granite ledge. She bent over to view the street sixty feet below. The terror of the height and the night before, punched me back into the shadowed loft.

"Aren't you going to help her?" said the young man. "Something pithy from your book of fiction?"

I stepped back to the window, I peeked at her. She braced against the stone building's Victorian columns. "Talk me out of it."

"Come inside, we'll talk about it," I said. "You can tell me your story."

"No," she said. "Tell me what God says with respect to all this." She waved her arm across the cityscape and almost lost her footing.

I tried to reach for her. "Don't move."

"Will you come out to get me? And why?"

"You have so much more life ahead of you, no matter how bad things seem at this moment."

"So come get me."

The eighteen-inch ledge with the sixty-foot drop, dismantled my feet. Across the divide, the neon, three-story-high roulette wheel spun me out of my body, sedating me.

"Do something," said the young man, breaking my stupor.

I couldn't move. "Inch back, take my hand," I said to the girl.

She leaned into the stone. "So, you won't come get me?"

I looked once more at the plunge. The wind warned me. "Never mind," she said with a laugh. She shuffled rather steadily back to the window. "I didn't think so."

"What?"

"Never mind." She stepped by me and back into the loft.

"What?" It was as if I myself had been rescued from the ledge, thankful I hadn't been pressed to test my fear. I propped myself against the wall.

The young man took Esperanta's hand. "See," he said. They both laughed. They disappeared through the metal door, cavernous footsteps coasting away, mixing with their laughter, their scorn ringing in my ears. Was it true what Father Toll had said, that I lacked faith? Or are there limits to it?

CHAPTER 10

Duke

I decided not to call Valerie; she'd got me all hot then cold-hosed me down. Too confusing. I'd done just fine without a woman for years. I didn't need the mind games and aggravation. A month went by. She called.

"Want to come over?" She said, as if nothing weird had happened, as if a month of silence hadn't passed.

"Come over, to your place?" I said. "You've never even told me what part of town you live in."

"Why not, I'll make you dinner."

"I don't think so." Yet a whiff of her wild territory promised a welcome distraction from the cramped air of the station house and my apartment.

"I know you want to come over, Duke. I *know* you do. So why not make us both happy?"

I didn't respond.

"Someone told you about my cooking, didn't they? Okay, so I'm not Julia Child. But that story about my brisket and the bathwater is simply not true."

I had to laugh.

"So, you'll come?"

I imagined the possibilities. "O-okay."

. . .

After the five-floor walkup, the first thing I noticed about her attic apartment wasn't the premature Christmas lights draped haphazardly around the living room, or the feline odor, but its untidiness. Not dirty. Just unkempt or maybe perpetually unfinished; a half-completed pastel drawing of a cat sat on the windowsill gathering cobwebs; a mirror hanging over what appeared to be an ornamental, non-functioning fireplace, framed indecisively on two sides in weathered barn wood, the other sides framed in polished cherry wood. It hung at a cockeyed angle, as if she'd taken it off the wall and absentmindedly re-hung it. Or had closed a door so hard that it went crooked.

A dowdy braided rope rug sat under the coffee table, and by its side, contradicting it, a stylish Persian carpet of some sort. A small marbled black-and-white composition book leaned against the coffee table. The whole room a diorama from the schizophrenia school of design. And a litter box—not piled with cat shit, but surrounded by a large scattering of litter, as if she'd spilled it and hadn't bothered to sweep it up.

She noticed me wince at the mess. "Damn Catalona. She's like a teenage daughter. Sorry." She waved me in, both her hands covered in large railroad engineer gloves, already frantic. A timer started beeping.

"Shit," she yelled.

She ran to the oven. Smoke began to waft out.

"Son of a bitch!"

She opened the oven and pulled out a blackened loaf of bread.

"Mother fucker!"

She threw the bread onto the counter; its charcoaled bite crowded the room. She turned to a large pot on the stovetop, started rapidly stirring it, and brought the spoon to her lips promptly burning them.

"Fuck that's hot!"

One of the engineer gloves caught on the pot handle as she faced me, overturning the pot of tomato sauce. It hit the floor with an ear-splitting clang.

"Mother fucker!!"

Chef Tourette at work.

A large cat, a stripped tabby, came bounding into the room, stood in the puddle and started lapping at the sauce. "Catalona," she screamed. The cat paid her no mind.

I'd never been partial to cats. Most made me sneeze and most of them were either intrusive, like that one, or surly and standoffish. Valerie shoved the cat away and began mopping the sauce back into the pot with her railroad mitts. "Sorry, this will only take me a few minutes to reheat. We'll have dinner, more or less, as scheduled."

I wasn't sure if the *more or less* referred to what I could expect from dinner or the time she planned on serving it to me.

She went back to cooking. I continued drifting around her living room, the only calming presence her choice of music, a muted mix of Stan Getz, Steely Dan, Sade and Erykah Badu—that sort of thing. It smoothed away the chaotic physical space that seemed to scream *I can't finish what I start.* "You have some tasty music," I said.

"Ordered Spotify in your honor."

The tabby quickly reappeared, leapt onto the fireplace mantel, and proceeded to lick a small black and white vase, crudely hand-painted with the yin-yang symbol. The cat gave off a loud screech.

"Catalona, no," yelled Valerie. "Get down from there." She stomped into the living room; the cat jumped down and slinked off.

"There's a bottle of Johnnie Walker in that cabinet," she said pointing below the stereo. "That's your drink, isn't it?"

"Yeah, thanks. Thanks for noticing." The cat hair had started to obstruct my breathing; not much, but the cat and I weren't going to be friends.

As I stooped to get the bottle, Valerie pulled a small pipe and a box of wooden matches from the mantel. "Care for a toke?"

"No, I'm good." I lifted the Johnnie Walker and grabbed a tumbler.

"You okay if I smoke pot?"

"Hard for me to say *no* holding a fifth of Johnnie Walker."

She struck the match, paid no attention as the aroused molecules burst free, devoured the oxygen surrounding the match head, and turned a heavenly royal blue and amethyst. She was oblivious to how it mounted the carbon particles and consumed them in an orange tongue of fire. She was too busy sucking the flame to the pipe, too busy to notice its beauty.

She took two hits, and with the same match lit the two candles on the dining room table. Just before the flame burned her fingers, she blew it out, gently tapped the black and white vase and moved on.

I regained my breath.

"Catalona," I called to her. "That's an unusual name. Is there a story behind that?"

"No," she called back. "I just like the name. I'm a Creative. That's why I keep notes." She pointed to the composition notebook. Just below it, a knot of extension cords and Christmas lights met an overloaded socket.

"Your lights don't exactly look up to code," I said.

"You going to turn me in?"

"No, but in an old building like this I'd be careful."

No response.

Five minutes later she'd turned off the overhead lights, the cat had disappeared, and dinner was on the table: spaghetti, blackened garlic bread and homemade coleslaw—the woman loved her coleslaw. But even in that dim light I could remember where the sauce had been.

"Thank you for coming, Duke. I do hope to get to know you, to understand how you think. I don't meet guys like you."

"Guys like me?"

"You seem nice. You're not an asshole."

I prodded my spaghetti. "Thanks." I waited for her to say something more, anything. But when she didn't I added, "I'd like to meet your friends some time."

She cringed. "I don't have many, really, a lot of friends." She twirled pasta around her fork and, loading it into her mouth, ended that conversation. Couldn't say she was dainty.

And who was I to ask to meet her friends when I had none of my own? "So . . .tell me about your work as a child psychologist."

She brightened. "Kids are great."

"You work with all ages?"

"Well yes and no. I mostly work with younger children, ages four to about eleven. After that they've lost so much of their essence. They gradually realize the inevitability of death and they build up internal scars, scars that bind them."

"*That* bad?" I said.

She went on. "They get it from their parents, even the well-meaning ones, and from the society around them—all the agreed constructs, the characters we become. The child should be allowed to develop himself or herself, but that never happens. Just look around. Are any of us living our true essence?"

"Gee, I don't know."

"Kids start out all so different, each born with freedom to understand the world and how to live it in their individual way. It's like you said to me about Miles Davis; they're looking for their true voice."

"Some are gifted cellists, some imagine their toothbrush is haunted."

A microscopic smile. "Yes." Her face flattened. "But it doesn't happen very often; almost never. It's criminal what we do to our children, how we regiment them . . . and worse."

There, again, an underlying anger. But I thought of it as her passion rather than a warning sign. "Do you have any kids?"

"No. I don't think it was ever meant for me to be a mom. Things might have been different, I suppose. But now I get to care for many children, to see how they tick, to see early on the difference between young boys and girls, to see what throws them off and what helps get them back on track. At least I try."

"Commendable," I said.

"Well, like I said, I try."

"Where do you work?"

Her face suddenly dour. "That's private."

An uncomfortable silence ensued. Much like I'd had to do with my mother, I worked around the hot spot. "That's an unusual vase." I pointed to the mantel.

"It's an urn," she said, still stiff.

"Really?"

"My mom and dad. You know, their ashes. I'm hoping to get a biofeedback machine, hook it up to them. See what they're generating now. That's why I painted it like that, the fusion of the two cosmic forces."

"Hmm." I pushed my spaghetti left and right. I couldn't tell if she was kidding. "Kind of early for Christmas lights." The slapdash network of decorations, some dark or missing, blinked and cycled.

"Not early, year-round. Keeps me optimistic."

"Right."

When it became clear I wasn't going to eat much of my dinner, and without asking why, she suggested we retire to the couch in the living room.

"Tell me about fire." She snuggled under my arm and put her head on my shoulder. Tension dispersed, her aroma ambrosial.

I marinated in it. "What do you want to know?"

"How you *feel* about it. How you work with it. That sort of thing."

"You're very existential, aren't you?" My lips swept her hair; I inhaled.

"Like you, right? You understand fire. It's what drives you. It gives you meaning. It's a core component of your authenticity." She was back.

"Wow. . . Yeah, I think that's true," I said.

"So tell me."

"Can I have another drink?"

"Of course."

I poured myself another. After the first sip warmed my throat, I drained it completely, reveling in its sting. The glow came—a steady freight train from my chest to the back of my neck. My shoulders dropped down a few notches. "Anyone who works with fire, not only me, should keep two constants in mind."

"And they are . . .?"

"Fire is power. And fires can suck."

She gazed up at me with awe, she ran her tongue over her teeth. She nestled again into the crook of my shoulder. "Positive and negative," she whispered.

I pulled slightly from her and investigated her face, as striking as a flame, more beautiful than any face I'd ever seen. She smiled at me. I drew her close again. "The fires you see in the movies and TV, those are romanticized. There's smoke in real fires and you can't see where you're going. The heat, it's excruciating."

"And you never can be sure how it's going to end," she said, breathless, into my chest.

"Exactly."

Her fingers slipped to my belt and gently unbuckled it.

I swallowed.

She pulled my jeans and shorts down and proceeded to arouse me.

She ruled my breath, more rapid with each immaculate touch.

I gazed down at her.

Her thick mane, her full lips, her large brown eyes. She glanced up at me briefly with admiration, then back to my member.

She studied it, stroking it stiff.

After she'd watched and smelled and licked every cleft on it, she balanced me on the crest—left me just enough oxygen to ignite—and understanding me better than any woman ever had, brought me to completion.

All at once I couldn't breathe. I was back in the hospital room. Black all around, pressing down on me. The end, finally. My body simply giving up exactly as the doctors had predicted.

"Just die." The whisper came strained and muffled, vaguely familiar but far away.

He or she pressed harder. A scent. Smoky.

I wasn't dreaming, I was asphyxiating, I was going under. Deeper. Powerless. Vanishing.

Then a shuffle. The dim light of my hospital room leaked back. The pillow slipped away, I heard glass shattering, I grappled for breath.

A moment later, nurse Shirley was fidgeting with my tubes, my machines; no one else in sight.

"My," she said, "how'd this tube get loose? And glass on the floor . . .?" Then whistling. A Bee Gees tune I think. Like a dream.

CHAPTER II

Duke

Who'd want me dead? The brother Valerie had mentioned? What did she tell him, how could he know for sure what I'd done? A friend of hers? What friend? My mind so unreliable, so freakin' unreliable. But someone *was* out to finish me off . . .weren't they?

Fucking Valerie.

After the sex I couldn't get enough of her. I wanted to get inside that mind of hers, to decrypt it, to pleasure her too. But she remained hard to pin down—both figuratively and literally. Back then it never entered my mind that I would murder her. Or try to kill myself.

Late one afternoon, I showed up directly from the station house, a cabbage, a pumpkin pie and whipped cream to jumpstart the festivities. I'd tried to reach her by phone for days, leaving messages, but she didn't return my calls. So I decided *what the hell*.

I rang the buzzer a number of times without success. Just as I was to leave, one of her brownstone neighbors recognized me from my earlier visit. He nodded and held the door for me. I made it through the lobby and up the five flights.

At the top of the stairs I heard a low rumbling coming from inside her apartment. Not music. I knocked on her door. She didn't answer, I tried the knob. Surprise, it turned freely.

I might as well have stepped into a meat locker; the apartment freezing, colder than the December streets. Like an air conditioner on full blast. A small windstorm throttled through the flat, vibrating the walls.

I called out. "Valerie?"

No way she could hear me over that gale.

After wedging the groceries onto the kitchen counter next to a small stack of undersized composition notebooks, I moved down the hallway. The first door on the left, the bathroom; the door at all times closed, a room with its own mystique. Valerie forewarned "Always ask first before using." After which she'd check it thoroughly before allowing me entry. I assumed it was a *female thing*. Beyond the bathroom: no man's land, to which I'd never been invited.

Her damn cat rushed past me.

As a firefighter, I entered unfamiliar homes daily, but here I felt like an intruder. Also, needy. My growing fixation for her was taking up space. Not only physically, but psychologically. All the music and comfort I was used to in my head was suddenly squeezed aside to accommodate thoughts of her. I shouldn't have come uninvited, that's the thing.

I turned to go. Above the coil of wind, I heard her groan, as if ecstatically . . . or maybe she'd hurt herself. I hurried to the end of the hallway. "Val?" I said through the door. "Are you all right?"

"What! Who's that?"

"It's me, Duke. I knocked. Your door was unlocked."

"Duke?" She sounded aggravated, and jumpy. "Duke, come back later."

"Are you okay?"

"I'm fine, I'm just . . ."

A deep male voice intervened from inside the room. "V, not now; don't stop now!" The wind blowing from her room began to subside.

"Sorry, Jimmy, sweetheart. Sorry to cut you off. You okay? Sorry."

"You can't do that to me," he said. "That was—"

"*Jimmy!*" she said chiding him. "Gotta go. Tomorrow, alright?"

A beat. "Okay," he relented. "You bet, okay. Okay."

I considered leaving. She called to me. "Duke?"

My feelings were tangled. What was going on? I stepped away from the door, "I'm sorry, I shouldn't have just shown up."

"Wait," she said. "It's okay, you can come in."

My fear of what and who was beyond that door with her, bound me in place.

"Duke?" she said again.

"Yeah."

"Come."

My fixation with her outweighed everything else; I opened the door.

"Hi." She looked up at me, eyes clear and smiling. Those big coffee eyes.

She'd tied her locks into a bushy ponytail, her face dripping with sweat. Her bathing suit soaked through; her nipples and the curve of her hips fully defined. The room barren but for the contraption she sat on; some sort of rowing machine mounted with a digital panel and speaker. It continued to whirl away. She reached for a towel.

"I'm sorry," I said. "I'll come around later." No man in sight, only nondescript industrial carpeting and a closed closet door. I thought about flinging it open.

"No, now is good." She pivoted out of the machine. "I guess you caught me."

Who was in that closet?

"Come here." She waved me closer. "I stink, but you're gonna kiss me. I'm progressing."

I leaned in, tentative. Was she trying to divert my attention? She locked around me like an octopus. She sighed in my ear, "I've missed you." She began to pull me out of the room.

So why didn't you return my calls? Over her shoulder I checked the closet door.

She pressed against me and commanded me out of the room. She closed the door behind us and ran her salty tongue over my lips. If it was misdirection, it worked. Despite my agitation, I could also imagine she was drawing me—at long last—to her bed. My fingers rested on her waist, then crept up her body. She pushed them away and pointed me toward the living room. "I'll take a quick shower, okay? We can decide about dinner after I'm done. Get yourself a drink."

While she showered I wrestled with returning to her workout room and opening the closet. Who the hell was *Jimmy?* But if she caught me back there . . .

She came out in jeans and a Navy sweatshirt, her hair damp, full and unfurled. Pretty spectacular. "From your look, I see you approve," she said.

Tips jutted from her sweatshirt. "I think so."

She plunked herself down on the couch next to me. "So Mister Duke, you caught me in a secret."

Contain yourself. "What's that?"

"Erging. Rowing. I compete. That machine, that's an ergometer."

"Pretty techno," I said, waiting for the other shoe to drop.

"It can be digitally hooked up to anywhere in the world, to other indoor racers. I'm training for a world championship in Boston."

I couldn't hold it any longer. "Who was the guy?"

Her eyes tapered. "You're not gonna get jealous on me, are you?"

"No, not at all."

"Good. He's . . . he's a guy I train with." Her inflection clear: *Stop this line of questioning.*

"Okay. Fine." I bit my lip.

She wet hers; she didn't believe me.

"Since you've now invited me in," I said, "what shall we have for dinner?"

She looked at the kitchen counter. "I see you brought me cabbage and pumpkin pie."

"Food of the gods," I said with a flourish, hoping to change my mood.

"Terence McKenna. Thank you."

"Terence?"

She waved me off. "It's not important."

We ordered pizza and beer. Was Jimmy still captive in the closet, waiting for me to leave? Her arm rested on my shoulder; she studied my face. Her head tipped and she hinted a smile. "You're a good man," she said.

What could I say? "You're a good woman; the work you do." I relaxed.

We talked for hours, touching on movies—she was partial to old westerns, Robert Downey Jr., Bradley Cooper and Coen Brother films. We touched on food—she was good with burgers and Japanese food and, of course, coleslaw. We touched on her affinity for astrology and "select" poetry. ("I get bored easily.") That didn't surprise me. We talked about growing up—me in lower Manhattan and she in Iowa.

"Why'd you leave?" I asked.

"Iowa?"

"Yeah."

"I might as well have been one of the hams being processed and canned down the road." Her eyes drew a line in the air that dissolved just before she turned back to me. "It's a spacious place, Iowa, but I needed to get lost."

"How do you mean?"

"The town, my family."

"Tell me about your family." *All ash, incinerated by flame, bottled in the urn on her mantel.* "Were they farmers? Conservative?"

She clucked. "Not at all." She clamped down.

"That's it?"

After hesitating, she granted, "I'd like to see my brother in a year or two."

"Why wait that long? He still live in Iowa? I'd like to meet him sometime."

Her eyes drifted to the window. "Do you believe in love?" She straightened up, rigid, to underscore the generic, almost academic, intention in her voice and of her question.

"Only when my brain stops working," I said.

"You mean giving up control." Stated with the same detached affectation with which she'd fired off her initial question.

I sucked air. Unsure if I was being tested, and if so, for how long. Should I be encouraged or apprehensive? I felt both. *Okay,* "Depends how you use it."

"You mean how you use *love,* or the word?" Her mind in many places at once.

"The word. I love my sister, Charli."

"Anyone else?"

"No. How 'bout you?" I sunk back into the couch.

"I love a few people. I've loved a few."

"Tell me about them." Again, I wondered if Jimmy was still stuck in the closet. Had he heard our conversations?

"I don't want to," she said.

Fuck, not again! "Well, shit."

"Why shit?"

"Because you ask me questions all the time and I give you answers all the time. But when it's questions about you—anything personal—you're always side stepping."

She clutched the sofa. "You didn't want to discuss your dad." She sounded like a petulant teenager.

"One time," I said.

"This is *my* time."

"You sound pissy."

She stood up. "Pissy?"

I tried to calm myself. "Maybe if you were more open and organized in your thoughts you'd understand."

"What?"

I slapped the table. "I feel manipulated."

"That's bullshit."

"You realize, we could have a real relationship."

"What does that mean?"

"It means I don't like being played like a yo-yo. I need you to open the fuck up."

She spread her hands on those perfect hips. "The poet Delmore Schwartz says, 'Time is the school in which we learn, time is the fire in which we burn.'"

"Yeah, well, Jude Cole and Prince both say something like 'At the heart of the fire there's cold.'"

"What's that supposed to mean?"

I took a breath. "You know what it means. Look, you confuse me. I'm not sure what you want from me. I can't seem to get closer. I don't know if this is what you call a relationship?" I thought, again, about bringing up Jimmy.

She blinked. "We have a relationship," she said dripping with condescension. "But I haven't figured out what I want from you."

I coughed a laugh. "Well, it makes me pretty damn uncomfortable."

She drew away, very coolly. "That's too bad."

A firestorm swept through me. "Listen, it makes me *fucking* uncomfortable, okay?"

She settled into the coach, still cool, indifferent. "Then maybe you should leave, because it's all I've got right now."

"Really." I stared at her, indignant.

"Really." She started to reach for The New Yorker on the coffee table.

"Okay, then." I lifted off the sofa. "I guess I should've known better."

"I guess so," she said.

I strode to her door, threw it open. I didn't look back.

...

Dr. Pak cleared his throat. He and Dr. Kirschner clustered around my bed, forcing my sister backward. The priest bided his time in his usual corner by the gurney.

Pak pulled my eyelids open as wide as he could and trained his beacon into each eye. He let my eyelids retract. He smacked his lip, turned to Dr. Kirschner, and shook his head, a signal that she fully understood given the way her shoulders fell backward. She faced my sister. "Mrs. Ryan, your brother's been here, what, seven months? I'm afraid we're beyond any reasonable expectation."

"Reasonable?" my sister said.

"Maybe if there were signs, but historically, even if this was LIS—Locked-In Syndrome—we could evoke some response by now. The handful of EEG blips mean nothing."

Charli stepped forward about to say something. The doctor put up both hands to quiet her. "He has no means of producing speech, limb or facial movements; his pons undoubtedly damaged permanently. Even if we could find something, anything, remotely showing brain function, the quality of life of a LIS patient is usually so poor that it's not worth living. We recommend taking Sean off life support."

Holy shit! No, no. I'm still here! I feel loneliness, anger. My brain works. I can still smell fucking Valerie! I still ache with what I've done. Don't, don't pull the plug, not now.

The color left Charli's cheeks, Father Blu quickly by my sister's side. He rested a hand on her shoulder. "Don't let them do this."

She wrenched away from him, from all of us. I thought she'd walk out the door. But her shoulders softened and her face reflected—I don't know—an *opportunity*, perhaps, to let go?

Charli, no!

She turned to the doctors. "Is he suffering?"

"He doesn't seem to be at all conscious, so no," said Dr. Pak. "But is this a life?"

"It *is* a life," said Father Blu without hesitation. He held his wooden cross between both palms. "God would have taken him if He'd chosen to. But He hasn't. Not yet."

His eyes were soft, he waited for Charli to meet his. "I'm so sorry. This isn't a choice anyone but God should have to make."

I'm here, I'm here! I writhed helpless, without movement.

"About ninety percent die within four months." Dr. Kirschner suggesting, I suppose, that Charli had already been luckier than most. "He has, we'd guess, a two percent chance of continued survival."

"In a vegetated state," added Dr. Pak. "And any medical coverage you still have will soon run out. Your additional costs must already be prohibitive."

"Two percent?" Father Blu closed his eyes as if requesting divine guidance.

Charli watched him, eyes disoriented, unable to grasp the choices dealt her.

He opened his eyes and with great kindness said, "Do you believe he wants to see you again?"

"Yes," she said. She sighed. "Yes."

"Then two percent is all you need."

The man was truly a savior.

CHAPTER 12

Father Blu

After the affronted doctors departed, Charli slumped into the chair by Duke's bed, draped in fatigue. She began snoring within minutes. I didn't have the heart to wake her. I waited.

While I did, I pondered her change in direction. For the first time she seemed ready, almost wishful, to give up the fight, to let Duke die. She'd run out of gas much faster than I'd have guessed, considering how testy she'd been initially.

Then to be charitable, it occurred to me that she might have good reason to let him go—his suffering, her suffering, maybe an insurance policy. An awful thought, that last one, which appeared out of thin air, but I'd need to follow up on it.

"I've got an idea," I said when she finally stirred and opened her eyes, realizing too late that I'd pounced on her rather abruptly.

She rubbed her temples. "An idea?" Her shield already being raised.

"About Duke. How about music?"

"What about it?" she said.

"I'm not arguing with you."

"Then what?"

"Music. He loved it, right? Maybe if we pipe some of his favorite music into the room, he'll respond. I'm surprised the doctors didn't suggest it."

"They never asked what he loved, but I'm not sure. They've tried talking to him. They seem nervous introducing unauthorized stimuli. They mentioned the possibility of a catastrophic seizure."

"Yeah, well, I guess it's a chance, if they say so, but so is the other. They don't seem to have much hope. They're ready to force him out of here, you heard that."

She startled at my break from dogma. "No prayers?"

"They don't have to stop. It can be a two-prong approach. What do you want for your brother?"

She put her head in her hands, her elbows on her knees. "I don't know." Her whole body limp.

"You're a scientist, I get it; I'm peddling superstition and the doctors have reason on their side."

Without lifting her head she said, "Counts for something."

"Okay, soul takes a backseat. Divine intervention is archaic, right? But what I don't get is that their numbers aren't doing your brother any good either. Let's ask one of the doctors about trying music."

She checked the almost imperceptible rise of Duke's chest. She rubbed the back of her neck.

I tapped the gurney. "Let me see if I can track down Dr. Kirschner."

She summoned a weary, dismissive wave, sending me out of the room, to do whatever.

"Okay." Down the hallway I went, searching for the doctor or a nurse. In either direction, the walls were draped with red and white garlands, cardboard Christmas trees, angels and a menorah. But the only life in the dark passageway was a janitor, dressed completely in a two-piece turquoise jumpsuit. A thin African-American man with a near-white goatee, he tied his graying dreadlocks into a single ponytail.

"Excuse me," I said to the janitor.

He leaned on his broom, his eyes tranquil. He didn't respond until I stood right in front of him. "Excuse me, have you seen Dr. Kirschner?"

He gave me a quizzical expression and pulled an earplug from his right ear. "You talkin' to me?"

"Have you seen Dr. Kirschner around?"

"She the one with the large . . .?" He cupped his long, thin fingers in front of him.

"Yes, that's her."

"Not usually around this late at night."

He scratched his goatee. "That all?" He started to re-insert the earplug.

"The Korean doctor, Dr. Pak?"

"He long gone." Once again, he raised the earplug.

"Wait. Are you listening to music?"

"Does seem natural, don't it?"

I put a hand on his arm. "Would you be willing to do a man a favor?"

He stared at my hand. "This for you, Father, cause I'm not Catholic?"

"No. It's a patient, in there." I pointed down the hall. "You might do him some good."

"What am I gonna do? I ain't no doctor. Is it a cleanup?"

"What are you listening to?" I asked.

"Right now?"

I nodded.

"Smokey Robinson. You know who that is?"

I laughed. "Yes, I do. Will you come with me?" I motioned for him to follow. "What's your name?"

"Arthur. Arthur Bridges."

We turned into Duke's room.

"Charli, I'd like to introduce you to Arthur Bridges."

Her mouth dropped open. She stepped closer to Duke's bed and pressed his hand in hers, as if alarmed.

"Arthur has been listening to some music and I've asked him to share his earpiece with Duke, just briefly."

Charli held up her hand. "Where's Dr. Kirschner?"

"Gone for the night. Dr. Pak, too. Let's try it."

"I don't know about that," said Arthur, his fingers tightening around the broom and retracing his steps.

"Wait," I said.

Charli's face twitched. "I'm not sure."

"I only thought—if Arthur is willing—that we could do a little experiment." I pointed to the digital flat line rolling uneventfully above Duke's bed.

"I told you I ain't no doctor. I shouldn't be in here." Arthur again moving to the door.

"Maybe he's right." She didn't make eye contact with him.

"Hold on!" I stepped toward Arthur. "Can I borrow this? Just for a second?" I reached out for his earplugs and iPod.

"This is on you, Father," said Bridges. "It's not my business." He looked to Charli for acknowledgement. She looked away, again squeezing Duke's hands.

Given everything else I'd seen from the doctors, there was no guarantee they'd approve the idea. It was now or never. I lifted the earplugs ceremoniously. "Smokey Robinson, right?"

"And the Miracles," he added cautiously.

I held the earpiece to Duke's left ear. "How do I get this thing to start?"

Arthur motioned. "That button there."

Charli's eyes were wide, sea foam green like Madagascar

tsavorite, but filled with uncertainty. Was I playing God? I faced her straight on. "He *loves* music."

A murmur. "Yes."

I pressed the iPod. I pulled the earplug from Duke's ear for a second, to hear for myself if it was running. I listened. A slow staccato piano began plinking, followed by a single loping guitar. I returned the earpiece to Duke's ear.

Arthur leaned on his broom, forehead wrinkled, unhappy he'd gotten involved. He needed his iPod back.

Duke remained expressionless, his brain apparently not taking to the Motown, because his EEG stayed flat as if he were listening to a fifth straight hour of Eckhart Tolle.

I scratched my head. "You got any Temptations? Martha and the Vandellas? Something more upbeat?"

"Give me the damn iPod." Bridges motioned for me to pull it from Duke.

"This isn't working," said Charli, her fear still evident.

"Just hold on. Give it a second. Duke couldn't not like Smokey Robinson."

But above him, the line remained level.

Another thirty seconds went by. Charli lowered her head.

"Okay," I said. "Well, it was worth a try."

"What's that?" Bridges pointed to the electroencephalogram.

Duke's brain registered a shallow ripple on the chart.

"The Miracles," I said.

Charli leaned closer to it, her lips parted, her mouth opened. *Mety*, the Malagasy call it. Possibility.

. . .

Arthur reclaimed his iPod and made a quick retreat. I went searching for a doctor or nurse. But the first I found who rolled back the EEG and reviewed Duke's brain waves, was Dr. Pak early the next morning, shortly after my duties at the parish. "Doctor, he responded to music. That's what that blip represents."

"You don't know that," said the doctor. "You have made a very dangerous experiment. Against hospital protocol." He eyeballed Charli who—having slept all night in the room, in the chair—appeared disheveled. Her long copper curls spiked chaotically, her eyes dull, blue around the edges; a beautiful but beaten-down woman. "You should have checked with me or Dr. Kirschner. You may have caused irreparable damage."

"You've gotta be kidding," I said.

Charli on overload, closed her eyes.

"We'll have to start an inquiry," the doctor promised.

I threw my hands up. "Thank you." I smiled.

"What?" He looked to Charli for interpretation.

Charli sagged. I wondered how long it might be before Pak and the crew of lab coats again pushed Charli to remove Duke's life support. And they'd use me as part of the justification for it. They'd claim that I'd somehow made the situation worse, though I couldn't see how. More important, Arthur Bridges might get dragged under for his part. I checked the clock, I was late for the rectory.

Dr. Pak thrust his finger at me. "No more experimenting on my patient, you understand?" When I didn't move, didn't answer, he turned and stalked out of the room.

My tongue had grown gluey. Father Toll was likely to demand an explanation, too. Things were getting edgy. "Charli, would you mind if I hunt around Duke's apartment?"

Haggard, she handed me keys. "You're wasting your time. I don't understand why you're doing this, some holy crusade? I've already looked. But I guess I should thank you." A feeble smile.

"Maybe I'll have different eyes. What did the cops say?"

"The cops are done with it," she said. "They're pretty uninterested. Said I could do what I like. But I haven't had the nerve to clean it up yet. The blood."

"Well," I said, "at least we're making progress."

She lifted her head, and with overcast eyes watched Duke's brainwave roll steadily along its previous flat and uninterrupted path. "We are?"

Having raised her hopes, I'd taken on more obligation, and apparently more culpability.

CHAPTER 13

Father Blu

Duke's apartment had been unopened for months. The bottled air made me nervous, as if the depraved thoughts that had shoved the gun to his mouth were still there, hanging heavy, breathing from the edges of the room. As if his hospital room and his apartment shared the same phantoms.

His front door needed painting; otherwise it was a compact first floor apartment in the rear of the building, almost everything in its place. But impossible to miss was the small patch of blood on the wall next to the shelves of record albums, where Duke's blood but not the bullet had exited his skull. A new trickle of nausea soured my stomach. I turned away.

Between the living room and kitchen, where most people would have a small dining room table, there were additional, carefully organized crates of albums, a shelf of books (biographies on Sam Cooke, Bob Dylan and other musicians, manuals on fire investigation, and a scattering of books on philosophy. Also, one small photo album of women sleeping, each photo hand dated five to ten years in the past.). Above them on the wall, a signed photo of Boz Scaggs and Donald Fagen.

The room confirmed what I'd already been told. He was a complex and insular man whose music collection probably offered emotional security—a way to organize the world—or tethered him to a safer past. Or filled a void, perhaps the *loneliness* Chuck Winston had mentioned.

There was no weapon, probably in police custody.

Under a small set of barbells, I found a stack of credit card statements on the kitchen counter, possibly pulled by Charli. They reflected a rather conservative and mostly unvarying monthly use of the card—for a cell phone, groceries, internet provider and the occasional clothes purchase, a one-time rental car, and a pair of concert tickets of some sort. Nothing that could be traced or that indicated an unusual variance of lifestyle. If the summaries told me anything, it was that the guy didn't get out much. But if he'd bought two concert tickets, who'd he go with?

My fingers ran along the wall of albums and CDs. A number of them had been pulled out from the rest as if Duke had planned on playing them. There weren't any scattered around, and none were on the turntable.

After walking through the apartment several times and noticing how clean and ordered it was, I returned to the stereo. The display on the CD player—easy to miss with a CD case wedged up next to it—gave off a pinprick of auburn light. The CD case, *American Myth* by a guy named Jackie Greene, was empty.

Why hadn't Duke put that CD away before pulling the trigger? Perhaps he'd been listening to it when he had. I'd have to ask Charli if the cops had found the stereo on when they found him sprawled on the floor. Or maybe they'd simply missed it.

I picked up the CD cover. The artist peeked from behind his right arm, smoke of some kind curling across the barren walls of a room. When I turned it over, one of the fifteen songs had been circled with a felt marker. I clicked on the cut, "I'm So Gone."

The tune opened with bongos and a strumming acoustic guitar, followed by a pulsing icy electric one that surged into the room with a bitter country-tinged vocal:

> *I'm not going to be civil*
> *I'm not gonna watch my tongue or what I say*
> *I'm gonna dance with the devil*
> *Gonna shovel out dirt for a stiff and shallow grave*

> *Oh, now nothing is sacred*
> *And it won't be long before one of us is dead*

Duke's suicide note? Misdeed or heartbreak often brings on that kind of despair, that kind of outrage. And from my own experience, there's no easy antidote.

I listened to the song several more times before turning off the stereo and surveying the room again for additional clues. Even silent, the tune plagued me.

I proceeded to examine the bedroom and hallway closet, thinking I might find an article of woman's clothing or bullets or I'm not sure what—something to pinpoint Duke's disillusionment or his self-condemnation. Things with which I should be accustomed. Anything to move my investigation forward. I found nothing unusual.

But there, in the kitchen, in a lower cabinet: almost 750 milliliters of amber Johnnie Walker, glowing like a garnet. A memorial to my imperfection. *What if my actions had wearied Charli to capitulate to Dr. Pak? Allowed him to terminate Duke's life? Or played into Charli's decision to reap the insurance rewards? One last monumental failure? Oh, Jory, I'm so sorry.*

I closed my eyes and sat on my heels. Duke's untold story had handcuffed me. I felt for Old Faithful, the flask of raspberry elixir in my hip pocket. A small sip. Very judicious. My breathing slowed. I uncorked the bottle of Johnnie Walker and inhaled its magic scent.

> *I'm not going to be civil*
> *I'm not gonna watch my tongue or what I say*
> *I'm gonna dance with the devil*

One scalding swig, just one, and I got the hell out of that place. But it was too late.

. . .

A bar, any bar, would do. The bronze warehouse lights flooded the tables and left everything else in shadow. The room lifted the chill from my bones and promised refuge. I'd barely settled in when I recognized two of the firemen I'd seen on my first visit with Captain Hoyle. They recognized me, with the same distasteful reaction. One guy, a shock of long black hair, gestured to one with wire rim glasses, identifying me on the bar stool. Both turned their back on me.

"Johnnie Walker Black," I said to the bartender.

"A celebration," he said, grabbing the pour.

"Yes," I said, the oft told lie no more true than the first time I'd told it.

Music from a jukebox battled the racket of the room. I didn't recognize the tune, though I doubt it would have mattered; the song from Duke's apartment kept running through my head. Christmas lights pulsed, strung in loping arcs across the backbar.

"Ain't no use knockin'. . ." hollered the third guy at the firemen's table, putting the finishing touches on a joke. He wanted me to hear it, because he looked straight at me. ". . . there's no paper on this side either." A surge of laughter followed.

I chose to savor my glow and the happy mood of the room. Safe from a repeat of my tortured ride atop the hook and ladder, I decided to go talk to them. Maybe assuage their concerns about me, whatever they were. Perhaps grab insight on Duke.

Scotch in fist, I stood over them. The one who'd told the joke, a buffed guy with a receding hairline and a large brown mole on his forehead, nabbed his beer and left. I faced the two remaining at the table. "You two, you're from Duke's fire station, right?" I held the table to fix my position.

They raised their heads, slowly. The guy with the long locks considered me with loathing. "Yeah, who wants to know?"

"Can I sit?" The room began veering side to side.

"Did ya miss some of the joke?" asked the other guy, blinking through his wire rim glasses. "It goes like this, 'A drunk staggers into a church, enters the confessional booth, sits down, but says nothing.'"

"Forget it," said the long-haired fireman to his buddy.

"No, no," says his friend, "the Father wanted to hear the whole joke."

Long Hair hung his head then focused on two women in the corner.

Wire Rims continued. "'The priest coughs a few times to get his attention, but the drunk continues to sit there. Finally, the priest pounds three times on the wall. The drunk mumbles, 'Ain't no use knockin', there's no toilet paper on this side neither.'"

I guffawed. It surprised Wire Rims.

"We're not gonna be converts, Father," said Long Hair, rejoining the conversation.

The guy with the wire rims downed the rest of his beer and pushed away his chair. "Want another?" he asked his friend without considering me.

I raised my glass as if they'd invited me in, and sat down. Wire

Rims whispered "fuck" under his breath and walked away. "So," I said to Long Hair. "You're in Duke's firehouse."

"Yeah so?" He pivoted the wooden chair onto its two hind legs and held the position with ease.

"I'm-I'm Duke's priest."

Long Hair laughed. "Really, that's sweet."

I took another nick of my scotch. "Look, I don't understand why you don't like me . . . "

"I never said I don't like you." He rocked forward, planting the chair with a loud snap to the floor. "I just don't fancy talking to you."

"Maybe I can buy you a drink."

He laid his large mitts on the table. "What do you need, Father? Behold, this is no chapel. We don't like being interrogated."

My head had taken on the weight of a sandbag. "I don't unnerstand."

"I think you do."

"Well, I don't. Really."

He ran his fingers through his locks. "Are you gonna make me leave my happy place, after the day I've had?"

I raised my hands in surrender. "I'm just tryin' to unnerstand Duke. Okay? I'm not interro—interrogatin' anyone."

"How bout I buy *you* another—what're you drinkin'?"

"Scotch." I waved my glass around in breezy brotherhood and splashed some on him. "Sorry," I said and fumbled for the small napkin on the table.

"Scotch . . ." he said, motioning to back off. ". . . and then you leave me and my friend alone."

"Sure, why not." I tapped my glass. "Johnnie Walker Black."

His eyebrows went up. "You've got expensive taste, Father."

"I don't usually drink this, but I had some at Duke's, and why not keep at it all night?" The chair and I, momentarily, didn't sync.

He scoffed. Then got clear eyed. "Duke's whiskey?"

"Yes, from his cabinet. You'd prefer I order Blue Label or a Macallan?"

His face curious, like how I'd gotten to Duke's whiskey. But he let it go of it. "Okay, and then you'll leave?"

"With jus a coupla questions."

"Geez, Father, you're really pushin' it."

"Okay, just one," I said.

He nodded wearily *bring it on.*

"Over the past few months . . ." I examined my scotch and pushed it aside. "Over the past few months did you see any change in Duke?"

"He kept to himself."

"Yeah, sure. But did he seem unusually sad? Angry?"

Long Hair sniffed and collected his thoughts. "Actually, he got happy, like I'm tryin' to do here."

"Happy! When was that?" In my excitement, my hand swept into my glass and almost knocked it over.

"About six months before he, ya know, pulled the trigger. Seemed, I dunno, happy. Like he was getting laid."

Wire Rims returned to the table with two frosty mugs of beer. Long Hair smiled up at him. Wire Rims gave me another exasperated look and sat down; slid a mug to Long Hair.

"Gettin' laid?" I asked.

"Well, ya know Father, for some of us it's okay. Sorry if that offends you."

"No, it doesn't. But he was happy?" I tried to focus.

"I don't know, maybe it wasn't a woman, but it sure had the feel of one. He even asked me once about them."

"Them?"

"Women." Long Hair winked at Wire Rims.

"What did he ask?"

"I dunno, just somethin' about how you figure them out."

"And what'd you tell him?"

"I said, ya can't."

Wire Rims crowed and clinked his mug to Long Hair's. "But it changed," said Long Hair.

"What?"

"His bein' happy. You could see it on his face."

"When was this?" I asked.

"Hey," said Long Hair. "One question; that was our deal. He rose up out of his chair. "I'll buy you that scotch."

"No," I said getting up myself and trying to maintain my balance. "I'm good. But thank you . . .?"

"Tony." A flat statement.

"Thank you, Tony." I bowed to him and Wire Rims. I made my way out of the bar. *Okay, a woman.* I could understand that.

CHAPTER 14

Duke

Hearing The Miracles' "You Really Got A Hold On Me" reactivated my self-contempt. I hadn't been able to separate from Valerie, even when I knew better. Once, I'd even tried to locate her name at a clinic through directory assistance and on the Internet. I'm not sure what I would have done had I found it. But it was moot, a dead end. Then, another few weeks after our latest row, she called. An early Sunday morning, days before Christmas.

"I was wrong," she said.

The wall of albums loomed above me, as if my response was buried somewhere in that vinyl. "What do you expect me to say?" I hoped my apathy came through loud and clear.

"I'd understand if you never want to see me again. But I'd like to explain a few things."

Unsure of what I wanted, I kept silent.

She continued. "Would you be willing to meet me somewhere? I'd like to tell you in person."

The thought of seeing her lit me up—both desire and fear; like nothing I'd ever experienced. It was as if I would be swept away by her current, so I clung to my glacial tone. "You can tell me over the phone."

"Please. I'll buy you a coffee and deliver it, I'll pay for your cab; anything, if you'll just give me a chance to explain."

The unusually dark morning offered raw drizzly cold. I had no appetite for it and I knew I should say *no*. But desire is a drug.

"Just one more chance. Please," she said.

Shit. "Let's not do this again," I said, attempting to sound like my legs and heart were firmly planted, while her current had already ripped me free of my mooring.

"Please."

She had a very specific place in mind. Not a coffee shop. Not a library or even a bar: a *graveyard* on the Upper West Side. "The grave of The Amiable Child." Typically warped Valerie. Yet her willingness to call, to divulge more of herself, gave me hope, stoking the fervor I thought I'd finally smothered.

The taxi, for which I fully intended to let her pay, looped cautiously around Riverside Drive and West 122nd Street, and—due to some sort of road construction and closure—dropped me at the park, in the fog, a ways from the gravesite.

The cab driver, a gaunt Ethiopian man, speculated that I had a quarter mile to go—a seven to ten-minute walk. But he said he'd never visited the grave and acted impatient to have me out of his cab, and to be done with the place. His cab crawled away, its taillights steadily devoured by the murk.

I'd guess that even without the vapors it was a desolate place, but the pea soup rendered Riverside Drive, and the Henry Hudson Parkway to the west, treacherous, mostly abandoned and voiceless given its thickness. Few cared to drive in it.

I hadn't thought to bring a flashlight, not that it could have pierced more than a foot or so of the black rolling mist. Lumbering along the path, mostly guided by the sound of my feet scraping against the asphalt, I bumped into a low iron fence dripping with condensation. The lancet-like fencing caught my palm and tore it open. I licked at the blood and swore at my own spinelessness. *You're doing this for some woman?* But, of course, at the time I thought she might be *the* woman.

No one passed me, though five minutes into my walk I thought I heard footsteps from behind. They quickly ceased, leaving the wail of a distant foghorn along the river as my only company. Luckily there were no alternate tracks on which I could branch off and lose my way. But the tarmac path and minimal light mirrored the claustrophobia that subways often roused in me.

I breathed easier once I arrived at the grave. It had taken me fifteen minutes, and I'd have missed it if not for the way the tomb rose up above me, at first a sensation rather than a visual in the dense mist. Valerie was nowhere to be seen.

Certain that I'd been stood up and again made the fool, the steely power chords of Van Morrison's "Mystic Eyes" slithered into my head. And up and down my spine. I paced. I cursed her (and myself). *Another five minutes, that's it.*

Five minutes later she arrived, out of the fog, out of breath, drenched, uncombed, and fucking ravishing. "Sorry," she said without explanation. She handed me a hot cup of coffee, taking my other hand and standing us both in front of the iron-fenced and very large marble urn. *She* held my hand; I did nothing to encourage her.

The brume swirled around us; my best instincts tested. My body vigilant, my breath weak. No one but a whipped idiot would be out on such a morning. I sipped from the paper cup. Caffeine. My breath returned. The inscription on the grave read:

"ERECTED TO THE MEMORY OF AN AMIABLE CHILD
ST. CLAIRE POLLOCK
DIED 15 JULY 1797 IN THE FIFTH YEAR OF HIS AGE"

"A young boy," she finally said without looking at me. "He fell off the cliffs," she pointed into the darkness, "onto the rocks of the Hudson River."

I waited for an explanation that tied me to the gravesite and to my relationship with her. Understanding her had become a compulsion. And I could hardly keep my eyes off her. I wanted to press my body to hers, I wanted to inhale her. I hated myself for it.

She pulled closer to me.

"So?" I said as dispassionately as I could, using the cup to anchor me, my eyes on the pedestal and urn. I took another sip of the coffee. It had a strange aftertaste that I couldn't place.

"I'm going through a confusing time," she said rubbing my shoulders. "And it's not you."

She pried the cup from my fingers and placed it on the ground. She took both of my hands.

"It's me. You're a wonderful man, a funny man, even poetic sometimes, which I know you appreciate is close to my heart. I find you very attractive, but . . ." Here she got choked up. It took her a minute or so to regain her equilibrium. "But something is dying and something is being born, and you're caught in the middle of it. And I'm sorry."

"What is it?"

She opened her mouth but could only shake her head. "I-I . . .I can't . . ." Then she pulled me to the other side of the urn. She tilted her head to the carved granite, a quote from Job 14 1-2:

"MAN THAT IS BORN OF A WOMAN IS OF
FEW DAYS AND FULL OF TROUBLE.
HE COMETH FORTH LIKE A FLOWER,
AND IS CUT DOWN:
HE FLEETH ALSO AS A SHADOW,
AND CONTINUETH NOT."

She was obviously touched by this young boy's death, which wasn't surprising given her work with children. But how it involved me, I couldn't understand. "How am I in the middle of this?"

"Because you showed up now, on the plane, at this time in my life. Because I care for you. Because this child represents me." She quickly appended her statement. "Any child that is cut short of being all they can be."

"You sound like a politician," I said. "Everything in circles."

She flinched; her eyes lost their shine. I'd hurt her.

"I'm sorry," I said. "I just don't understand. I *want* to understand."

"*I'm* sorry. I thought I could explain it this way, but I see that I'm only confusing you." She collected herself. "When I first left Iowa I knew I wasn't right. I was in the wrong world and wasn't sure where the right world might be. Maybe I shouldn't have brought my parents along." She snapped back to the present. "My parents were good people until they weren't, but not always generous—especially my mom. I'm still not courageous because I've seen what courage can do. Things in the world are never as certain as they seem."

She had a way of filling my head with a series of detours; impossible to keep up. But I thought better of interrupting her.

"I got to New York," she continued, "and applied my license, and the work I did with children became an exploration rather than a career. And all at once men seemed to flock to me. Which was only more confusing as almost no one noticed me in Iowa."

I found that hard to believe.

"At any rate, I became overwhelmed." She let out a long breath. "I got pregnant." She lowered her head. "I had an abortion."

"And you love children." I was trying to connect the dots.

"Yes, but this wasn't a child yet. It was about me."

"Did you love him, the father?"

"I did. Well, I think I did."

I braced myself. "Are you still with him?"

"No, not at all. It couldn't work out."

"Why?" I asked.

"That's what I'm still figuring out. I guess I'm not ready to explain what I don't even understand myself. But look at me, what do you see? Do you see someone who would play with your feelings purely for fun?"

Purely? Truth, I wasn't certain she understood her own seesaw emotions. Nor did I care to be her guinea pig. I resisted meeting her eyes. She stood her ground waiting for my answer. As soon as I met them their magic again dragged me in, just like the first time on the plane. "Mystic Eyes," I muttered.

"What?"

"It doesn't matter," I said. "I'd like to believe you, but you're not consistent." *Maybe not stable. A beautiful wreck.*

She seemed relieved. "But I'm reliable. You'll see. Stick with me a little longer; let me untangle this, so someday you'll understand. So, at the very least, we can someday be friends?"

"Friends?!"

"Would that be such a terrible end? Neither one of us has many of those."

Of course, she was right but it felt like defeat. "I'm not sure what to do with you," I said.

"And I'm not sure what to do with you, either. But you'll consider it?" She ran her fingers over the crown of my head, and cupped my chin. She looked lovingly into my eyes, like a campfire in that cold morning gloom.

"You'll give me some answers?" I said. "You'll talk to me about your family, your experiences?"

"I promise. Maybe not all at once, please be patient. But yes."

I tried to sound uncommitted. "I'll consider it."

And then it all went blank. Apparently for quite some time.

Ultimately, Val's voice edged me into consciousness. "Duke?"

I opened my eyes.

"Duke, lean on me."

Fog everywhere. "Is he okay, lady?" An unrecognizable female voice.

"Just help me get him into the cab," Val said.

"Is he drunk?"

"No, he's not well."

When I fully cleared, we were on my bed, in my apartment. It wasn't how I'd imagined we'd be there, together, for the first time.

"Are you sure we shouldn't get you to a hospital?" She propped me up and passed me a glass of water.

I made sure I took the glass in both hands. "No, I told you, I'm fine."

"Duke, you toppled over. You're not fine."

"I'm fine, okay? Just got a little woozy."

"Has this happened to you before?"

I adopted an offhand manner. "No."

"Should I call your team at the firehouse?"

"No!" I softened. "Don't make a big deal of this."

She angled away from me. "Are all men so stubborn?" Slushy rain pelted the window. "Suit yourself. Can I get you anything else?"

"No, thanks. It was great of you to get me here."

She pulled back, as if I was an extraterrestrial. "Seriously? That's what friends do. You're sure you're okay?"

"Positive."

A wind kicked up. "It's a mess outside, I'd better get home." She started grabbing her things.

"Stay."

She paused and squatted next to me. "Do you remember us walking back?"

"Walking back?"

"We were almost to where the taxi met us when you fell, but I sensed you were . . ."

"What?"

"Distant, even before you fell."

I didn't remember any of it. I reached for her arm. "Stay. We'll be warm, we'll listen to music."

Her eyes told me she knew I was hiding something. She touched my cheek.

I asked again. "C'mon, stay."

She stood up. "Hold that thought."

She left me staring at the ceiling, shaken, though I tried not to show it, more certain that the acoustic neuroma was gathering a foothold in my brain, and that every second with her was precious.

CHAPTER 15

Duke

Charli walked to the door to shut out the rest of the hospital. She returned to my bedside, her mood unusually sober. "Duke, I don't know if you can hear me or not." She watched my eyes, but of course they reflected nothing. "I'm going to hope that you can, that somewhere in your brain you can understand why I need you to stay, I need you to get better." She angled her head to the ceiling, sniffled and dabbed her eye then returned to me.

"You remember when Dad was dying, how Mom pretended to brighten up to make it easier on him. Either one could've begun crying. But they didn't. I think we both learned that from them.

"Three days later, it was all over; Dad gone, only forty-three, Mom's already meager spirit draining out of her, you impervious. Me? Don't know what to say about myself. But *I* had to find the job in fucking Jacksonville just to be near her. *I* had to visit her in that miserable assisted home, even after she had no idea who I was. I don't know how they could call it that, *a home*. You didn't want to deal with it, and I understand why. But shit, there's no one left but you and me."

I couldn't reach for Charli's hand. Too late to be brotherly.

She tugged at a strand of her hair. Panic knotted her face; she no longer resembled my sister. I'd never seen her come unglued. And I could do nothing.

She started to cry and struggled to squeeze out her words. "More than ever, I need to know I'm loved, that I'm not alone. I'll always know that from you, because you're the only one left who was there. You've got to get better."

She wiped her tears, she studied my face. "Or maybe you want to let go, I don't know."

She lowered her voice. "And there're questions that need answering, questions only you can answer. Not just about why you did this. But the Arson Squad contacted me the other day. They asked a lot of questions that I don't follow. Their tone upset me. Fires intentionally set, people dying ugly deaths. That kind of shit. I need you here, you understand?

"And . . . one other thing . . . There's a lump in my breast. You understand? I'm going to need money, I'm going to need emotional support. Every penny went to Mom's care."

The door opened and Father Blu came into the room looking like he'd spent the past forty-eight hours propped up next to or in a dumpster. His dog collar had sprung loose around his neck, his clerical shirt smudged with what appeared to be dried spittle. The dark outer jacket wrapped over his right arm managed to accentuate the stubble on his face. Not very priestly.

Charli daubed at her red eyes, squared herself and grimaced. "What happened to you?"

He rubbed his hands over his face and scalp as if that would make him appear whole. "Just haven't gotten much sleep."

She assessed him as he laid his jacket over the gurney in the corner. Despite his bloodshot eyes and panhandler appearance, if he hadn't been wrapped in a diocesan suit, I could see how she might have been attracted to him.

He proceeded to tell Charli what he'd heard from the fireman in my station house. Given his description to my sister, it was clearly Tony S whom he had spoken to. Not my biggest fan.

Father Blu went on to mention my music collection and the suicide note I'd left for Charli, the Jackie Greene song. I'd wanted her to recognize my anger so if the police ever made a connection to me and Valerie's death, she might understand that there was something more going on. Now I realized it wouldn't excuse me in anybody's eyes, not even hers. I'd fucked up everything.

Just then, Doctors Kirschner and Pak, the bulky intern and two hospital administrators barged in to my hospital room. One of the administrators, a tall black man in a suit with the physique of a New York Giants running back, moved immediately to Father Blu with the intention of grabbing his arm. "You'll need to leave the building, Father."

The Father sidestepped the administrator. "What?!"

"You've broken hospital policy and endangered this man." The administrator pointed to me.

"That's ridiculous." Father Blu looked to my sister for support.

"Wait a minute," she said. "You're not talking about the other night?"

"We have protocol that has to be followed."

"You're concerned about your liability, your insurance. That's what this is all about, not the safety of my brother."

"Miss, we have rules. He could have caused a problem."

The Father bent forward. "Playing Smokey Robinson and the Miracles?"

Unmoved, the administrator took another step toward Father Blu. "Interfering with Mr. Ducotty's treatment."

Then Charli said something that I'd never have expected. "He's our priest." She turned to the other administrator and the two doctors. "Surely you're not saying we can't have our priest by my brother's bedside."

Dr. Pak jumped in. "It's not that, it's—"

Football administrator raised his hands cutting off Dr. Pak. He closed his eyes, channeling his irritation. "You understand that we may have to ask you to remove your brother from this hospital if you insist on letting this man"—he indicated Father Blu—"remain around your brother. And if you do, there will be a risk moving him, which will be on you."

"I'm sure," said Father Blu, "that the Communications Director at the Archdiocese will have a heyday with that." He smiled.

"Yes, that's right," said my sister.

"Well, I'm, I wouldn't be so sure," said the administrator searching for his next parry.

"Ya know," piped up the intern, "I just read a paper that suggested that any stimuli might be—"

"We didn't ask you." The administrator turned back to my sister. "What's it gonna be?"

As far as I could see, the hospital wasn't going to send me anywhere. I'd already overstayed the normal welcome. Thanks to Smokey Robinson and the Motown Blip, they'd let me dwell in their room, in their valuable bed, because *I* was most valuable to *them* as a test subject. I'd become a public relations coup, and a formidable grant and fundraising tool, if it turned out that I had Locked-In Syndrome. *If.*

Father Blu spoke up. "I'm going to recommend to Ms. Ducotty-Ryan that we bring in a simple sound system and play Mr. Ducotty some of his favorite tunes."

Dr. Kirschner's head bobbed, seemed to warm to the idea.

The administrator cut her off. "We'll have to check with our carrier, but I don't think it's a good idea."

"I think it would be very therapeutic." Father Blu made a show of taking my sister's hands in his and smiling down at her.

She was somewhat surprised and less comfortable with his gesture, judging by the way her shoulders constricted, but she played along. She relaxed, nodding affirmation to the hospital hit men and woman.

I had a team!

· · ·

The next morning, Father Blu, considerably cleaned up, had a small stereo system installed in my room—a CD player and a turntable. A rustic sound but who was I to complain. The next day, he came in with his first stack of CDs and albums from my apartment.

Thing was, I wasn't sure I wanted to hear that music—at least some of it. The ones I'd shared with Val; songs that made her cry, and laugh, and hug me. And profess love to me. Staked to a bed I couldn't even feel, those tunes would be like fire ants chewing on me.

Sure enough, the very first song tripped me. One of my more recent CDs. A cut called "No Place Like Home" by the English band Honne. It took me back to one week after the graveyard incident, after she'd put me to bed with my dizzy spell. She'd insisted we spend the whole day together rather than just a few hours. The plan began as a long New Year's walk in Central Park. But the weather turned brutally cold and wet. One step out the lobby, we turned around. "I'm happy being inside with you," she said. We went back up to my place.

The log in the fireplace spit sparks onto the floor. I brushed them away with my bare hand and she applauded.

This might be the night. And then . . .*Maybe I've peaked sexually.* It'd been three years since the last date. What was her name?

I pushed those thoughts aside. And when this tune, "No Place Like Home" came on, she started to cry. She rested her head on my shoulder and fastened to my arm. "You okay?" I asked.

"Not really. But I feel a lot better next to you. As close to home as I feel these days." She snuggled tighter.

We sat like that, listening to music, the icy rain whipping against the window, the fire crackling. Neither one of us spoke again for at least an hour, with something wonderfully old about us. Serene in a way I'd never experienced.

"I brought something over I'd like to read to you, if that's okay," she said.

"Of course."

She lifted and kissed my wrist, leaving her coral imprint. She went to her backpack and pulled out a piece of paper. The lipstick left a trace of vanilla, but there was none of *her* detectable aroma. She returned to the couch. "I'm an amateur astrologer, and maybe you're not into that sort of thing, but I believe it's referring to us."

"Well, not usually. But if it's referring to us, I'm all ears." I said.

She read off her handwritten sheet. "Tonight's full moon is in Aries and things are out of balance. Confusion and anger are everywhere. Don't you feel it?"

"If you say so."

"Aries is a fire sign. Aries is green fire, impulsive."

"A fire sign," I said, "seems up my alley."

Another one of her rare mini-smiles. "Good." She revisited her notes. "Don't ignore your confusion—I'm not going to ignore mine. Or my anger."

"Are you angry with me?"

"No, not at all."

"But you're angry?"

"I am, but I'm not sure who I'm angry with." She pondered. "Maybe my family; because, except for you, I'm alone. And afraid."

"Afraid of what?"

"I can't tell you yet."

"I want to help you through this, whatever it is," I said.

"Anyhow . . ." She began reading again. "We should be speaking about our fear—with courage, not with aggression. Our inner fires are key to communicating wisely. Use that fire; we're not victims. Thinking we are is only dodging our responsibility."

I wasn't sure what she was talking about or where she was going with her astrological analysis—nothing new there. But I held her gaze. It had a certain ferocity, as if her spirit had been set on fire.

"If we take action for our thoughts, speaking our truth without striking out at anyone, from a place of self-knowing, we'll peel away layers, one at a time, and, I believe, we'll change the frequencies around us. Fearlessness over convenience. And if we do, there will be movement. This moon wants you and I to act as friends through these difficult times." She folded the paper in her lap. "Can you do that? What do you think?"

"Well . . ." I gaped. "I think you're a special woman." She intertwined our fingers. My eyes journeyed around her face; those lips, those eyes. I could smell her. "And beautiful."

"You just want to fuck me."

"Wow. And smart too," I said.

She cracked a smile, she wagged her head slowly. Astonishment grew in her mocha depths. She pulled my hand to her heart and held it there as dew clouded her eyes.

I didn't have a clue what to say or do. I pulled her to me. She wrapped her arms around me, laid her head to my chest and cried. She seemed happy, relieved.

I was giddy; I was disoriented. But we were peaceful. No other place I wanted to be. She fell asleep in my arms.

After about a half hour, I gently uncoiled myself, grabbed my cell phone and took a number of photos of her as she slept. This one would be different.

Later she told me, "I looked it up; that song, "No Place Like Home." The group's name is pronounced 'honay.' It's Japanese. It means 'real intention.' Isn't that perfect for us?"

CHAPTER 16

Father Blu

"The gun came from Pinky's. It matched his list and later he identified it." Detective Zhōng rifled over his desk, equally preoccupied with an upcoming press conference and his daughter's basketball game. But not with me. His armpits splayed with perspiration.

Having pressed him for the visit, I was the usual unsought distraction.

"I hate public speaking." He explored the wrecked hills and valleys of his cubicle, searching for something. The small fan clipped atop it looked ready to join the heap on his desk. Cantilevered out, it panned left and right with no practical effect. Despite the freezing temperatures outside, Zhōng's office was a sauna, but without the fresh cedar.

I tried to get him to stay focused. "Pinky's."

"Pinky's, yeah, the gun shop. Off Canal, around Broadway. The gun . . . makes sense. There'd been a fire—hold, damn, wait a minute!" A pile of papers slid like a wave off his desk.

"Sonuvabitch!" He grabbed for them, and in midair came up with half a clump. Then half of *that* relapsed to the linoleum floor with the dust balls, pennies and Tootsie Roll wrappers. He threw the few remaining sheets to the ground and faced me with frustration, like I had pushed him over the top.

"Where the fuck was I?" He refocused on my attire. "Sorry."

Half the people I met asked for forgiveness. The other half rebuked me. "Pinky's."

"Freaking Pinky, you never can tell with him." The detective panned across his desk's grim territory. "A fire; roughly two years ago. Maybe Pinky set it himself. Wouldn't be the first time, but Arson couldn't prove it. A few of his weapons went out the door."

Detective Zhōng closed his eyes, went to his *inner place*, released his breath. He resurfaced and tried to find direction for himself. He started picking the papers off the floor. His arm leaned up against his desk; he got a good look at his wristwatch. "Shit!" He stood up. "I gotta go."

"The gun, it went out the door?"

"With three-four others. We got numbers and descriptions. Two of them were ours. We got 'em all back."

"Ours?" I thought I'd misunderstood.

"Our personal handguns—weapons we'd sold or traded to Pinky, guys from the force—look, sorry, gotta go." He grabbed at his coat and turned to the door. "You can't stay here."

"Right. But Duke's gun?"

"Couldn't trace it initially, that's the one that wasn't returned until, you know, the fireman. . ." He poked a finger in his mouth. "But Pinky says it was his and it matches the inventory."

I weighed the information: Duke used a gun, and fire was part of how he got it. Not much to go on, but something.

Detective Zhōng grew pensive. "What do you reckon, Father? Was it God's hand or the hand of the guy loading the powder?"

"What do you mean?"

"The bullet, it must have been a squib, that's my guess since it's still in there, in his brain. Probably wasn't enough powder—maybe no powder—in the cartridge to fully eject it. That's why it lodged in his head and didn't exit. If it'd been full powder when that firing pin struck the primer, that guy wouldn't be in a hospital, he'd be underground. I can't figure if he's lucky or unlucky." He glanced again at his watch. "Anyways, I gotta go. You need anything more, go talk to Pinky." He shooed me out of his tiny cell, into the lobby.

"Last questions. Did Duke have an insurance policy and who was the beneficiary?"

"Yes, his sister. Public knowledge."

I pressed. "A considerable amount?"

"I'm trying to be polite, Father, but you're pushing your luck."

"Please."

"Not bad. Look, it's a suicide, plain and simple." He tapped his pockets to make sure he had everything. "She was in Jacksonville at the time."

"Did you ever do a forensic swab of Duke's locker to check for gun powder?"

"At the firehouse? No, no need for that. Now, out of my way." He lurched from the building, on the run.

· · ·

By the time I got to Pinky's it was mid-day. Dim sum and a swig of my raspberry medicine restored me. My support liquids weren't so bad.

Pinky, it turned out, was Chinese, too. Short. Balding. Maybe sixty, sixty-five, a gold chain draped around his neck. "Sure, burned most the place. Shitheads took guns, I got 'em back. No nearly so bad as they torched the place. What mess."

The cheap laminate walls appeared new and gave off trace toxic fume. They were hung with defensive sprays, silhouette targets, and other firearm accessories. In the glass counter, shelves of handguns. Up the wall, ammo and rows of rifles rose to the ceiling. Nothing fancy, but organized under the fluorescent glare, the small space almost felt cozy, unless you took into account that everything in there was used to kill. He must have noticed my reflex to the shop.

"Look nice, right? Insurance pay. I don't need cops thinking I did it. Pain in ass. They prejudice against me."

"The fire was set?"

"Sure. If I do it, nothing be here now. I smart; I still own building. I walk with lots insurance money. But then I have less money a year from now, so stupid. I'm not stupid. I run honest business." He began unloading boxes of ammo onto a shelf.

"They set the fire to get the guns," I said.

"Sure, not first time. Tong shitheads."

"Brothers?"

"Gang, Ghost Shadows Two. Shit always up nose, needles in arm. Not smart, hotheads, crazies. Kill people. But got my guns back. Fourth one found when guy shoot himself. Don't want that gun. Bad luck."

"All from the fire?"

"Definitely my guns. But I say to Dave Zhōng *No thank you, you keep fireman gun. Bad luck. Diu mianzi.*"

"What's that?"

"You say, *loss of face.* When you embarrassed and everyone knows. Face is lost. Might as well be dead. So people do."

"You're sure the tong started the fire?" I asked.

"They caught with my guns, didn't they?"

"They take ammunition too?"

"No, they just want guns. All thing bad luck."

. . .

Driving sleet dripped into my collar. The back of my neck raw. I mulled Detective Zhōng's question, *Was it God's hand or the hand of the guy loading the powder?* Could Duke have purposely faked his suicide? Buy why? And if so, how had it gone wrong? Or did someone else shoot Duke and try to make it look like a suicide? If that were the case, I was mucking around in an attempted homicide— way above my pay grade—with a murderer still at large.

"Come in, come in, Father." Chief Winston ushered me into his office, his left hand wrapped in a bandage decorated with colorful childlike stars.

The photo of the Madden Cruiser crowded me. I angled my chair to avoid it. "Thanks for seeing me again."

"Come on in. I only have a few minutes."

"Your hand?"

"Trying to do two things at once. The avocado won. My granddaughter had fun with it though. What can I do for you?" Instead of sitting behind his desk, he sat across from me. But the motor coach photo ruled my periphery.

"So, you investigated fires?" I asked.

"I did. First, as a fire marshal, then in the AIU, the Arson Investigation Unit. The last three years of my tenure."

I pushed my luck. "Would you examine a gun, the gun that Duke allegedly shot himself with?"

He winced. "Wouldn't that be a police matter?"

"The police are done with this case. It's not even a case to them because it's pretty clear that Duke tried to kill himself. Would you be willing to requisition it?"

"What's the purpose?"

"I'm not sure. Maybe you'd see something that was missed." I pointed to the handgun collection over his shoulder. "You know guns. And the gun came from a fire, possibly an arson fire; a gun shop downtown. Owner doesn't want the pistol back; the police still have it."

"Does it matter where Duke's gun came from?"

"Maybe not," I said. "But I don't have much to connect to anything. If I knew with certainty where the gun came from, maybe I could figure out how he got it and from whom."

"You seek certainty?" He chuckled. "Maybe in your line of business, Father, but not in mine. But okay, on what grounds do I tell the police I need to see the gun?"

I hadn't thought of that. "Tell them . . .Tell them that Duke's sister, Charli, wants you to do it as a favor, as a family friend. Ask for Detective Zhōng."

As soon as I said it, I knew I'd overstepped. Hard to stay within *all* the rules.

"If you think it will help, sure." Chief Winston stood. Curiosity or minor irritation crept into his mood; I wasn't sure which. "You're taking this very seriously."

I scrambled for an answer that sounded real. "I'm on duty."

"A priest?"

"Clergy can question facts." I was making it up as I went along.

"Can they? Well, you're certainly sticking to it."

He showed me to the door. I stopped. "Were you aware that Benny Stein and Duke had a serious falling out just before Benny's death?"

He didn't look surprised. "Where'd you hear that?"

"Jean Stein."

"What was it about?"

"I thought you might know."

"No," he said. "Did she?"

"No. Okay, thanks for checking on that gun."

I set off to find the tong, amazed to have re-found some spontaneity, and leery that later—just as I had in the past—I'd have to atone for it.

. . .

The Chinatown streets bustled with activity. Purple strands of light hung across Mott Street dangling canopies of giant illuminated snowflakes. Below, a man bulging out of his blue leisure suit pushed a shopping cart brimming with baskets of fresh flowers for sale. Orange ribbons and bows trailed over and around him.

In the alley, a line of lion dancers, in preparation for a performance, donned bright fluorescent outfits. Above them, a "Gift Center" sported two decorated Christmas trees with tinsel garlands and a plastic Santa waving a candy cane, embellishments suggesting apostasy.

For about two hours I ducked into shops and inquired around. Without exception, the mention of the Ghost Shadows generated fear in the eyes of men and women, young and old. Proprietors chased me out of every shop and office, scanning in every direction, it appeared, to avoid exposure and peril.

Ready to give up, I measured my energy and next move. The sky had turned canescent and forbidding. An emaciated man passed me holding above him a dark brown silk kite, a large predacious-looking moth, each wing marked by large warning eyespots, reminiscent of the Madagascan *angatra*. Despite its menacing appearance, its intricacy and craftsmanship something to behold.

I attempted to hail the man down, curious if the Chinese, too, believed in the phantom gods on earth who hover between the living and dead. Those tales seemed to be in many cultures. Even Dad with his grandfather's Mohawk legends had such stories. But the throng surged against me and the moth jagged away above it.

When I looked down, a dog that looked eerily like Ataraxy grinned up at me, wagging its tail. "Where's your person?" I stooped to pet her and a stocky young man bumped into me. "Sorry," I said. Then thought to ask, "Ghost Shadows Two?"

He stopped, impassive. "What are you looking for? And why?" He sported a diamond stud in one ear, a business suit, no tie, and a serious, clean-cut face, largely masked by his sunglasses.

"I'd like to talk to their leader, whoever's in charge."

He popped and chewed gum, deliberately. My edginess reflected in his shades; a clear target. "Because?"

Stay upfront. "A fire, I'd like to ask them about a fire."

"You think that's smart?" he said.

"I'm not a cop."

He remained tepid. "How do I know that?"

"Isn't there a rule that if you say you aren't a cop, the cops can't touch you?"

He stopped chewing his gum. "Entrapment."

"That sounds right."

He added, "Same goes for a firemen cop."

"I'm not a fireman of any kind, as you can see."

"Uniforms mean nothing. You speak Chinese? If so, which dialect?"

"I wish."

He said something in Chinese and watched my expression.

I had no idea what he said.

He pulled a cell phone from inside his finely tailored suit pocket and hit an auto dial. Within seconds he responded in rapid Chinese to someone on the other end. They volleyed back and forth for no more than thirty seconds while I knelt. The Husky with the creamy coat had vanished.

The young man addressed me. "Are you willing to trade?"

A nervous laugh. "Trade?"

"You're Catholic, right?"

"It's past Halloween. Would I dress like this?"

"I already told you about uniforms. Dress up like a cockroach for all I care as long as you're straight with me." He looked at his watch. It had the radiance of a Chopard. Pricey. "I'd like to help you but . . ."

My throat restricted. "What kind of trade?"

"Bibles, *Studium Biblicum*. Nineteen sixty-eight."

I'd heard of them, of course. "Chinese Catholic bibles."

"At least twenty." He tracked my reaction.

"Twenty."

"Everything comes with a price." He looked down the street.

"I'm not sure if I can find twenty."

"Then never mind." He shoved the cell phone into his jacket and began to stride away.

"Wait." Twenty seemed doable, a small price to pay for the information.

"I'm busy, Father."

"Okay, twenty *Studium Biblicums*."

"Nineteen sixty-eight."

"Nineteen sixty-eight."

"Follow me."

Asking additional questions seemed imprudent. Besides, he moved fast and like a needle through the foot traffic. I fell behind. I dodged head-down stevedores and elderly women intrepid in their shopping.

"Here," he said as I caught up, designating the nondescript, aluminum-framed glass door. He tapped on it three times. He awakened his phone, said something in Chinese, and just as quickly shut it down. "Wait here. If no one comes down within three minutes, forget it."

"What do you mean?"

"I think my English is pretty good." He disappeared into the crowd.

The white lettering on the door read:

GST
Youth & Community Group

GST
青年和社區團體

There were no hours or phone numbers posted which seemed strange.

A young woman in her twenties came down the stairs, peered at me through the glass and unlocked the door. She wore a blue work shirt, sleeves rolled up, and jeans. On the back of each upper arm were tattooed two ghostly eyes with pupils of orange flame, not unlike the predator eyes of the moth kite. "Go ahead," she said.

Smudged grime lined the narrow stairs—and what looked like several wide swatches of dried blood.

God guide me.

The young woman said nothing but stayed close as we ascended the stairs. She almost crashed into me when I stopped short on the landing. "Right," she ordered. "Down the hallway. Second door."

When I got to that door, a textured glass with a single Chinese character engraved on it, she waited for me to open it. When I didn't, she did it for me.

Once inside, I glanced over my shoulder as the door snapped shut. Her shadow pressed against the door. She didn't move. A dark Dracut cloud closed over me, with no Ataraxy to hold on to and no Jory speaking softly.

What light there was, filtered down from a cathedral ceiling and an old, industrial skylight with wires embedded in it. A trapeze-like canvas swing was tethered to it, hoisted high with pulleys. It struck me as a tool of torture.

Below the swing, the unexpectedly large room seemed prepared for an AA meeting, twenty or so chairs circled around. It was otherwise devoid of posters, furniture and people. In its vacuity, I sensed the storm coming.

"Hello?" My voice bleated, a timid quality I'd never heard before.

I took a few steps to the chairs. A door closed in the distance and from across the room an unseen door opened. A person came my way, looming larger with every step. The affect was of Poe's *The Pit and the*

Pendulum, the individual and the walls converging on me.

She was directly across the circle of chairs from me before I realize it was a woman. Missing the lower part of her left arm. "Sit," she said, cheerless, her voice bouncing off the barren floor and walls.

I did.

She sat some twenty or so feet away. "Speak. Wait. Twenty *Studium Biblicum,* nineteen sixty-eight."

God direct my path. "Yes."

"Delivered how soon?"

"I don't know how quickly I can find them. I have no experience with this."

"If it were easy," she said, "we'd do it ourselves. Two weeks. No bullshit. And discreetly."

"Okay. Can I ask—?"

"Cardinal Kung Pin-Mei," she offered. "You heard of him?"

"Yes, the Catholic underground in China."

"That's all you need to know, passing on the good word of Jesus." A warning bubbling in her eyes. "What's your fire question?"

Old Faithful beckoned. My head filled with beating wings. "Well?" Her boot struck the wooden floor, setting off thunder that rebounded around the room. If I wasted any more of her time, I imagined she'd swing the closest chair across my head, crushing it.

"A fire set in Pinky's Gun Shop eight or so months ago," I said. "You know the place?"

"Get to the meat of this."

"It was arson," I offered. "Guns were stolen and eventually retrieved from members of your . . . community."

"And?"

"I'm not a cop. And I'm not a fireman cop."

"Are you any kind of cop?" For a second, I caught the suggestion of a sadistic smile, as if she was hoping I was.

"I am not a cop of any kind. I'm a Catholic priest with the—"

"Stop! I don't care about your parish. We can always find you. Why do you need this information?"

"A friend shot himself and it would help to know some facts."

"A fact." She got up, turning away from me; the same apparitional eyes as the young woman tattooed on each upper arm. Her stump hung like a club.

"Okay, well . . ." I took a full breath " . . . did your members start the fire?"

"No."

"You're sure of that?"

"I said so." She latched onto a chair.

"But they were prepared for the fire?"

"That's it." She started walking away.

She took several steps before I could find my voice. "They didn't just happen by Pinky's at the moment it started smoking."

She stopped and turned to me. "They got a phone call."

"From whom?"

"Good luck, Father. Not a day more than two weeks. You like that pretty face of yours? Don't fuck with us." Her threat hung in the pressed air. She vanished like a spectre through the hidden door.

As I hit the street, the pressure left my head and shoulders. I started making calls. To friends who'd been in seminary with me, parishes in New York and around the country with large Chinese populations—Jersey City, Los Angeles, Oakland. In less than an hour I had five of the bibles on their way to me. I was in dangerous company, but this would be easy. Then I'd be done with them.

CHAPTER 17

Father Blu

I made my way to the AA meeting, congratulating myself for my cleverness; small steps toward uncovering Duke's story, freeing myself from him, and more importantly, from Father Toll's bridle. A block away, squealing tires and the rasping of tortured metal on metal jolted me, re-opening the wound that wouldn't heal.

Jory had called me, said he needed to tell me something. "It's serious," *he said.*

"Okay, tell me." I propped myself up on one arm.

"No, it has to be in person."

"Jory, can't it wait?" The woman lying next to me, fondling me. *There always had to be a party.*

"No," he said.

I don't even remember her name. She kissed my chest and moved *down my body, licking me. "I'm kinda busy," I said.*

"Please, just meet me tonight half way? Like I said, this is serious."

"How bout Friday?" I said.

Silence.

"Jory?"

"*Yeah?*"

"*Come here if it's that important. You can tell me your story. We'll have a beer.*"

"*Damn it, Jamie.*" *A strained sigh.* "*Ooh. . .Ooh, alright.*"

He never made it, crashing head-on with a 40,000-pound motor coach on route.

My cell phone rang.

"Father Bluterre." Father Toll's voice light and sociable, yet his imperative conspicuous.

"Father Toll."

"I haven't seen you in a few days. I figured I'd check in. Any progress?"

"I'm still gathering, but perhaps something more substantial in a few days."

"Nothing to report?"

"No sir," I said. "But I'm working on it."

"Keep at it, God is on your side."

"Father Toll?"

But he'd hung up.

My parents never knew the backstory to the accident, except that Jory was coming to see me. The three of us disoriented and forever bonded by the unimaginable. What was so urgent? Why couldn't Jory tell me over the phone? I asked around, I tried. For quite a while. Plenty of condolences, but no one knew. Nothing. I had to let it go. I had to. I had to.

Old Faithful and my black raspberry tonic lifted my mood. I rarely got the nausea and headaches anymore. Becoming immune, I suppose. I took a circuitous route to the Church of the Resurrection.

Through La Fiamma's window, past the etched golden lettering and the neon Moretti and Peroni signs, the pub was even more alive with firemen than my first visit. Risk and opportunity.

Once in, above the din, I motioned to the bartender. "Ginger beer."

He placed a stubby bottle of Genesee in front of me. Cream Ale. Alcohol. *Hey!* Before I could correct him, he walked to the other end of the bar, responding to a slew of loud and waving off-duty firemen and cops in need of refills.

The bottle of beer, a cheerful malachite green, exuded cold promise against the dense air. *But no.*

A body bumped hard into me—almost knocked me off the barstool—and left the beer spinning in a wobbly orbit. I regained my balance. Whoever bumped me, gone. An appendage of the larger unwelcoming crowd. And my fist had wrapped around the Genesee, steadying it. *Happy holidays.*

"How is a Catholic priest like a Christmas tree? The balls are just for decoration." Laughter. Mean-spirited eyes burned across my neck and shoulders. I didn't have to look to know.

The Genesee spoke to me. It said, *I'll make everything alright. I'll take away the sting of their hatred and you will turn the other cheek.* I said, *Bullshit! . . .*

A couple to my left banged a leather cup to the bar. Dice clattered in front of them.

. . . But let's try it.

"Yours," said the woman, ready for another drink.

Then from a table behind me. "Did you hear about the priest who became a marathon runner? He never finishes first; he's always coming in a little behind." More laughter.

I swiveled around. Clustered directly behind me, three full tables of guys leered my way. Wire Rims raised his frosted mug to me. He hadn't shaved for a couple days and his reddish stubble gave him an even more ill-tempered look.

I swiveled back. *Just one.* I mean, it was already there. I took a sip. Smooth, as promised. I took another.

"Father Bluterre?" Captain Hoyle squeezed in next to me at the bar, that familiar trace of cigar smoke settling with him. "I didn't expect to find you here. Merry Christmas." He smiled.

"Was walking by."

"Hmm." He finished off the deep caramel liquid in his lowball and spun the ice around. He looked tired, but his ease relaxed me.

"It's been a long day," I said.

"I'll say." He stared into his empty glass. "One of my guys just pulled an eighty-two-year-old man off the Canal Street tracks."

"That's tough."

My lethargy must have shown because he gave me a concurring shrug. "Too late. Some kid—I guess he's autistic—a teenager, a big kid, knocked the old man onto the tracks just as the E train came into the station." Hoyle blew away sour cigar breath. He gazed at his empty glass. "Can I buy you another drink, Father? Maybe something stiffer?"

"What was the name of the kid? The teenager, the autistic kid?"

"Don't know."

"Hispanic kid?" I asked.

"Don't know."

"Ribbineros?"

"Maybe, I haven't seen the report yet. Why, you know him?"

"If it's him I'm afraid so." I downed the remaining beer. The last thing the Ribbineros needed was another tragedy.

He pointed at the bottle. "Something stiffer?"

"Sure, why not."

"Ice?"

"Neat."

"A man of my stripe," he said with great satisfaction, and ordered two whiskies, straight. After knocking back mine, and chatting about everything *but* the Ribbineros kid: the Knicks' host of injuries, next year's Mets, and my previous life as a gem dealer, he asked for guidance regarding a small marital issue he was having with his "perfect" wife, Anne.

He was amiable enough and the hostile peanut gallery had dispersed. I felt pleasantly numb, and easy to give advice. "Do you love her?"

"Of course!"

"Then tell her; see if she wants to talk about it. Never miss a chance to love."

Another sip for both of us. A bit more chit-chat. My turn. "You have any idea about a woman Duke might have been seeing before his . . .? Maybe a name you overheard?"

"Duke had a girlfriend?" Something akin to appreciation played around Captain Hoyle's mouth. "No, nothing. But good for him. I'm not sure where I'd be without Anne."

"Maybe one of the women firefighters?"

That startled him. "In my station? I think I'd know."

"But it would be okay, I mean, if he had been having a relationship with one of them?"

"As long as it didn't impinge on their performance and they didn't flaunt their romance, sure. Naturally they couldn't sleep together in the firehouse."

"No, of course not." The lights around me diffused. *Sleeping with a woman. No matter how much I prayed, the earlier Augustine— rather than the latter—was always my partisan.*

"Well, Father . . ." He began to rise.

I brought myself back. "Captain, you remember . . .you remember you told me about that trick Duke pulled?"

"Which one?"

"The one with the energy-efficient car."

"Oh, yeah, that one. What a mind."

"Who was the owner of the car?"

"I'd rather not say." He searched his pockets for cash.

"Ah, but it's long ago," I said, still grasping at straws.

"So why do you care?"

There'd been several times when I sat in front of the motor coach driver's home, ready to confront him. His home meager. He had at least three kids and a wife as worn as he. Forgiveness isn't always easy. Some grievances last a lifetime.

"Just background on Duke," I said.

"I guess. By now one of the guys will likely tell you anyhow. And he probably already knows. But don't say I told you." Hoyle dropped a twenty on the bar.

"No."

"Lieutenant Vaughn. Of course, he wasn't a lieutenant back then."

"Vaughn," I repeated.

"Hmm." Hoyle ready to leave.

"Hey." I reached to stop him. "Duke lost his best friend—Ben Stein was it?"

Taken aback, his happy mood derailed, Hoyle squared me up. "Yes."

"A subway fire," I said.

He stretched his neck and shoulders. "Yes."

"Tough memories, I'm sorry. I . . . But I heard that fire was purposely set."

"Where'd you hear that?"

"A rumor I picked up. Do you think Duke blamed anyone for his friend's death?"

Hoyle shook his head. "Why would he do that? Arson was never corroborated."

"Yeah, just fishing." My brain had slowed to a crawl. I'd run out of questions; we'd run out of small talk. I was fairly shit-faced. Even if I *could* walk steadily, I wasn't going to my AA meeting.

Hoyle tapped his watch. "Anne." He clapped me on the shoulder and made his goodbyes.

I turned back to the bar and had a couple more.

"Father, you alright?"

My head lifted off the bar. I'd drifted away. "Yeah, I'm fine." Grit scored my eyelids.

Standing above me, Long Hair and an older, crew-cut firemen, regarded my abasement. "You sure? You want me to call you a cab?"

My tongue foraged for saliva. "No, thanks."

He didn't look convinced but the other guy said, "I gotta get home." Long Hair shrugged and they both left. I sat there slightly dazed. Though the place had thinned out, I could still hear the click of pool balls colliding in the back room.

A thin-waisted, full-figured woman in aquamarine sequins and a Santa hat, shimmied in next to my stool. She swayed gently and called to the bartender. "Teddy." Right there, he poured her a tall glass of water. My urinary tract called for attention.

She lifted the glass to her lips, she stumbled back into my arms. My hand caught her shoulder and slid onto her breast. I lifted my hand and mumbled an apology. She didn't object. Instead, she reached behind her shoulder, curled her arm around the scruff of my neck, and pulled my head onto the nape of hers. She smelled of sweat and sweet perfume, her pulse thumping. I was already light-headed.

"Well, hello, sweetie," she said.

I tried extracting my hand.

"No, it's okay." She replaced my palm on her breast. She contorted over her shoulder to see my face. "Cute. We can celebrate together."

Again, my familiar struggle between the crusade and my desire. I hoisted her up and she rotated to face me. "Oh," she said seeing my collar, followed by a quick once over. "Well, why not. If you're willing I am."

I straightened up in more ways than one. I slipped unsteadily off my stool. I grazed inadvertently against her backside and excused myself.

Toddling through the crowd and holding the railing, I bumped unevenly side to side down the tight stairs to the basement, almost missing the last step and landing on my face.

At the bottom, a single uncovered light bulb—scarcely enough illumination to make out the matchbox dimensions of the passageway. The smell of bleach, fresh paint and turpentine attacked my high. My bladder screamed at me. *A war zone of the senses.* With hardly enough room to rotate between the ladies' and men's rooms, or the utility closet next to it. If anyone had come out of one of those rooms, I would have had to squeeze by them. If there had been a third person, we'd have had gridlock.

The Men's Room door handle wobbled—one of those old glass types. Wobbled like it might come off. I stepped inside the men's room. It held the foul residue of a past occupant, an old water heater, and me. Tight. Very tight. I hooked closed the flimsy door, unzipped and released. I closed my eyes in relief.

Sulfur joined the air; the joy of grease and charred burger, I assumed. From the kitchen above. Or maybe a woman in the adjacent bathroom purifying her air with a lit match. But it was strong.

I hurried to conclusion, the chemical fetor starting to choke me. I unhooked the door and reached for the doorknob; it came off in my hand. I pushed at the door. It jammed against my shoulder. Then the hiss, combustion and explosion lifted me up and knocked me through it.

. . .

"You say, *hiss, combustion and explosion?*"

"Yes." The ice in the towel seemed one with my head. I passed it back to Teddy, the bartender. I remained clouded.

The EMT took notes—off duty but apparently he'd stopped in for a nightcap. "You sure you're alright?"

"Thanks to you guys, I guess."

He patted lightly over my arms, shoulders and legs for feedback. He checked my sleeves a second time. "Just that one burn on your leg. You're very lucky, Father. God must be on your side." He reached for my forearm. "You ready to try standing up?"

I tried and fell back. The pressed-tin ceiling filigreed in blackened dust.

"Take your time," the EMT said.

Someone with an anvil beat on my forehead. Chemicals embedded my clothes. I gagged. "Give me a moment."

"I'll order you a cab," said Teddy. "That okay, Barry?"

The EMT agreed. "Father, the cops'll need to see you at the Ninth Precinct, East Fifth Street, sometime between nine and eleven tomorrow morning, to fill out forms. You understand?"

"Sure."

"One last thing, Father . . ."

"Yes?"

"D'ya hold a grudge against any of the firemen?"

"A grudge? No, not at all. Why the heck would—?"

"Right. Okay. Go see the cops tomorrow."

CHAPTER 18

Duke

"You want me to go where?" Valerie squinted. She'd pulled on my lucky black Steely Dan tee shirt, her nipples rising to the occasion. The tee fell mid-thigh above her strong, naked legs.

"I want us to go away," I said. "I've got three days off and you said you didn't want us to ignore our confusion. You said the fire moon wants us to be friends."

"Aries moon. And you're making fun of me."

"I'm not. Let's go, what d'ya say?"

She checked me for mischief. "Where?"

"I'll rent a car. *I'm* driving. Historic Charing Cross Castle. Upstate, near Little Falls. A three-hour drive; maybe a bit more. My parents met there, talked about it often. And they're having a psychic fair."

"I can't leave Catalona; who'll feed her?"

"A neighbor."

"I'm not that friendly with any of them. I wouldn't ask."

"So that's it? You can't leave enough food and water for your cat for three days? We'll share a bed but, hey, you're not required to do anything but dare to *reveal yourself.* And I'll do the same. That's what you want, right?"

"Wow. You're for real. You're taking me up on this. I just don't know. A psychic fair? What kind of castle?"

"A haunted one."

. . .

Whether it was the crisp, sun-drenched January day or the adventure, Val stepped into the car perky and more youthful. The mid-morning sun teased out her advancing gray strands, tempting me, once again, to run my fingers through them. *She* was the scenic route. All I wanted was to pull off the Sprain Brook, release the growing tightness in my pants, and smell her body next to mine. The rest would come naturally.

Though I'd brought a ton of music on my iPhone, we talked all the way up.

She faced me, her expression soft. "You ever been married?" Her shoulders set against the passenger door. Her head cocked to the left, almost resting on the seat back. Beyond her, rolling by in pockets of shadow, the earth had been baked hard and jeweled with frost. Occasional mounds of still-virgin snow dotted edges of the parkway.

"Married . . . ?" I bowed my head and beamed at the absurdity, "No."

"Why not?"

Got time for a freakin' essay! "Never found the right woman, I guess."

"Or the right man?" she said.

"What?" My mouth ajar. "What? NO, absolutely not." I laughed and pressed into the steering wheel.

Her neck stiffened. "Why not?"

"Well, it's. . . it's disgusting."

"Really?"

"Well, yeah, with another man. I'm sorry, that's not for me." I thumped the wheel.

For a moment, she morphed into a female Larry David, naïve, blameless, arms open.

"It was just a question."

"Really? You think that about me?"

Her head twitched. "Think what about you? That you might have had a relationship with a man?"

"Well, I haven't. And look, let's be straight about this . . ."

"That's clever." She deadpanned.

"Yeah, that's right. Look, I'm not saying other people shouldn't have their ya-ya's."

Her head twitched again.

I knew what she was thinking without her saying a word. "Yeah, yeah, and their *loving* moments too. But it's not for me, that's all I'm sayin', okay?"

"But maybe someday . . ."

Shit! "No day, no way, no never. It's not for me, okay, got it?" I said.

She let out a breath. "Okay, it'll be what it'll be."

"Val, I'm telling you."

"Never mind." She opened both palms, flags of truce. "What were you searching for? In a *woman*, a partner?"

"Searching for?" I pretended to be distracted by the rough road. "I don't know."

"Yes, you do."

"No, I never thought about it like that."

"Give me some idea." She brushed her fingers across my right arm. Like a small bolt of electricity, it made me jump. "Whoa, buddy," she said. "I ain't gonna bite." She rubbed my shoulders—kind of hard, maybe a minute. I uncoiled. "Okay?" she asked.

"Okay." I breathed.

"Stop!" she called out.

"What?"

"Pull over." She pointed.

An oxidized brown pickup had left kamikaze tracks off the road onto the bank and idled, coughing balls of smoke into the frigid air. Just beyond it, on the lip of the woods, two men grappled, kicking and punching each other. The bigger of the two, wearing a red flannel jacket, took a boot to his privates and went down.

"Pull over!" Val yelled.

I slowed toward a turnout. "Shouldn't we let them work it out?"

"Violence escalates."

"I think it already has." Before I pulled to a stop she opened the car door and started to get out. "Hey," I yelled at her.

"Hey!" She hollered at the two men and leapt out of our car.

The smaller guy in camo, unruly beard matted in blood, looked at her. The Red Flannel guy picked something off the muddied snow—a crowbar.

"Hey!" screamed Valerie.

I slammed on the brakes, turned off the ignition and ran toward her. "Val!"

She never looked back. She waved at the big man. "Put it down."

He stood there stupefied. "Who the fuck are you?"

The little guy charged him. The big man raised the crowbar.

I hit the big man in the midsection and threw him into the snow. "Fucking stop it, you want to go to jail."

Valerie kept moving toward him. "Put it down."

He swung the iron at me. My left wrist caught part of the blow; lightning coursed up my arm, shoulder and neck. "Motherfucker." I lost control; I nailed him on the right cheek, I nailed him on the left, and was ready to reduce his nose to splinters.

"Duke, stop it!" She grabbed my arm.

The little camo guy barreled into Val's waist and they both went down.

I jumped off the big man and pulled the other guy off Val. "You don't touch her." I hit him in the mouth and he started to bleed again.

He waved his hands at me. "Okay, okay."

He bounced back up, bounded for the bigger man. "Fuck you, Howie." He vaulted onto him, hammering him with his fists. "You're a selfish sonuvabitch, just like mom said."

Just as Howie took hold of the crowbar again, Valerie pulled it from the big man's grasp and hurled it into the woods. I put a knee into the little guy's back. "Stop fucking around, both of you. One of you will be dead if this keeps up. And the other will go to fucking jail."

The two brothers wrestled some more but less fervently. I thought Val was going to kick the one on top. "Hey," she said, "we're trying to help you."

He rolled off his brother, panting.

"What the fuck is the matter with you two?" she said.

Jack spoke to the air above him. "Go on, Howie, tell her what-the-fuck's the matter."

Howie didn't seem compelled to answer until Valerie kicked him gently in the side. I pulled her back. He spit blood and ran his tongue over his lips. "I fucked his girlfriend—so big deal, they're not married. I did him a favor."

Jack propped himself up. "You motherfucker."

"Listen boys," I said, "don't kill each other over a woman. She obviously likes you both. Can you see it that way?"

Val gave me an approving look, like I was using psychology when all I was really demonstrating was the obvious. "Get up and go have a beer together," I said.

Val withdrew her approval. "Maybe a cup of coffee."

"Fuck you," Jack said to Howie.

"Fuck you," Howie said to Jack.

"You're an asshole." Jack dusted himself off.

"Yeah, well it ain't like you're just findin' out now, douchebag." Brotherly detente.

"You guys ready to calm down?" I pulled Val closer to me, just in case.

Howie looked at us. "What are you, some kinda avenging angels?"

I put my arm around Val's shoulders. "I like strong women."

"Hmm." She gathered her mane in her right fist, the left pulled it straight back. "That's admirable."

"You think so? Thanks," I said, "I've always been partial to the seas."

She grimaced. "Really!" Faked exasperation.

The two men traded a punch-drunk look. "Look," I said. "Our work is done here, right guys? You finished beating the shit out of each other? Because we've got an appointment with ghosts and we weren't planning that one of them would be you."

Jack took a theatrical swing at Howie. "Yeah, I guess. Till the next time."

. . .

Back in the car, heat from our bodies fogged the windows and maybe my perspective. I could smell her, but barely see the road. I swiped at the windshield. The narrow two-lane pavement whizzed by, uprooted in places and in need of serious rehabilitation. "Have we got a problem?"

She braced, prepared to defend her actions. "You think I took a big chance back there."

"Yeah, you did." I gave it a moment, the windshield defrosted.

"But I get it. In some strange way, I get it." Her recklessness unnerved me *and*, in this situation, I saw something of myself in her.

"Good, that's who I am," she said. "But what happened to you? You kind of went off."

"I don't like people messing with me."

"Yeah, I see that."

The car scraped across a chunk of ice. My teeth hurt.

"You certainly have a temper." She motioned to the brawl disappearing behind us. "Maybe you need therapy." She pinched my shoulder.

"Got a couch handy?"

She turned to watch the road ahead.

I squeezed the steering wheel. "I just want to keep it simple. Like with women; I don't want to be a guy that's always looking for the next best thing. I want the best thing to be the woman next to me, from the start."

"An ideal." Her tone intolerant of such foolishness.

"The thing is, she has to feel the same way about me. I don't want to worry when other men are hitting on her, because other men *will* hit on her, she looks that good."

"You have high standards."

I made brief eye contact. "I'm not afraid of heights."

"Ha. Okay."

The tires buzzed along the old roadway, shuddered over a gap, and began droning again. I glanced at her. "And you?"

"Me?"

"You ever been married?"

"I was." She yawned.

"You were?"

She shifted upward in the seat. "Uh huh."

"Was this before or after the guy with the abortion?"

"*I* had the abortion."

Oh, oh. "Understood."

She reset herself. "Before."

"Tell me about him, about the marriage?"

"Why do you assume it was a *he* that I was married to?"

"Was it?"

"Yes. We were so unsure of getting married, we did it twice and of course we failed. It was vicious and I hated it. It was as far from home as I ever want to be. I'm still bruised by it."

"But you'd consider a woman?" I said.

"I have. But don't you want to know why the marriage was so awful?"

"You've considered a woman or you were with a woman?"

"Both."

"Really?" I said.

"Yes, what-the-fuck, *really*."

"And . . .?"

"And a flame always burns itself out. At least in my experience. No different than with a man; she was cavalier. Anyway, I'm naturally drawn to men."

My stomach loosened. "It was an experiment?"

"I wouldn't have called it that at the time, but I guess, yes, it was an experiment."

"You like to experiment."

She stared at the road ahead, mulling my assertion, focused on some point beyond the landscape. "I suppose that's true."

Verbalizing it seemed to disturb her. Her shoulders slumped and she repositioned herself, her back to me. She watched a broad hedge of smoke bushes whisk by. I tried to break whatever spell had come over her. "Flames don't always burn themselves out." I reached over and touched her shoulder.

She returned to me. "No?"

"No. There's a flame not far from here, not far from where

we're going, that burns year-round—from beneath a waterfall. Natural gases."

"Yes, but people . . ." She hung her head.

"The right man," I said surprising myself, "he'll stand by you."

"I told you, I was married."

"You did."

"Well, you know how in the movies the fireman always saves the woman in distress?"

"Yeah."

"Well, he didn't." She concentrated on the road.

"*One* man," I said.

"One fireman."

My foot slipped off the pedal. "He was a fireman?"

She nodded.

"Where, what precinct?"

"No." She shook her head. "I'm not going there. Put that question away. Besides, he's long gone. Died young, heart attack."

Could I track him down? Did I want to? My jaw tightened.

"I told you," she said, "it's over. History."

"Okay, what fucked things up?"

She scraped at the dashboard. "A power struggle; we negotiated everything: sex, kitchenware, family politics—always his family; mine didn't exist."

"Highbrow categories. I haven't made the rounds like you."

"Watch yourself." A caution, not a jocular one.

I held up a finger. "One live-in. Eight months but it was over at four. We never got beyond *gimme your tits* and *fuck you!*"

"Pleasant."

"Well, not quite that bad," I said. "But what's a man to do? Her basic intent appeared to be to control, and for me, I closed down shop; *my* control restored."

"Another struggle for dominance." She crossed her arms, as if we were both coming to the same conclusion.

"Anyhow, to add to the levity, she and I switched roles every so often. Mostly I kept offering my tits and, mostly, she told me to 'fuck off.'"

"I see."

I pressed on the gas. "Then you won't hold it against me?"

"What?"

"Being a man."

She studied me then turned to peer through the windshield at the countryside and the twisting road ahead. "We'll see."

CHAPTER 19

Father Blu

4:00 AM. I showered, marginally awake, until the water re-set the fire in my leg; a reminder of the debts I'd taken on. The church housekeeper wouldn't arrive for another six hours; Fathers Toll and Quade, Sister Maryann and the resident cook, slept peacefully.

The corridor lights, dimmed as usual, led me by rote to the dining hall. From my room, maybe thirty steps and down a slow ten-foot slope, into the church's basement. It might as well have been hundreds of miles given my hangover and the tender leg I dragged along. The impending visit to the Ninth Precinct made me uneasy. Then I just waved it off.

After unlocking the dining hall doors, turning on all the lights, the place still had the feel of a large windowless meat locker; thankfully not as cold. My head throbbed. The fluorescent lights, the refrigerators and the freezers all hummed, and occasionally gave off errant shudders as I set to making the first pots of coffee.

The EMT's question from the night before, *Did I hold a grudge against any of the firemen*, seemed more appropriately *How badly did someone want to stop me from my inquiry?* Or maybe, simply my imagination.

Regardless, a lineup of homeless people—all carrying pain—would soon be at the kitchen's door and I needed to be ready for them. *Old Faithful*, I thought, putting my hand on my hip pocket, searching for the flask. A little fruit elixir in my coffee to ease into the day. And there was a pint of Johnnie Walker Red that I'd separated from one of our visitors, and hidden—

"*Ola*, Father!" Herberto Ribbineros came down the stairs, his teeth white as selenite, his grin wide as ever. His receding gray thatch combed back, and at the peak, his signature black tuft. As always, cleanly shaven and deeply tanned. His skin announced his vibrancy—almost no sign of wear from the sun. "How are you this fine morning?" he asked.

If his autistic teenage son had pushed someone onto the Canal Street tracks, it didn't show.

"Herb, you're on today?" My thoughts of Johnnie Walker Red went into hiding.

"On prep and on the line, a full morning." He watched as I continued to put the final touches on the first four carafes. He smoothed over his charcoal mustache. "I'd love some of that when you're done."

"Anyone up at this hour gets two cups. And we've got treats this week." I gestured to the woven basket of powdered creamer packets. He came over and shook my hand, then to the large open vestibule and pulled one of the aprons off the row of hooks. I asked casually, "How are Carmela Irene and Gonzalo?"

He slipped the apron over his head. "Fine. She's still at the law firm, still moving paper from one desk to another, but content. And Gonzalo, the medications work most of the time." Herb tied the apron around his waist. "He's doing okay, thank you. And you? You look tired."

"I touch the sky when my knees hit the ground, but He sleeps so much better than I. Shall we . . . ?" I motioned to the unassembled kitchen and dining room.

We proceeded to lay out the chafing dishes, fill them with water, turn on the service line burners and start wrapping the silverware in paper napkins. The coffee began to tempt. We took down a couple of chairs from the long tables and sat for a moment.

If Herb had gone to the men's room or pulled eggs from the storeroom or checked the vat of corn syrup . . . But Herb stayed planted. No morning tonic, no whiskey; the coffee would have to do. Divine intervention?

"You know, Father Jamie, I actually enjoy getting out of the stacks once in a while, even if it means getting up at this hour."

Stacks? I'd forgotten his occupation. "The library doesn't need you today?"

"They need me every day, but so does the Lord. So do these folks." He raised his cup to the sky, his smile a reminder: selenite is a stone used for contacting and communicating with angels or other spirit guides for guidance.

"We appreciate you pitching in."

"It's probably their one real meal of the day."

"'Jesus said to them, 'Come and have breakfast.'"

Herb raised his cup. "John 21:12, I believe."

I nodded, impressed. "You know your scripture."

His eyes twinkled. "With all those books around, I try to read some of them too."

"Are you acquainted with the official Chinese Catholic Bible?"

"*Studium Biblicum*, isn't it?"

Herb knew his books. "It is," I said.

"I haven't read it. My Chinese is limited to pot stickers and duck, anything duck."

"Do you know where I can find some?"

"Duck or Chinese bibles?" His eyes lit up.

"Bibles."

"Strange you should ask. You know it's out of print. Well, maybe that's not true. But when I called and wrote the publisher in Hong Kong, I never got an answer. And I really tried reaching them."

"For the library?"

"I thought it'd be a good idea to have three copies, given our Chinese population."

"The 1968 edition?"

"No more of that," he said. "But the 2013 edition is identical. Regrettably, the cost of a *Studium Biblicum* is prohibitive, if you can find one. They're certainly beyond our means at the library. So I just bought generic American-published editions, under twenty dollars each. Who'll know the difference?"

"*Studium Biblicum* is costly?"

"Here in the U.S. quite a bit pricier than the standard bible, if you can find one, but I guess in China they go for about thirty-four thousand yuan; something like five thousand dollars."

I coughed. "Five thousand!"

"Each."

Whether they were destined for the black market or clandestine parishioners in Mainland China, I'd probably never know. I cringed at the probabilities. I'd become a trafficker in contraband.

"You look pale, Father."

"It's absurd."

He downed the last of his coffee. "The other volunteers will be here soon. We'd better get a move on. Okay if I turn on some music?"

"Sure, absolutely." I headed for the eggs contemplating how I'd handle the tong.

He switched on the small portable radio next to the microwave and began humming.

· · ·

Compared to Detective Zhōng's workplace and many of the other precincts I'd passed in the city, the Ninth Precinct presented a bright and recently remodeled exterior, the archway flanked by two patina deco lamps. Inside, as I negotiated the small knot of hallways and offices, I wished I'd stopped for a shot. The combo of coffee and rancid morning mouth had only intensified. I was taken with light claustrophobia—laughable under the circumstances—but still . . .

I announced myself and the female officer waved me in. "This way." They expected me. She led me into a windowless, empty room—vacant except for a table and two very uncomfortable metal chairs bolted to the floor. She closed the door behind her as she left.

I sat there for what seemed an eternity drenched in a callous indigo light. Father Toll would soon hear of my evening encounter at La Fiamma. *That* would initiate an entirely different and more difficult interrogation.

In the meantime, with Duke's story and Charli's pain still eating at me, maybe I could learn something from the inevitable cross-examination I was about to undergo, something that would track back to the firehouse or an enemy I'd provoked. Just thinking about Duke and Charli, rather than myself, allowed me to breathe, just a little.

When the door at long last opened, two cops entered, one in uniform and the other in a bright green holiday cardigan, festooned with a hokey moose, Christmas lights in its antlers. I began to stand. My leg hammered back.

"Don't get up."

I sat.

"I'm Detective Saunders." A no-nonsense African-American woman in her thirties with braids pulled stiffly back.

I offered my hand. She didn't reciprocate.

"This is Detective Rouben Parsamyan." Late forties, he of the sweater. Parsamyan carried a foot-long cardboard box and sat at the table as Detective Saunders lingered above us.

He leaned over and shook my hand. "You came close to immo-lation." The room got smaller. He continued. "Turpentine rags in the utility room; you may have noticed that the men's room had been recently painted."

Vaguely.

"And a can of D-D mixture in the men's room, possibly near the water heater. You're lucky, unusually lucky."

Detective Saunders interjected. "You know what D-D mixture is? You, by any chance, bring it into the men's room?" She pulled a pad from her skirt pocket and a stubby pencil that had been nested in her cornrows. Her pencil loomed above the pad.

"Me? No. What is it?"

Her face told me she wasn't convinced.

"Why do you look at me like that?"

Judging by her starched posture, she didn't give a hoot about my pique.

Parsamyan lifted the cardboard box to the table, pulled a plas-tic bag from it, and laid it in front of me. Inside the plastic bag, he uncovered a tall, completely blackened aerosol can, the top of which was jagged and blown open. "D-D mixture is flammable, especially dangerous in enclosed spaces; particularly when near sparks or open flame. Breathing it is also a no-no." His index finger delicately tapped the can to an unheard beat.

"Not so great on your skin or clothes, neither," added Detective Saunders, "unless you're partial to blistering your skin to the bone." She lifted her chin. "You washed your garments?"

"I did."

She seemed displeased and glimpsed at Detective Parsamyan. "Hmm."

"Shouldn't I have done that?" I asked.

"Never mind," said Parsamyan. "The EMT should have known

better. It would have been useful evidence."

"Say," I said, "what is this all about?"

The two detectives shared a look that lacked the sympathy I expected.

"What do *you* think?" asked Saunders.

If there was a good cop and bad cop, I knew where Saunders fit. Even the option was insulting. I directed my question to Parsamyan. "What is D-D mixture used for?"

"You see, Father, that's the strange thing. It's for fumigating soil before planting, to keep away pests."

Saunders broke in. "We understand you work with plants at your parish."

"Yes, occasionally." Now I was fairly certain that Father Toll had spoken to the police or whoever had, had reported their conversation to Father Toll. This seemed to be going in the wrong direction.

Parsamyan put his palms on the table. "You have a grudge with any firemen?"

"No, of course not. Why would I have a grudge with them? I'm hardly acquainted with any of them."

"There have been suggestions."

My body heated up. "What kind of suggestions? By whom?"

"Apparently you've been asking a lot of questions about a fireman."

"What's the big deal? Yes, a member of my parish, who almost *died*."

"Some people have insinuated that maybe you started this fire to put pressure on them to talk. Like maybe you were setting them up to look bad. A fire in a firemen's watering hole."

"And," Saunders added, "maybe it backfired."

"You've gotta be kidding."

"Well, "said Saunders, "it could be that someone was sending *you* a message. We've heard you were seen going into Ghost

Shadows Two. They're friends of yours?"

"Church business."

"Or," Parsamyan jumped in, "it was just an accident. But what's a can of D-D mixture doing in the bathroom? The folks at La Fiamma never heard of it."

"I can assure you I'm no arsonist."

Saunders tapped her pencil on the table. "That's good to know."

The young man in Chinatown was right; contrary to Father Toll's reprimand, wearing my collar and the sanctity my priestly trappings presumably conveyed—none of that mattered. Not at all. My forbearance was growing thin.

. . .

"So," I said after I'd finished retelling Chuck Winston the past day's events (leaving out any mention of the tong), "what am I missing? To whom am I threat?"

He appeared apathetic. "I presume if someone really wanted to harm you, you'd be dead. You're a man of God; this was probably coincidence. Still, I'm not surprised that you're getting pushback from the crew; firefighters are a tightly knit bunch. For days on end, we eat together; we sleep in dorms together; we share dangers that most folks really can't comprehend. We have our own internal ways of dealing with problems. You may have the best intentions, Father, but you're an outsider."

"Okay, but why would Duke's station mates not contribute to his relief fund?"

"Can't say. He wasn't the most gregarious guy although I don't think he was disliked. Maybe it's because he's insured—through the department, by the way—until a final disposition is reached. His care is expensive. Some may be convinced it comes out of their pocket or out of their future care. Maybe because he's only got his sister surviving him, no children like some of the other men and women.

"Maybe some of the men—and this is pure conjecture—aren't too happy with him trying to kill himself while the rest of them are fighting every day to save lives, often times their own. But listen, I did take a look at the gun."

"Duke's?"

"Yes. And I passed the information on to the AIU."

"The arson unit."

"Yes." Winston hesitated. "There's been an ongoing investigation." He quickly clipped the subject by searching for something in his desk.

"And?"

"Well, it's news; I don't know if it's good or not." He pulled out a folder and opened it. "Duke's gun didn't come from that fire. There was no soot on the nostrils."

"What does that mean?"

"That gun wasn't in a fire. You said it was one of the guns stolen during the fire. It wasn't."

"That's what the gun shop owner said."

"It may be what he said but it's not true." Winston patted the folder. "If that gun had been in the fire, it would be like the others, have similar traces. Just like a human. And I examined a couple of the other pistols that were returned, to be sure."

"I don't get it."

"If a human dies in a fire they have soot around the nostrils, from breathing in the fire."

"Makes sense."

"If they were dead when the fire started, there's no soot on the nose. The body may have been planted there to cover up a murder. Duke's suicide weapon showed no signs of being in a fire. The others did."

"So, if it wasn't, it's either not the suicide weapon or he got it from someone other than the kids who trafficked the guns from the fire."

"It *was* the weapon Duke used. I checked with Detective Zhōng. There's no question. Police ballistics confirms that. They compared the beveling around the entrance wound, the bullet casing and the striations the MRI detected on the lodged bullet. You keep reaching, Father; I don't understand why. As much as it hurts me to admit it, Duke attempted to kill himself. Why, and who sold him the gun, may be questions needing answers, but perhaps not germane to his motivation."

"You're probably right, Chief."

"But," he said standing and ending our conversation, "if you're right about what happened to you last night, if it was intentional, you might reconsider what you're doing and leave it to the cops. You're a priest not a hero, Father, and—except perhaps existentially—nobody expects you to investigate life and death matters on the street."

. . .

As I made my way back to the rectory, shapes sharpened around me, colors grew more vivid. I was alert in a way I hadn't been for months, maybe years. As if taken over by something nebulous but familiar and intimate. Like stalking through the tall reeds of Long Pond with Jory, or when Miss Lili re-kindled the animal in me.

Looking beyond the skyscrapers, past the broken clouds, to the ether, to Heaven, I stirred with the sense that investigating a life and death matter on the street was *precisely* what I should be doing; perhaps what God intended. Or, as both Charli and the chief had intimated, I was simply consumed with being a hero.

Nevertheless, instead of entering Our Lady of Sorrows from the rear and the basement, I came up the front steps through the vestibule and nave, scanning for Father Toll. When he was nowhere in sight, I strode through the tiled hallways, past volunteers stacking boxes of bananas onto a cart for distribution, and down three stairs to Father Toll's office.

I knocked. I prepared for recriminations, maybe worse. But he'd be heartened to hear I'd made progress on Duke's attempted suicide.

"Come in."

All at once, a vibration in me; I wasn't so sure.

"Father Bluterre, you've deemed us worthy of a visit. Sit down."

"I can explain."

"Yes, I'm sure you'll try." His hands formed a pyramid in front of his face as if to physically block any such explanation. "You were in a bar, drunk."

"It's true. But I was there to investigate Sean Ducotty's attempted suicide."

"With several drinks in your hand."

"It didn't start out that way."

"It seldom does. Anyway, it doesn't matter anymore." A punishment about to be delivered.

"Father Toll, I'm making progress."

He sat forward. "What have you learned?"

"Really, nothing conclusive, but soon . . . "

"Then it doesn't matter, I don't want you doing anything more on this Ducotty business." He sat back.

"What? No, you don't understand—pardon me, I'm making progress. Don't hand this off to anyone else, I'm on top of it. The drinking, I know, I had a setback. But look, I'm here. I'm done. I won't need drink anymore."

He didn't blink. He rested his pyramid hands on the desktop. "Good, I'm glad to hear it. Let's trust it doesn't happen again. But we're not going to bother Ducotty's family anymore. Or anyone else. They'll call me if he comes out of his . . . his state. If he ever does."

"I think there's more to this suicide attempt," I said.

"Be specific."

"I can't. Not just yet."

His left hand curled tighter. His right hand walked toward the solid glass Saint Florian paperweight. "There always is, but we're done with it. It's becoming too much of an issue. Go pray to Saint Monica."

"But you were adamant—"

"Father, there's already too much talk. Do you want your escapades to leak to the Vicar?" His voice had the quality of flint.

"I told you, my drinking's under control."

He shook his head gently and with a chaste smile said, "And I hear there are more delicate issues, issues that have been previously raised."

"What? What delicate issues?"

"The kind the Vicar might want to discuss with the Bishop: sequins, licentiousness, your usual account. *Again.* You draw so much attention."

"That won't happen again," I said.

"Perhaps they'll have you transferred to another parish—if anyone will take you. Maybe somewhere far, far away."

"On what grounds?"

"Don't test me. Just stop your investigation. You're a priest, I think, not a cop."

"But you were the one—"

"What are you waiting for? Go work on your homilies, plant flowers or help clean up the rectory. I don't care. Just get out of my sight."

Even before I lifted out of the chair, the room seemed to shimmy. I steadied myself, stood and moved to the door. I looked once more at him, hoping I'd see something in his face that would explain his sudden turnaround. And his anger. "If it's the drinking, I promise—"

He cocked his arm, threatening to hurl the paperweight at me. "Get out."

"But, Father . . ."

His left hand griped the edge of the desk. He glowered at it, as if to command his left to channel the enmity in his right, to bridle it from following through.

I stepped out of his office, on my own.

. . .

I couldn't take my eyes off the flame hanging above the ark.

Cantor Jean Stein noticed. "It's called the *Ner Tamid*, the eternal flame. A symbol of God's eternal presence." She looked resplendent in her vestments, all white. The synagogue empty and still.

"Yes," I said turning back to her. "I seem to be preoccupied with flame these days. And that song, *Outcast*. I listened to it, not three hundred times, of course. But it got me thinking; was there another song you remember, maybe another that Duke related to, one that also says something about him? Anything you can remember?"

"Another song?"

"Yes?"

She closed her eyes, she caught something, her head tilted.

"Yes that, what's that?" I asked.

"It's not a song, it's a composer."

"That says something about Duke?"

"Yes, in a way, it does."

"Who?"

"Beethoven."

"Why?"

"One evening Duke went on about him, and Benjamin mentioned Duke's Beethoven broodings several times. Duke related to Beethoven's tragedy, the loss of the composer's hearing in the prime of his life, the depression. According to Benjamin, Duke's mother suffered from it, the depression. At one time she was institutionalized. I don't know if that helps. But I called you because I found this." She leaned against the pew and withdrew a heavy book from her satchel. "It was Benjamin's book. I was cleaning things out."

The cover read, *Scientific Protocols for Fire Investigation*.

"Look inside. That bookmark." She pointed.

I opened to the handwritten note wedged in the section titled "The chemistry and physics of combustion." It read, "Surveillance never breeds trust."

"A note from Ben?"

"No, not his writing. I think it's Duke's," the cantor said.

"What does it mean?"

"No idea. But like I said, Ben and Duke had a falling out just before . . . you know."

"Right. Do you mind if I keep this?"

"No, that's why I called you. I don't know if it helps."

"At this stage, everything helps," I said.

I sat there, not wanting to go. Her prayer shawl bore delicate dark blue embroidered leaves that ran over both shoulders to small crowns on each end. Her elegance somehow calming.

She smoothed out the shawl. "You're hurting."

"I am." I let out a breath. "I am."

"A wounded healer," she said.

"You overestimate me."

"I don't think so." Her eyes so kind. "The brain can't always tell the difference between physical and emotional pain. Anything I can do?"

"Thanks, no. You've already done what you can. I'm just tired."

"I get it. I do. And on to the next."

"Yes," I said. "On to the next."

CHAPTER 20

Duke

As Val and I drove up to the castle, evening had already begun to descend. A delicate blue arc of remaining sky backlit the limestone merlons, ivy-covered battlements shaped like angry teeth. Orange light flickered through the windows.

"What a great idea!" Valerie cupped both hands around my face and gave me a hungry unhurried kiss before jumping from the car. "Let's go."

As I unloaded our small luggage I noticed that the parking lot was deserted.

"Sorry," said the undersized desk clerk, his nasal tone grating. "We had to cancel the psychic fair. Not enough participants. Early winter mid-week can be like that."

Valerie, clearly disappointed, fingered her duffel bag. Lambent candelabras circled the empty lobby. "And the other guests?" I asked.

The little man, head down, wrote in the guest registry. He'd knotted his sparse bleached bristle into a small bun above his head and his matching khakis were pulled almost as high, belted just below his chest. I was surprised he could breath and his pallor suggested that.

"Oh, well, yes . . ." He resumed scribbling into the large ledger. "You'll be very comfortable," he said talking into the book. He raised his head and dangled a key. "You've got the Tóirse Room. Probably the nicest room in the castle. Still has no electricity, thank goodness, a modicum of the Lauthrey's history still being respected."

"The original owners?"

"Yes. The whole history's in your room by the bed stand. But please respect our rules concerning candles. We have a variance grandfathered in." He offered a crooked smile that implied he was being humorous.

"Three candles a night. You can blow them out or relight them. We'll provide the refills the following morning when we make up your room. Please do not use your own: fire department rules. At any rate, the Tóirse Room is certainly the quietest room, it's in the rear, near the postern gate. Do you need a hand with your luggage?"

"No, I think we can manage." I checked with Valerie; she'd let go her minor disappointment and was enthralled with the surroundings. "Val?"

"Yes, of course." She bent down to pick up her sport pack but I was ahead of her.

"I've got it."

"One last thing," said the little man, still not meeting my eyes. "A lot of people assume we use the castle's legends as a marketing ploy." He glanced up at me then quickly returned to avoiding eye contact. "You can believe whatever you want, but we haven't wired your room—any room—with sound effects. Or any special mumbo jumbo." He tugged at his bun.

"Okay." I winked at Valerie. She pouted as if I were embarrassing her.

"Believe what you want," he repeated. "I don't suggest leaving your room after midnight. Or until there's daylight."

I buried a smirk. "Right."

Valerie looked like she was going to kick me. "Let's get to our room."

"Where's the restaurant?" I asked.

He pointed across the lobby to a darkened space. "Not open during the week in the winter." He checked the book. "Friday night we'll be open for dinner. You'll find it's quite good. But the bar's open . . ." He checked his watch. "In about an hour."

"Friday night!"

"There's a vending machine at the top of the oubliette stairs. There's usually soup available in the bar."

"The oublee-what?"

"The stairs above the dungeon."

. . .

By the time we'd navigated the castle's drafty stone corridors and dim lighting—some wired with primitive electrical, most candlelit—we found our room on the second floor, exactly as the little man had said. Not large but spacious enough to accommodate a canopied king-sized bed. I fantasized Val spread across it.

Two nightstands bookended the bed, while a dark oak dresser, a free-standing armoire, and two red side-by-side antique wing chairs filled out the room. Cozy and romantic. In the rudimentary bathroom, a claw-foot tub and shower. Like the bedroom itself, the bathroom offered a scenic view over the ten or so acres of grounds that lay behind the castle, most of them now in darkness.

A fire had been lit in the small fireplace, muting the winter wind that occasionally licked through the room. Three long candles, each surrounded by an etched glass holder, illuminated the space. This would be a night to remember.

"You were teasing that odd man." Val pulled out one of her composition journals and tossed her tote in the corner.

From the same spot, a large brown moth took off, traveled across the room, and landed on the upper corner of the bed, slowly flapping its wings.

Val turned back to me.

"I was not," I said, "not making fun of anybody." The moth tarried above us. "Should I get rid of it?"

She threw herself on the bed. It chirped like a cricket. "Come here." She opened her arms. I dropped my duffel and stood above her, admiring her.

She grabbed my belt and pulled me down next to her. She got very close to my face. "Don't diss the ghosts."

"No?"

"No. They'll come after you if you're not respectful."

"I'll try to keep that in mind. Do they get to read your journals?" I waved at the composition notebook.

She grabbed for it and put it on the nightstand. "No one gets to read my journals. And, please, with the ghosts, do more than try." Her lips close, her breath warm.

"I'll do more than try."

She lifted herself up on an elbow and lowered herself on top of me. "Good boy."

"So . . .?" My hands rested on her hips, unsure if she'd push me away, again. At worst, I expected her to turn cold; at best, I expected we'd finally make jungle love. Instead she grew silent, her eyes afraid.

"What's wrong? I'm not gonna hurt you, really. I live by my agreements. No pressure."

Her eyes filled with tears. "It's not you, it's me."

This time I considered making it into a joke. *That's a pretty standard line, lady. You've used it on me several times already.* But her pain was genuine; something she feared in me, something I couldn't fathom because I didn't remember ever having that effect on other people.

"I won't hurt you," I repeated, not knowing how to allay her misgivings, whatever they were.

"No . . . but I may hurt you." She pulled me closer and buried her lips in my neck. My chest rose and fell with hers. A seamless fit. She hooked her right leg under mine and tightened down on it, not so she hurt me, but so I knew that she had the strength to pin me down, if only for a little while.

She whispered in my ear. "I'm pretty sure I'm in love with you. But I can't promise you a thing."

Her hair fell over her shoulders onto me. I whispered into it, "You've made that clear before."

"Are you willing to take that chance?"

"I am." Caught up in her magic, I was confident of the outcome.

She pushed herself up. She took my face in her hands and she came at me, mouth open. She bit at my mouth, and I bit back, our tongues inside each other with no room to breathe. Along every point of our bodies, boundaries disappeared. Still, we didn't have enough.

She reached between our bodies and down the outside of my pants until she felt me stiffening. "Would you like me to complete you?" she asked.

Yeah, I wanted that. But I wanted something more, something I never could have verbalized until that moment. "I already think you do."

"Oh my God!" She began to cry.

I held her. Muffled in my shoulder, I think I heard her say, "What am I going to do now?"

The moth watched from above.

. . .

We lay in each other's arms like two warm well-worn rugs, separate from the rest of the room, the walls, the floor, the ceiling, the castle, and all else that escaped into the night. When I opened my eyes, the candles that lit the room had melted down to a third of their length. "Uh oh, wake up little Suzie."

"What?" she said, stirring from the magic.

"We need to eat something." I checked my watch. Close to midnight. "We slept a long time."

"Sleeping? Were we sleeping?" Insinuating we'd been very much awake but in a different reality.

"Seriously, I need to eat something, and you must be famished."

A light came on in her eyes. I knew what she was about to say; I said it with her. "The bar!" We hopped out of bed and repossessed our shoes. I grabbed the keys. She blew out the candles.

But when we arrived at the bar, we could only peer into the dappled light. I shook the door. It rattled but no one appeared. "Closed," she said.

I checked my watch again. "Well, it is midnight and we appear to be the only guests."

"That can't be true."

"True or not—"

That same light came on in her eyes. Again, in unison, we said, "The vending machine!"

We tore down another maze of hallways suppressing giggles. We loaded up on the worst snack food I've ever deliberately put in my body. Valerie stared nervously down the stairs leading to the dungeon. Cool damp air rose from it. "Can't you hurry up?"

"Do we have time for the dungeon?" I juggled the packets of our coin-dispensed dinner.

She wagged a finger at me. "No, no, no. We ain't goin' in no dungeon."

"You're the one that believes in the afterlife."

"I do, and that's why we're heading back to our room to devour the few morsels technology has bestowed on us." She slapped my ass and led the way.

In our room, Valerie relit the candles and I laid our loot across the bed. "Where shall we start?" I began dividing the packs into piles of sweet, salty and indecipherable.

Her eyes flashed in the candlelight. "The time to hesitate is through. No time to wallow in the mire." She snatched a Kit Kat bar.

"Impressive," I said. "You weren't even born in nineteen sixty-seven."

Another rare smile. *She was going to tell me her age.* "No, I hadn't quite arrived," she said. "But the song's a classic and one of my dad's favorites. He said my mother and he used to make love to it, and that I might even have been conceived to it. I said, 'Dad, TMI.' But he just laughed. 'Get over it,' he said."

"Tell me about your parents."

The enthusiasm drained from her face. "They're in an urn on my mantel."

"Yeah, I've met them." I waited for her to expand on her history. She unwrapped the Kit Kat and plopped into one of the wing chairs. I grabbed a bag of peanuts and sat next to her. "So?"

"You don't really want to know."

"I do."

She flexed her hands as if about to lift a great weight. "You'll be sorry."

"Bring it on."

"Thad." She said with a hint of reverence.

"Like Thad Jones?"

"Thad my dad. That was his name." She sighed. "He died way too early."

We had that in common.

She continued. "A land surveyor, he loved the outdoors. Happiest man I ever knew."

"What happened?"

"You mean how'd he die?"

I nodded.

"My mother killed him." Said with such indifference she might as well have been ordering pizza.

My mouth opened but, of course, nothing came out.

"Well, you asked." She took a bite of the candy bar. She chewed it slowly. Her face no longer exactly covered in skin, more like a thin layer of elastic. "She caught him with another . . . another man. On the floor, in front of the fireplace. She ran him through with the fireplace poker."

Electricity arced my shoulders. What could you say to *that*? "I'm sorry."

She bent forward, took both my hands in hers. "Oh, but it gets better." A rictus smile froze her face. "The other man . . . was her brother."

"Her—?"

"And he killed *her*, choked her to death. He told me he was resolute." Val's eyes settled on our paired hands. She took me by the wrists, hard.

The way she held them, I wasn't sure what to do . . . "Your uncle, oh geez." I tried to pull away. She gripped tighter.

"*Resolute*, that was his exact word. Meaning he never equivocated." She kept staring at our locked hands, her pupils enlarged, glassy and out of reach. "I so respected him for that." She tapped the heel of my hand. "He's in the Bennett Correctional Center dying of metastatic colon cancer."

Her story for real? "I don't know what to say." *A warning? A ghost story for the castle?* She wasn't smiling. "Of course you don't." She let go my wrists. "But that's what I want to be, resolute in my choices." She took another bite of chocolate. "And you? What about your parents? You said they met here. How'd that happen?"

Her seismic shift—away from the horrors of her childhood—left me searching for footing. It reminded me of my first time in her apartment, the schizophrenia of it. It knocked the breath out of me.

"Yours had to be happier than mine," she said as her lost femininity regenerated, refueling her skin, restoring her color.

Faced with a gale of questions I dealt with the easiest. "Happier?" I said dully. "I guess so."

"And it started here at Charing Cross?"

The candle fluttered.

"Duke?"

I grabbed hold of her question. "Yes. I never knew precisely how my parents found each other at Charing Cross." A lie. "He was filling in for a friend, a security guard, I think, just for the weekend. She was on a day field trip, from someplace close by, I guess." From the asylum.

"He was working here at the castle?"

"I don't know, they never talked about it, not specifically." Which was true enough.

"You never asked?"

"We did—both my sister and I. But they were vague."

"But they hit it off." Val hopeful. "And it lasted."

"Well, I'm here aren't I?"

"Unless you're a ghost."

"Anyway, my dad had a way of making Mom sunnier, and she had that effect on him too, though he hardly needed it."

"Was your mom pretty?"

"She was. Not flashy, but when I see photos of her, the ones with my dad, she has flower innocence." *The later photos less upbeat, more withered.* "I think my dad was the only one who could properly water her."

"How lovely. Certainly not how it played at our house." She squeezed her eyes together, packed away the remnant of that brutal evening then said, "Sorry, go on: your dad."

So, I told her about my dad the cop; how he died. I told her the whole story except the part about the acoustic neuroma invading his brain, how it affected him, how he fell over dizzy, just like I had begun to do, how his face went numb and he could barely swallow, how the tumor couldn't be removed without further and more extensive injury to the surrounding nerves, before the work he loved was taken away from him, and he died.

"Cancer." I lied. Treatments hadn't significantly progressed since his death. The doctors would turn me in. If I remained dexterous, at least I'd have a few more years of the work I loved, on my terms.

"Your terms!" Benny's face intruded, raging at me, dredged up from the past. One of the last times we were together.

Val said, "You and your sister were even younger than my brother and I. Is your mom still around?"

"No." *No point going into Mom's depression.* "My father's death pretty much did her in."

"So . . ." Valerie laid the remaining candy bar to the side and opened my palms in hers, as if reading them; the same hands that only minutes before seemed to hold me prisoner. "We have a lot in common after all." She ran a finger along a line. "I thought so. It's the kind of sadness that even years of laughter can't fix."

I touched her cheek. "Maybe not, but we can try. Let's talk about something else."

"Okay." She picked up the Kit Kat and took a final bite. She chewed. "What shall we talk about? Relationships? Death? Death of relationships? Relationships as the cause of death?"

How to respond? So I laughed. "I'm not sure what to talk about, but I want to talk about it with you."

She dipped her head, affection implied on her lips. "If not death, name a subject."

"The best things about your past boyfriends."

"You really are digging it all up." But her eyes welcomed me.

"I care. I want to understand what worked, not what didn't."

"Fair enough," she said. Without warning, the windows brattled and the candles sizzled. The large moth reappeared, drifted across the room and seemed to travel through the glass and out into the night.

Down below, maybe 200 yards into the castle's gardens, a flame moved among the trees. "What's that?" she asked. As quickly as it had appeared, it was gone. "What was that?"

"Can't tell. Let's take a look." I started to rise out of the chair. She pulled me back down.

"It's after midnight."

"The best time to tell tales." But perhaps this wasn't a night to make fun of ghosts, skeletons maybe. "Alright, the best of the boyfriends."

Suddenly overloaded, her eyes cast downward. "They were *boys*, most of them. *Friends*, I'm not so sure."

"Has it always been so bitter?"

"You think I'm bitter?" she said.

"Could be."

She thought for a moment, then acquiesced. "They were men."

"And . . .?"

A vastness drained her eyes of focus. They were still large and striking but they drifted away, far away. "They couldn't love me."

"But you're magnificent."

"It's what you see."

"Sure, of course," I said.

"That's not me."

"I don't understand."

She swallowed. "I know. I'm an object, cut down to a manageable size."

"Oh, c'mon on!"

"No, you come on. It's late. Let's get in bed and just hold each other. We communicate well that way. We can dig a little deeper tomorrow." A plucky withdrawal, but clearly defeat ran along the edges of it.

"No, I want to understand," I said.

"Don't push me."

"Please."

"Okay, alright. My mom would say, 'You're so attractive.' And I'd say, 'I had nothing to do with it. You're not taking *me* into account.' She'd say, 'But your hair, your eyes, your skin—you've always looked so good, you're a beautiful young woman.' 'That's exterior, Mom, I'm more than that.'

"But she'd bull ahead, 'And your shoes; those shoes, so nice looking.' I expect she had her own legacy in mind. That was short lived." Val lagged, exhausted by her explanation or her exposure. "Do you understand?"

Words bubbled in my throat, words that scared the shit out of me. Words I'd never uttered, not even to my dad. "I love you."

"I don't think so." Her tone steely, intended to put a quick end to my brash fantasies. Or hers. A painful strike to my heart; I regretted telling her. And maybe she was right.

"Is that so impossible?"

Her mouth tensed. "Can you really love *me*?"

She wanted me to convince her, a lifeline I grasped ahold of. "I do, I think I can. Who are you? I suspect I know but . . ."

She stood and took a step away from me. I grabbed her wrist. "No, you're not walking away from this."

She slapped at my hand and tried to wriggle away. "Let go of me."

I held tight. "Is that what you really want?"

She waited till her breathing steadied. "I believe I'm kind. I believe I'm compassionate. Maybe a little scattered, and afraid.

That's at my core." She threw off my hand.

"But you're also angry. Why?"

"Like I said, it always burns out."

"So far," I assured her. "So far."

"Shit, you're such a believer in love?" She measured me with wounded eyes. "We should take off our clothes and get into bed." She ran fingers up my arm and led me to the four-poster.

When I revisit it now, I imagine that bed and The Doors song. Because our love did become a funeral pyre.

CHAPTER 21

Father Blu

The early New Year's Eve Mass came to a close, and with Father Toll's clear reprimand to stay out of his sight, I returned to Duke's apartment, shaken by the warring information I'd invoked. But also slightly drunk on the modest progress I'd made.

The apartment appeared untouched since I'd last been there. Detective Zhōng had said, "I've never seen a cleaner, more organized man cave in my life. The guy must have been a saint." Without qualifying Duke for canonization, I could vouch for his orderliness.

I went to his computer. It opened without a password. He didn't have an address book. He didn't have an email account—at least not on that computer. And his Internet search history was mostly confined to—what else—references to various songs and musical acts, and to fire and fire investigation.

There *was one* orphan link to mind-altering plants, and I put in my mind to ask Detective Zhōng and the hospital doctors if toxicology reports had been run immediately following Duke's suicide attempt.

I closed down the computer and went looking for his cell phone.

Whether he'd put it there the day of his attempted suicide, or Charli had placed it there, I found it easily in his desk drawer, below the computer. Calls dated back almost a year. By referencing the limited address book on his phone, I quickly attached most of the calls to 411 information, the firehouse, an occasional call to Charli or to Chuck Winston, and to someone identified as "V." One letter, but it energized me.

There were several other unidentified numbers. All activity had ended a week before his bungled suicide.

I slipped the phone into my jacket pocket and felt for Old Faithful. A little black raspberry sounded about right. But Duke's liquor cabinet also called to me. Opening it, I stared at the bottle of Johnnie Walker. I reached for the bottle; I unscrewed it. I smelled it. I headed to my AA meeting.

Along the way I'd rid myself of the bibles. They'd metamorphosed from useful currency into a hazardous, unholy burden, though I had no clear answer how I'd handle the shortfall. I told myself the Ghost Shadows Two wouldn't physically harm me, but a pastor in Boston had gotten too close to a Chinese gang and had incurred burns over three-quarters of his body. He wouldn't talk about it. Locally, there was the man found in the East River, *bào chou* ("to take revenge") crudely carved into his forehead. I was already in deep water.

Their building was locked.

I walked away, the Good Books now impious and hatching under my arm. They were restless, like a venomous bin of Madagascan Moth caterpillars clambering to break out. I imagined them crawling over my arms, my face, stinging me. Weird paranoid stuff. I just wanted to be rid of them.

In the basement of the Church of the Resurrection, I stashed the box of bibles below my chair. No one around to distract me from my anxiety. Every time I closed my eyes, tattooed eyes of orange flame stared back. Or I'd picture the Ghost Shadow woman, her grisly upper arm swinging, a slow menacing club. Then, again, the moths, thousands of them.

People started filtering in around 6:30 PM. Most were regulars, easing some of my unrest, but as usual—except for the occasional nod—no one approached me, until Teresa arrived. She came over and sat next to me. "Father Jamie, we've missed you. It's been almost a month. You been sick?"

"A little bit."

"You look better tonight." In her mid-to-late fifties, Teresa's homey moonstone face and unaffected smile reassured me.

"I feel better, thanks."

"I wanted to ask you something, Father, if it's okay. I really shouldn't bother you about such things."

"No, please, go on."

"I know this chapter decided early on not to keep a roster of any sort; we want to maintain everyone's privacy. But some of us are between sponsors—you may have heard of Silvie Martin's death."

"I hadn't." Not only did I not know Silvie Martin, I didn't want to take on anyone else's pain.

"Anyhow, what do you think about initiating the idea of a roster? With people coming in and out of meetings like they do, we could be sure everyone is covered if they want to be. Perhaps bring it up to remind everyone that sponsors can come from everywhere, and at any time—even for those of us who have been involved with the program for years. We can't ever take our cure for granted."

My hand went to my chest. "I think you should ask the group, but I'm probably not the one to bring it up."

"Oh, why not?"

"I don't have a sponsor," I said.

"No? But you could. And you could be one."

"I don't think I'm the right person to sponsor anyone."

"Would you be my sponsor?"

That's what she was getting at. I was barely afloat and she wanted to attach an anchor. Still, I felt derelict. "I think you should ask the group if they want a roster and if anyone would like to offer themselves as a sponsor. I'm honored that you would ask me, Teresa, but I can't commit to being there for you the way you deserve. And you know it's not advised for a man and a woman . . ."

Her face conceded; the palimpsest of previous disappointments now more visible. "But you being a priest . . . I thought of all people. . ." She stood up. "It's okay. Sorry to have bothered you, Father." She walked away with the gait of a way-worn soldier.

I faded in my chair. *Go after her, say yes.* But I knew it would be wrong. I didn't have a year of sobriety. I'd be angry if she called. I didn't have the internal flexibility to add another soul to my flock. I could barely keep myself together; was only starting to fantasize about my reclamation. One sip away and I'd be falling down a flight of barroom stairs. Or I'd be pushed.

When the meeting came to order and we'd gone through the usual agenda, Teresa spoke up. "Hi, I'm Teresa. I'm an alcoholic."

The group responded. "Hi, Teresa."

"As I look around this circle . . ." She made eye contact with everyone, even me. "I see people are missing from the last meeting and the meeting before, and the meeting before that. I recognize that a roll call is inappropriate. But I'd like to know who's missing and I'd like those people to know we're here anytime they want or need us. We say that every meeting, but well, I believe it might be useful to have a voluntary roster available to us—maybe to make an occasional call. Maybe to let those who desire to be sponsors to identify themselves. To let them know we're a team, a family."

A fine idea, I guess. But after that, my mind drifted. Hands went up. Mine followed in support, though I was already traveling through an inventory of places I'd lived or been assigned: Scottsbluff, Lincoln, Lexington, Madagascar, Reunion Island, the Chestnut Hill Seminary, Boston, Pittsfield, Amherst, Boston again, Worcester, Flushing, lower Manhattan.

Jory and I had always thought of ourselves as explorers. Even in the seminary, I still carried a scintilla of it. But through the years the energy for it had emptied from my body, a grain of courage at a time. I'd lost tone, and found myself sitting alone and immobile in Father Toll's damp undercroft bedroom.

I wouldn't have guessed that Duke's tenuous struggle would lead *me* on a forward path. Yet he tugged at me with his paralytic presence. I *owed him* for the lifeline I'd been thrown, considering how little I still knew about the man.

Just then, Teresa's blue pantsuit caught my eye, rushed in an otherwise easy stream of people exiting the meeting. "Teresa," I said as she hurried by, and reached for her arm without thinking. I caught her.

"Father?" Her eyes said the evening had left her wiped-out.

"Please sit." I scooted to the next empty chair so she could sit next to me. The last eight or nine people were filing out.

She sat. She looked at me, more hurt than anything. Whatever youthful vigor she'd sustained in front of the group had drained from her mouth and eyes, probably not for the first time; heartbreak her backfill.

"I'm sorry," I said. "Your roster idea is a good one." *You're not doing enough.*

She composed herself, a moment of stateliness. "I'm glad you support it."

I wrestled with the impropriety . . .

"If you'll still have me," I said, "I'd be honored to be your sponsor." *Have you lost all reason?*

The Younger Teresa re-emerged, illuminated. "Really?"

I nodded, governed by some long-lost compulsion. She hugged me, her body soft and warm with a hint of orange.

And me with a bundle of misgivings.

. . .

The next morning sleet returned saturating the air. Teresa had given me an idea. I surveyed the Firehouse 27 landscape for resistance. Wire Rims and another fireman moved around one of the trucks, washing it, their voices careening off the concrete and metal.

I darted behind the hook and ladder to avoid them seeing me. I headed up the stairs to Captain Hoyle's office. Long Hair came down. His head drooped in displeasure. "What is it now, Father?" On one shoulder he wore the emblem, "Engine 27" with the Ghostbusters image spitting on a flame. On his chest he wore a nametag, "Tony Scalzo."

"Fireman Scalzo, happy New Year. I'm here to see Captain Hoyle."

His fist locked onto the bannister.

"Is Captain Hoyle around?" I asked.

"He's expecting you?"

"No, but I'm sure he'll see me."

Scalzo hooted. "Father, I've got to give you credit for persistence." He crossed his arms. "But I think Captain Hoyle is out at the range or with the apparatus. Something didn't square in the journal this morning. Why don't you come around later?"

"What?"

Scalzo clarified, "He's probably checking out the engine truck."

"Well," I said inching my way past the fireman, "I'll just leave him a note."

Scalzo laid his large hand on my shoulder to stop me.

"Father Bluterre?" Captain Hoyle stood directly above me on

the second landing. "What are you doing here?"

Scalzo lifted his hand and belched. I began moving up the stairs again. "I just need a minute of your time."

Scalzo gave his captain a questioning look and Hoyle just flexed his hands in acquiescence. Hoyle started down the stairs. "*Just* a minute; we've got battalion drills this afternoon. I'm very busy. We all are." He blocked my way up. "What is it, Father?"

"I understand most of your men may not want to talk to me, but you said it was up to the individual."

"It is."

"May I have a roster of the crew here in the station house?"

He motioned me to head down the stairs. "Like I said, we're busy."

I didn't move. "It's public information, isn't it?"

He stopped. "It's public information, but I wouldn't usually just hand a sheet over. Anyone can file a request for a document with the department."

"I'm sure that could take some time."

"It might, that's not my job." He tried again to move me down the staircase.

My hand wrapped more firmly around the rail. "What could *you* do to support Duke and Duke's family?"

"His sister."

"Yes."

He huffed. "The roster, it's more than a year old."

"That's fine."

"It won't have personal phone numbers or emails on it. It's just a manifest, the roll call that we use."

"Then that will do. I can send individual notes to each of them, I'm sure."

"I suppose." He didn't budge.

"So?"

"Okay, okay, hold on." Hoyle left me standing on the stairs. Below, Scalzo, Wire Rims, and three others had gathered. They looked up at me as if I were an incendiary device that needed permanent diffusing. Their stares left small hateful incisions. I turned my back to them.

Hoyle returned with a sheet of names. "Here." He extended the sheet to me and, his hand against the small of my back, steered me down the steps, through the group of firemen and women, and out of the building onto the pavement.

Storm clouds had darkened the city, the air wet, settling on my hair, hands and cheeks. *What would Father Toll do if he knew I'd run through his stop sign?*

...

By the time I reached Our Lady of Sorrows, my clothes adhered to me. To avoid Father Toll I went around to the rear and through the undercroft to my room, as always unlocked. A humble sanctuary, for which, that morning, I was thankful.

Throwing aside my overcoat and muggy tunic, I toweled off. The frigid air of the church basement as bullying as the frozen rain above. Inside my tunic the roster sheet had become soggy. As if it were the shroud of a saint, and careful not to tear it, I unfolded it onto the small table that I used as a desk. The sheet displayed a head count of approximately thirty men and women, listed alphabetically. Scanning the list, I assumed that the men and women who'd already made clear their hostility—like Wire Rims and Tony Scalzo—would be non-responsive to an interview.

Then a name, halfway down, caught my eye: Christopher Toll.

I stretched out on my bed. Christopher Toll? I fell asleep, a restless sleep.

...

The 2 PM choir practice brought me out of my deep slumber. The wind rapped at my subterranean window, a constant chipping that ultimately goaded me out of bed and hastened me to wedge a pair of socks between the frame and glass, muting it. The glass raw with cold.

Outside, the wind scolded, and from above me in the chambers the choir chanted the Latin "*Improperium*," though Good Friday was many months off:

> *Thy rebuke hath broken my heart; I am full of heaviness.*
> *I looked for some to have pity on me but there was no man,*
> *nor found I any to comfort me. They gave me gall to eat,*
> *and when I was thirsty they gave me vinegar to drink.*

A mourning; words that reflected God's generosity and forgiveness despite man's cruelty.

The Ghost Shadows' deadline had arrived with only five bibles of the twenty I'd promised. They weren't likely to forgive; the club-armed woman made that clear. Were they above torture? What would that gain? They wouldn't kill me, same thing. Maybe a combination of torture and leveraging me into some unholy payback—if I was lucky.

I considered sacrificing myself, sending the bibles back to my fellow priests. But they wouldn't have an avenue to the Chinese black market. Selling them in the city would only fetch a fraction of their worth. Of course, I could run. But I'd already been doing that far too long. And the tong would track me down anyhow. Phantoms circled me.

With the $25,000 worth of canon in the cardboard box, I gathered whatever cash I had on hand and in my thin bank account.

$283 wouldn't appease the tong for my shortfall, but the effort would show good intent. Laughable optimism.

Lacking a name or a phone number, I set out by cab for the gang's community center. I trusted that someone would let me in. To my surprise, the front door was open, and no amount of calling up the stairs brought any attention.

The lower hallway disappeared into a dark, unlit cavity. Only one of the two uncovered fluorescent lights held steady. I hefted the box up the stairwell, through the smothering dankness, past the smeared blood, to the door where I'd previously met the large woman with the mutilated arm.

The door was locked.

Too afraid to stay, too intimidated to leave, I knocked, I called out. No one responded. It was, after all, late afternoon New Year's Day, the wind still reproachful. *Get it over with.*

On the floor below, the fluorescent ballast flickered with crisp little explosions—scurrying cockroaches of sound that might well have been cockroaches. The light outside was falling away and there was nary another sound in the building but my heavy breathing.

More than an hour passed.

"You were running out of time, Father." She stood over me, much closer this time, the Tong Woman, the most massive rock of woman I'd ever encountered. Not that she was just tall or bulky, but her muscle mass defined her; her arms—even her fraction of an arm—like sculpted basalt. And though I wouldn't have called her a beauty, she possessed unmistakable sexuality, though I'm sure that was far from her mind.

I started to rise, stiff. I'd been sitting too long on the box, in the stagnant air. "You might as well know I'm not able to deliver what I promised," I said to her.

"What's going on here?" Father Toll stood thirty feet down the hall at the top of the stairs, marking me.

I hadn't heard his steps, not the whole time, not one, even in that cavern of a building. As if Toll drifted up the stairs, a revenant. A chill ran through me.

He came toward us. "Father, can you explain this?" His arm swept over the scene. He bore into Tong Woman, as if he could knock her over with his fervent eyes and Godly arsenal. Then to me, cold, so my back froze. "Well?" His eyes heavy. He didn't let me respond. "You have no shame, do you, Father? This building, this woman . . ." He waved at her. "*These* people . . . What are you doing with these people? This *gang*?" He charged atop a white horse, devoid of any doubt.

Tong Woman spoke up. "It's a community center."

Her thick, bass tones startled Father Toll, finally reminding him of The Devil with whom he was dealing. "Selling what?"

She stood like a rock. "It's a community center."

He charged again. "If I called the archdiocese and asked them to make a few calls—you know, for inspectors and others to hang around, monitor things a little more closely than we already do now—I can't imagine the mayor's office would think twice before they'd have people on the roof, in every corner, at your doors. *I* can see it happening." He was enraptured. So much so I thought he might levitate. *Where was the damn choir?*

He continued. "What do you think I'd learn? Sex and drugs, of course; the cheapest way to people's false happiness. But what else? Because I'm ready. Do you kill people? That man in the East River?"

Something flickered in her eyes. A tiny spasm in that magnificent physique.

He didn't take his eyes off her, seeing he'd punctured her armor, but he spoke to me. "And here you are, Father Bluterre. Have you done quite enough, Father? *I* think quite enough."

"Father," I said. "I don't know this woman very well but I think we should be respectful of her organization."

"Organization?" It came with spit. He zeroed in on her. "Blasphemers, whores, savages preying on the flesh and fears of our populace. You've been on the radar. This is no community center." He turned to me. "And you're no priest."

"Father, I'm here as a messenger of The Church, *our* church."

"I'm no fool, Bluterre. You drag your sordid history behind you, wherever you go, like the Devil's Tail."

I thought to strike, but I didn't. "I'm here to donate five bibles to the center." I looked to her for the name.

"GST Youth & Community Group." Her face didn't show it, but the ever-so-slight retreat in her voice validated to me that she'd rather not cross swords with The Church, not over this.

I saw, or imagined, her face overlaid, two faces at once. Neither was decipherable. "It's so generous of you . . ." she said then glanced at Father Toll. ". . . and your parish to donate these holy books."

Father Toll slapped the wall. This time leaving an echo. "You two underestimate me. You'll be very unhappy that you did."

I knelt to the box and pulled out my keys. I ran one along the seam. Cold bled into my knees, paranoia again wended over me. On opening the box, would I be met with *Studium Biblicum*, or a new swarm of phantom moths?

"Father Toll," I said, "I don't think either of us—myself or Ms. . . .?"

"Archie," she injected.

" . . . understand what you're talking about. But the Lord's words are the clearest, and they are all in here." I tapped the box. "In Chinese." I tore open the seam and exposed the bibles.

Archie bent down and pulled one out. Balanced on her stub, she ran her lithic hand over the cover then opened it. "It's magnificent." Her teeth slid back and forth as if gnawing on something—but again, the quality of watching two people at once. "Truly magnificent."

I lifted the box and held it out to her. "For your community."

"Let me see that." Toll grabbed for a bible. It took him one, two, three attempts to secure it, which only further infuriated him. He turned it over in his fists. He began to thread through it and paused to read the title page. He stared at me. "I don't believe it."

He flipped more quickly, fanning the pages as if there were cut-outs in the book, little hideaways for drugs, an approach I'd used in my earlier days.

"I'll need to go now, Father," she said. "But what a wonderful way to start the New Year."

I motioned to Father Toll to replace the bible to the box.

"And I'll need to lock up," she added, nodding at me; what I took to be settlement.

Toll picked up another bible. Repeated the fanning.

"Father," I said. "We're guests here."

He dropped the *Studium Biblicum* into the carton. Archie organized it so she could close the box. "Bless you," she said.

"Bless you," I said. And Father Toll followed me down the stairs and out onto the street. Fuming.

Both the Tong Woman and I had benefited; perhaps I wouldn't hear from her again. I'd paid $25,000 for *one* answer, but after all, I'd moved forward, hadn't I? *Hadn't I?*

Father Toll emerged from the building decidedly less content. "You'll be done very soon, Father. If this keeps up, very soon." He walked away, his fury merely a whisper on the wet pavement, yet lodged fully in my chest.

I turned my collar against the wind, buried my hands in my overcoat and lowered my head. Father Toll had confronted me in the building looking neither cold nor tired. Yet he must have waited for me to connect with the Tong Woman, as I had, for over an hour. Had he already been in the hallway shadows waiting for me? Had someone followed me and tipped him off?

The wind came at me again. Like those days in Boston,

foretelling a formless but certain affliction to come, even when things were going just fine. It felt inevitable, just around the corner. I needed a drink.

· · ·

A number of pubs were on the way, many of them bustling with good cheer. I kept my head down. My stone-cold sanctuary in the rectory would put the final touches on a bleak New Year's Day, Teresa's congenial face the exception.

The wind drubbed my chest and shoulders, and continued to thin out the pedestrians around me until I found myself almost alone on the pavement. Less than five blocks from Our Lady of Sorrows a woman, her head also down, crashed into me. She wore a purple dress with a white stripe.

"Sorry!" I said. She bent forward. Rain dripped from her blonde ringlets. The load of pain she carried was palpable. "Are you okay?" She didn't answer. She just crouched there, as if I were the latest wall she'd hit, searching for breath, scraping herself together.

"Miss?"

She didn't look up. I put a hand on her shoulder. She turned to me with childlike, blood-fractured eyes. She began to sob.

"What is it?"

Her knees buckled and I caught her, the first woman in my arms in years.

"Go away." She sunk to the wet concrete in tears. In chorus, the wind began pitching sleet on her and leaking over my collar.

"C'mon." I raised her up, her body portable in my arms. I walked her under the awning of a closed cigar shop. "It's going to be alright. It always is." *Was I a liar too?* I held her with one arm and opened my overcoat with the other. I extended her a handkerchief.

She swept aside bangs and her pale innocence rushed at me.

She'd once been quite pretty and still retained a shade of it, even carrying the pain. "Always?" she said. Then a grunt came out of her—a vibration that *couldn't* have come out of her. "What the hell do you know?" She wiped her eyes and forehead; she noticed my clerical collar. "Shit." She eyed the sidewalk. She held up my handkerchief, in disgust, like she was sorry she'd taken it. She tensed. "Take the fucking thing."

I let go of her. "Keep it. You want to talk about it?"

"Go away." She tossed the handkerchief to the ground.

"It might help."

"When does fucking talking about anything help?" she said.

"Let's try."

"*Let's* means *let us*, that requires both of us. Ain't gonna happen." She started weeping again.

I went to console her. "What's your name?"

She sidestepped me. Despite those baby eyes, she had more history than I'd first assumed, probably mid-forties. Her low-cut dress hit me between my legs, a place I kept hoping to forget. The woman was a jewel in the otherwise dreary conditions.

"This is out of your league." She started to pull herself together.

"Try me."

"You a crusader?" A raindrop spiraled off her cheek, twined down her neck and rested in the well of her naked collarbone.

"Try me."

"Two kids, no job . . ." She fell against my chest. "No fucking *nothing!*" The warmth of her body against mine unnerved me. She began to pound on me with her fists. Then she began swinging.

I grabbed her arm.

"You know what that's like in this . . . fucking godforsaken fuckin' city?"

"It's not God forsaken," I said.

Another grunt, this time apocalyptic. "He's fooled me."

"Where're your children?"

"None of your business." She started to pull away.

I caught her elbow. "Wait. Do you have a place to stay tonight, some kind of shelter—you and your kids?"

She straightened just a little. "I told you, *out of your league.*"

"Try me."

"I can't talk about it." Her right eye quivered.

"Why not, you in danger?"

The oncoming sleet pelted her eyes. She clammed up.

"Come to our church, Our Lady of Sorrows. Bring your children. I'll make sure you'll all eat, have a warm meal and a safe place to stay tonight."

"Not that fucking simple."

"Why not?"

"Never mind." Again, she stepped away.

I caught her arm. "I want to help."

"You want to help? Okay, I need two hundred bucks. Can you give me two hundred bucks, right now? Three hundred would be better, but I'll settle for two. And I'll do whatever you need." She opened her coat fully and displayed her body. "Because that's what *I* need."

"Stop," I said.

"I can't promise you'll get your money back, but I'll try."

I leaned closer; no trace of alcohol on her breath. She cupped my neck and pulled me toward her, her voice raspy. "I'm ready to do anything for a couple hundred dollars. Isn't that what *you'd* like?" I tried to pull away. Her strength surprised me. She tilted my head to her breasts; no bra, now visible down to her nipples. I jerked to focus on her face. She smiled. "Right?"

Even her smudged mascara couldn't hijack temptation from my mind. My heart hammered. "Of course not. Close yourself up."

"Last look." She bent forward.

When I refused, she rewrapped herself. "Like I said, out of your league. To hell with you." But she didn't budge.

My hand went to my heart. The Ghost Shadows' $283 cash sat in my breast pocket. "Why can't you tell me where your kids are? I can go with you."

"You can't protect me or my kids. I'll find somebody who'll pay me." She turned to go.

"Wait!" I reached into my pocket. "If I give you money, you'll come to the church?"

Her face suggested victory. "Maybe, maybe in the next few days. It won't be tonight."

"But you'll be safe?"

"As safe as I can be." She waited to see the money withdrawn from my pocket.

"And your children?"

"They'll be safe, *if* you give me the money." She indicated I should hurry up.

"Won't you tell me—?"

"No!" The awning flapped and stung the air; the sleet rained down harder. "And don't follow me, you'll make things much worse. You'll risk us all." She seemed to include me.

I pulled the bills from my pocket and began counting out two hundred then handed her the whole wad. Like a different woman, a woman in control, she said, "Bless you." Then further surprised me by placing her palm against my chest and kissing me on the cheek.

Again, *that* surge. "Bless *you*," I said. "Be safe—*please* be safe—and come visit. And no worries about repaying me, okay?"

The bills went into her pocket, her lips parting—but not in gratitude, as I'd expected—but rather in *appropriation*, her eyes narrowing. She turned abruptly down the block, and away.

CHAPTER 22

Duke

That night Valerie and I did get naked together for the first time. I don't know if it was her rowing regimen that kept her body so well-toned, but it was a body to be admired—her breasts not as big as I'd originally envisioned, her legs and thighs larger. But all of her a miracle in my eyes. Freckles on her chest and along her shoulders, a wash of stars tossed across a galaxy.

In the castle's stillness, in that large four-poster bed, our fingertips ran along each other's, and then went separate ways of discovery. Mine down her neck and shoulders, her spine, along her hips and thighs, calves and feet. All the while, her perfect pungency mine for wonder.

Under the sheets, time slowed as I rubbed her feet, my fingers tracing the inside of each toe on each foot because . . . because I craved to dwell in what Kierkegaard called her "unknown divinity." I didn't want to miss an inch. I was home.

She began at my face and chest. But when I'd slipped under the covers, my head at her feet, she ran her fingers over my belly, my thighs, my balls, my knees and eventually she began nipping at and sucking on my toes. We went on like this for more than an hour, murmuring a language of our own.

Finally, I pulled her to the base of the bed with me, with its redolence and lack of light. We rejoined mouths, my legs opened hers. I descended deep into her, fusing with her for the first time.

. . .

The next morning the distant strike of a hammer fetched me out of my sleep. Wood smoke layered the room, her smell coated my lips. I ruffled the sheets. Her aroma drifted up from the base of the bed. But she was not next to me.

Steam billowed from the open bathroom door and I waited with bated breath for her return. Whether it was five minutes or fifteen, the wait felt interminable. I threw off the covers and made my way to her.

The claw-foot tub, surrounded by a plain undecorated opaque shower curtain, clouded her face and figure.

I called to her but she mustn't have heard me over the shower. So as not to scare her, I pulled the curtain back slowly. Her was head tilted skyward, and water coursed over her hair and closed eyes. Deep in thought, I assumed. So I spoke softly, "Good morning."

Her head dropped forward, she snapped the curtain shut. I stood there dumbfounded, short of breath. A moment passed. "Good morning," she finally said, a hoarse whisper, then pressed her lips to the curtain and waited for me to meet her there, a thin film between us that, at the time, I found off-putting.

In retrospect, it presaged our fortunes.

At any rate, I let it go and returned to bed where I must have fallen back to sleep, the remote pounding gone and the castle hushed, devoid of the city's constant rumble. It helped to know that a fire alarm wasn't going to interrupt my sleep.

When I looked up, Benny was hunched over me, his face strained.

"You just keeled over. You okay?"

"I'm fine."

"What happened?"

I tried to get up, but I had no arms or legs, just a head.

"Just stay down," he said.

"Just stay down," he said again. And again. "What's going on?"

"Nothing."

"You're full of shit."

I floated in a tunnel of some sort. Dark. No sound except his voice. And then mine. "You can't mention this to anyone."

"Tell me."

"Promise?"

"Don't be ridiculous. You need to look into this."

"Not a word," I said. "Not a fucking word to anyone."

"Bullshit. What if this happens in the middle of a call? You need to get checked out. This isn't normal."

"Probably not enough sleep," I said.

"The fuck it is."

"I'm fine."

"It's not just about you." Benny had never turned his anger on me before.

"I've got it handled."

"You're being an asshole. You gotta tell somebody."

"Keep your mouth shut."

Benny intransigent. "I'm gonna have to tell somebody."

"I can't let you do that," I said.

"What are you up to?"

Then Valerie's voice. "What are we up to today?"

Val, fully dressed, lit a pipe of marijuana. The castle room came back into focus. "Come on, wake up." Eager, the bathroom incident erased, she offered me the pipe.

I declined.

Across the room, over her shoulder, watching from the head of the red wing chair, the large moth had returned.

Val proceeded to lay a carton of takeout breakfast in my lap: eggs benedict garnished with greenery, and slices of apple, orange and cantaloupe surrounding it. Breakfast in bed. No one had ever fed me breakfast in bed.

"I took the car; I hope that's alright," she said. "It's a lot longer into town than I'd remembered." She pointed into the carton. "Eat up."

When a piece of muffin protruded from my mouth and I shoved it back in, she commented, "So debonair, Duke."

Mumbling through the muffin. "That's me. Debonair Duke."

"I like it! From now on you're *DD*."

I wiped my mouth. "And you're *Cabbage Patch*."

"Lovely." She actually smiled. "So, what would you like to do today, DD?"

"Well . . . let's explore the grounds, CP."

I reach over to the nightstand and pulled the laminated flier to my side:

Charing Cross Castle
& the Lauthrey Legends

I began reading aloud. "Charing Cross Castle, so named because of the abandoned graveyard on which it was constructed, was originally built in eighteen-eighteen by Niall Lauthrey as a mansion for his bride-to-be, Maeve O'Sullivan."

As I read to her, Valerie fed me the rest of my breakfast, every so often picking up the napkin and wiping the edges of my mouth. I wasn't sure I liked that, but I supposed it was her way of being tender, maybe even romantic.

I continued. "Maeve was true to her surname, and with raven eyes the color of obsidian, she refused to move into the castle until Niall Lauthrey had completely finished construction and had dutifully married her. But Niall was unrestrained for her, and every day without her by his side, his trust in her faded. In the evenings he would begin pacing the castle's parapet—sometimes until dawn—hoping she would acquiesce to his entreaties and arrive with open arms."

Val interjected, "Men are so cocksure on the outside."

"Cabbage."

"Go ahead."

"When he could bear the separation no more, Niall convinced Maeve that the castle was only days from completion, and that she should travel to it immediately so they could be married.

"When she arrived from the city, she straightaway insisted on seeing every room to ensure the castle had been properly accomplished. Being a man of simple tastes and great economy, Niall Lauthrey had not yet brought on a cook maid or footman, but he showed Maeve the sturdy castle, from its highest room to the first-floor dining room. But not the cellar.

"Maeve was displeased with the utilitarian, stolid design of the castle. She showed her displeasure by storming off and locking herself in the room that Niall Lauthrey had built especially for her, a room at the top, above the postern gate, looking out over the gardens."

Valerie and I surveyed our room.

I went back to reading. "No amount of cajoling could entice Maeve from her room that night. But when Niall finally went to bed, disconsolate, in his own quarters, Maeve slipped out of her room and began to reconnoiter in the hope she could reevaluate and find benefit in Charing Cross despite its spare assemblage.

"As she made her way through every room, she began to moderate her disappointment in Niall's hard work. That is, until she stood on the ground floor, at the rear door, surprised to see narrow stairs leading to a cellar."

"Stop," said Valerie. "I don't like where this is going."

"I imagine it's going down those stairs, the same ones we saw last night. Shall I keep reading; I'm almost finished with the page?"

Val didn't look convinced, but she gave me a small nod.

". . . Until she stood on the ground floor, at the rear door, surprised to see narrow stairs leading to a cellar. Lighting a candle from a wall torch, she descended the stairs into the bowels of the castle."

A knock on our door broke our concentration. Valerie jumped off the bed. "Who is it?"

"Oh, sorry," he said through the door, the desk clerk's nasal tones unmistakable. "I thought by now you'd be out of the room so I could clean it and make your bed, and get out of here."

Valerie opened the window and started swatting the smell of marijuana out of the room. The room filled with winter's edge. I called to him. "I can be out of here in five minutes."

He grumbled something. Valerie pulled the carton and silverware from my lap. I ran to the shower.

. . .

"So how do you think it ends?" Valerie sidled to my left and passed me a steaming cup of coffee—so strong you could walk across it. We were a hundred or so yards from the castle, the garden's curled brown remainders looking desolate buried in snow. We passed into the woods.

I took a sip. "The legend?" I caught her hand in mine. She accepted it willingly. "I don't think it ends well."

"Relationships." Her voice weary.

"Hey now." I let go of her; I lifted her chin and looked deep into her eyes, still mystical and slightly mahogany in the late morning light. "We can do this. We *are* doing this." I thought of my parents.

She forced a smile. "Yes." She kissed me but her worry lingered.

"This way." I pointed into the woods and reclaimed her hand.

She zipped her jacket tighter and off we went again, hand in hand, the pristine smell of pine and coffee auguring my optimism. The woods seemed to embolden her. "I should tell you why I'm hesitant, why at times I run from you."

"We're all frightened at times. We all live with ghosts, don't we?"

"Every time I walk towards somebody, down this romantic path, down an aisle, I'm walking toward someone who doesn't know me, not really. The results have been grim."

"Everyone we meet is struggling with something we know nothing about."

"Yes, exactly." She touched my face. I lifted her hand and kissed it. "But," she continued, "knowing *that* is not the same as understanding the struggle. And I don't help. Because . . ." Her eyelids closed searching for the right words. "Because I send mixed messages to every man and woman I meet; I persuade them that I'm something I'm not."

"You don't strike me as being disingenuous."

"No, that's not my intention. But you're blinded by something you see in me. I can see it in your eyes."

"I see some of that in your eyes, too."

"Perhaps, but your faith in me doesn't change who I am."

"Try me," I said.

"I'm getting closer to it, but you may not like the outcome."

"I doubt that."

"Yes, I know." She shrugged and started us walking again. "Be careful what you commit to. Men, and women, like their prearranged order of things." She left it at that, conflict simmering close by. I didn't press her. We penetrated deeper into the woods; the forest grew darker and colder. She drew her jacket hood over her head and stared at the path forward, strewn with its pinecones and fallen branches.

She was a complicated woman, no question. But every fire had had its complications and I'd weathered those. Her willingness to admit to her demons a sign that she wanted me to help her slay them. And, of course, I was sure I was up to the task. Like fighting a fire, I shifted the energy. "How's your rowing going?"

"It's good." She didn't elaborate.

"Could I come watch you at your next meet?"

"It depends."

"On what?"

She stared straight ahead. "Your ability to push me."

"How do you mean?"

"I mean you need to push me beyond my comfort zone. Physically. Basically, torture me."

"You don't seriously mean—"

She finally looked at me. "Oh yes, I do. And that's why you might not be the best for me at an event. You regard me as some dainty thing. I'm not."

"Your rowing means that much?"

"I'm much more competitive than you think."

In the thicket, the wind began to pick up, white flakes twisting out of control, whole sheets of snow sweeping off the evergreen limbs. "That's okay with me."

"Good."

I felt light-headed.

That's all I remembered until we were back in the garden, me lying on the ground, snowflakes wetting my cheeks, eyes open to an angry sky, the wind tangling her hair across her face.

"You think you can get up now?" Valerie knelt over me, spooked.

"What happened?"

"We were walking, we were talking. You got wobbly. I helped

you out of the woods. You don't remember?"

I tried to clear my brain. I rubbed my head. "What were we talking about?"

"We were talking about fires. You were telling me about the 'lake of fire.'"

I knew the reference, but I didn't remember ever telling her about it.

. . .

That night at the bar, we each ate a big bowl of clam chowder with crackers, her appetite as large as mine. "So," she said, pushing the bowl away, "are you going to tell me what's going on? And please don't tell me it's normal for a fifty-five-year-old man who looks to be in great shape to get dizzy, to not recall twenty-five minutes of conversation, and to pass out."

If I shared my assumptions about my condition, she'd probably abandon me for someone healthier. "Okay, I'll see a doctor. But I'm sure it's nothing. Too much hollandaise, perhaps."

She wasn't amused.

"Hey," I said turning to the twenty-something bartender. "What happened to Maeve O'Sullivan when she went into the cellar?"

He put down a jar of stuffed olives and stepped toward us, the bar otherwise unoccupied. "The legend?"

"Yes."

"Of course I wasn't there to verify it," he said.

"I'd guess not." I smiled at Valerie to join in the joke but she remained somber.

He continued. "They say when Maeve got to the bottom of the stairs, the cellar was a maze of building materials: straw bales, wood stacked high and piles of lime and clay, in addition to the several remaining large blocks of granite. She moved slowly in the candlelight, not pleased, seeing the construction incomplete. Then, according to what I've been told, she heard footsteps on the stairs, and receded into a corner. It was Niall, perhaps having heard her leave her room or—I've heard it said—he hoped to seal off the unfinished basement before she'd discover it."

Valerie finally turned to the barman.

"After that it's mostly speculation. But whether it was Niall attempting to destroy the evidence before Maeve found it, or whether it was an accident caused by a fight between them, no one knows."

"But . . .?" said Valerie.

"But the cellar became engulfed in flames. Before the fire was out, almost everything down below was in ashes. The floor above the kitchen caved in, the heat so intense in the walled-in cellar it became a crypt. Maeve's body was completely incinerated, never found."

"What about Niall?" I asked.

"Apparently, he escaped. They found him on his back in the garden, half his clothes singed off, his arms, chest and half his face burned. He went quite insane and lived out his years in the Willard Asylum. It's still around, a prison facility now, about two hours from here." He paused. "Can I get you two anything else before I close?"

I looked at Valerie. She was brooding.

"No," I said. "Thanks."

CHAPTER 23

Father Blu

Christopher Toll. His name on the fire station manifest mere coincidence or related to Father Toll?

But first, I decided to call "V" and each of the most recent unidentified phone numbers on Duke's phone. Perhaps Christopher Toll's was one of them, although even those phone numbers were seven days prior or more from the time Duke had shot himself.

I called V's number. No longer in service. Then the five completely unidentified numbers, starting with the oldest chronologically, a call just before the Christmas past . . .

"Morgensterns." An older woman with a horseradish voice. "Hello, can I help you?"

"Yes, sorry. I'm calling regarding . . ." *How was I going to phrase this?* "A friend of mine called you just before Christmas the year before *last*."

"Yes? We get lots of calls, mister. What is it you need, we're kinda busy here."

"Well, ah, what kind of business are you?"

"Is this a prank call?"

"No, no! Please, I'm sorry." *Try the direct approach.* "My friend . . . died shortly after he called you the second time. He called your number . . . let's see . . . twice. Last December and then a month or so before his death." Not exactly the true explanation but . . .

"Listen mister," she said, "I'm sorry for your loss, but I don't see how I can help. That was more than a year ago."

"Well, first off, what kind of business are you?"

A deep sigh filled the space. "We're a grocery store. Does that help, because I gotta go?"

"No, no, please, one last question. If I give you his name, can you check your records to see why he called?"

She laughed. "You gotta be kidding. You got any idea how many people call here each day to find out if we have organic strawberries or canned yams or an Excello mop. You're not even talking this past Christmas. I gotta hang up." And she did.

I found the address and went to the store, a rather large, well-lit upscale store with customers streaming in and out. I'd never gotten the name of the woman I'd spoken to. "Excuse me," I said to a clerk checking out an East Indian woman and her two children. "Can you direct me to the manager's office?"

He pointed to the back of the store. "On your right, next to dairy."

As I arrived, an older man, stubby like a hydrant, exited. "And tell him," said a voice from beyond the door, "that we're done. I can't charge my customers that price. We'll find another distributor." The horseradish voice.

"But Marcy—"

"That's it, Joel, no more." And Joel left with his orders.

I knocked on the door. She looked up, over dark-rimmed glasses, from a pile of papers, clearly unhappy with my intrusion. "We've already given, Father." She looked back and forth between two of the stacks.

"I'm not asking for a donation," I said. "I called earlier."

"*Everyone* called earlier."

As if on cue, my cell phone rang. I looked; my heart sank. Teresa. I turned it off, guilty.

"See," the woman said and went back to organizing papers.

"My call to you, it was about my friend who died."

She shrunk a little. "Oh *you*. Look, we sell groceries. We can't be held accountable for what people put in their bodies and what happens to them after they do. And we don't offer taxidermy either." She lifted up a file and after holding it midair for a few seconds, put it down in the same spot it had come from.

"No. As I mentioned on the phone, he called here twice. I'm hoping you can check your records. Perhaps he made a special order. You keep those?"

"What's this all about, Father? Why *us*?" She took a swig of her Starbucks. "I need this just to keep up with people like you. Maybe the stress will kill *me* next." She flinched, realizing she'd gone too far.

"Would you look? His name was Sean Ducotty."

She lifted and lodged the glasses in her hair. "And then you'll leave me alone with this pile of crap?"

"Sean Ducotty," I repeated.

"Okay, okay." She turned to her computer, lowered her glasses back onto the bridge of her nose, and after checking with me on the spelling of his name, she typed his name into the computer. "Figures." She scanned the screen. "We get all kinds."

"You found him?"

"Special order, just like you said. Sean Ducotty. Deliver weekly."

"Deliver what?"

She looked up from the screen. "One cabbage."

"That's it? He wanted a cabbage delivered to him weekly?"

"Not according to his billing address."

"Then to whom?" I said.

"I'm sorry, Father, but I shouldn't even be telling you this much."

"It's important."

"A few blocks from here, that's all I'm gonna say." She clicked off the screen so I couldn't read it.

"And the second call?"

"To cancel the order. Now if you'll excuse me, and even if you won't, please let me get back to my work."

I'd need to get that address.

. . .

Just as my phone lost its charge, and I took the last dram off Old Faithful, I finally found Teresa. It was slightly after 4 PM in Brooklyn, in Green-Wood Cemetery. The sun might have been setting on the bone-chilling day, but snow blew vertically and hard, and in giant swirls making visibility impossible. She leaned against a tombstone—bundled, thank God—drinking from an almost-completed two-liter bottle of something called Zombie Antiserum. She wiped away tears congealing on her eyelashes.

"Aren't you freezing?" My breath billowed and quickly dispersed in the descending light. The stone slab against her back was caked with ice. *My bones* shuddered.

"Happy Three Kings Day." She sipped from the bottle then offered it to me before withdrawing it. "Can't have."

"No?"

"No. It's basically rum and coke. Always loved it. Seems fitting," she said.

"The Feast of Epiphany," I said, somehow following her twisted logic.

"Very good, yeah, and that's why I called ya. I thought this would happen. And look, it did." She pressed for a smile but it didn't come.

"C'mon." I gave her my hand. She had no gloves. "Let's get out of here."

"No, come sit with me. You, me and Lola." She tapped the tombstone. "Lola Montez."

"Looks cold down there. You're gathering snow."

"It is." She waited. I squatted. She wet her lips. "That's the best you're gonna do?"

"I'm here to listen, not to freeze."

"Do you ever cry?" When I didn't answer, she said, "Oh shit, okay." And reached for me.

"Let's walk." I helped her up. She clung to her drink until I stopped us in front of a trash barrel. I eyed the bottle with ill will; well-rehearsed bullshit. Old Faithful sitting empty in my pocket.

"I guess," she said. She threw the bottle and its remaining contents into the trash.

I put my arm around her. "Tell me." We began to walk, heads down, snow bombarding us.

"Look at me, Father Jamie. What d'ya see?"

Immediately on dangerous ground. The little I'd seen in the past, she was a punctilious woman, always acting appropriately, showing attention to her appearance, and more often than not, showing concern for others. But in this inebriated state she'd emerged more disheveled, somewhat ursine in form. *And what did I look like when I got like that?* "I see a strong woman who has briefly stumbled."

She looked up at me. She kissed me on the lips, surprising me. "That's the kind, redacted version," she said. "You're not telling the whole story." She wiped the flurry from her eyes.

"That's all I see, that's all I know."

"I suppose that's fair. Can we get somethin' to drink?"

My head jerked.

"Water," she assured me.

I stomped my feet to get some feeling back in them. "Well, we'd better get out of here. It's late, weather's already serious."

She huddled into me, arm around my waist. Then slipped her hand onto my butt. I removed it. We continued walking.

"See, I thought I could be Lola Montez." He voice dragged. "You know who that is?"

"The name sounds familiar, but no."

"Eighteen hundreds. Irish-born Eliza Gilbert ran naked through the streets of County Sligo at age ten, traveled Europe in her teens, passed herself off as Lola Montez, a Spanish dancer, in her early twenties. An actress, a mistress, a Bavarian Countess, self-assured, obstinate—generally a shit disturber her whole short life when women weren't supposed to do such things. She slept with wealthy older men, like Franz Liszt. She died not even forty, here in Brooklyn."

"*The* Franz Liszt?" I said.

"Yup." She clutched tighter to my arm. "Wanna know how we're alike, me and Lola?"

"All ears."

The gale cut across our faces, howling and tapering into high-pitched shrieks. She tripped, I caught her. "Faith," she said. "I always had faith in myself. I was *already* Hispanic."

"Halfway there," I agreed.

"That's what I thought." She punched my arm. "That's *exactly* what I thought, *halfway there*." For a moment she turned glum. "I didn't run naked in the streets until I was in my twenties, though." She shoved the hair out of her eyes. Shoulders back, she lifted her chin. "Did try sleeping with wealthy older men."

"How'd that work out?"

She wiggled her fingers. "*Menza-menza*. But's okay." She pulled me to a stop and tilted her head. "You should try it sometime, a woman, I mean." Snowflakes matted her pumpkin cheeks.

"Let's keep moving," I said.

She started walking again. "My papa said *go for it*. My momma took me aside and told me I'd end up in hell; that I should be thankful for what I'd got."

"Got?"

"She meant these." Teresa pulled her coat apart and showed me her cleavage. Before I could seal her back off from the elements, she rewrapped herself. "And damn, if she wasn't right."

"I doubt that's true."

"Faith," Teresa continued, "it's a kind of neurotic obsession, a private fantasy, a weakness. And I've been following it too long. Even as a priest, don't ya ever think that maybe people created God, not the other way around?"

"If you can't find a traditional view to fit into, what's wrong with personal faith?"

"Right, a personal religion; my very own. A god in every man."

I kept her moving. "Why not?"

"I failed the fuckin' bar exam, again!" She staggered. "You know what that word means, right?"

"Bar exam?"

"No, the other word."

"Failed?"

"No, the other word."

"Yes, Teresa. You want to be an *abogado*."

"Multi-lingual, too. What a man. You sure you don't desire taking me home?"

"Keep your faith."

"Ya mean, if I build it, they will come? I'm getting a little old for that."

"No one's too old for that," I said.

We'd made it to the entrance gate. Chained, locked for the night. I joggled it; couldn't even hear it rattle, the wind had picked up again. The storm caught her hair, convulsed it left and right. "Build it and they will come," she repeated, trying to keep tresses out of her eyes and mouth. "Now what?"

Everything swirled white and gray beyond her shoulder. I could barely hear her. I felt for my phone. But of course, it was dead. "Give me your phone. We gotta get out of here."

"Don't know where it is. Lost it in there somewhere. Wanna go look?" Eyes expectant; she tugged amorously at me. "Could be fun." Still drunk.

Squinting into the slate night and the blizzard, I estimated the wrought iron fence to be about eight feet tall, a swell of spikes crowning it along the top. No more than twenty yards away, wraith-like cabs and trucks occasionally rumbled by (I could only assume from the vibrations beneath my feet). If pedestrians were braving the wicked cold and unknown, they weren't visible.

I yelled. "Anybody there?" The storm swallowed my shouts, though in the skein of sound I thought I heard Jory's voice. Well, why not? *The god* and *animal in every man.* "You like to climb?"

"We can't climb that." She shook her head.

"Another hour in this cold . . . Lots of famous people buried here. You hoping to rub caskets with them?"

She squirmed like she had to go to the bathroom. "How we gonna do this?"

"Instinct." I cupped my hands. "Right foot, left foot, alley oop."

"No way."

I signaled for her to step into my hands.

"What a man." She lifted her leg, reached for a vertical post.

"There're two horizontal bars below the spikes. Can you see them?"

She dropped her leg back to the ground. "What spikes?!"

"Along the top. Ornamental. Once you've got hold of the first horizontal bar, pull yourself up, put your foot on the horizontal, you can step over the spikes. Then hang from the other side and drop down. Stay flexible."

"You go. I'll wait."

"Too cold, can't take a chance. Could be hours in this mess," I said. "What would Lola do?"

"*Dios mio.*"

"Yes, exactly," I said.

She looked up into the turbulent night then to me. "What about you? Without a hand up, you could be stuck here."

There had been a time in my life when I could have scaled that fence easily. "What choice do I have but to trust?" Once again, I cupped my hands. An icy blast rocked us back and forth.

She put her arm on my shoulder, her leg in my hands; I hoisted her up. "Can't reach it," she said.

"You can." I strained to push her higher. My arm burned to the bone.

"My hands hurt; they're freezing. The fence is freezing." She motioned to let her down.

I lowered her down. We could easily die here, a half block from ten thousand people. "Okay," I said removing my overcoat, then my shirt.

"What're you doin'?"

"Wrap the shirt around your hands." I slipped the overcoat back on.

"You'll freeze."

"We'll both freeze. We've got to get out of here, now!"

She waffled. Despite her resistance I bundled my shirt around her hands. "Now get back up there." I cupped my hands once more. My body trembled, but she saw that I wasn't going to compromise.

"Alright." And with her hands protected from the biting metal, she made her way up—teetering on the top—then over and down, though she slipped and fell the last six feet, landing awkwardly on her right leg and grabbing it in pain as she crumpled to the ground.

"You okay?"

"I'll be okay, just get over here."

After several tries—my overcoat always getting in the way—I removed it, tied it in large knots and threw it over the fence. It left me bare chested but more flexible. I wrapped my hands around the wrought iron and began my climb. It bit like fire. My fingers and palms went numb, I lost hold of the fence. I crashed back to the frozen earth.

"Father!" Teresa part of the wind.

The pain of a thousand arrows shot through my shoulder and ribs. My back cramped. Voltage overtook my body at the slightest movement. A single breath drew lightning to my ribcage. I lay as still as possible. The wind sang to me. The pain began to ice over. The cold ground and spirit world drew me closer, inviting my return. And Jory whispered, "Are you really ready for *Ohronte*, your walk along the stars? What about your earthly obligations?"

"Jory?"

The white squall lulled me with promises of painlessness.

"Are you of the good mind, the *Kahnekonriio?* Are you ready for your transition?"

"Father!" Teresa disappearing in the wind.

The ground kissed my cheek. I braced myself against it. I struggled to my feet. Convulsions shoulder to toes. In a dream I attacked the barrier again. Jory propped me against gravity and with no recollection of anything but wind and its siren song, I made it over.

Teresa limped to me with my shirt and coat, both stiff with ice crystals. "Your hands!" She pointed at my bloody palms, each a dark-iron red. The spikes must have pierced them as I'd gone over. I didn't feel a thing.

"I'll be fine." I re-tied the shirt around her hands and wrestled my coat back on. "Come on."

She could barely stand, but she hobbled along next to me, my arm around her waist. Her skin gave way. Something gave way in me too. We'd made it out, miraculously.

"You may not be a believer in a traditional God," I said to her, "but your personal gospel helped us through."

She leaned in, her arm around my shoulder for support, her wet curls in my mouth. We shambled toward a muted light.

. . .

I deposited Teresa in her apartment and returned to my room, released from the icy grip but still bearing the battle. I started again on my research, dinnertime forgotten. I waited for the phone to recharge.

The storm whistled through my lone window, under my closed door, and scattered down the basement hallway, jangling door-frames. I shifted gingerly, checking the phone frequently, quaking with each strike to my ribs and shoulders and back. Eventually I got a signal.

The next number on Duke's phone linked to an auto racetrack in New Jersey. A third and fourth number to the Crash-B World Indoor Rowing Championships. The fifth and last number, I realized after several tries, was a voice mailbox without a greeting. It allowed me to leave a very brief message, ten seconds at best. No amount of calls or reverse-engineering to trace its origin manifested any results. No one ever returned my calls.

Finding Christopher Toll became the priority. However, the idea of confronting Father Toll directly (if in fact there was any family connection) or walking back into that hostile firehouse, didn't appeal to me (nor could I foresee getting any new information there). I rather doubted that I'd be all that welcome at La Fiamma either, given the explosion in the pub's men's room.

I decided to take on the first of two V's that showed up on the fire company's roster: Vaughn, Hakim (Lt.), *the fireman with the energy-efficient car.*

"Is Lieutenant Vaughn on duty tonight?"

"Yes, who's calling?"

I hung up. I couldn't go into the firehouse to identify him, so I decided to send him flowers. But on a night like this?

"Confucius Florists, how can I help you?" The man sounded tired, his voice slightly rote and officious.

"I need flowers delivered," I said.

"Very well, sir, what kind of flowers?"

"I don't know, something simple."

A small cough or guffaw, I wasn't sure. "Well, whom will these flowers be going to? Your wife? Your mother? A girlfriend?"

"No, a fireman."

"Okay, sir, a fireman." He'd been unprepared for that, and from the sound of his voice he'd found it curious, and therefore worthy of his consideration. "What kind of flowers?"

"Not exorbitant."

"No." His tolerance once again waning.

"Can you recommend something?"

"The occasion?" he asked.

Stumped again. "Years of loyal service." No idea where that came from.

"Let's consider this. How about a *Gloriosa*, a Glory Lilly? Orange and yellow petals shaped like flames. We just got some in, unusual for this area. From East Africa. Gorgeous."

"Great. Can you deliver them to the fire fighter *outside* the fire-house? And the flowers must be delivered *only* to him, no one else," I said.

"Why outside?"

"It's a surprise."

"Hmm, I see," said the florist. "What kind of card would you like on it?"

"No card."

"No card?"

"Yes, can you deliver it within the hour?"

"Tonight? It's freezing out there." I thought he was going to hang up.

"Tonight, please," I said.

"My, we are in a lavish mood." He totaled it up. I gulped. $204.00. *I* almost hung up. I gave him my credit card.

I waited across from the firehouse to see who would accept the flowers, the snow still curling over the empty streets. More than an hour I lurked, staying as inconspicuous as one can in clerical black, hopping carefully from foot to foot, pounding my gloves and scarred palms together. The rest of my body begged for sleep.

Flowers in a blizzard? There wasn't any movement in or out of the station house.

Finally, the florist's van pulled up and the driver knocked on the firehouse door. Captain Hoyle opened it and motioned the guy to come in. But the guy explained, with clumsy body language, that the flowers had to be delivered in person, outside.

Hoyle frowned, looked around the frosty circle of light, and with a shrug closed the door. Moments later, a forty-something African-American man, bald, medium build, came to the door with a tote bag and a knit red jacket tossed over it. He took the flowers, thanked the driver and, after considering going in with them, slipped into his jacket, picked up the tote and started down the street, away from the firehouse, walking briskly.

I followed at a distance. The gap quickly grew between us. I picked up my pace, the frigid night and unplowed snow banks fighting me all the way.

Hakim Vaughn never looked back. I assumed he was unaware

of me following, especially in the dark vortex of snow. He hung a left on North Moore Street, heading for the Hudson River piers. He turned up Hudson Street and then onto Laight, a warehouse district gentrifying into condos and lofts. Between buildings, he disappeared.

When I got to the spot, panting and swaddled in cold sweat, the alleyway snow had already been plowed to the walls, three or four feet high and wide enough for a small delivery truck or van to enter. The alley was illuminated by a series of industrial lamps that lined the left side of it. Moths danced frantically against their light, perhaps laboring for heat.

Taking small, exaggerated steps over the patches of snow and ice, I followed under each pool of pale-yellow light, each billowing and collapsing with dun clouds of rabid moths, then into darkness, then back into the chaos of moths until I reached the only door, three quarters of the way down the alley.

A horn, traffic hum, and a lone siren came from many blocks away. But in the alley, only muted, snow-covered trashcans and the desperate sound of the insects bouncing off the lamps. Desperate intermediaries?

The sign on the door read:

Deliveries

Vaughn Memorial ONLY!

I tried the door, expecting it to be locked. It opened, emitting a blast of heat, into a wide, pitch-black, sixty-foot-long hallway. Bright light filled the room at the end giving the hallway its only definition. Hooks of some sort spiked across the wall near the light. White shirts on hangers.

Three or four steps into the corridor the bite of formaldehyde hit my nose. My arm was wrenched back, almost torn from its socket. "Who the fuck are you?!" the man snarled.

The new pain joined the old; it pinched my voice into a screech.

"Please, no, *no!* I'm looking for Lieutenant Vaughn." The wounds of the cemetery circled me. I thought I'd lose consciousness. I craned over my shoulder. He threw me against the wall.

"Who wants to see him? And why-the-fuck are you following him?"

"He's-he's an officer at Firehouse 27." My breathing difficult. "Thought he could tell me about Sean Ducotty."

"*Sean?*"

"Duke. Yes, Duke."

He eased off my arm.

"Why-the-fuck are you following me?" He turned me around.

Even in the darkness I could sense he was an inch or two shorter, but he pinned his arms on either side of my shoulders, hemming me against the wall. His breath objectionable. Only small swatches of him were visible. He pulled at my collar, then my shoulder and pushed me forward into the light, against a large gurney which carved into my hip. I let out a howl. He didn't withdraw.

Over his shoulder, across the aisle and a couple yards away, a large brushed metal furnace rumbled, two green steadily blinking lights illuminated on a larger panel of LEDs.

When he saw my clerical attire, he backed away, hands up, like he'd encountered a ghost. He held a small pistol in his right hand. "What-the-fuu—? Who are you?" He waved the pistol at me then answered for me. "You're that damn priest asking all the questions."

"Please." I motioned for him to direct the weapon away from me.

He did, unenthusiastically, with a sour, unrepentant face. He slipped the gun into his waistband. "Don't you get it? It's an internal fire department investigation."

"What is?"

"Don't play coy with me. Father Toll won't give this thing a rest, so he sent you. He's been told, it's an internal affair now."

Despite the cramping snaking through my arms, I went to

shake his hand. "I'm Father Bluterre."

He regarded it with distaste. "Even if you were my father—which judging both from your outfit and your chalky hide, you are not—the investigation goes on without you and the church's interference. Father Toll will hear any results when and *if* there are any."

"What does Father Toll have to do with this?"

"Just stop the charade," Vaughn said.

"We just want to help the family, Duke's sister in particular. To understand what happened."

His face corkscrewed. "I find that hard to believe."

Stretching my shoulder reignited the spasms. My voice thinned to a whisper. "We're trying to ascertain why Duke tried to kill himself."

"Oh," he said sarcasm dripping, "so this isn't about Chris?"

"Chris?"

"Father Toll's younger brother."

"I don't understand."

"No? Forgive me if I'm skeptical after Father Toll harassed the shit out of the department for close to a year."

"But," I said, "Duke's suicide attempt was eight months ago."

"Right. But it's been at least a year since Chris died in that fire. But you know that." He must have seen my bewilderment, though it didn't change his mood. "Get out of here."

I pressed. "You knew him, right?"

"Chris?"

"Duke," I said.

"Duke? I'd say so. We were partners for a while. Now get out a here."

"To your knowledge, did he ever do drugs?"

This only raised his rancor. "Hell no. Just scotch. Do I have to throw you out?"

"He never said anything about psychedelics?"

"No. Duke? No."

I kept pushing. "Was he depressed before his-his attempt?"

"More of this shit. Let it go." His hand went back on the gun.

I motioned for him to please calm down. "It's about Duke."

"We weren't that close after the subway fire. Maybe I reminded him how close he came to death. Maybe it was . . . " His voice trailed off, as if he'd caught himself saying too much.

"What?"

"Nothing."

"What about the subway fire?" I asked.

"Look, Duke was a terrific firefighter. I had great respect for him. I was pleased to serve with him."

"There's a *but* there."

"You know, Father, you're a pain in the ass. I never subscribed to any rumors, if that's what you're getting at. He was brave and that fire on Spring Street proved it. He saved eight or nine lives. Maybe mine too." His face softened at the thought of it.

"I'm trying to help his sister," I said, "to come to grips with his suicide attempt, nothing more."

He looked away, visibly struggling to withhold *something*. Finally, he said, "Subway fires are rare, and that one was particularly unusual."

"Because?"

"It was a three-alarm and it kept on coming."

I could see he was re-imagining it.

"That's all." But his face said *it wasn't*.

Try something simple, non-threatening. "Did you recently discontinue your phone number?"

"I've had the same cell number for five or six years. Why-the-hell—?"

"Duke had a V in his address book. I thought it might be you."

"He never called me. Maybe once at the station."

"The other V at your firehouse, Penny Velez? Was Duke close to her?"

Vaughn recoiled. "Get out of here before I toss your sorry ass into the alley. Clergy or no clergy, you're trespassing. Duke didn't have anything to do with her, may she rest in peace."

He grabbed hold of my shoulders. More spasms. "No, please!"

He lifted me up. The man was strong. *Rest in peace?* "What about Chris Toll?"

"I don't want to talk about it." He started dragging me to the door. My body flared again.

"You said he died."

No response.

I went limp and tried again. "Was Chris Toll a good firefighter?"

"Very good."

"How'd he die?"

"Ask Father Toll."

A small but sudden shudder emitted from the furnace. The panel of lights animated rapidly, the red lights convulsed. Lieutenant Vaughn didn't flinch.

I did. "What was that?"

"That?" said Vaughn. "That was the retort burner kicking in. Eighteen hundred degrees: the skin ripples and burns away, the fat sizzles, the organs shrink. Muscle turns to carbon. In a couple of hours only small fragments of bone and surgical enhancements will remain. This is my family's crematorium." He never took his eyes off me. "And you're not welcome. Get out and don't come back."

He threw me, with ease, into the alley, with the moths.

CHAPTER 24

Duke

We returned to the city. Valerie demanded that I see a doctor immediately. Several days later, as I joined her in her garret apartment, I told her I'd seen one and that he'd given me a clean bill of health. "'Except,' he said, 'you need to cut out coffee.'"

"The dizziness, the lack of focus, the loss of memory?"

"Yup, coffee," I said to her. "I guess I'm allergic to it; hypersensitive to it. Especially as it builds up after several days and I get dehydrated."

"That was his diagnosis?"

"That's it." It sounded good. I wasn't going to lose her now. And I wasn't going to lose my spot on the team fighting fires.

"You should get a second opinion," she said.

"That's spilled milk under the bridge and you can't lead a horse to drink it," I said.

"Debonair?"

"Cabbage?"

The doorbell rang. She'd offered to cook; I had beer and sushi delivered.

"And no soda either, that has caffeine." She almost sounded motherly.

"Sure." I brought the unagi and yellowtail to her small dinner table. She put on some music. We sat, a votive candle flickering between us. I pushed away the damn cat with my leg. The beer was cool, the bottle wet to the touch. Steve Winwood and Traffic played in the background. *No more health questions.* "You mentioned the 'lakes of fire,'" I said, hoping to divert her. "What'd I tell you about them?"

"That they were the most horrific fires."

"Of the ones I've dealt with, yeah."

She rested the chopsticks on her lips. "You mentioned one in a subway before you passed out." She caught her indiscretion. "Sorry, maybe the stress of reliving it—?"

"No, not at all. It's okay. I remember that one," I said. "The one in the subway, *that* lake of fire, yeah."

"If you don't want to talk about it, I'll understand."

Anything but the status of my health. "No. No, it was . . . it changed things for me." *Was I setting myself up for her psychoanalysis?*

"Tell me everything, your process, your experience."

"Everything, huh?" *What the hell am I afraid of?*

"As much as you're willing," she said. "From the beginning. Details."

Loving her had made every day more alive, made every day more worth living. Under the table, she rested her warm hand on my knee and waited. "Okay. Okay," I said. "Well . . . The lake of fire . . . We saw the loom up—the billowing smoke—a block away, pouring out of the Spring Street subway station. But no way we're going down that hole."

"People were down there?"

"Somewhere," I said.

"And?"

She wants process. "Protocol is to attack from uninvolved to involved, you understand? Away from the fire *to* it, so we have an escape route if necessary. If we start at the fire we run the risk of pushing the smoke and heat to other parts that aren't involved yet. Make sense?"

She nodded with the rapt attention of a child. Snow spilled from the sky and caked her windowsill.

"Subways are alien places, we're not very familiar with them. First thing we gotta know is that power is turned off because—like in this fire—there's usually zero visibility. We're going in blind and it's often staying that way; there's no place for the smoke to go. And if one of us touches the subway's third rail, six hundred and twenty-five-volts of current goes through us, and *adios*, our hearts stop, we're fried."

"That right there would scare the shit out of me." She rubbed my leg.

"So," I continued. "I get the key that allows us to go down the unmarked emergency exit. It's a block or so away from the station, a stairway off an alley on Vandam. It's two in, two out, as usual; we don't go down alone.

"I slip on my breather, my mask, and my partner Hakim and I submerge into the black. It's a very steep, very long, metal stairway. I've walked up and down plenty of stairs. This one seemed to go on forever. Even the sound of our boots on the steps got sucked away in seconds. It was as if we were descending into a void. Then all of a sudden we could hear a deep rumbling coming from below."

"Descending into hell." She sounded like a child about to leap from a high perch into a lake, breathless but excited.

"Definite similarities," I said. "We're carrying our rolled-up hose, so we don't have to stretch our line down the stairs. Once water starts through that hose we lose way too much flexibility— most of it—and we need to stay flexible.

"This particular morning I've got the pipe, I'm on nozzle, so I'm down first. Even at the bottom of the stairway neither of us knew where the hell we were exactly, except that we're supposed to be looking to the right, for the blue light. That's the cabinet with the emergency power shut off and a phone directly to the MTA, to let them know we're turning it off.

"Of course, those MTA folks don't like us turning their electricity off. Shit, they've got tens of thousands of customers packed in trains throughout the city. Something like eight hundred miles of track. Even one downed subway line brings on migraines and serious acid reflux. But not our problem.

"For us, one touch of that third rail, and like I said, it's a three-D headache—our eyes kick out of our sockets, we're crisp."

"Oh god."

"So, when we get to the blue light cabinet, I can't find the switch. I call some jerkoff at MTA dispatch. He doesn't know why there's no working switch, but he says 'Hold off for a few minutes.'

"I say, 'Buddy, we can't see shit down here. We've got limited air and we gotta get your folks off that train."

"And he says, 'Okay, judging from your box, you've got at least another two hundred fifty yards to go. Stay to your right and I'll have it off by the time you get there.'

"I say, 'No, man, we don't work with the third rail on.'

"And he says, 'Oh and there's standing water down that way too, so be careful.'

"Like he didn't hear me the first time.

'We're not going down that fucking tunnel until you turn off the fucking power, and if you lose those folks on the train, it's on you.'

"But he just repeats the same crap on how he guarantees the power will be off by the time we're down to the station.

"I look at Hakim and he grabs the wooden train boot. Even if the power's off we'll need to boot the train and the rail—there can be residual electricity or standby power. We decide to stay to the right of the tracks and hope for the best.

"We feel our way along the tunnel's cement wall, tripping over all sorts of shit—I'm *guessing* empty paint cans, beer bottles, a bicycle wheel. I can't even see the hand in front of my face. And here come packs of rats, hundreds of them, screeching and scurrying over us away from the fire.

"Rats?"

"Hundreds of them. Some ran up my leg and over my head and shoulder. Anyway, we've got no idea what started the fire. Good bet it was started by homeless folks living down there. Whatever started burning seemed to still be producing a shitload of smoke, though I couldn't see any flame.

"But even with the power off, if the fire was caused by a break in the insulator—the grounding third rail—the minute that power goes back on, the fire will spark back up again.

"So, leaning into the wall as my lifeline, I came to an opening. Like someone had taken a sledge hammer to it. I almost fell through.

"With all that smoke, I barely made out a makeshift tent, a can of campfire fuel and a pile of rags; probably someone's home. But it wasn't burning. There wasn't any sign of life. We kept moving."

Valerie took a drag of my beer and handed it back to me. I took a hit and launched back in. "Another emergency cabinet and hose hookup mashed my right arm, so I figured we're within fifty or so yards of the train and the fire.

"In my first few years I could tell from my earlobes how close we were to the heat. But since then they've issued newer hoods and helmets, it's more of a guessing game.

"Anyway, an orange fog rolled over us; we were close to the seat of the fire. Hakim yelled 'working fire' into the handi-talkie, to our chief on the street above. Hakim hooked up the hose and, in the process, lost the talkie somewhere at our feet. He bent over to search for it. I grabbed him. No telling if the power was truly off."

"Oh, geez," Val said.

Even retelling it, my heart raced. She patted my leg. "You okay?"

"Yeah, sure." I said. But I could smell the smoke all over again.

"So go on."

"Around a bend in the track we saw flame. Five or six people were bent over running, coughing toward us. 'Stay to your left,' I yelled. 'Run along the wall, past the blue light." Don't know if they heard me, or if they'd make it before being overcome by smoke. 'Keep going,' I told them, 'no matter what!'

"Thirty yards beyond us was the station, two side platforms and four tracks—engulfed in a lake of fire. The entire track beneath the train a pool of flames. The paint on the first car burbling from the heat—people trapped inside, pounding the doors. Two arms in a small rear window reached out, caught fire. And then a single voice, screaming from below the car, as if we had fallen into hell with the bunch of them."

"You've gotta be crazy to do this shit, you know that." Val spellbound.

"The heat was unbearable. Without knowing if the power was off, I attached the fog nozzle. A solid stream of one-inch wide water would conduct the electricity back onto me, possibly Hakim as well. But the fog stream breaks up the water into droplets so it's not solid water. In theory the electricity can't return through the stream electrocuting us. In theory. You understand?"

Val, still enthralled, mouth open, blinked but said nothing; a stoner drifting on a high.

"I gave Hakim the sign to release the water. I opened the nozzle. As soon as the fog stream started, steam started to build. I gave it short bursts because the steam can burn you as bad as the fire."

"Jesus."

"After a minute or so the inferno started to come down. Hakim drew closer. I handed him the pipe. 'What're you doin'?' he asked. 'I'm goin' in.' 'You're out of your fucking mind.' And of course, he was right.

"I found the side of the first car. I started attacking the window with my pick axe. It ain't dainty, but it gets to the guts of things quicker. No forms to fill out.

"The people are screaming. I'm telling whoever's in there to stand back. With five or six strokes I broke through, easier than I thought. I directed the first woman at the door to press the safety door release on her upper right, which she did, freeing her and four other people in the car. Apparently it was the only car whose doors hadn't opened.

"Why they hadn't realized that safety switch on their own, I don't get, but— helter-skelter and hacking and coughing—they followed Hakim's instructions to make their way out. Except for the smoldering body in the back of the car. Too late for her. The rest of them quickly disappeared.

"I heard the scream again—the one *under* the car. Shrill. I couldn't tell if it was man or woman, boy or girl. I jumped off the platform, staying along the tunnel's wall. 'Hello?' I shouted, but my facemask muted it.

"I lifted the mask—just for a second—and shouted again, 'Where are you?' Fine glass particles cut into my throat, my eyes, my lungs. I started choking.

"Then blubbering, barely audible above the roaring flames, I heard the voice again. 'Please help me.'

"It came from below me as I re-sealed my mask, locking smoke in with me, further lacerating my throat. I coughed up blood, splattering the inside of my mask."

"Blood!"

"I'd swallowed a mixture of charcoal, iron and something smelling like chrome. A caustic I never did place. Anyhow, I stooped and squinted under the train. There, not more than ten feet from me and less than a foot from the third rail, backlit by flames, was a gentleman in a brown dashiki huddled below the train. He wallowed in a small puddle of rank water, untouched by the lake of fire around him. But the water was beginning to bubble.

"When I reached for him, he receded from me toward the third rail. As if he believed he was safer *below* the train than unprotected above, where the blaze circled us.

"The heat began to sear the dashiki off him. I watched it curl. His shoulders combusted in flame and he came within inches of the third rail.

"I called to Hakim, 'Hit us again.' And he gave us three blasts of steam, enough to allow me to grab the guy. I know this sounds weird, but I asked *the train* to please not shift as it sometimes does.

"I dragged him out—no small feat; he was much bigger than me. I tamped out the flames covering him. I pulled him back along the tunnel. There are times I don't know where my strength comes from. This was one of those.

"I passed the guy to Hakim and told them to get out. The man would surely die of smoke inhalation within minutes. It was a miracle he was still alive."

"You could share your mask with him." Valerie still awestruck. "Like divers do."

"Never with civilians," I said. "They panic and you'll both die."

"Oh."

"Anyway, the flames weren't out, but they were laying down pretty good, at least temporarily. That's when the bell on my breather sounded. Down to reserve air.

"I could stay a little longer, but not much. I grabbed the downed hose. I gave the fire a couple more blasts of water. Black and orange smoke ballooned around me. Time to go.

"I left the hose on, laid it at my feet, and moved along the tunnel the way I'd come, following the hose line, running my left hand against the concrete wall.

"And then, I can't tell you exactly when or how, something knocked me backwards; some small, otherwise inconsequential hand that wouldn't let go. It jerked me back, hung me up. Like a giant spider had dropped its web over me. The air container of my breather got tangled in something—bailing wire, plumber's tape, some sort of fucking mesh melted or burned by the heat. I don't know. And my warning light flashed, only seconds of air left.

"I couldn't take off the mask. At that point I'd choke on the soot, die instantly from the blackened air. The more I turned around to loosen myself, the more tangled I got, the more trapped I became.

"Oh, my god."

"Just before I panicked, an inexplicable calm came over me. In front of me, hung in pitch black, photos of myself carouselled past; framed photos of my life as a child. Photos that had never been taken. One, as a young boy growing up in the city running through Central Park chasing pigeons. Another on vacation upstate on Lake Kanawauke fishing with my dad among the lily pads. Visiting Cooperstown with Mom, Dad and my sister Charli, Dad pointing at the great Roberto Clemente's plaque. Snapshot memories. Then I ran out of air.

"My face piece, with its airtight seal, suctioned onto my face. I took the hose out of my second-stage regulator, like they train us to do. I put it into my jacket to offer some kind of filtration from the outside air. Did no good; the air was toxic, even in my turnout jacket.

"I began hacking and convulsing, fire blistering my throat. Like fucking razors slicing inside my chest. My entire body was being torched from the inside out—toes, legs, fingers. I felt *This is it. This is how I go. This is where I go. This is how I die. Stay calm.*

"The only light, a bronze dust with wings, nothing more. A gauzy marker, offering a direction; not the sun, but where I was to end. Through the smoke, I moved toward the light and my extinction.

"Oh my god."

"But it was real light. A portable spot lamp. Someone from one of the other fire companies, very heads up, had put the high-powered spot down the entrance to the subway."

"How'd you get free?"

"Don't know. To this day, I haven't a clue. Maybe the heat of the fire melted or burned away whatever had trapped me. I woke up in a hospital, major smoke inhalation. But I didn't die on the fireground." I latched onto the leg of Val's dinner table to ground myself. My throat in flames. "I didn't die on the fireground."

"My god, you're fearless," Val said, her voice buried under the sound of my pile-driving heart. I shouldn't have relived the story in such detail. It had *all* come back to me, again. I gripped the bottled beer in my other hand. I took a swig. And then another. And another.

When Val could see the beer had calmed my tremors, she asked, "Did he make it, Dashiki Man?"

I finished off the bottle. "He did."

"You're so brave."

As usual, her adulation set off mixed feelings in my chest. I stayed moored to the dinner table. "Everyone in that stationhouse is brave, women and men."

"You're modest."

"I do what we all do." I wanted another beer but I couldn't let go of the table.

"You respect them," she said.

"I do. And I have to trust them, to survive."

She acknowledged that with a small nod. "I can see that."

"That's when I decided, conclusively, that I should fight fires till the day I die. Just consent to give myself up, to face the risks, if that's what it takes. If I get engulfed and used up, so be it. At least I lived."

"Oh," she said, panting, her face ingenuous. As if something close to her had been affirmed. "The hero is the man who can go into the spirit world, the world of the dead, and return alive."

"What?"

"You're the classic hero," she said. "You see reality. You've died and been reborn."

"Well, let's not get carried away."

She got up from the table, came around to my chair and laced her arms around my neck. She whispered in my ear. "Real living is to play at the meaning of life." She kissed the crown of my head, patted my shoulder. She began to remove our plates from the table. I let go of it.

She was a miracle! "And you," I said, placing my hand on hers. "Your work has edges. Sit, please. Tell me, tell me a moment in your work that changed you."

CHAPTER 25

Father Blu

Following Mass the next morning, I intercepted Father Toll on his way to his office. Pain and misgivings had kept me tossing much of the night. As usual his walk signaled assumption and loftiness. The absolute conceit he carried around his shoulders begged to be knocked off.

"Father, may we speak?" I said.

"What is it Bluterre? I'm very busy this morning."

"We need to talk."

"*We?*" he jeered. "About your gang connections?"

"No, about your brother."

Color emptied from his face. He crooked his neck over his shoulder, down the corridor. He motioned me into his office and shut the door. Eerie, how he affected temperance after that, sitting casually on the edge of his desk. "Please, take a seat."

Which I did.

"So, what about my brother?"

"He died in a fire," I said.

His body compressed, as if bound by rope. "This is old news."

"I'm sorry for your loss."

"Thank you, Father." His tone nearly appreciative.

"But you should have told me," I said.

"For what purpose?"

"Your probe of Sean Ducotty."

"There's no connection." He turned his back on me and re-established himself behind his desk. He clasped his hands together. "It's that vivid imagination of yours again, the one that keeps getting you in trouble. I don't want to get into a discussion of your bible delivery, but the company you keep is alarming. Again, the Vicar . . ."

"I know it was a suspicious fire that took your brother," I said. "I can imagine your pain."

"You have no idea. And so what?"

"You've been using me to construct some sort of dossier on Duke."

"That's laughable." He grabbed a pencil and began tapping it against the desk.

Find common ground. Admit. "I lost a brother too. It's not something I'll ever get over. I understand, I do. But the arson squad—"

He slammed the pencil down. "A bunch of incompetents and worse."

"Father, let the process play out."

"Did you do that with *your* brother? Did you forgive the driver of that bus?"

Suddenly I was unable to breathe. "You know about that?"

Father Toll stoic. "Have you forgiven him?" Lights blinked silently on Toll's high-tech desk phone, an expensive leather-bound headset close at hand. The set conspicuously incongruous with his otherwise fossilized office. However impervious to outside thought Father Toll might be, he was ready to respond to the call of his flock. He wouldn't heedlessly turn anyone away. "Well?" Father

Toll raised his nose and looked down on me.

"I had to," I said. "I had to forgive him."

"And you forgave yourself? Or did you let your brother down? Because I won't. I won't harbor a crippled conscience. I'd *have* to bare it to the open air."

"Father Toll—"

"What if the driver had been drinking? Or on drugs? What if he simply wanted to pleasure himself? Or perhaps he had some ulterior motive?"

"But that's not what he intended." I reached for the last thread of decency and impartiality within my grasp. "That's not what Duke intended."

"You don't know that." His beady eyes fastened on mine. "In fact, I think you already know better. Yet you defend him."

"Well . . ."

"And the department knows there's an arsonist in their midst," he continued. "Ducotty's their prime suspect. Their *only* suspect. They've had more than enough time; they just won't do anything about it. They're afraid the media will eat them up. They're embarrassed and impotent."

"But the arson squad—"

He smashed his fist to the desk. "If you wait on them, you're easily duped. They protect their image and their own. A *false* hero so this will all go away. They're sacrificing my brother."

"We can agree that pride is the sin from which all others arise," I said.

"Pride!" His neck and cheeks flushed crimson. "Watch yourself, Father."

"And anger is not far behind."

His fist smashed the desk again—with such force I thought his hand would splinter. His cup of pens vaulted from the surface, spilling across it. He pulled back, a bit more under control. Veins bulged along his forehead. "You're an impudent man, Father. Leave, please." He pointed to the door.

"You only tried to stop me," I said, "because I was becoming too obvious. But, again, please share a different narrative, if you have one."

He got up from the desk and came toward me. "I don't have to share anything with you, Father. Get out!"

I stood, but held my ground. "You used me for your own purposes."

"You don't know what you're talking about. My brother died a hero. We can't say the same for Ducotty."

"We can't say anything yet about Duke. You hoped I'd link Duke's suicide attempt to his guilt?"

"We know, don't we Father, that in Revelation 20:14 John describes the eternity of hell, the final resting place of the devil, the antichrist and false prophet, as the 'Lake of Fire.' There's enough evidence. Let him burn in hell, the eternal place of conscious torment. Day and night forever. There's justice in Ducotty's frozen eyes. Now get out."

"With all due respect, Proverbs 18:17. 'He that is first in his own cause seems just; but his neighbor comes and searches him.' You've become Sean Ducotty's judge and juror."

He sneered. "Get out. I'm sure now you'll be hearing from the Vicar."

"There's nothing there. He won't believe you," I said.

He leaned into me. "With your track record? And more incriminating reports. I'd say your time is winding down." His eyes spun, his spittle pelted my lips.

I wiped my mouth. "What kind of incriminating reports?"

"Like so many out there," a deprecating wave, his tone belittling. "Your loss of spiritual ideology has—perhaps among other things— created your shameful serial dependency on physical partners."

"What?"

A hot scornful laugh. "You're done." He pointed once more to the door. "Keep your distance from me, Bluterre, until the process is completed."

I passed into the hallway, reverberating—from Toll's rage, his invasion of my personal ache, and his unequivocal assurance that Duke was a killer.

· · ·

I quickened my steps back to Morgenstern's Grocery in search of answers that would free Duke of culpability. His untold story ever more important and in need of defense. Yet niggling uncertainty seemed to follow every facet of him I unearthed.

Down aisles of fresh produce, pausing in front of the cabbages, then past baked goods and frozen foods, I kept my head low and on the watch for the manager. Until I bumped into a clerk labeling bottles of bleach. "I'm wondering if you can help me?" I said.

He laid his coding gun on the shelf. "Of course, Father, what do you need?"

"A friend of mine had a weekly delivery order sent a few blocks from here. He became very ill and it's come to my attention—well, I'm hoping you can check to be sure the delivery has been canceled to that address."

"I'll be happy to check for you. What's his name?"

I gave him Duke's name and reminded the clerk to confirm the deleted address. The clerk set off to retrieve the information while I kept watch for The Horseradish Voice.

He returned in five minutes with a satisfied look on his face. "Yes, Father. The order was deleted last May. I liked what he said."

"Excuse me?"

"With the order for cabbage. His note read 'Off with her head.'

Get it?" He lit up, a goofy smile.

"Yes." I reached for the scrap of paper in his hand.

He clung to it. "It's from *Alice In Wonderland.*"

And the French Revolution. "Yes, I remember. And the address?"

He handed me the torn piece of paper. "Does that look right?"

I glanced at it. "Yes, thanks, you've been very helpful." I pocketed the address.

"I hope your friend makes a full recovery, I really liked his note."

"I'm sure he'll appreciate your thoughts. Thanks again."

Out of the store, I plowed into the current of pedestrians. I navigated the four blocks to the address the clerk had provided: an older five-story brownstone. The address indicated "Apt. #8." I climbed the stoop and made my way to the directory. Apartment #8 was at the top and the tag indicated that the resident was Valerie Dunn. The V?

The buzzer had been bound over with gray duct tape.

I stepped back. My eyes scaled the building to the uppermost floor. The entire top of the structure, a charred hull. The window facing the street was gutted, without glass, and the gable above—that which I could see—a makeshift patchwork of black tarps and crisscrossing boards indicating a collapsed rooftop. A smell of ash, I came to realize, still marked the air.

. . .

"I'm only here because of Duke's sister, you understand?" Hakim Vaughn slid into the booth, a cup of tea and a cruller already in his grip, a sulk on his face.

"I appreciate you coming." My body still ached from his assault and my fall in the cemetery. "She's pretty distressed."

"How's he doing?"

"Not great." In spite of Father Toll's edict, I'd continued to sneak my twice-daily visits to Duke's hospital room, hopeful that

Toll or one of his acolytes wouldn't cross my path. "But there are signs, every once in a while, that he might understand some stimuli." I watched the lieutenant's reaction.

"What kind of stimuli?"

"Music," I said. "Occasional peaks on his EEG."

"Makes sense. He once confided in me that a tune was always running through his head." Vaughn's large hands wrapped around the mug of tea. "Anyway, he didn't deserve this."

Vaughn's face told me nothing. I questioned why the lieutenant never visited Duke. But I could see why there might not be a point to it. "Well, he did it to himself." An uncharitable thing to say?

"I guess that's true, but the pressure . . ." He lifted the mug to his lips and blew the steam away.

"What kind of pressure?"

"Wrong place, wrong time," Vaughn said.

"What does that mean?"

He looked conspiratorially around the coffee shop. "You didn't hear this from me—ever."

"No, of course not."

"He's had a good run. But those fires . . ."

"Specific fires," I said.

"Yes, questionable ones. He always seemed to be there." Vaughn fingered the rim of his cup. "Either first in, first out. Or somehow involved. And everyone knew he knew more about starting a fire and getting out of one than the rest of us, even the chief. Maybe even more than the arson squad guys. He always got out."

"I'm not sure I follow."

Vaughn shrugged. "Never mind."

"No, please, finish your thought," I said.

Vaughn was beginning to sing like Father Quade's choir. He clenched and massaged his hands. He wagged his neck, hoping to unbind it. He struggled.

"There's something I should know, isn't there?" I said.

He leaned over his cup of tea. He lowered his voice. "I'm not sure how it started, but there was talk, ya know, that maybe he was involved."

"Involved?"

"To save his job. Maybe to show his worth. Maybe to show up the captain. One time he even got testy with me and a couple other guys. He said, 'You get one of these nut cases that sets fires, you'll be sorry you don't have me around.' All I know is that the case against him seemed circumstantial. But Duke has always been a loner and that never rubbed the guys the right way."

"What other guys?"

"Eisler, Chris—a couple others."

"Chris Toll?" I said.

"Yeah." Hakim blew on the tea once more and took a sip. "I stuck up for him a couple times but it didn't seem to make any difference; the guys just went back to their gossip, and I'd get frozen out for days. So I gave up, especially as Duke did nothing to put a damper on it himself. And maybe he wasn't even aware of it; he could be like that sometimes, with his damn headphones on all the time."

"There were ongoing arson investigations?"

"Still are, which is why you and Father Toll are so unwelcomed. Look, you gotta understand that the department is no happier with a torcher in the company than you are. Father Toll has a right to be angry. There's a good chance the fire that took Chris Toll was arson. But it might not have been anyone from our company. It might not have been arson at all. But pressing on the chief and Captain Hoyle, and all of us, ain't gonna do a bit of good. We're like crabs; poke at us and we'll just retreat into our shells."

"Yeah, I get it."

"Do you?" he said. "Look, I'd like to help his sister—what's her name?"

"Charli."

"Yeah, I met her once. Is she as hot as she used to be?" He caught himself. "Sorry, Father, that's probably not your domain."

"No," I said, "it isn't. But, yes, she is."

"Anyway, I'm sorry to see her suffer. And Duke. But this is out of our hands. It's out of *your* hands."

I hadn't encountered Charli for a few nights. It left me a little disappointed; she gave life to a room. On the other hand, it allowed me time to consider how I'd introduce her to Valerie Dunn, and to Valerie's untimely and fiery death, which had been officially corroborated by the authorities. I asked, "Duke ever mention a woman named Valerie Dunn?"

His head yanked, his eyes widened, his mouth opened. A definite disturbance. Yet he said, "No."

"You're sure?"

His jaw tightened. "I'm sure he never mentioned her."

And then there was Penny Velez, also deceased. Vaughn's first response to her name had also been anything but normal.

I persisted. "Do you believe the department is trying to turn Duke into a hero so this all, I don't know, will fade away?"

"No."

"How about Duke?"

"What about him?" Vaughn's attitude still acidic.

"Did he encourage the hero talk?"

"Give me a break!"

"Is that a yes or a no?" I said.

"No."

"Penny Velez. Were you and Duke both interested in her?"

He stiffened. He measured me. "You know George Washington was a volunteer firefighter before he was our first president?" He stood up and threw a crinkled dollar bill on the table.

"Really?" I said.

"Yeah. Some people naturally feel it's their duty." He left, a small pond of his tea darkening the bill.

When Washington became thoroughly saturated, I called Chuck Winston. I asked him if he could find a report on the 77th Street fire. "And what can you tell me about Hakim Vaughn? Or the late Penny Velez?"

"Oh, Penny. A tragic story," he said. "But I'm not going over it again. Go read the reports for yourself." Impatience in his voice. "They're thorough enough. I can't tell you more than they do."

"Were they a couple? Vaughn and Velez?"

"I don't know," he snapped.

"Who would?"

"Probably Lieutenant Vaughn."

"He and Duke got along?" I asked.

Winston curbed his restlessness. "Mostly, I think. I was pretty much gone by the time Vaughn came along."

"What does that mean?"

"As far as I know neither of them ever had a chance with her, okay?"

"Popular, huh?" I said.

"Murdered. I told you, go read about it."

"Chief, tell me, just briefly."

I heard him strike a match, light a cigarette, and blow the smoke away. Then he barked out the overview. "It happened about a year before Duke shot himself. Cops guess she interrupted a robbery at her Montauk beach house. Died of gunshot wounds. It was in all the papers. Go read the archives."

"Arrests?"

"None so far," Winston said. "Now leave me alone. I'm getting a little tired of this."

CHAPTER 26

Duke

"And you," I said to Valerie, "your work has edges. Tell me a moment in your work that changed you."

There were few times I knew Val was fully in the room with me. This was one of them. "Fair enough," she said.

I poured myself a whiskey while she thought a moment. I settled into the sofa and motioned for her to join me. She filled her pipe with weed and took a couple hits. She offered it to me. I raised my glass. The snow hadn't abated for hours and would be thick on the streets. This was a night I would spend in her bed with the hope she'd begin to accept my affection, a tenderness I'd only begun to recover.

Stopping first at the table for her glass of water, she reunited with me on the couch. "You know anything about the chakras?"

"I know Chakra Khan and Rufus."

Val patted her chest, feigned indigestion and cleared her throat. "The body has seven chakras, seven areas of energy."

I started tapping around my body.

"Your body, too, Debonair. And the third chakra is the solar plexus, your navel area."

"I got one of those."

"Yes, you do. It's the center of our will, self-confidence and self-esteem. The element associated with it is fire."

"Ah, yes, fire. I can identify with that."

Her eyes shut in mock restraint then reopened. "It relates to our individual power, our ability to make an impact on the world. But when there's tension there, there's the feeling of being overwhelmed and out of control. Not developing that third chakra may raise issues of feeling guilty when saying *no*. Or an inability to assert yourself, which might cause a feeling of helplessness."

Where she was going with her story, I couldn't guess. But a clear calm settled in her eyes and in her breathing; almost as if counseling herself. "Imagine that a healthy child—or a healthy adult, for that matter—has four faucets emptying into a very large sink. Imagine that each faucet represents an emotion: one for joy, one for fear, one for anger, and one for sadness. All four functioning faucets are necessary for a healthy being. If one or more are jammed, problems—often serious problems—arise."

Valerie took a sip of water. "An eight-year-old girl came with her parents to see me. She had horrible, debilitating stomachaches that often lasted weeks. And had for years. They were getting worse. Doctors found nothing physically wrong with her. No amount of pills suppressed the child's pain. Her parents entrusted me with solving that pain.

"Ironically, the girl was super-easy going, agreeable, compliant, pleasant and delightful at home and at school. She was even wonderful with her younger brother. In fact, she was always joyous except when she writhed in pain under the covers in her bedroom in darkness."

"What did you do?" I asked.

"Session after session, we drew, we painted, we worked with clay—even played with puppets. And I assessed her. She was stuck on joy, which meant her fear, anger and sadness faucets were jammed. She was way out of balance. But when I asked her what made her mad, she said 'nothing.' When I asked her to tell me what she liked about her dad, she said 'He's really happy in his new job.' When I asked what she liked about her brother, she said 'One thing I like about my brother is that he really likes school.'"

Valerie held eye contact with me. "Do you see what she's doing? She's making no *I* statements, it's like she's impersonalized everything. Instead of saying 'What I like about you, Dad, is that you read me the Sunday comics,' the story is about them, *not* her. She's inauthentic about *herself*. She's observing people rather than interacting with them.

Val continued. "You've heard of acting out? Well, she was acting *in*. Somatic issues like stomachaches and headaches are usually connected with unexpressed anger and aggressive energy."

I found myself wondering if it was the little girl she was talking about, or herself. Or me.

She resumed. "The girl's father was a relatively easy-going guy. But often at work and exhausted when he came home late. And the mother . . . a strict religious woman who maintained a very traditional home. She dressed the kids very conservatively and spanked the kids—nothing illegal or anything that would need to be presented to Child Protective Services. But it was a home in which the kids knew better than to express their desires or anger. Because if they did, mom was going to come down on them. The kids learned to bottle it up, and keeping tension in like that, the body rebels."

Val's expression still abstract, her tenor academic.

"So, as a therapist I tried to get the girl to draw pictures of anger, have her make a clay bucket of things that would make her angry, and so on. I tried to bring anger out in the open, normalize it so it was an okay thing. But she'd say 'Nothing makes me mad.' So much resistance from her that I had to scale back the experiment.

'What kind of foods don't you like?' Getting her to make any kind of negative statement was difficult. But ultimately, she admitted, 'I'm not crazy about Brussels sprouts.' And we worked from there. Slowly, she started to open up.

"After months of sessions, the stomachaches began to subside. I gave her a rubber mallet and said 'Tell your mom what you're most mad about. Say it out loud. Yell it.' She took the mallet and with a big breath pounded the table with it. 'I'm so mad that you always want me to wear dresses, Mom. I'm old enough to dress the way I want!' I applauded. 'Great,' I told her. 'That's great.'"

"Fantastic," I said. Val deeper, more generous and beautiful every time she revealed herself.

But Valerie slumped. "The mother didn't like *that* anger released. She stopped the sessions, saying that the child was already feeling better; there was no need to continue her therapy. I argued for the child but the mother was immovable. I don't know what she told the father. I never saw the child again."

"That's awful," I said.

"What's awful is that the child eventually poisoned herself, I'm sure of it."

"Oh no."

"She survived. The parents said it was an accident and they moved away. I've never heard about that little girl since. Hardly a day goes by that I don't think of her." Valerie wiped moisture from her eyes. "And that has changed me."

Unsure how to comfort Val, I stared into my whiskey. "I'm so sorry."

"People speak in codes. Children less often, but even they do. You need to understand codes."

I twirled my drink around and finished it off. "You mean people don't say what they mean."

"Sometimes. But it's more than that. Sometimes they don't

know what it is, exactly, themselves. Current society doesn't offer a plan for heroism that youth can relate to, or most people can relate to. We've lost courage, we've low self-esteem; we're not convinced our lives have meaning. I think most of us doubt how brave we might be in a dangerous or deadly situation. Which is why we so revere true courage, courage like yours." She sat back. "Sometimes people can't just come out and say the things they want or need to."

"I'm not good at guessing," I said. "I like things straightforward."

"Have you found life to be like that? Have you found people to be like that?"

"Well . . ."

"No, I didn't think so." She got up from the couch and took my glass with her. "Another?"

I nodded.

She poured me another Johnnie Walker. She sniffed it. "Have you ever considered taking something more . . . expansive?"

"What does that mean?"

"I don't know, maybe a drug that might *expand* your vision," she said.

"Cabbage, I'm not sure what you're suggesting."

She handed me the glass. "You know I like alcohol. It makes me happy—temporarily. But it doesn't provide me much insight."

"And pot does?"

"Sure, a little."

"So you want me to try pot?" I said.

"Maybe. And maybe we could try some other things. Together."

I probably scowled. "What kind of other things?"

"Never mind. It was just a thought." She squeezed in next to me.

"Have you tried other things?" I asked.

"I'm sorry I brought it up. I just hope to get closer to you."

"And we need drugs for that?"

"Sometimes," she said. "For some people it can be very illuminating."

"Illuminating?"

"Let's drop it, okay?" She put her arms around me. "I love you and I want to get as close to you as I can. I want to dissolve the boundaries between us. It was just a thought. Don't get all bent with me. Okay? Can you drop it and just hold me?" She brought her mouth to mine.

Once more, she'd unsettled me. But we'd had such a sweet evening, I had no interest in damaging it. And those lips! I pressed mine to hers; I let go.

CHAPTER 27

Father Blu

I considered mentioning Valerie Dunn and Penny Velez in front of Duke, to goad him, to see his reaction. Would his response to their names be as agitated as Hakim's? Would they kick up his EEG? But I had to consider Charli, so I took her aside. We huddled in the hospital hallway. A portion of her torpor had burned off.

"Duke depressed?" she asked. "Because he was going to be forced into retirement? He never mentioned anything like that to me." Luster had replaced the worry in her eyes. "And the way his EEG spiked."

I'd been encouraging her, raising her hopes. Now I wasn't so sure. I didn't want to smother her optimism, but I needed my doubt to be out in the open. "That would have been a blow to him, don't you think—forced retirement?"

She mulled it over. "Maybe." But clearly undaunted, she tossed back her ginger locks; the way women both inspire and wreck men.

Did Duke fall into that trap with Valerie Dunn? I vacillated. Until I knew more, I'd already injected enough negativity for one day. "Did Duke ever mention a rift with his buddy Benny Stein or a feud over a woman with Hakim Vaughn?"

"No. Why? What woman?"

"Probably nothing," I said.

"What do you know? Tell me."

"When I have something solid, you'll know." I checked my phone; time to call Chuck Winston. I motioned to Charli that I had to make a call, and stepped into a nearby corridor for some privacy. He picked up on the second ring.

"Chief, it's Father Bluterre. You find out anything as to that Seventy-seventh Street fire?"

"I think you should meet me at the site," he said. "That was one hot fire."

"Aren't all fires?"

"Some more than others." His tone less combative than the last time I'd spoken to him, but suggesting discouraging news. "This obviously means a lot to all of us that knew Duke." For the first time he spoke of Duke in the past tense. "You should meet me here. I'd rather not discuss this on the phone," he said.

. . .

When I arrived at Valerie Dunn's scorched apartment, Chief Winston quickly ushered me into the building and up to the last standing apartment, the one beneath Ms. Dunn's. He unlocked the door but didn't open it.

"Stay close behind me. I'm here on borrowed time," he said. "This has become a larger investigation and a drawn-out one. Eight months now. And since I'd asked about it at the department, the Arson Section Commander requested that I take a look at it too, give him my opinion."

He opened the door.

Over his shoulder, charred devastation. Nary a vertical support still standing. Those that were, were blackened stumps, no more than a third off the floor. My body still ached, and that green, sickly feeling lodged in my stomach again.

"Most of this floor is safe, Father, but we aren't going out to the middle. And you shouldn't even be here, but I thought . . .Well, you'll be talking to his sister. You should see for yourself. You probably have a better bedside manner than I do."

Extremely debatable. And ominous.

He directed my attention along the remaining blackened wall. "We'll stay on the edge. And obviously we're not going over there." He pointed to the missing back wall and the clear view across the open thirty yards to the next building. The paint around the scorched windows of *that building* had melted off. The queasiness advanced through my body.

An icy wind raged through the open space, trilling the bright yellow tape crisscrossing the threshold. It warned "Extreme Danger: Keep Out." The thick scent of ash revitalized.

Ducking under the tape, he started to inch forward. He looked over his shoulder. "You okay?"

"Sure, I'm fine." I followed, unsteady.

"This was an inferno," he said. "It reduced almost everything to ashes, as you can see. The owner was lucky the entire building wasn't razed, which was strange."

"How so?" My ribs spasmed every time I took in too much air. I *couldn't* look around. I kept my eyes on him.

"This fire was set. Arson. Yet, only the apartment above was targeted."

"The owner of the building?"

"No."

I kept my hand against the wall attempting to channel his comfort with the dizzying height surrounding us. "What makes you say that?"

"Why would he torch one apartment? He was asleep in his

apartment downstairs, with his wife and two grandchildren when the fire was finally reported. He wasn't the least bit unhappy, suicidal or looking for insurance money. From all accounts, he had a good relationship with Ms. Dunn. She paid rent on time; she even babysat his grandchildren once or twice when they were out on the town. No, this was someone else."

"But you're sure this was arson?" I asked.

"The arson unit is, and let me show you why." He squatted and I copied him, bracing against the floor. "See that?"

There wasn't much to look at. The entire floor, for the most part, empty; all but one lamp removed. Bits of debris had fallen from the floor above littering the charred carpet.

He dropped to a knee, pulled out a pair of tweezers and lifted a one-inch square piece of thick brown and red cloth material for me to view. "You recognize this?"

"Clothing?" I guessed.

"No, it's the remains of a braided rope rug. You notice the carpets in this apartment are not of that type."

"Is that meaningful?"

"Could be. Like I said, this was an unusually hot fire, probably seventeen or eighteen hundred degrees. The average house fire runs about eleven hundred. At eleven hundred degrees our bunker coats catch fire. This piece of rug must have been wedged into something for it to have survived temperatures like that."

"How'd the apartment get so hot?"

"We're not sure." He stood and looked around. I remained anchored to the floor. "But it burned without abatement for almost two hours because it wasn't immediately called in—the fire being late at night, I suppose, many of the local residents asleep. And smoke, initially, almost non-existent.

"Luckily, the folks here in this apartment were on vacation, Hawaii. And Dunn's attic apartment was thoroughly sealed off, not many windows. Once it had gathered heat, no man could have gotten in there without incinerating himself."

I considered what Hakim Vaughn had told me. "Did anything survive, fall down to this level?"

"Silverware, a few pots and pans, part of the stove, some jewelry, mostly trinkets."

I hesitated to ask. "What about Ms. Dunn?"

He bit his lip. "She couldn't survive this. She was seen going in to her apartment around six PM. We presume she was sleeping when the fire really took hold. It got up on her quickly and ran very fast; so hot that everything was consumed, the floor, her bed, even most of her bones. Calcium can be pretty indestructible but at that heat . . ."

"She's dead?"

"I'm afraid so. Arson squad is very thorough. They'll even check remaining skulls when they can."

"Skulls?"

"There wasn't one here—probably blown apart—but yes. If a body cooks up enough, the head explodes from the boiling liquid in the skull. When a body is found, we check the blunt force trauma to the head, inward or outward."

The floor seemed to move again under me. "That's important, why?"

"If the force is outward we can say the person died from the fire: the head exploded. If it's an inward blow, the person was struck over the head. The body was planted there after he or she was already dead."

"And in this case?"

"Some small bone fragments and her fingerprint-verified carbonized left little finger, that's it." He took a deep breath. "There's no evidence of her escaping. What's more, all these months since the fire, her money's untouched in her bank account. And according to logs her credit cards and cell phone have been unused since the fire. She never showed up at work the next day, even though she had several appointments scheduled. Not a single trail of any electronic record. I'm told her brother's given permission to fully authorize her death. She'll be an officially-certified fatality very soon."

I wondered. "Could this have been a domestic dispute?"

"Doubtful. Those fights are usually spontaneous; they escalate. Someone tosses gasoline down a hallway. They light it and run. It's sloppy, it's obvious, but it works. Ninety percent of all arson fires start that way. This was more sophisticated. For one, whoever set this was able to get far away before the burn was visible. Or she set fire to herself; people don't usually do that."

"I wouldn't think so," I said, hoping we could finish our discussion on the street.

"Religious zealots making a statement, maybe. If people want to go, they want to go quick. And the smoke detectors, even in the hallway, had been disabled. No," he raised the cloth again. "This is what's left of a rope rug. Remarkably, the AIU found the dense, stapled end of a matchbook embedded in a slightly larger piece of this rug when they sifted through the rubble. "This fire, even when it was called in, was very difficult to put out. That leads to the possible conclusion that the arson set a lighted cigarette with the unburnt end into the matchbook, then buried the matchbook in the rolled-up braided rug. Very flammable and very hard to put out because the flame is protected.

"There were undoubtedly more accelerants used that were consumed—maybe magnesium or some of that crap they use in meth labs: acetone, lithium, toluene. Hard to say. That would give him at least thirty to forty minutes to get far away, even establish an alibi."

Winston surveyed the devastation one last time. "Anyway, the rest of the investigation is ongoing; someone was targeting her." He paused. "You see now why I wanted you to be aware of all this?"

"Duke," I said.

"In the past I couldn't imagine that he'd be involved. But he's been on the arson squad's radar." A flake of ash floated toward me like a maleficent moth. Chief Winston pointed us back to the door and safety. I was more than ready.

A cheerless silence hung over us as we went down the stairwell and out into the street. I welcomed the pavement. We both looked up at the incinerated top floor, our cloudy breaths lifting toward it.

Without facing me, he said, "Duke had some sort of relationship with Valerie Dunn, didn't he?"

"Yes," I said. "But I don't know what kind of relationship." Wind whistled through the remains of Dunn's apartment. "Have other women been lost in those arson-set fires?"

"Yes, of course. Why?"

"Their ages? A pattern?" I asked.

"Oh, I don't know. That would require going through years of old fire and police logs—possibly thousands of pages—which I'm not about to do. No one is. And how would you tie them together?"

"Just a thought."

He pinched the bridge of his nose and rubbed it. "I'm hoping that, as I've helped you, you will keep me apprised if you find out anything more about their relationship."

"Certainly. Can I ask you something else?" I said.

"Shoot."

"Where does a firefighter make enough money to have a Montauk beach house?"

"You're still on the Penny Velez thing." He pulled lip balm from his jacket and ran it across his lips.

"Just wondering."

"It's a family of firefighters. I broke in with Marciano Velez. That house had been in Penny's family since the nineteen fifties. But there's one more thing."

"Yeah?" I said.

"I checked the files on Hakim Vaughn. Many years ago he was married to Valerie Dunn—twice."

"Whoa. Do you think—?"

"Don't know what to think," Winston said. "But he was on duty most of the night of the fire, I checked."

"And Duke?"

"Didn't show up for his shift." He returned the lip balm to his pocket. "You're gonna keep me in the loop, right?"

"Sure."

I called Charli and made my way back to the hospital to meet with her. How was I going to tell her about Valerie? What I'd uncovered that the police hadn't? Your brother is a murderer? Even if he survives he'll live out his life in a cell. Or maybe they'll condemn him to death, fry him in The Chair. God and faith traps; that's the legacy I'd leave her? This wasn't the story I'd hoped to uncover.

. . .

Deep purple tentacles spread like serpents beneath my skin. My bruised ribs, shoulders and back manifesting the still-tender memories of my cemetery fall and Hakim Vaughn's violence. Now, with the new information, I couldn't shake the notion that Lt. Vaughn was somehow involved.

I dabbed at the wounds. I needed a drink. Just one to drive away the pain. To settle my nerves. To restore my confidence. To neutralize the disturbing details I'd exposed. I argued with myself that it was, after all, early evening, happy hour. I met with Old Faithful for a slug of raspberry tonic. Then another. I made my way to the hospital cafeteria, more cauterized than confident. Maybe the auxiliary beer I had as I waited for her wasn't such a great idea. Charli finally arrived.

"I thought it'd be bedder to meet here." *Away from Duke.* I tried to focus.

She tilted her head, appraising me. "Aren't you excited? Duke seems to be coming out of it. You were right."

Where to begin?

"Well?"

"The meeting with Chuck Winston . . ." My eyes had the consistency of crushed bone. Rubbing them did no good. She shot me a mistrustful look. I attempted to rearranged myself. "We met at Valerie Dunn's apartment, a woman I think Duke was seeing." I scratched at the beer label. My lips and throat were chunky dry too, but there was nothing left in the bottle.

"You found her! How does she know Duke? What can she tell us? I want to meet her?"

"Charli . . ." I reached for her arm and missed.

She pulled it away. "You've been drinking."

"Just this beer. D'ya want one? I could use another."

"Doesn't look like one beer." She folded her arms. "Why'd you bring me down here?"

My head heavy; it was all I could do to keep it up. "Valerie Dunn is dead."

Charli shifted almost imperceptibly. Whatever joy she'd embodied drained away. "Who was she?"

"Doan know yet but guessing she's somehow key."

"Okay." Her face and body suddenly taut.

"She died inna fire." My eyelids weighted. "Purposefully set, probably for her."

"That's awful." Charli appropriately aghast, but nothing more. The connection to her brother remote.

"Department thinks Duke may have been involved," I said.

A belligerent chuckle. "What do you mean *involved*?"

"Arson, Charli. There been arson fires set. More than one."

"So?" Her cheeks and neck started pulsating. "What does this have to do with Duke? He's the good guy, the guy who saves lives."

My forehead beaded with perspiration. I couldn't look at her. "That's what I'm hoping." Even to me it didn't sound convincing.

She leaned forward, eyes flaming. "I'll live with the images of my brother as he is now, if that's the best I can do. But I'm not going to drag him or me into a witch hunt, now that he can't defend himself. Not by a band of jealous firemen. And certainly not by a drunken priest, a priest who longs to be the hero."

Sweat trickled into my eyes, burning them. I reached for the handkerchief in my back pocket. Old Faithful fell with a hollow gong to the floor. "Cough medicine," I said as I bent over to pick up the flask.

Charli shook her head in disgust. She stood up. I tried and capsized onto the floor. She looked down at me with pity. "Maybe you drink to ward off your own despair."

I grabbed for the chair to lift myself up, but it toppled with a clatter. The whole room looked at me. Charli turned away and marched out.

I picked myself up. I did my best to walk straight out of that cafeteria. Nonetheless, what she'd said about my desperation, about me wanting to be a hero. . . She was right. And now, with Duke's motivation even more suspicious, leaving Charli with the wreckage I'd created was no longer an option. But I could barely keep myself upright.

CHAPTER 28

Duke

The opening strings of Etta James' "At Last" flowed over my empty hospital room, burying the low but incessant hum of my EEG and the other equipment surrounding my bed. Etta's earthy and reassuring voice transported me to March when I had everything I desired without ever having known I'd thirsted for it.

Valerie had been in fine spirits; our early spring a series of jaunts through Brooklyn's Prospect Park, Randall's Island and Riverside Park. She seemed relaxed. Cherry blossoms overhead animated her every step. Lavender and orange crocuses teased the air when we knelt close. All of it and all of her, breathtaking and relaxed—*except* when I pulled out my phone and started taking photos of her.

"Put that thing away." She held her hand in front of her face.

"Just a few."

"No pictures."

"Just shots of you, so when we're apart—"

"Give me the phone!" She grabbed for it.

A quick side step. "No."

"No more fucking photos."

"Okay."

"I mean it." She lowered her hands.

"Okay, okay." I slipped the phone in my pocket. *Excuse me!*

Otherwise, it was nirvana. Valerie and I consumed almost every free night together; a virtual feast, even with her questionable cooking and the expletives she served with them.

She traveled every ten days or so to Miami; conferences, she said. Or client-related. Or she'd be oblique. But no time for me to question my good fortune. I had my shifts too, often weird hours, and she never complained. I don't think we spent more than five consecutive nights apart.

They were sweet times. We played cards together—Double Solitaire, Sixty-six and Egyptian Rat Screw. We tried *once* to cook together—not a good idea. We listened and danced to music in our apartments—The Manhattans, Phil Collins, Coldplay, Zayn, Emancipator. I'd toss in some King Pleasure, Bill Evans, Django Reinhardt, Billie Holiday and Alphonso Johnson, just to keep her ears wide open. She found she liked Joni Mitchell. She even got me to dance in public a couple of times.

We bowled once. She beat me bad. We went to a Bonnie Raitt concert. We went to two (!) of her NASCAR races. They left me with terrible headaches. She sat in on a public lecture the captain roped me into giving—much to my discomfort—on fire safety building construction. And with her goading me on, I managed to sit through a coffee-klatch astrology group (mostly women) at an Upper East Side club.

For two people who tended to be fairly insular, together we were getting out more often, albeit without chaperones. And of course, we spent hours in front of my fireplace or on her couch discussing relationships, the world situation, and bemoaning the lack of serious coleslaw artisans. We kissed a lot and made love.

"That's not what I want," she said when I tried kneading my

finger in her. Okay, no sticky fingers. And of course, I tried the standard approaches, front to front then front to back.

"No," she said and went down on me.

It's not that I didn't like it, but I felt controlled and not particularly spontaneous. What's more, she didn't seem physically satisfied after much of our lovemaking. I wondered if I were somehow letting her down. She said *no*, but she clearly preferred giving oral and receiving anal sex.

During that period, I had only one shaky spell and no memory loss or blackouts. It happened at the firehouse doing maintenance on the apparatus. None of my company noticed. I never mentioned it to Valerie. And it entered my mind that soon we might need only one apartment. I suggested we exchange apartment keys. "In time," she said. "I'll leave the door open for you when I'm home."

One evening late in March I let myself in. She was in her workout room, on her rowing machine. From the sound of the machine she was cooling down and talking to *Jimmy*.

The guy made me nervous; well, jealous. I'd never met him, and I didn't know how often—if ever—Val saw him in person. But since she spent so much time with me, I grit my teeth, said nothing and let it go. At least I tried.

"When am I going to see you again?" I overheard him say. I moved a little closer to the door.

"Not for a while," she said. "Not until I get this all sorted out."

"This is getting a little weird," he said.

"I'm sorry, but it's got to be this way for at least a little while longer."

The room hushed as her rowing came to a rest. Feeling threatened and humiliated, I stepped back from the door.

"You know I love you, right?" he said.

"I love you too," Val said. "Gotta go." I could hear her get off the machine.

I tinkered in the kitchen clutching a beer as she walked into the living room. She had a towel around her neck and her workout clothes were drenched in sweat. I didn't want her thinking I was spying on her or prying into what was probably a perfectly appropriate relationship. But my insides screamed for answers.

She was taken aback. "I didn't realize you'd made it in yet." Her face quickly softened. She walked over, grabbed my ass and gave me a passionate kiss, full tongue. Her pong, exquisite.

I pulled away.

"You okay?" Suddenly she was mother hen?

"Tough day." I swigged my beer.

She wiped the sweat off her forehead and dropped onto the couch, patting the space beside her. "Come, tell me."

"Maybe I should go."

"No, don't be silly. Come here. What's going on?"

I maneuvered in, still stiff. "It came pretty close today."

"You're okay?" She laid her hand on my knee and rubbed it.

"I'm okay." I rested my head on the sofa back. I stared at the ceiling and the cobwebs and the fly caught in one, struggling to get out.

"Tell me." She rubbed playfully against my shoulder.

"It's over now." Another drag on my beer.

"Please. You know now it isn't healthy to hold it in, not talk about it." Ironic and galling, considering her duplicity. The cobwebs fluttered to a hidden draft. "Please." She rubbed my neck.

Drop the grudge.

"Come on, out with it," she repeated.

"Okay." *Where to begin?*

"Where'd it happen?"

"Newly remodeled lofts, an alley over on Liberty Street. Rosen, the fire marshal, was on overwhelm and behind schedule. Captain asked me to step in, do a simple check off. Building's vacant. Not quite done."

Valerie's eyes said *Keep it moving.* I almost said *fuck it* and left. I rolled the can of Miller across my forehead, cooling it. "Anyway, halfway round the top floor I smell smoke. All I can tell is that it's coming from the elevator shaft. I called it in."

Valerie interrupted me. "No elevator. That can't be good." She ran her fingertips down my neck. I tried to resist, but she had *the touch.* "So?"

"So, yeah. I scrambled down the stairs and within minutes the upper floors were well involved. The fire had engulfed the upper floors."

"That fast?"

"Yeah. When the crew arrived, we laddered the building. We had to get up the roof, cut a hole in it, ventilate it to let the heat and gases and smoke out, so we could get inside and put out the fire.

"So, we're up there, and it's pretty bad. We're getting smoke and fire out of the holes we're cutting. In other words, we're standing *over* fire the whole time; never good. We've only got a certain amount of time and then we've gotta get out of there; the roof's not lasting forever. . . "

The fly had stopped struggling; only the cobweb trembled.

"Duke?"

"Yeah. . . Plus there's a small breeze fanning the damn thing, so my internal clock is ticking. I start looking for more signs. Captain too. The roof's showing clues that it's weakening—in particular where the roof meets the parapet wall."

"Like the castle." Valerie put her palms together as if she was praying.

"No, different. It's where the wall comes up and the roof sits on it, on hangers inside the wall. When you see smoke coming out of that seam in the roofing paper, where it meets the wall, it's a really bad sign. The roof's beginning to flex and give way. Only a matter of time before catastrophic failure.

"I pointed it out to the captain. He nodded. I motioned to the other team members. 'We're off, we're off the roof. Let's go!'"

"Oh, Duke." But she was eating it up.

"We proceeded to get off the way we came on, back to the ladder. But as we did, the roof caved in cutting off our escape route, trapping us on the rooftop. Flames were fifteen-twenty feet high.

"We got to a corner that felt relatively stable. Captain got on the radio saying we were trapped and needed another ladder on the west side of the building. But there was a lot of static. So Tony S tossed his helmet over the side, so the guys on the ground knew we were in extreme danger. And when they saw it, they raised a hydraulic ladder. We started throwing our chainsaws and tools off the roof."

Val's hand tightened on my knee.

"Ouch, Cabbage!" I pried her off it.

"So?" She faced me full of worry . . . but also a hunger.

"The guys were down the ladder except me, Gracie and Captain Hoyle, the two of them the closest to it.

"A high-pitched cracking sound and the rest of the roof began to give way. I said 'Go, I'm right behind you.' And they did. I was the last one.

"Less than ten feet from me, the roof disappeared, smoke and flame rolling toward me. I leapt head-first grabbing the ladder as the whole roof collapsed below me."

She stroked my head. "Oh, god."

"It was close. Too fucking close."

"I'm sure. The fire, so fast. What caused it?"

I shrugged. "That's what everybody will want to know."

"You're the most courageous man I've ever met." She hugged me and bit my ear. "And now you're safe here with me."

Even then I knew I wasn't safe with her. *Sure, the park's cherry blossoms could be breathtaking. But like many aspects of nature, their beauty is short-lived.* I knew it, yet I did nothing about it. I kept inhaling her.

CHAPTER 29

Father Blu

After my poorly executed explanation to Charli, and my humiliation in the cafeteria, I parked myself at the nearest bus stop, waiting for the bus to Duke's apartment. When it arrived, it swung close to me, tires hissing, brakes rattling, doors opening like fangs, purging any false sanctimony I might still harbor.

I found a seat next to a young Hasidic man. He gave me one look—suggesting I was unclean—before turning away. The billboard panel above me full of censure: the grizzled face of a New York City fire fighter and the headline

"When others ran out,
he rushed in."

The bus gained speed, a pothole shocked its steel skeleton. "Sorry," said the bus driver.

"It's serious," Jory said.

"Okay, tell me."

"No, it has to be in person."

"Jory, can't it wait?"

My life had an uncharted linearity to it. That first step seemed to have informed all the rest. Whatever felt right, whatever felt pleasurable. *A fool gives full vent to his spirit* . . . Like women. All the women in whom I put so much faith. All the love songs claiming heaven on earth, suggesting the divine ideal can be embodied—not in heaven—but in a love partner. I followed that line straight ahead.

The gems, too. Searching for meaning in stones. My decision to skip college and find my way traveling the world, ending in Madagascar. My mother said *geophysicist*, I said *nah*.

I never could substantiate which gems healed and which lacked purpose. Did hematite and obsidian really ground us from avoiding worldly tasks? Did jade offer serenity? Fluorite cleanse negativity? Black Phantom bring awareness of one's personal addictions?

So many wrong turns on such a linear path.

Why I thought serving the Lord would wipe away the litany of defects in my DNA, I no longer recalled, if I ever knew them in the first place. They all laid heavy on me, joining the motor coach parked on my chest.

The bus stopped within a block of Duke's apartment. I got off. Duke and his methodically-ordered, bulletproof world pissed me off. What had I missed?

As soon as I walked in, it was all by the numbers: the meticulously organized crates and shelves of albums, the painstakingly uncluttered countertops, the fastidiously clean floors, the perfectly hung and spaced memorabilia. The guy had created a flawless environment for himself, so damned immaculate I wanted to fill the room with thunder and shake it apart.

I went to his liquor cabinet, pulled the Johnnie Walker and set myself a glass from his scrupulously-organized cupboard. Hair of the dog. The bottle cap twisted off, out of my fingers, and fell to the floor. Even that pip-squeaky sound offended me.

I poured myself a full one. Then a second. Reaching for it, I knocked the damn glass over, spilling the gold. The glass rolled off the countertop and shattered on the floor. That's when I lost it. *Holy war!*

I reached into the cupboard and with one sweep of my arm brought all those impeccably-stacked mugs and glasses to the ground. *Oh, I beg your pardon.*

Felt so good, I took hold of some plates; dropped *them* to the floor. The rest I started heaving against the walls, splintering them left and right. I laughed. *Kiss my ass, you assiduous little shit!* Delightful. Satisfying.

I stumbled to the living room. The self-consciously categorized books, down they went. Even the philosophers. I kicked a few across the floor before going back to the kitchen and the bottle, this time feasting directly from it.

Cabinets to the right—pots and pans diligently stacked. *Screw you.* Pulled them out, punted them in every damn direction. Made as much noise as I wanted. Made sure heaven and earth heard me.

His exemplary drawer of utensils? Tugged the stinking bin right out of- and off its tracks. The silverware scattered with thunder over the kitchen floor. Picked a few up. Looked at the Johnnie Walker. Threw the forks aside and went for another, and then another swig. *Keep the fires burning.*

Last I remember, I'd ransacked the inviolate pantry, slicing open a bag of flour and letting it fly. Powder and grit hung in the air, then coated the geography like so much ash. His rigorous, unerring space, spotless and unsullied no more.

Jory nudged me. "Wake up, we'd better get home."

I woke up on my back watching the ceiling smoke detector liquefy in and out of focus. Duke's bottle of scotch cold and empty in my hand. Boz Scaggs and Donald Fagen crooked on the wall, staring unsympathetically at me. The place torn apart; a sliver memory of the night before. I'd toppled everything standing so it could all be at my level, the bottom.

My temples ached, alternating with the drumming of my body. Even massaging them was a chore. I lay there, wreckage and remorse all around me. I tried once more to make sense of it—*not* my world, which repeatedly had proven to be swamp-like and beyond sense—but Duke's.

If Duke was being forced out of the department, he might start fires, then show how valuable he was by putting them out.

But as AIU closed in on him, he might have started the fire in the gun shop so he could have an untraceable weapon if the investigation got too close. He could die a hero before anything could be proven. He could reap immortality with a single bullet.

Would he do that? Courage isn't so unusual in those who see themselves as historical icons. Look at Father Toll. Look even at the saints. What is a little pain next to guaranteeing immortality?

Penny Velez as a focal point now seemed a little remote, though Hakim Vaughn's accounts still left me unsettled. But what about the other woman, Valerie Dunn? How did she fit into Duke's life? And why would he set her apartment on fire? To frighten her? Why? Did she know something about Duke, about the fires he was lighting? Did he kill her because of what she knew? Was she one of his many victims?

I tried to stand up and failed, falling backward *hard* against a cabinet below Duke's vinyl collection. Vomit stuck in my chest. All body fluids leached out. Sandpaper along every nerve. My body complained.

Using the edge of the cabinet door, I raised myself up to view the topography. The thrown dishes had left scars on the walls, the kitchen backsplash and the cabinets below. The floor and countertops were littered with the scree of cheap, brightly colored tableware.

Using the wall, the LP crates and the desk, I groped to an

overturned kitchen stool. I righted it and landed on it. Looking over the room, it appeared more lived in this way, all trashed, rather than the meticulous cosmos Duke had fabricated. I clucked. But I was only mocking myself.

At the sink, without a single unbroken glass to drink from, I splashed my face and doggy-slurped from the faucet until the water ran down my arms and pants. My head began to clear.

Several of Duke's books lay open, the closest a Buddhist text with something written inside the cover. Even reaching for it I thought I might be sick.

Please mail back to me:

Tamar Beryl

242 W. 41st Street, 27th floor

A trip to mid-town was in my future.

I surveyed the room again. Duke had his patterns. He evidently wanted everything simple, uncluttered, easily at his fingertips, whether it was his music, his kitchen wares or his meager technology. I'd undone all that.

All except a simple white candle, the only vertical item that had withstood my meltdown. It sat on a small shelf to the right of the vinyl collection, almost hidden, because several albums leaned against it. Behind the candle and its plain glass candleholder I detected another object; its placement, beyond first reach, contradicted Duke's routine.

On closer review, wedged behind the candle, I uncovered a small black and white composition book. The kind we had in junior high school. I slid the candle aside and pulled it out. I opened it to this handwritten scribbling:

10048:

IRR/mir – 12:1-6

CAM/des – 9:4-7+22

HOL/lad – 5:3-8+11&12
VAS/leg – 9:24-27
MOT/whe – 1:2-6+11-12

The notations reminded me of quoted scripture, bible verses, with these only a bit more cryptic. For Duke, they were probably a way to organize and categorize his life, and his music collection. A manual for his life. *And where had it gotten him?*

I tucked the notebook under my arm, knowing I'd need to return to clean up the mess I'd created, though neither Duke nor I would likely savor order again.

CHAPTER 30

Duke

"Who was Valerie Dunn? And why would you be part of an arson investigation?" Charli hung over my bed, eyes darting around my face and then to the EEG. She knew! How? I cascaded still deeper into self-loathing.

"You can hear me, can't you? she said. "I see it on your electro-encephalogram. Who was she?"

Someone had made the connection between me and Valerie. Once it all came out, even my sister wouldn't see me as a hero any-more. My sins would be block headlines across the Post and Daily News, every tabloid and Internet site in the country following suit. Scandal and dishonor would tear through the department; my leg-acy as a monster, a pariah. All because . . . Val had egged me on.

"You're so smart about these things," Val said. "That fire at the Liberty Street condos, did they ever determine the cause?"

An early April shower had left the Central Park paths glisten-ing and the air a touch cool. The sun made a show of returning in full force. She dug into her pockets looking for something. She thrust a few items at me to carry—a small comb, lip balm, some coins; *her apartment key*. She found her pipe. She dragged from it. We held hands as we walked.

"It was arson. AIU found remains of a plastic gallon milk bottle—one way to start a fire."

"Explain," she said.

"You're one inquisitive broad."

"Inquisitive *human*; about you, about what you do. Now explain about the milk bottle."

"Sorry. You fill one of those bottles with gasoline, then stuff a kerosene-soaked rag in its handle, and *presto*."

"And *presto* what?"

"A smart pyro, or at least a more sophisticated one, wants to be far from the scene when the fire takes hold, right? A kerosene rag—which burns slower than gasoline—provides a built-in fuse. Burns down through the handle into the gas and boom! You've got a helluva conflagration. And if he or she wants to watch—"

"Why, do they like that?"

"Who knows," I said. "Maybe they want to see firemen and women in action. Maybe they like the flames. Maybe they hope to outsmart the fire department—even show the department they're needed. I'm told some get a sexual charge from it."

"Firemen start fires?"

"You bet. Like I said, we have a unique relationship with fire. I'm guessing most people do. Firefighters just happen to be ultra-special."

"Hmm," Val said. "Can they catch the guy, the pyro?"

"I'm pretty skeptical this time. He was smart. But they're still investigating."

We walked on in silence for a bit, past Sheep Meadow and north to Cherry Hill, her arms entwined with mine. She leaned into me and occasionally turned to me and kissed me. We stopped to watch a group playing cricket—mostly East Indians and Pakistanis. A bright red ball left the hand of one player, and the batsman wacked it. Hollers erupted as a player converged on the ball.

Their exuberance enchanted her, like a little girl. "They're so happy. They know how to play." She turned to gauge my reaction.

"Yes," I admitted.

She flinched. "You sound wistful."

"A little. I realize that I've only begun to play."

"We play." She fussed with my hair.

"We do, and it's marvelous."

She cradled my neck then grabbed my ears. "You're the only adult I play with." She beamed. She kissed me like a jackhammer attacking concrete.

I pulled away. "Is that true?"

Her face kinked. "Yes, of course. Do you doubt that?"

"It *feels* great, but my mind starts twisting things. I know there's something you need to tell me. It's been there a while. And I believe you *want* to tell me. But that *thing* that you're not telling me is making me a little crazy, making me *a lot* crazy." I held her at arm lengths and admired her. "Despite your magnificence. Do you understand?"

"You're right," she said. "It's time. You and I are mostly a perfect fit."

"Mostly?"

"I love and trust you," she continued. "You love me but *trust*, not so much. You have every right to question me. And to expect an answer, a truthful one." She separated from me, a step. "But what if I can't answer the question you need answered? I don't want to lose you, but I don't want to lie either. Do you understand?"

"I do," I said. "But I can't imagine anything that would change my mind about you."

She raised her hand to interrupt me, but I went on. "You're dedicated to helping people, children. I love that about you. You're creative; you're quirky. I love those things about you. You're pretty good with cabbage, a master with coleslaw in particular, and pretty shitty cooking all other foods. I even love that about you."

She lifted an eyebrow, feigned disbelief.

"I salute the urn flakes; the physical package your parents gave you is breathtaking. It's my physical home. I love it. Oh, and its own special fragrance, an odor so raw that it makes my dick stand up, as you've noticed."

She prepared to rebut me then stopped. She looked me in the eye. "I'm ready to commit to you one way or the other. I'm sorry there's a fork in the road at all. But there is."

"I can't imagine . . . Please, I want to go forward."

"Either fork will take us there," she said.

"I want to go forward with you."

"We will." She wrapped my fingers in hers and we began walking again. "It's clear your drug is alcohol. Mine, pot more than sweet rum drinks. But obviously I won't say *no* to any of them, if the time is right. But I need help and I'm hoping we can go to the next level."

Like a kid, my heart sprung open, but then wavered. "What kind of help?"

"I need a completely new perspective. I need to shed as much ego as possible to know the answer to my question, which will be the answer to your question."

"Always riddles, Cabbage."

"I'm untangling my own code, okay? Can you love me for that, even though if feels shitty?"

"It scares me, whatever you're suggesting."

"It scares me too. But not for the same reasons, I think, scare you."

"I don't like drugs deciding whether we continue or not," I said.

"It won't be the drugs deciding, I promise you that. Because I only have one question going in."

"If there's another man, just tell me."

She began to say something, then pulled back. "There isn't."

"You're sure?"

She chuckled. "Yeah, I'm sure."

"Then can't I answer your question for you?"

"No, no. Only I can answer the question. Going in with you should make it clear."

"What exactly is *going in?*" I asked.

"I want you to take mushrooms with me, out here in nature, all around this park." She spun around embracing the greenery. "What d'ya say?"

"Mushrooms? Psychedelics?" I said.

"Naturally psychotropic bourgeons. Know what *bourgeons* means?"

"I'm not into drugs."

"Yes, you are," she said. "Just not the same ones I'm into. Here," she held out her pipe and lighter. "Take a hit."

"I've tried it, it doesn't do much for me. And I've got to be careful about testing."

"In your blood, a day or two. Urine, maybe eight days." She lifted her chin. "And then urine the clear. Get it?" Her palms flattened to the sky, she even *looked* playful.

"Clever."

"Take a puff for me." She jabbed the pipe forward.

"That'll make you happy?"

"*You* make me happy." She pulled back her mane. "But yes, I'd like us to take this last hurdle in friendship."

"It sounds ominous."

"*Bourgeons* means 'To grow or develop rapidly; to expand; to flourish.' We can do that. Take a hit of pot; tell me if you're willing to share a day of bourgeons with me, sometime in the next ten days. After that there may be questions, but there'll be no barriers." Her eyes sincere, pleading *I love you, please.* "Maybe you'll see for yourself, all hidden in plain sight," she said.

Her muscular confidence surrounded me. And I knew I loved her, loved her deeply. . . in my *solar plexus*. I didn't want to retreat. Retreat felt stupid. *Have faith. Why not?*

I put the pipe to my mouth, cupped the lighter and inhaled. Then, either by chance or on purpose, Val never asked for her comb, lip balm or apartment key to be returned. And I didn't offer them back.

CHAPTER 31

Father Blu

Tamar Beryl's address in the cover of the Buddhist book, led me to the New York Times building and the corporate offices of Your Land, Inc. on the twenty-seventh floor. I asked to see Tamar Beryl, and the receptionist immediately became resistant, asking if I had an appointment. I told him, *no*, but that I was returning a book Tamar had lent a friend. I showed him the book and he made a call. I was ushered into a sparkling, glass-walled office with spectacular views of Manhattan. Greeting me from behind her desk was an African American woman in her mid-forties, fitted perfectly in a business suit and blouse.

"You're not Duke."

I explained the circumstances of my visit. She expressed sadness, offered me a seat, and sat across from me. "I only have a few minutes. And I only met him that once, when we sat next to each other at the lecture, when he showed interest in my book. Now I understand why he didn't return it."

"How long ago was the lecture and what was it about?" I asked.

"About ten months, right around Easter."

"Can you be more specific—I'm sorry to ask."

"No, it's okay." She went to her desk, scrolled through her computer, and returned. "April twentieth. Is that helpful?"

"Two weeks before his attempt," I said. "What was the lecture about?"

"Impermanence. Kind of a basic Buddhist concept."

"And did he say anything to you? What was his demeanor?"

"He was agitated; sad and agitated."

"Did he say why?"

"No." Ms. Beryl sat back. "He just asked me why I thought people were so dangerous—I guess he asked because I told him I've been a practicing Buddhist for many years. Maybe he thought I had some insight."

"He used that word, *dangerous?*"

"Yes."

"What did you tell him?"

"I told him I believed that we are all part of nature. That my belief was that mountains, trees—even weather and animals—are equitable, unbiased, dispassionate. And in that raw expansive view, nature could be both generous, abundant . . . and dangerous. And if that's so, then man—who is also, in my view, a part of nature—can be both."

"Did he have a response to that?"

Ms. Beryl didn't hesitate. "He said, 'So it's okay that I'm dangerous.' And I said, 'Well, I lean toward the well-intentioned.'"

"And his response?"

"He said, 'That doesn't guarantee a positive outcome.' No, I said, but bad intention is certainly more likely to create a negative result."

"Anything else?" I asked.

"No," she said. "Will he survive?"

I shrugged. Her impeccable yet unembellished office gave no

indication as to her business or her position there. "Can I ask, what do you do here? And what is your role?"

"I negotiate with private and corporate land owners on behalf of the public. We try to buy or trade to increase or maintain public lands. I'm the CEO. But not for long."

"No?"

"I'm not doing enough," she said. "I'm stepping down the end of this month."

I wondered what was next for her—how could she do *more*? But it seemed too personal a question, and I'd already imposed enough.

· · ·

Charli drew me out of Duke's hospital room, closing the door behind us. "This isn't my brother's handwriting." She handed the notebook back to me. "Why are you even here? Do the Christian thing, and leave." She started to turn away.

I pulled out the handwritten note Jean Stein had given me. "Is this Duke's handwriting?"

She glanced at it. "No."

"Look, I'm asking for your forgiveness. Please. I've been clumsy, I know. But don't you want to know why he did this?" I weighed telling her about Jory, about what it's like to *never* know.

"You're barely able to stay sober." Again, she pivoted to go.

"And still I've made progress."

She paused. "You've said that before."

"It's true, isn't it?"

Her hand rested on the doorknob. She swept her hair over her shoulder. "I want to believe, but you're dredging up baseless innuendo and accusations."

"But you want to know, I know you do," I said. "I'm willing to try if you are. Let's find out the truth."

"You have nothing to lose."

"I know brothers are memories, and not easily set adrift."

She closed her eyes and leaned against the wall, as if needing ballast.

"Do you need to forgive him?" I asked.

Her eyes opened, downcast in resignation.

"Look, I'm committed to you. And to Duke. I won't stop now," I said.

"Even if I ask you to?"

"No. Maybe in the past. But not today, not anymore."

She wouldn't look at me. "So, it's all about you. It's about your ego. You're going to produce a lot of pain, for others."

"I'm doing what I can to expose the pain to the light. Hopefully to release it."

"To cleanse yourself." Her contempt contained a whiff of fear, and some truth.

"Perhaps. To once and for all finish what I started, yes. More important, to free you and your brother. To free his soul. He deserves that now. You both do."

"More religious hogwash," she said. "The church turned sin into a self-serving condition for salvation. I don't need to be freed. Only medical science and good luck can save my brother now."

I hoisted the notebook. "I found this in your brother's apartment. Don't you think these notes are worth exploring?" I slipped the journal back into my satchel. "Because I do."

"Then give it to me." Her eyes blazed. She reached for my satchel, her breath brushing my lips, our bodies coming in contact for the first time. Fever flooded me.

She didn't retreat. "Well?" She held out her hand.

Mere inches apart; Duke's legacy not top of mind. My breathing rapid, the animal in me undeniable. Her chest rising and falling heavily. She swallowed hard, apparently as surprised as I at our intimacy. It took all my willpower and commitment to God to step back. "Let's do this together, okay?"

"Together?"

"I'm sorry, I've got to try," I said.

She wasn't so sure. She too backed off, lowered her arm. "You'll keep me informed."

"Of course."

The air still electric. The tension still visceral. The moment still cumbersome. Denying the most natural order of things. Her hand went back on the doorknob. "I'm going to spend some time *alone* with my brother now."

Like the gems cubanite and magnetite, we *had* to be pulled apart. "Of course."

. . .

Hakim Vaughn walked away from the firehouse. I caught up to him around the corner. "Lieutenant?"

He never broke stride. He spit. "Why am I not surprised to see you?"

"Can we talk?"

"No." He sped up.

"Please. You once said that Duke might have wanted to show up the captain."

"I did?"

"You said maybe to show his worth." Keeping up with the lieutenant wasn't easy.

"He probably wouldn't; that's not really Duke's way."

"But there was something you had in mind."

"I don't want to get any more involved." His forced march continued.

"But you're Duke's friend."

"I was."

"Well . . .?"

The lieutenant halted and confronted me. "What good is this gonna do?"

"Maybe save Duke's reputation."

"Or ruin it," he said.

"I think that's already in motion."

"You must really want this, to be such an incredible asshole all the time. That's probably not how people usually talk to you, Father, but something bad's about to happen. I got a sense. And I don't want any part of it."

"You don't have a choice," I said.

"Bullshit."

"Your life and his—they're intertwined, aren't they?" I said. "You were twice married to Valerie Dunn. You said you'd never heard of her."

He glared. "No. You asked if Duke ever mentioned her to me. And he didn't. That was the first time I ever heard that the two of them even knew each other. She and I never spoke after our second divorce. Now leave me the hell alone." He accelerated.

"Wait."

Out of nowhere, a bright yellow bike jumped the curb and circled us. A young African boy—maybe five, maybe six—corralling us.

"Whoa, Jamison," said Hakim. "I appreciate the attention, but ya gotta give us some space."

"I can come back later?" the little boy asked.

"You got three blocks and this gentleman. . ." He pointed to me. ". . . he's got less than one."

"Okay," the boy said. He glanced at me. "Hi, mister." He waved.

"Hi," I said, still wondering from where he'd appeared.

"See ya, soon." The boy gestured to Hakim, made a motoring sound and peddled up the block. Hakim turned back to me, his face a tad softer.

"Cute kid," I said.

"Yeah. Smart too."

"Your son?"

"If he was my son, he wouldn't be biking eight blocks from our house, not in this city. But he's got his own three-block turf and that's enough for him, for now."

"You want to know too, right? About Duke?"

Vaughn shook his head. "Oh, we're back to this."

"I'm interested in what you have to say."

"Oh, shit." His barrel chest swelled. "Okay, maybe there was something." He began walking again.

I followed. "Between the two, Duke and the captain?"

"It's probably nothing. Hoyle's a good guy. Maybe a little stiff, but a good guy."

"But?"

"But earlier on, I'm sure most of us thought Duke would be captain before Hoyle."

"But Duke wasn't interested in being captain," I said.

"No, he wasn't. But Hoyle wouldn't believe it. He seemed to be looking over his shoulder, considering all of Duke's heroics. And I'm sorry to laugh, but that lottery thing wasn't lost on Hoyle."

"The lottery thing?"

"Yeah, captain buys a lottery ticket a week. Says *'You'll see'*—meaning he'll hit the jackpot. He's absolutely sure of it. He's sure about a lot of things, but anyway . . . Every freakin' month he pulls rank, takes over the station house TV for the televised lottery drawing. Meanwhile, the rest of us sit around waiting—there're Mets *and* Yankee games on.

"Duke goes home, watches a mega lotto drawing, records the show with his phone and marks down the winning numbers. A month later, captain is stuck in the station all day and Duke offers to get him a 'quick pick.' Captain is much obliged. Duke buys a ticket with the winning numbers from the month earlier."

"Oh boy."

"Ya see where this is goin'," said Vaughn.

"Well, I . . ."

"Before captain comes in, Duke hooks up his video to the TV. It's already rolling when captain sits down with us. Captain's checking the numbers as they're called. He starts chortling. When numbers four and five are drawn he gets real quiet. Rubs his hands together, shows teeth.

"When the sixth number is drawn, captain jumps to his feet and starts pointing at each of us. 'You wouldn't believe me. I've always been lucky, but you wouldn't believe me.'

"He's gloating, waving the ticket. 'I'm going to buy myself that titanium gold Desert Eagle and maybe a *little* something for each of you, *to remember me by*.' He's so freakin' pleased with himself. Until the group explodes in laughter.

"'What?' Captain asks. Duke pauses the video."

I leaned in. "Whoa, how'd Hoyle take it?"

Hakim seemed to enjoy the memory. "He *had* to laugh. But he was steaming. Who wouldn't be? I mean, all that money."

"Hmm."

Vaughn startled, like a man waking from a dream. Or a man ambushed. He'd done exactly what he'd set out *not* to do. "Listen, don't tell him I said so."

"Of course not," I said. "Any other tension between them?"

Still apparently unsure where he found himself, Vaughn studied adjacent buildings. "Not that I could tell." He rested in the idea, then surprised me, and went on. "Captain seemed to let it go, even joked about it months later. But he stopped forcing us to watch the lotto show. We have Duke to thank for that."

I slowed to pull the black and white notebook from my satchel. Hakim kept moving.

"Does this look familiar?" I held up the notebook.

He finally stopped, perused the book. "No."

I handed it to him. "Look inside. Tell me if that makes sense to you. Some kind of fireman jargon?"

He opened the notebook and scanned the page. "Not at all. Some kind of code? What is it?"

"I thought you might know."

"Got me." He began walking again.

"One last question, what's a Desert Eagle?"

He shrugged. "Some sort of collectible rifle, I guess. One of captain's things. I'm pretty sure he can't afford it without the lottery." He winked.

"You have a gun."

His demeanor shifted. "Sure, what of it? I'm licensed."

"Right, of course," I said.

"How long you think you got cross-examining me . . .?" He looked back and forth across the street. He seemed to have re-found his footing. ". . . Because this was your half block of credit; it just run out." He shuffled in place. "You never talked to me. Don't come round me no more. You're looking for trouble, and you're gonna find it. I've got folks waiting for me, so *adios.*"

With a clear hint of ridicule, Hakim saluted and wandered off down the block, scratching his head and whistling. Before he even reached the corner, the little boy on the yellow bike began circling him again.

The lieutenant was an uneven man. Feeding me reasons to distrust Duke *and* Hoyle's intentions? And . . . I still needed to get to Our Lady of Sorrows.

A hulking Chinese man—bald with dark glasses and a knit cap sitting high on the back of his head—came toward me. I froze. More than once I'd found myself looking over my shoulder, sensing someone watching me. But two weeks had passed without any push back from the Ghost Shadows gang. I'd begun to relax my vigilance for them.

The man continued past me without lifting his head. Time to stop speculating and stick to facts.

Within blocks of the church, I walked past the cigar shop where I'd crashed into the desperate blonde woman in the purple dress. The money long departed. It had been Pollyanna to expect her to return it, but I'd hoped she would at least come to the church for assistance. But like the tong, a couple weeks had passed since I'd run into her. The reality finally settled in; she wasn't coming back. *Something bad* dogged her too.

I refocused on what Hakim had told me.

I reached the rectory and made my way to my room. Thrust partially under my door was a large, thin manila envelope. No markings. I grabbed it and opened the door.

My room had been ravaged. A war zone, not unlike how I'd left Duke's apartment: ransacked, tossed upside down. Except that my space was sparse and so much smaller. The mattress had been pulled off the bed, inverted, the sheets pulled back. My desk drawer thrown three feet away, a large crack through its belly. My small closet and bureau drawers breached. My other papers and books scattered around the room. My laptop open on the windowsill, battered and open, apparently invaded. So much for the sanctity of the physical church.

My whole body vibrated as I returned the room to its former semblance. In doing so, I found scattered along the floor, in a corner by the window, the Black Phantom Miss Lili had given me in Madagascar. I slipped it into my pocket, and with my overcoat thrown aside, I sat on my bed and opened the manila envelope.

Inside were three 5x7 color photos. The first, the blonde woman in the purple dress, coat spread open, offering herself to me. The second, the woman accepting the fistful of cash from me. The last photo, her arm around my neck and her hand on my chest, embracing and kissing me.

It *was* a war, with amorphous enemies on a nebulous battlefield. Whether someone was trying to find something in my room or trying to scare me off, I couldn't tell. The photos seemed to have been left *after* the room had been ransacked, another warning. My cloth no shelter from any of them.

CHAPTER 32

Duke

When I awoke, Charli had her head down on my bed, muffled crying. *Had she learned what I'd done?* The Doobie Brothers "What a Fool Believes" wafted over my hospital room chronicling those last few weeks with Valerie.

"Ms. Ryan?" The Jamaican nurse took a tentative step closer to my sister. "Are you okay?"

Charli lifted her head and wiped her eyes. "I'll be okay. Thanks."

"You see he's showing more and more signs of responding to the music." The nurse nodded at the EEG above my head. "It's a good thing."

"Yes," Charli said and pulled a tissue from my bedside. She blew her nose. "Yes."

"I thought I'd just check in on him before I go off shift." She had a round, friendly face, and gave my sister an expression that implied *it'll all turn out*. She examined my drips. "I've heard some stories. He's a hero, you should be proud of him."

Charli dwelled on my helpless arm. "Yes, thank you."

"Well, goodnight."

"Goodnight." Charli laid her head back down on my bedside. I drifted off . . . back to Valerie.

"Think of it as play therapy." Val filled a water bottle and handed it to me.

"Just like with your kids." I paced her small kitchen, already feeling boxed in.

"*Exactly* like with my kids. Except you and I are both layered with so many years of rust and build up as adults that we need a little help. That's where these come in." She held up a baggie of slender, white-stemmed mushrooms, small with light-orange caps.

"You're sure about this?" My stomach skipped around.

She put the mushrooms in a small food processor, ground them into a coarse, yellowy powder, and after carefully eyeballing the finished pile, scrapped and shuffled them into a baggie.

While she did, I peppered her with questions regarding our safety while on the mushrooms, short- and long-term health effects, and what to expect from the trip. I already knew most of the answers because I'd done my own research. Still, I was nervous.

For obvious reasons, I never brought up my continued dizziness and memory loss. She'd seen enough of that herself. It didn't seem to faze her. What's more, I wasn't going to use my debility to undermine her resolve. I could back out if I wanted to. She'd made that perfectly clear. But I'd be backing away from the woman of a lifetime. That would've just been stupid.

She weaved around me in the kitchen, gathering water for us, juice, fruit, her pipe and weed. She answered every question deliberately, even quoting scientific studies. She corroborated what I'd read.

In time, she stopped moving and faced me head on. "DD, I'm not going to force you. If I thought doing these, in any way, would recreate the conditions you had with the coffee, I wouldn't suggest them. This is my issue, I know. But you are so much a part of my decision. *And* what I'm asking you to do is out of your comfort zone.

I know that. That you're willing . . . Well, it's more of that bravery of yours, and more of why you're so special to me. But I promise it will not endanger you. In fact, I suspect, you'll find it euphoric, spiritual and transformative."

"Spiritual, me?"

"*You*, Debonair."

"How 'bout a beer instead?"

Her eyes closed gently, just for a moment. When she looked back at me, it was with tenderness. "Stop resisting. Really." She moistened her lips. "It's your choice. Yes or no."

"Transformative, how?" I asked.

"Is that *yes or no*?"

"How?"

"To be determined for those willing to board the Play Train." She was being completely reasonable and it gave her the polish of truth. "And it's okay if you don't. I understand it's scary facing our demons."

"I don't think I have any demons," I said.

"Well, I do," she said. "And I want to be rid of them. Or at least try."

A standoff. I leaned against the counter. "Have you ever taken them?"

"Once."

"And?"

"Euphoric, spiritual and transformative." A musical lilt to her words.

"How'd you transform?"

"I left Iowa. I started a new life."

"And today you want us both to transform."

"Not necessarily," she said. "I want each of us to fully understand what we want—no, what we *need*. And what's most important to us. That way we'll be free of barriers."

"I don't have any, not with you," I said.

She pinched my cheek and kissed me.

"If you're gonna continue to pinch and poke me," I said, "should I take off my clothes?"

"Sooo debonair," she said. "C'mon, let's play. It's a perfect day to be in the park. Let's strip away all the crap, mine and yours." She went to the urn on her mantelpiece and carefully began pouring the ashes of her parents into a large cellophane Ziploc bag. While totally preoccupied with harvesting every flake, her resolve inspired me. I pulled my phone, took a quick couple of photos of her, then stashed my phone. I pointed at the baggie. "Are we going to ingest those too?"

She stuffed the bag into her jacket pocket, along with the apples, tangerines, pipe and lighter.

She laughed out loud. "Now we're talkin'!"

. . .

We walked the few blocks to the park. We sat by the pond near the bird sanctuary. Swallows and thrush celebrated the baseball-like weather, flitting from magnolia branch to water, with a race around four horse chestnut trees, before returning for more of the same. A persnickety heron officiated.

"Beautiful, no?" She tamped the ground. "A bit damp, but let's sit."

The sun pampered us. And maybe because the temperate weather had been unexpected, there weren't more than five or six people within fifty yards of us. They seemed to be tagging along with the colors, the breeze; the reassuring warmth on our shoulders.

"You ready?" Her face widened, she smiled. Her big nut-brown eyes held me in admiration. She epitomized *peaceful*. "I love you. I do."

My lips landed on hers, a perfect, soft landing. "I believe you." I ran my fingers over her lips.

She passed me the pipe. "Let's start with one hit of this. Then we'll drink the shrooms. It'll ease us in."

"Can you do this without me?" I said.

"Of course, if that's what you want. But without your participation I'll never know for sure. It's a journey of the heart. And we're both good with whatever happens, right?"

When would I ever fully trust her? "Okay, let's play."

"We're *both* good with whatever happens, right?"

I didn't want to believe anything but the best could happen to *us*. "Right." To show my commitment, I reached into my pocket and gave her the keys to my building and my apartment. "Copies," I said. "For you to come and go as you please."

She studied them as if they were foreign objects. Her fingers rubbed them. She held them away from her body. I couldn't tell what she was thinking. At one point I thought she was going to return them to me. But she skewed her head in *that* way that melted me, and stuck the keys in her pocket.

We each took a toke from her pipe. I coughed. She handed me water and I sipped it. Then she pulled the powdered mushrooms from her pocket.

"You're sure that's not your folks," I said.

"Sure." She poured the powder into a large jar of grapefruit juice and shook it. "Half for you, half for me. Drink up." We did.

We began walking north, past men and women playing chess and checkers, a group of millennials walking a tangle of dogs, and the occasional jogger, until we found a quiet, dappled spot on the edge of Sheep Meadow looking west.

"Let's sit for a while," she said.

Far to our left, our closest neighbors played with their two young children. Their joy spread like soft wind around my shoulders and heart. I didn't want to take my eyes off them for fear I'd lose the delight. Valerie watched too. For the first time I felt a connection to children and parenthood that I'd never before experienced. But I wasn't sad. I accepted that both Val and I were too old for children. *Although we could adopt.*

"Feel anything yet?" She placed her hand on my shoulder. We were one.

An insect cruised by me, leaving a trail of light. "I think so. What was that?"

"Whatever you want it to be."

Along the skyline, trees and buildings began to soften and sway, the childlike laughter of others far in the distance setting the rhythm. "Hold me," she said. Her eyes rotated with wonder, her skin glowed like a young girl's in bloom. I did willingly, our bodies coalescing into one warm organism on the ground. My eyes closed. I spilled into a waterfall of greens and yellows. We breathed as one. *I'm home.* With no desire to speak. No desire to spoil our time-lessness with words, words that she already understood from my embrace, and I from hers.

I cannot tell you how long we lay there together in pure bal-ance—temperature, tactility, *aroma*—before she kissed my neck and let go. I could have remained there forever. And, in a way, I knew she and I *were* forever.

My eyes danced across her face, now aged like melted wax, deep crevices crisscrossing her cheeks, as if she had fallen to her death-bed, no longer man nor woman, then almost dust.

Her aged fingers reached for my face. With great tenderness she stroked my cheek, though it was *more* than physical. As if she were setting roots. "Do you see?" she said. "Do you see that we will soon be gone, without ever leaving? Time is our illusion?"

"I'll love you always," I said.

"Yes."

Her scent shifted, as if it too was dying.

"We must have faith," I said, unsure where my voice had found such words. And then it added, "Kierkegaard."

"Yes, but let go. Untangle from any construct. Let's *be* the source not talk about it." She managed to get to her feet.

For an instant I felt betrayed. It evaporated just as quickly as it had arisen. She held out her hand, lifting me upright. "Let's explore."

She led me under the blue stretch of sky, across the great meadow, past the old cricket grounds to Strawberry Fields and the empty bench by the John Lennon Memorial. Someone had laid pink, red and white petals around and through the mosaic, circling the word Imagine. *Harmony and tranquility with all things.*

I didn't sit long, lured by a tiny thatched gazebo at the end of a small stone path, sitting in filtered sun on the edge of the lake. I tracked the footpath through a tunnel of kaleidoscopic emerald light, touching and smelling the bark of trees that led me to the spot.

Valerie followed slowly behind, eventually sitting opposite me under the canopy. Beatific, she stared at the water, which like her was protean, fluid, shifting yet peaceful. Her hair flowed of its own accord, lengthening and retracting around her magnificent face, transmuting from charcoal to gray back to charcoal. Her face flowered, peaked and withered before me several times.

I spread my palms. My own hands breathed with a million tiny breaths until I lost track of my body and found myself shoeless, dangling my feet in the lake.

"I'll always love you." She murmured in my ear. Or I imagined it. She was beside me, *her* toes digging into the mud. She reached into the goo and pulled up a handful. "May I?" she asked.

"You may do anything." I leaned into the direct sunlight as a dog might lie on its back, subordinating itself to its master, and the ensuing pleasure for both.

Using her right hand as a paintbrush and her left as the palette, she dipped her fingers into the mud and began drawing upon my face. The contact brought tears to my eyes. And laughter.

"Oh what a man!" she said and took a deep mysterious breath. But at that point it was *all* mysterious.

I took her muddy hands in mine. I buried my face in them, the cool loam infusing and purifying me. I was earthen, needing nothing. Neither of us moved for a spell until I reclaimed my body and lifted my head out of her hands. She passed me the water bottle and I drank from it.

That's when I first heard the voices beginning to intrude. But, again, I let go of any feelings of encroachment.

Two large Hispanic women walked toward us, arm in arm.

Valerie took mine.

I must have looked ghastly, veiled in mud. But at the time it never occurred to me that I should move or wipe my face.

The two women were no more than a few feet from us when they stopped and with mouths agape, looked at each other. "Sorry," said the more corpulent of the two, who filled every inch of her white dress. "I see you've made this your special spot too."

I'm pretty sure I nodded. Not sure what Valerie did. But neither of us said a word; it just seemed too much work. And unnecessary.

The woman looked at her partner, squeezed her hand, and faced us again. "We were married here. I hope you'll be as happy as we are." They looked at each other with such tenderness that I almost joined them in an embrace, but Valerie kept me grounded, both physically and metaphysically, to the bench.

As they turned to go, the other woman said, "Blessings." And were gone.

"Beautiful, no?" Valerie offered me a tangerine.

I nodded, the smell ambrosial, but I abstained.

"Drink water." She offered a small handkerchief.

I accepted.

She wiped my face and kissed it.

I drank water. Many hours seemed to pass, only because I was aware that the sun was now above the western skyline, still high and even warmer than before. We moved on.

As we approached Belvedere Castle and its small lake, a homeless man in a filthy, brown three-piece suit was removing items from a shopping cart and dumping them into a fire he'd apparently started in a fifty-five-gallon drum. An odd sight on such a beautiful spring day. But both Val and I stopped to watch the man divest himself.

The man smiled at us. His teeth suggested tobacco and pain, but butterflies danced around him, leaving trails of dust-like whimsy on the edge of every movement. "You want to throw anythin' in," he pointed at the drum, "yo welcome." He pulled a cherry pink bra from a knapsack and tossed it in.

A fire can crackle and send off sparks. This wasn't one of those. This fire offered a few muted pops but mostly it sounded like sheets on a line, confiding to the wind.

"Be my guest," he said rummaging through his treasures. "No charge today."

"You're right," Valerie said to the man, surprising me. Neither of us had spoken for what seemed like hours.

She moved to the lip of the lake. Across the water, a few shadows had begun to fall along the castle's reorienting rock outcroppings. She took a handful of grass and tossed it to the wind. It pulled the blades into the lake. "I need to start over, fresh."

"You will," I agreed.

"I will." She hunted through her pockets and pulled out her parents' ashes. She unzipped the bag and, without a word, let the modest breeze carry her parents away, across the small lake.

It all happened so unexpectedly. We both stood there for quite a while, watching the gray powder rise and twist in fitful knots above the water but never into it, like it was wresting with itself, until the sunshine seemed to swallow it from our view, as if her parents never met the water's surface.

Val's head angled to the sky, tears rolling down her cheeks.

Neither of us said a word, words were poor things for things so vast and so simple. I knew she had faith in what she was doing. And that gave me faith in her, faith in myself. Faith in our friendship.

After a while she whispered, "I can be anything. Can you?"

My words came gradually, bit by bit. "I can give up fire . . . if you're by my side."

She waited to see what I might add. When I didn't, she looked contemplative and bowed to me. She said, "Shall we travel some more?" Her eyes clear; she didn't wipe her tears. She began walking and I followed her, up and around the expanse of the reservoir. We just kept going. We passed the tennis courts. She intended for us to walk the entire length of Central Park. But her energy and mine were in sync. Not only was I willing, I was at the center of her determination. I wanted for nothing.

As we passed a waterfall, the air cooled and cleansed me. I bent to feel the stream and the rocks. She did the same, pressing the elixir to her cheeks and then mine. For the longest time, she watched the water drip from my cheeks.

"Val?"

She put her finger to my lips. *No words.*

Then, without a sound between us, we stood, the babbling cascade bidding us to keep moving. And we flowed again, to the North Woods.

There, she made a large sucking sound and wiped her hand across her nose. She sat on a bench and hucked phlegm into the bushes. "We made it!" Her grin goofy.

I fell in love again.

"How're you feeling?" she asked.

I surveyed myself. "I feel good. Maybe a little tired." I moved my jaw around. My world still saturated in color.

Her pipe and lighter came out. "One hit. Make the transition smoother." We took puffs.

She raised our empty bottles. "Maybe some juice to get us back home?" I have no idea how she was able to talk.

She placed the bottles in the recycling. She tugged at my arm. "You okay leaving the park for a little bit? Let's see what we can find before we head back."

So far so good. "Sure."

I remember heading west, south of Morningside Park. There wasn't much in the way of grocery stores, and the landscape all bathed in a different color: bluer, cooler, the sun lost behind the buildings. She pointed, "There's a place."

The sign read *Dreadlock Draw*. "Looks like a bar," I said.

"They'll have some kind of juice," she said. "Then we'll head back."

"A bar?"

"Juice."

Going *inside* wasn't as a weird as I'd thought. Evening had begun. Lights were low—mostly blue and green. Vicky Sue Robinson in the air. I didn't look to see the number of people. We were there to get in and out, Valerie doing a good job on the practical logistics and I with no capacity for them. I followed. "Let's sit for a moment," she said.

"D'ya get the juice?"

"They'll bring it." She nodded toward the bar.

Fine, we sat. "I could use some water," I said. "How bout you?"

"Sure."

I motioned to the bartender, indicating two. "We have some waters, please?" My voice actually worked.

That's when two guys came bumping down the hallway, one with no shirt. They embraced each other and locked in a deep kiss. I turned around, expecting that I'd misread what I'd seen. But I hadn't. "Val."

"Yes?"

I looked again; the place a third full, unless there was another room. No one seemed to notice the couple who'd crashed into the room, still grabbing at each other. "Cabbage?"

She wasn't paying attention, either.

"Really?!" I circled my barstool to her. Then all the way around. There were a lot of men, a few annoyed by the spectacle. Most didn't seem to care. And then there were two holding hands. Another couple intertwined. All men. "Val. It's a gay bar."

"They're getting us the juice." She said, unconcerned.

Words formed in my brain, but not quite in my mouth yet. "I'm not comfortable here."

"Why?" She swung her stool to face me. Ever beautiful and open. There completely, for my answer.

"You know," I said.

"Tell me."

"Men on men."

"You okay with women on women?" she asked.

I leaned against the bar. "What other people do is their business. But in public . . . "

"But not for you."

"You know where I'm at with it," I said. The two men finally pulled out of their indulgence, still pecking and growling amorously at each other. "I find it . . . unnatural." I turned away from the men, making my aversion fairly obvious. She frowned at me. As if I didn't give her the right answer, the answer she'd already decided for me.

The bartender brought us two lemonades. I reached into my pocket and paid him. Valerie grabbed one of the bottles and started walking out. I reached her on the sidewalk. She'd already hailed us a cab. She waved me into it. "I'm tired. Our playday's over."

She settled into the cab's pickled smell. We traveled back to her apartment in silence; the city lights splashed and darkened across her face. She held my hand, though she was clearly someplace else. She stared forward, with an unwavering, open-eyed detachment from our surroundings.

I wasn't sure what to say. Nor did I have the desire to talk. Apparently, she didn't either. So we never spoke.

We arrived at her place. She went directly to bed and I followed. Just before drifting off, she spoke softly, "You'll always be my hero."

CHAPTER 33

Father Blu

My brain swarmed with theories: the attacks on me—like a siege of moths—too frenetic for any one of them to land conclusively. Exhausting.

Someone was trying to disgrace me or frighten me. Or both. Father Toll would disavow taking the photos, might even disavow having seen them, though surely he'd sent copies to the Vicar. He might have stripped my room searching for whatever research I had on Duke and *later* camouflaged his entry by slipping the photos under the door.

Hakim, too, might have raided my room looking for evidence that would incriminate him. But for what? Penny Velez' death? Valerie Dunn's? Arson? Protecting Duke? Incriminating Duke? Or he planted the photos to discredit me and get me off my investigation. Why?

Were the Ghost Shadows looking for ways to extort more money from me, the church, or for my priestly cooperation in one of their schemes?

Maybe the blonde woman. Would she soon be calling with demands?

What of Chuck Winston, Captain Hoyle and even Tony S or one of the other firemen?

The only thing certain were my bruises. They'd settled in, turned a dark maroon, except on the edges where they'd feathered to a stylish chartreuse.

What does that have to do with anything?

I tried matching Duke's anonymous phone numbers to Valerie Dunn. Nothing. The Crash-B Championships *did* have her name. But her involvement in the rowing competition had come to an end in February, more than two months before her death. Yet Duke's call to the rowing competition had come only five days before her death and six before his attempted suicide.

It wasn't much, but I could imagine Duke trying to track her down. Whether failing or successfully doing so, their linking was indisputable. It also opened up the possibility that Duke had an even more perverse side, perhaps as a stalker. Valerie Dunn the last of a series of victims?

An unkind wind and freezing rain drove at me as I turned onto 77th Street and headed for Dunn's apartment building. I rang the buzzer. Mr. Metaxas, the owner and landlord of the building, greeted me and invited me in.

A lively eighty-year old gentleman with one bright blue eye, the other a dull gray, Mr. Metaxas seemed particularly happy to have company and offered me tea. "Greek mountain tea," he said stroking his white bristle. "We get leaves from cousins in Lakonia."

I demurred, he insisted. "From dried flowers of Sideritis. Very calming. Natural anti-oxidants. Your blood pressure is good? You must try it."

"I can use calming, thank you," I said.

He hobbled off and returned quickly with a pot and two cups. He didn't look like a guy who'd torch his own building. Or have the capability for it.

"Let's let sit for few minutes. I'm glad you called." He sniffed at the tea and eased into his chair. "Not ready yet. What can I do for you, Father? Something about Ms. Dunn."

Hearing his own words, he was all at once downcast. He chewed on his gnarled right thumb. "Such a tragedy. Her brother is devastated. You've spoken with him?"

"Her brother?"

"Yes," Mr. Metaxas continued, "he came from out of town. Iowa, I think. I'm surprised he didn't call you."

"To take care of her estate? Finally get it all closed out."

"Yes, a nervous guy," Mr. Metaxas said. "I guess I understand, under circumstances."

"Any idea where I can reach him?"

"He said he was going back home. I don't think he's around now. But I should have his mailing address somewhere. He was very clear that he wanted all his sister's affairs cleaned up properly. To get closure on grief, I suppose."

Mr. Metaxas propped himself up and out of his chair. He walked with a slight painful limp over to a small antique desk with multiple drawers up and down its face. "I told him, she was always good with rent; we were up-to-date. The insurance will cover the material losses, both for her—for him—and for me." He proceeded to search through the desk drawers.

"Did the police suggest that arson might have been a factor?"

"Yes. And I hope they catch the sonuvbitch." He sifted through a few more papers and gave up, slamming closed the last drawer. "My wife. I can't find anything she puts her hands on. But I'll find you that address." He moved tentatively, retracing his steps to his chair. He poured us each a cup of tea. "You'll enjoy this, Father. Good for your heart."

"She had a friend or a boyfriend, a fireman named Duke," I said. "Did you ever meet him?"

"She was very private. I don't think so. Over the two and a half years, there weren't a lot of men or women in and out of her place, just a couple. Surprising considering." Something almost lecherous crossed his mouth before he composed himself. "A lovely woman. I would even say—" he looked over his shoulder to the interior of the apartment and lowered his voice, "—quite attractive. I would never say with my wife around, you understand."

"Do you have a photo of her?"

"No, no, would never do." I could see he was puzzled by my question.

Better to change the subject. "She babysat your grandchildren occasionally."

He perked up. "She did. She was wonderful with the children. She was a child psychologist; did you know that? Well, you were her priest, you have known that."

Mr. Metaxas had misunderstood my reason for calling on him and I thought better than to correct him; another transgression, morality becoming less clear in pursuit of truth. Or was that just my rationale?

"No, I didn't," I said. "But can you remember this man visiting her?" I pulled out a photo of Duke and showed it to him.

"Yes, *this* man." He pouted. "He made her unhappy."

"Sir?"

"When I saw them together, I knew he was trouble. I didn't thought he was her boyfriend. She deserve better."

"Why would you say that?"

"A week or two before the fire. They didn't look happy. She deserve to be happy. But I thought he was a friend of the other guy."

"The other guy?" I asked.

"The thin one. The only two I saw. My wife thinks I'm pushy as it is, so I avoid getting into Valerie's—Ms. Dunn's—private life too much. But I notice. I invite Ms. Dunn down for tea when Myrto, my wife, away. I ask. She say they were just friends, the two men, I mean. But now you mention, she and fireman didn't look like *just friends*."

"Why do you say that? Can you recall anything with respect to the last time you saw Ms. Dunn and the fireman together?"

He hung his head in thought. He stroked his stubble. "Well, I remember next day Ms. Dunn had bandage wrapped around her arm."

"A bandage?"

"Yes. Up and down her arm, her left arm. I ask her about it. She said it was nothing. She burned herself cooking."

"Do you think she could have killed herself?" I asked.

The earth seemed to move beneath him. "Valerie? Oh no. She was sad, but she was *apofasisménos*—determined. No, she wasn't the type to do that, I don't think." He paused and studied me for a moment. "You don't seem to know much about her. You *were* her priest; that's why you're here, right?"

I swallowed. "I'm trying to get to the bottom of what happened."

He scowled. "Are you here for the family or not?"

"I'm here to help all the families sort this out."

"All *what* families?"

"There are other people involved," I said.

His cheeks grew crimson. He grabbed hold of the armrest and tried to stand. He fell stiffly back into the chair. "You should leave."

I rose, passive, doing my best to deflect the shame—my métier over the years. But this one stung. "Thank you for your time," I said, hoping to immunize myself with the fresh information.

. . .

I plodded around Duke's hospital room waiting for Charli. Underneath the low streaming music, his roomful of diagnostic equipment maintained its irritating whir, but hadn't offered an iota of new data or fluctuation since I'd been there. I'd intended to wait for Charli, but my impatience got to me. I spoke to Duke. "You see this notebook?" I held up the black and white composition book. "Your sister says it's not your handwriting." I opened the book. "Take a look." I shoved it in his face. "If you know what this means, give me a sign. Blink your eyes, think of a song that will trigger your EEG. Something." To my surprise, the EEG spiked. "Duke, Duke you can hear me!" But I wasn't sure. What was the dirge playing behind me?

I saw the fireworks
I believed that I was dreaming
Till the neighbors came out screaming
He's a third world man

"Duke, let's do this again. If you've seen this book before, think of a song that will boost your electroencephalogram. Or blink your eyes, raise an eyebrow, move a finger."

Scanning his eyes, his mouth, his fingers; nothing.

"Duke, try. I know you're in there."

Soon you'll throw down your disguise
We'll see behind those bright eyes

Still nothing. "Do you recognize the writing in this book?" The EEG edged along and then. . . and then it moved again. Chills ran through my body. I called out, "Nurse!" I didn't want to leave his bedside, didn't want to miss a moment. I grabbed his dead arm. I squeezed it. "Duke, Duke that's great. Nurse! Nurse, come in here." I fumbled for Duke's call button. I pressed it. Nurse Shirley and Charli almost collided at the door.

"You rang?"

I orbited over Duke. "He spoke to me."

"What?" Charli stood halfway in; the nurse came to my side.

"Father?" Nurse Shirley uncertain.

"He responded to my question," I said.

"What kind of questions are you asking him?" Charli's tone bordering on defensive.

"Yeah," said Nurse Shirley, "what kind of questions?"

"I asked him about the notebook." I patted it.

Nurse Shirley eased up and jumped in. "How? You sure it wasn't the music?"

"You know, I'm not sure exactly. I guess it could have been the music. But he responded directly to my question. He'd seen this notebook before. No, he knew the handwriting. I don't know, maybe both."

Charli stepped next to me. She placed a hand on her brother's. "Ask him again."

"Duke," I held up the notebook. "If you've seen this handwriting before, blink your eye once." We watched him, suspended in time. Then it came, one solitary flutter of his eyelid.

"Oh my God!" Charli lay on her brother's chest. "Oh my God!" Nurse Shirley's mouth opened in astonishment, and possibly, uneasiness.

"Valerie Dunn," I said looking him in the eye. "Penny Velez."

"Who?" asked Charli.

"Just guessing," I said.

The EEG spiked again. Charli looked up at me, renewed effervescence percolating in her eyes. All that hope, while I contemplated, once more, the mounting evidence that Duke's story might condemn him for life.

I saw the fireworks
I believed that I was dreaming
Till the neighbors came out screaming
He's a third world man

CHAPTER 34

Duke

Shortly after our play day, Valerie headed to Miami "on business." Indefinite about her stay, she said she'd call me when she returned.

"We'll talk while you're gone," I said. "I need to know what you learned about yourself, about your big decision during our day in the park." But I already felt something slipping away. She'd warned me about a letdown after the euphoria of the mushroom trip. I wanted to believe that was it.

Her response, "I'll be pretty busy." I never did reach her.

When a week passed and I hadn't heard from her, I decided to go by her apartment after work, to make sure everything was okay. *To assure myself.* To free the tension building in my neck and shoulders. She'd never asked for her key back, and I'd taken that as a sign of trust. I wanted to believe that I was overthinking the recent chill.

I knocked. No answer, so I let myself in. In the living room, her suitcase lay open, her clothes scattered around; classic Valerie. She'd returned. And from the looks of things—dishes in the sink, her garbage bag a third deep—she'd been back a few days. "Shit."

I wandered into her bedroom, the air stuffy with sex. Her blanket and sheets twisted, a vestige of undulating bodies. I leaned into them. Her smell was barely present, replaced by another more-manly smell; ammonia or . . . a smell similar to my crotch. A stench thick with betrayal. "Whatthefuck." I began to hyperventilate.

On her nightstand sat a phone number, written on scrap paper in her typically messy scrawl. I dialed it. No greeting, just a beep. I slammed the phone down. A secret number?

I slipped open the nightstand drawer and sifted through it: a ring, matches, a small pipe, *photos! Naked* photos of Val. Recent. Full length and not a stitch of clothing on her. The whore! Who had taken them? I didn't recognize the background. There was no pose. She looked almost innocent—possibly embarrassed—in the way she stood there. Who and why? There were four of them, one a duplicate. I took it.

I opened her closet. Hanging to the right of her clothes, a man's dark blue pinstriped suit, a casual sports jacket and slacks, a white dress shirt, a pair of jeans, a pair of men's shoes. Above, on a shelf, a stack of men's t-shirts, informal socks and *underwear.*

"Motherfucker." She might as well have ripped out my guts. I roamed the apartment like an animal, yelling profanities. The damn cat hid. I was gonna break something. Anything. Everything. So I left.

. . .

A day later Valerie still hadn't called. I went directly to her apartment. I talked to myself the whole way. *Be calm. There's a logical explanation. She'll explain all of it. She loves you; she said so.*

I knocked on her door, afraid of what or *who* I might encounter, what I might *do*. My stomach in knots—over a woman! I knocked several times. I considered using my key. She came to the door. With no look of surprise. Also, no look of admiration or excitement, a look I'd become addicted to. She wore jeans, a sweatshirt. She'd cut her hair shorter and pulled it tightly to one side. She looked delicious and I hated myself for it. "Come in," she said.

No *I was going to call you*, no nothing. Like I'd fallen into an alternate universe and reincarnated as a plumber she'd requisitioned to fix the sink.

I went to pull her close. She sidestepped me. She waved me into the living room. She'd tidied up, marginally. "What's wrong?" I said.

She sat on the sofa; I sat next to her. She had nowhere to go. "Nothing. I'm tired."

"Weren't you going to call me?"

"After I got settled," she said.

"How long have you been back?"

"Just got back."

I tested her. "Last night?"

"A couple days." She stretched her neck.

I wanted to kiss it, chew it; smell it. Maybe grab it and shake her. But I rubbed it. At first, she was reluctant, even wincing a little. But she melted into it and let me continue. *Who else's hands had been on her?* "I've missed you," I said.

"I've missed you too." Her voice deep and emotionless.

Kierkegaard wrote "Dread is a desire for what one dreads. Attraction and repulsion. An alien power." "How'd it go in Miami?" I asked.

She seemed to relax. She actually faced me, her eyes more chocolate than ever. "It went very well, thanks for asking."

"Of course. Are we okay?"

If only for a second, she pondered her answer. "We are." Again, her voice flat, lacking affection, as if there was no joy in our union.

"Well," I said pushing off the couch, "I just wanted to make sure you were okay, that your landlord was feeding the cat." Surely my distaste for gay encounters wasn't *that* critical. *Unless her brother . . .*

"You've never cared for Catalona."

"I wanted to make sure she was okay because *you* care about her." She gave me a disingenuous smile.

"Cabbage, tell me, is there another man?"

She hissed. "You're going to start that again?"

"Just tell me."

"No. Now leave me alone, let me get organized. We'll get together in a couple days."

"A couple days?" My body went limp. At the same time I wanted to rock her against the wall.

"Don't push me." She stood. I could imagine her taking a swing at me. I could imagine swinging back. "You've got your own life," she said. "Don't cede control to me, no matter how freeing that may feel. I'm not your parent."

"Wow, that must have been some fuckin' trip to Florida," I said.

Hands on hips. "Just get out."

There were all sorts of things I wanted to say, all sort of questions I wanted to throw in her face; all sorts of clothes and beds and odors I wanted to smash into it. But I was afraid, afraid of losing her. *Pathetic, right?* I'd become a wuss. My stomach coiled. And I felt guilty. Not sure why. "You know there's danger in drugs. Too many possibilities," I said. "No one's perfect."

"Go," she said.

. . .

The next morning at the station, I came in running nightmares through my head, then fantasies. One minute she was fucking some skinny sonuvabitch with a bolo, and enjoying it. The next she was wrapped in my arms, stroking me and nipping at me, telling me she loved me. *It had all been a mistake.*

Maybe an hour after we were into our shift—after General

Orders, updates to information, the first of a half dozen cups of coffee, and roll call from Captain Hoyle—Tony S noticed me stumbling and bumping around the hook and ladder. He made some remark about the guys spotting a zombie in the station. "They catch fire easy," he said. "Better call a fireman."

I stopped. "Hey, wait."

"Sorry, I'm already taken," he said with a swish. "But there are other firemen in the house." He pointed up the stairs.

"You're so smart about women, how do you know what they're thinking?" I said.

"You're fifty-five, right?" He threw his hands up. "You're still asking that question? Holy shit, man . . . you can't."

So I waited for her call.

The day drooled on; one of the slowest days we'd had in months. Every minute ticking loudly. Normally I'd be busy doing something—even just coiling hose or checking pipes—but hell no. I listened to music on my headphones, first in the kitchen then on my mattress, springs squeaking through the phones because I couldn't stop tossing. I got stuck in a Steely Dan phase; all I could think of was Val, fuckin' Val.

"Ducotty?" Captain Hoyle and Hakim were holding on to me, one on each arm. Captain looked concerned.

"Yeah, Captain?" I wasn't on my cot.

"What happened?" he asked.

"What do you mean?"

Hakim loosened his grip. "You were walking kinda funny, Duke," said the captain. "You okay? You been drinking?"

"Me? Come on, you know I wouldn't do that, not on duty." They had me in the hallway; no idea how I'd gotten there.

"Slowly, man. Slowly," said Hakim.

Clearing my brain took a moment.

Captain studied me. "You okay to stand on your own?"

"Sure, yeah. I'm fine."

"You remember asking me about scheduling?" asked the captain.

"I don't need a day off, I'm fine." I brushed down my shirt. "I'm probably drinking too much coffee."

Captain didn't look persuaded. "That wasn't exactly what we were talking about."

"What were we talking about?"

Captain glanced at Hakim and back to me. "You really don't remember?"

"No. I get that it sounds crazy. I must have hit my head or, like I said, the coffee. Who needs that much coffee?"

"I don't think you're ready for duty. Take the afternoon; I'll call in Eisler."

"No, no. Look at me." I met him eye to eye. "I'm ready to go."

Captain shook his head. "I don't think so."

"Too much coffee, I'm tellin' you."

One more look at Hakim.

"Captain, I'm fine. I'm fine," I said.

"Shit. Okay, okay. But in the next coupla days, you gotta promise me that you'll see the doc."

"Sure. Sometime in the next week or so."

Captain stared me down. "That's not what I said."

"Right, okay," I said. "Next couple days."

He pointed at me. "Don't fuck with me."

I retreated to my kip. Sat on the edge, wrestling with images of Val.

. . .

Val had said, "A couple of days," and surprisingly, her call came the next morning as I got off my shift. "Are you available tonight?" she asked.

I wasn't, but I was pretty sure I could get somebody to switch with me. "Are you asking me over?"

"I was thinking of your place. But sure, we can do it at my place."

I tried for a little levity. As soon as I let it go, I knew it was a mistake. "We can *do it* at your place?"

Silence on the other end of the phone. "Just come over around six-thirty, okay?"

"Sure."

It took me most of the day trying to find somebody who would switch—most everyone already had commitments—but eventually Captain Hoyle said he'd take my shift. Just before leaving the station he sat me down and handed me a beer. "You okay?"

I took it. He and I had never been close. I assumed he always thought I wanted his job. But at any rate it was kind of him to offer the beer and a shoulder.

"You seem . . . upset," he said. "Something you want to talk about?"

"It's nothing," I said.

"A woman?"

Don't know if he'd overheard me questioning Tony S, or if my problem was so universal or so transparent. I'd never had the hook so deep in me. Mostly, I dodged the captain's questions. But even after the conversation switched to the Yankees and just before I left, he said, "If she starts crying, you're done for. Don't let yourself get manipulated." He slapped me on the back. "Take care of yourself."

I headed for her apartment, chewing my nails. I had no idea what to expect. I hated my clumsiness, the unknowing, and if she was taking advantage of my good fucking nature . . .

She opened the door with more warmth than before. But without the sizzle. She'd ordered sushi and we downed a few beers. We made small talk.

I couldn't resist putting my arms around her. "Something's not the same between us. Was it the gay thing?" *Surely that would blow over.* "We can have differences of opinion."

She drew a serious breath. "We're still friends, aren't we?"

"I don't want to be your friend."

She pushed away from me. "But you said you would."

"Yes, but I want more."

"What is more?"

Even as I detested her, I risked my luck. "I want you as my partner, my *woman*. Don't you want me as your man?"

She took my hand and hoisted us both off the sofa. Without a word, she walked me into her bedroom where she painstakingly removed every piece of my clothing.

"Stay," she said, then slipped into her bathroom and closed the door. I stood, disordered and slightly chilled, until she returned moments later, dressed in her striped railroad engineer's bib.

Despite my best efforts to lay her on the bed, remove her clothing and mount her, she persisted on moving down my body until she had control of my member, sucking on me until I could hold off no longer.

I lay there, her body fragrant. But not the same. Like another man had infused her.

"Is that what you wanted?" She wrapped a blanket around herself.

I could barely speak. "I love you, you know."

Her lips pursed. "I love you, too."

CHAPTER 35

Father Blu

"Death's a tragedy, Father . . ." The medical examiner, a heavyset man of about forty with a ruby birthmark above his left eye and deep fissures along both cheeks, rested stubby hands on the stainless-steel table buttressing himself. He'd been going on for about five minutes.

I was reminded of Great Grandfather's rule, "Great Spirit gave you two ears and only one mouth, so you can talk half as much as you listen." So, I did.

The examiner went on. ". . . But a death every nine minutes is a statistic—on a conveyor belt. I don't know how the others do it. I'm not sure when it happened; I seem to have lost feeling, not at once but in increments. Folks keep droppin' dead every nine minutes after every nine minutes all over this city. As a forensic pathologist I thought I could acclimate. But this job; I'm not sure if I'm alive or just breathing."

Whether on this afternoon he'd objectified one too many dead bodies, or my clerical black had released him, he'd maxed out on death. We weren't so different.

"I'm sure you do what you can with those who are living," I said.

He huffed. "Not many of those left in my life either. My wife filed for divorce last week."

"I'm so sorry." I'd come in service to Margaret Stott, but also for information about Valerie Dunn.

He hung above Margaret's body, ready to let the sheet and darkness fall forever around her. "You know, this lady spent years becoming . . ." He glanced at the printout with her name on it. ". . . Margaret Amelia Stott, a unique being, seasoned over eighty-seven and a half years. And then . . . after those eighty-seven years of effort and suffering, she probably fashioned a little dignity; she'd become an *individual*. Then she was only good for dying." He teased a wisp of hair from her forehead. "Just like you and me." He pushed away from the table and composed himself. "So, that's her?"

"It is." Margaret lay on the slab; more peaceful than I'd ever seen her in the five or so months I'd been visiting her.

"You're sure?" the examiner asked.

"Yes," I said.

"Thank you, Father. You saved me so much *b taie de cap*; you have no idea."

"Do you want to talk more about how you're feeling . . ." My hand circled around the morgue. ". . . about all this?"

"No time, but thank you for listening." He scribbled something on a form and indicated where I should sign. "I've got another one coming in any minute. Mind if I eat?"

"No, of course not." Nausea nipped at my throat and belly. I signed.

The dead room smelled of pickles. Not unlike Hakim Vaughn's funeral home, although the city's tomb lacked the warmth of Hakim's. Where the Vaughn Funeral Home had several ovens, the morgue had long rows of stainless steel refrigerators, row after row of them, built into the walls. "What will happen to her?"

He flipped off his emotions and the halogen lamp illuminating

Margaret. The lamp seemed unnecessary given the brightness of the room. "There's no family?"

"Sadly, no."

"The city will be legally responsible to find her a burial spot. At least we can cremate now. That used to be a problem. Saves the county money and space." He stripped off his blue latex gloves and tossed them into a nearby receptacle.

"Her ashes?" I asked.

"Still need to be interred somewhere; still plenty of paper-work. Always the trail of death." From a hidden drawer beneath Margaret's slab, he withdrew a white wax paper object, unwrapped a jumbo chopped liver sandwich on rye, placed an accessory pickle to the right of Margaret's bloodless hand, and took a bite of the sandwich, a portion of which plopped onto her outstretched palm.

He scrapped it off and sucked it from his finger. "Pickle?"

"No thanks," I said. "What kind of paperwork?"

"Usual bureaucratic stuff: my examiner's case number, affidavit of removal, the death certificate. That sort of thing. Buried one way or the other."

"What if there's no body," I said, "but there's surviving family?"

"How do you mean?"

"In a fire, death certified but no body remaining. Is there a form for them, for the surviving family member?"

"Of course, always rules and regulations."

"So you'd have a mailing address?" I asked.

"Like I said . . ." He placed his free hand on his laptop computer and tapped it.

"All alphabetized?"

"Yes," he said. "Or it can be referenced in any number of ways."

Somewhere beyond my sight, a door opened and voices could be heard. "Here comes my next one," he said, rewrapping his sandwich and tucking it back into the drawer.

"Don't forget the pickle." I pointed.

"Right." He picked it up and tossed it into the receptacle.

"I need an address," I said.

His face impassive. "I can't share the database."

"You'd appreciate the hassle *I'm* dealing with. It's just *one* death, but the parish priest is on my case." Faces of everyone tied to that one death flashed before me. "All I need is her next of kin's address. Nobody can tell me where she's from originally."

He glanced at Margaret's swathed body. "Name."

"What?"

He waved *hurry up* and sat down in front of his computer. "Quick."

The voices grew louder.

"Ah, Valerie Dunn. Died last May."

"Dunn with an *e*?" he asked.

"No."

He punched the keyboard. He was fast. "Brooklyn Heights or West Seventy-seventh Street?"

"Seventy-seventh Street."

"Professor James P. Dunn, Storm Lake, Iowa. You didn't get it from me." He snapped close the laptop. They rolled in the next body.

. . .

Going from the morgue to the Westend Rifle & Pistol Range seemed somehow appropriate, deadly force being the theme of the day. But whereas the morgue had been cold, modern and massive, the Westend Range was hot, broken-down and claustrophobic. A narrow, linoleum hallway with aging lime green paint and water-stained acoustic tiles lead me to the counter. There I waved off safety ear muffs from the woman behind it. I explained that I was waiting for Captain Hoyle to finish his target practice. She might have been the same woman I'd spoken to earlier, who'd correctly assumed he'd be in at his usual early evening time.

She pointed to the free coffee machine and a row of tables flanked by a wooden bench along the shooting range wall. An assortment of uncomfortable chairs bottlenecked the other. I thanked her, but the accumulating facts were already driving me like caffeine.

Glass windows offered a view of the shooters. I chose to sit on a chair watching them, because the pop-pop-pop of the firearms would have been more unnerving if I hadn't been able to connect the sound to the visual.

I must have waited about thirty minutes, wishing I'd accepted the ear protection, when Captain Hoyle came out wearing a Yankees cap. He shook the hand of another man and bid him farewell. That's when he saw me. He sighed heavily, rubbed his brow. He was unenthusiastic. "Father Bluterre, you're a gun buff?"

"No, my mother was for a time. I have an uncle somewhere . . ."

"You're taking lessons?"

"No," I said, "I wanted to talk to you, away from the firehouse so the men wouldn't stare at us." The building continued to echo with a cacophony of rounds being spent.

He laughed. "You have been kind of pushy."

"I'm sorry about that, but Duke—"

"Yes, I know: Father Toll's obsession. You're forgiven, my son." He squeezed my upper arm. An attempt at being playful, I suppose, yet somehow unnatural for him.

"You understand, I'm just the messenger," I said.

"Or the inquisitor. But understood." He pulled out a cigar. "Do you imbibe?"

"No."

"Well, maybe a drink? I have a favorite place around the corner. I'm headed there."

Hearing him above the firing range din would be impossible. I could hardly say no. But I'd have to be strong. "Sure."

He ushered me into the saloon, a small, under lit room with several tables in the rear away from the bar. "Let's go there," he said pointing to a darkly lit corner, "where I can smoke." He smiled. "They're fond of me here." Then he said something to the bartender and walked me to a two-top in the back. "You okay here?"

"Fine."

We sat, and as we did, the bartender himself appeared and placed two old fashioned glasses on the table. A thank you nod from Hoyle and he was gone. "I remember you like good whiskey." He lit his cigar and blew the smoke out the side of his mouth, away from me. "Let me know if this bothers you."

"No, I'm fine, Captain."

"Call me Rick; we certainly have seen enough of each other these past three months." He raised his glass and looked at me to do the same.

I must have shown my apprehension.

"Johnnie Walker Black, right?"

"Right." I wanted to say *I don't drink anymore*, but I needed him to be pliable. Maybe I could get away with sipping it slowly. I clinked his glass. "Thank you," I said.

He took another puff. "So, you have more questions for me." But before I could answer he added, "I know nothing, or close to nothing, about the arson investigations regarding Duke, so please don't ask. Although I do hear that they're close to a determination. I hope for Duke's sister's sake that AIU's findings aren't disheartening."

I put the glass down. "No, actually I wondered, does the name Valerie Dunn mean anything to you?"

He dove in, unreserved, his face lacking guile. "No, should it? Who is she?"

"I'm not entirely sure." *Where could he help me?* "Regarding the gun that Duke used in trying to kill himself . . ."

Hoyle squinted. "That's a question for the police. And isn't that old business? It's been over eight months."

"I understand you're an expert on firearms."

"I'm a collector; I mentioned that to you before. I like to shoot." Trace laugh lines surfaced, implying a curious amusement with my question. "I'm no expert. Besides, what would I know about the gun Duke used?" He held the whiskey to the light.

"It was a handgun, a Rossi," I said. "It came from a gun shop downtown—Pinky's. You know the place?"

"I'm aware of it."

"There was a fire there. Were you in on it?"

He cocked his head. "What do you mean?"

"You help put out the fire?"

"Probably, with medical emergencies and fires we average five to ten *a day*. You do the math. But listen—"

"But you know the Rossi?" I said.

"Yeah." He swallowed some aggravation. "It's a mini." He tossed back the whiskey.

"So you know it?"

"Not my style, but sure. It's pretty common. Easily concealed." He lay the glass on the table, tenderly. Like reposing a baby in a crib.

"What else can you tell me about it?"

"The Rossi thirty-eight? Look, this really is beginning to feel like an inquisition," the captain said.

"Sorry." I settled into my most rapt attention.

He relaxed back into his chair. "It's a five-shot. Made in Brazil. Cheap."

"For not being an expert, you're pretty good."

His lips curled back, more than comfortable with the compliment. "That's hardly expert knowledge. Hakim Vaughn could have told you the same thing. Probably a couple of others in the fire house too."

"How do you think Duke got his hands on it?"

He shrugged it off as obvious. "Whether from Pinky or out on the street, if he wanted to find a gun in this city, he could pretty easily. Anyone could." He relit his cigar.

"But that doesn't tell us *who* he got it from."

He dragged from the cigar. "I certainly have no idea."

I tossed it aside. "No, I guess not."

"And what difference does it make who he got it from?"

"Maybe no difference at all," I admitted. *Or perhaps a lead to Duke's motivation.*

"I wouldn't think so," the captain said.

"Probably not."

Hoyle began absentmindedly scanning the room. "Maybe Duke was feeling the heat of the investigations."

"What?"

He turned back to me. "Maybe that's why he bought the gun. He's a proud man, he had a reputation to protect."

I pawed the Johnnie Black.

"But who knows?" Another scan of the room. "Listen, Father, good talking to you, as always, but I'd better get home." He stood, we shook hands. He pointed at the tumbler. "Don't waste that good whiskey."

"No, I won't." I sat down. "Thanks again."

He beckoned to the bartender, fastened his jacket, stuck the cigar between his teeth and pushed out the bar room door.

How did he know it was a five-shot .38 special? I'd never mentioned that.

The lovely amber played at my fingertips. I stroked the glass. I lifted it to my nose. I inhaled. I was closer still to some kind of truth or open sore, a key piece of Duke's story. It wasn't in that glass.

CHAPTER 36

Duke

Yes, I was angry, angry enough to kill her. And here's why: After that night with her, that last week in April, she shut me out. Stonewalled me every possible way. Whenever I called, she claimed to be tired or not feeling well or busy.

"Too busy to see me?" I said.

"Right now, yes," she said and promptly got off the phone.

Feeling even more the patsy, I went to her apartment to see exactly how busy she was. All the way there, I cursed my body for wanting her so bad. I missed her touch. Even more, her aroma.

Early evening had settled softly on the city block, but not on my shoulders or in my belly. Seething, I positioned myself across from her building. I played out different scenarios in which I was inquisitive and thoughtful, gracious and understanding, determined and insistent, and demanding and dictating. The battle within my body, of disbelief and anger, had become a cancer, rotting me from the inside out. What was I going to say to her that would make her stop pulling my chain, this woman who supposedly loved me? What could I say to her to get us back on track? What was it that *she* needed?

Reaching for her keys, I realized I'd left them at home and prepared to leave. Then *he* showed up—the motherfucker I'd seen at the raceway in late October, the tall, skinny guy with the stringy hair and the Native American bolo. Except this time the son of a bitch wore a sports jacket, shorts and fucking sneakers, no socks. His few strands pulled into a fucking ponytail. *This was the guy she was trading me in for?* He rang her buzzer and brushed himself out. He slipped his glasses into his breast pocket. I wanted to crush them *in* his pocket. I thought I'd pull him down the steps and slam his scarecrow face into the pavement.

She responded almost immediately, like she was expecting him. She buzzed him in.

It was roughly eight PM. Despite the remaining glow in the sky, lights shone in several apartments, including hers. From off the curb I tried to get a glimpse of her front window. Not possible from that angle. But almost directly across the street sat the West End Collegiate Church.

Moving up its steps helped my aspect a little, but the church doors were flung open, so why not? I went inside and up to a second story portal, ironically next to a door marked "Ministry of Music." It gave me a clear view of Valerie's living room window.

They appeared there, Val and The Scarecrow, hugging. He separated from her, gave her a wide smile, touched her hair and hugged her again. She looked up at him, she returned the warm embrace.

He sure didn't look anything like her sibling. They disappeared from view. I circled the parapet. I considered ringing the buzzer and confronting her. Then running down the church's steps and across the street, I did.

The little speaker, her voice tinny and shrill, offended me. "Who's there?"

"It's me," I said.

"I told you I was busy tonight."

Her clipped superiority raised my blood pressure even higher. I organized my breathing and played ignorant. "I want to see you. Can I come up?"

"No, you cannot."

She wouldn't squabble with me meeting her brother. "Just for a few minutes," I said.

"Duke, I said *no*."

I know there's a man with you. "You're hiding from me."

"I'm hiding from everybody," she said.

Not everybody. "Just for a minute," I said as courteously as possible.

"I said no."

Confronting her with what I knew—gloating I could taste— was reckless. She'd have known I was spying on her. "What happened to 'speaking about our fear?'"

"Go away," she said, straining to hold back her anger.

"Who's up there with you?"

Silence.

"I know you've got a man up there," I said.

"Go away."

"You're fucking with me."

"I'm not."

"Then buzz me up." I tugged on the locked foyer door. I pounded it. "Let me up."

"You're scaring me."

"Good, you've fucked with me enough," I said.

More silence.

"Val?" I stepped back to see her window. She'd closed the curtains. My whole body baked. *I'll wait for him and I'll beat the living shit out of him when he comes down. And if it's tomorrow morning, I'll fucking kill him. I'm not taking this any longer.*

She broke the silence. "You just don't understand."

"That's a fucking understatement."

"You've got nothing to be jealous about."

"Hard to believe."

"If I promise to meet you tomorrow, will you go away and not make a terrible mistake?"

"What about the guy?" I said.

She didn't deny him. "He's a friend."

"I thought I was your only friend."

"He's not a friend like you," she said.

"You mean he's not a sucker?"

"That's not what I meant. It's not romantic."

"*Romantic*, is that what we are?"

"Please." She finally sounded unable to cope. "I'll meet you tomorrow night, a restaurant or a—I don't care where, if you'll just trust me."

"Trust? You gotta be kidding."

"You can still be my hero. Please."

Fuck you. "My apartment," I said.

She responded quickly. "No." A pause. "Pick a restaurant."

"No. Someplace private. Your apartment."

"Fine, fine," she said. "Just go away. Just don't hurt anybody."

"What time?"

"Around now. Goodnight." The speaker clicked off.

"Valerie?" The intercom dead; she'd switched me off.

I decided to wait for one of the other tenants to come home. Maybe I could slip in, beat on her door; catch that skinny son of a bitch.

The night cooled. I patrolled for thirty minutes or so. When no one showed up, I went home. In a way, I was relieved—distraught and relieved. I still thought I could make us work.

. . .

The next night I was scheduled on shift, but I wasn't letting Valerie off that easy. Again, it came down to trading with Captain Hoyle. "What's going on, Ducotty? You sure you're alright?"

"It's nothing" I said.

He saw right through me. "It's a woman. Another man?"

"Nothing I can't handle." My answer apparently anemic.

"Want to scare him?"

"Who?"

"The guy."

"There is no guy." Lame, nobody would have bought it.

But he did. Or I thought he did. Or maybe he just let me off the hook. "Okay. Just take care of yourself. We need you clearheaded and you sure aren't acting that way. Women can fuck with you, and if they're doing that they're usually not worth it. Take the night off, but come back whole."

Whole?

. . .

The Johnnie Walker almost slipped from my hand about the time I reached Val's door. A mostly full bottle. That would have been a waste. Just before eight PM. My jaw tight, my stomach tight. Everything tight.

She greeted me with all the enthusiasm of an acned movie ticket taker. And her neck bore the blotches of her amorous encounter with the scarecrow the night before. "Nice to see you," she said and led me into the living room where I plopped down the bottle of whiskey. "Ice?"

"What did I do, Val? I can make it up to you." *Don't plead.* "I don't get what's going on. What do you need?" Three feet separated us, but it might as well have been miles.

"You didn't do anything, Duke, really. It's just that I looked at my life and made some decisions about it. Everything comes with a price." She took a step toward the fireplace mantel.

"Just like that—I'm not part of your life. Why?"

She faced me stolid. No, in fairness, *composed*. "To you it seems sudden, but for me it isn't. You're just not the man for me." *There, she said it!*

My whole body chilled with the impact. "But someone else is."

"I don't mean this to sound cruel," she said, "but I hope so."

Sonuvabitch!

She pulled her pipe from the mantel and took a toke. "Can I pour you your drink?"

"I can pour it myself."

"Of course you can. I thought maybe we could put a friendly cap on all this."

"A friendly cap . . . *on all this*." I swung the bottle around. "You gotta be fuck—"

"Please don't get hostile or I'll have to ask you to leave."

"You ain't seen hostile yet." I drank from the bottle.

"Duke, please."

"Don't fucking placate me. No, wait, you're not that fucking rational. Nothing goes one-two-three."

She had the nerve to respond with nonchalance. "Maybe one-two-three is only rational to you."

"What! In other words, let's play with *no* rules? Complete fucking chaos."

"I warned you . . ."

I jumped up, stepped toward her. She flinched. "*Warned me*, you bitch! You women talk about liberation, about being holy and wanting a man who is true, true blue—as long as you have control. How fucking true blue is that for the man? You don't want a man who stands up for you *and* for himself. In fact, you don't want a man; you want a blowup toy. One of those punching bag clowns; smack it to the ground and it bobs back up. You're a fucking hypocrite, a pretender."

She was grim. She studied her feet. That's all I remember.

· · ·

When I woke up, I was on her couch, still chafing on fuzzy resentment. Warm morning light streamed into her apartment. She stood in the kitchen in a man's pajamas, biting her lip and whimpering. "What the fuck happened?" I asked. She kept her head down. "Hey, what the fuck happened?"

She took hold of the counter top. "You don't remember?"

"I remember you pissing me off. Telling me that everything we'd meant to each other was bullshit."

"I didn't say that. I'd never say that." If I hadn't been able to see her, I'd have imagined her a foot smaller, her voice miniaturized . . . and thin.

"The fuck you didn't." I rubbed my eyes, pinned her to the wall with them.

"You want tea?"

"No, I want fucking coffee."

She flinched. "You shouldn't have coffee."

"Sweet. You still have a memory of *me*." I shook my head back and forth hoping to clear it. "What happened last night?"

Her eyes red. Her mouth puckered. She turned away from me and hung her head. Along her left arm, a bandage wrapped around her wrist to her elbow.

"What's with your arm?" I asked.

"You should probably go."

I took a step toward her. She retreated further into the kitchen. "What happened?" I said.

"You have great qualities, you don't need mine."

"Don't spread your psycho-babble bullshit on me. Save that for your patients."

"Duke, please go." She started crying again.

"What the fuck happened?"

"You don't remember?"

"Stop screwing with me."

She held up her hands to say *don't come any closer.* "You had one of your dizzy spells."

"And?" I closed my fists, ready to rip flesh. *No more fucking retreat.*

She wiped a dishtowel across her swollen eyes. I had no recollection whatsoever, and felt alone, completely alone. "You're pissing me off."

As if unveiling a precious work of art, she unwrapped the bandage. "You really don't remember?"

I could have shredded her.

"You won't hurt me?" Her eyes begging.

"I should. Like you've hurt me. But no, of course not."

She continued to unwind the bandage, then let it fall around her wrist and the counter top. Deep diagonal cuts formed a ladder up the inside of her forearm.

"What's that? What happened?" A step toward her.

She retreated. "Please go."

"But—?"

"If you ever loved me, please go."

"How did this happen?" I said.

She stifled a sob. She closed her eyes and opened them again, apparently attempting to gain strength. "You were so angry with me."

"Sure, I was. Still am. But I didn't do this? Impossible."

"Please go away. Don't make me call the police."

WTF. "The police?"

"Please Duke, don't make this any harder than it is."

"I don't believe you. It was that guy, that motherfucking scarecrow."

"There's no other guy."

"I'll find him, and I'm gonna kick the living shit out of him. And he'll never bother you again, I promise."

She pointed at the door. "Just promise that you won't come back."

"Val."

She peeked at me, terrified and pitiful, her eyes ringed in purple, the whites ruptured by blood red fibers. "Maybe someday we'll be friends again. But not now. Please go."

I'd never seen her so delicate, so frail—not even that first time on the airplane. Yet I felt no pity. She turned so the kitchen counter separated us.

"Fine." I slipped on my shoes. "I'm not gonna make this so fucking easy for you. We're not done—not by a long shot. . . Not by a fucking long shot." I hurled the door shut on my way out.

Morning cloud cover had dropped gauze over the city, coral suppressed the sky. But all I could see were the cuts along Val's arm and the fucking scarecrow. They were messing with me in more than one way. Whether it was by her, by her new boyfriend or by my own freakish knack, I was out, dumped like garbage.

Kierkegaard said, "I see it all perfectly . . . One can either do this or that. . . . My friendly advice is . . . do it or do not do it—you will regret both."

I intended to fight back.

CHAPTER 37

Father Blu

Though temperatures still hovered in the teens, a dense winter fog enveloped the city. The same cold fog clouded my view of the events, eight months earlier, of the night Valerie Dunn was murdered, a mere eighteen or so hours before Duke shot himself—too close to Valerie Dunn's death to be coincidence.

"Is James there, James Dunn?" The phone tight in my fist. God, or whatever spirit was guiding me, wanted me fully awake to talk to Valerie Dunn's sibling.

"James? No, he's away. Who is this?"

"My name is Father Jamie Bluterre. I'm calling from New York City. Is this Mrs. Dunn?"

"It is. Is James okay?"

"Yes, I didn't mean to alarm you. Do you know where he is?"

"Who did you say you were?"

"I'm a Catholic priest in New York City. Father Jamie Bluterre."

An extended silence on the other end of the line.

"Mrs. Dunn?"

"Why do you want to talk to James? We're not Catholic. And none of that money's going to the church, if that's what you're thinking."

Money. "No, no, it's about Valerie," I said.

A deep exhale from Mrs. Dunn, apparently a sore point. "Oh." The line hummed. "I suppose you know she's dead, died in a fire."

"Yes," I said.

"Did she tell you that you'd get some of that money?"

"No."

"Good, because you're not. Anyway, James has been attending to her estate since her death, six months—even more now. Cleaning up her mess as usual." She caught herself. "Sorry, that's unkind."

"Messes? What kind of messes?"

"Is that why you're calling? She had another one of her—what do you call them—epiphanies? She came to you before her death?"

"I couldn't tell you if she had," I said.

"But you want to know *something*, don't you? That's why you want to talk to my husband."

"She was involved with a friend of mine. I just want to know *how*?"

Mrs. Dunn cackled. "A man, a woman, a shrink, a drug dealer, a priest?"

"A fireman," I said.

"Not her first. Why don't you ask him?"

"She had a *thing* for them?" I asked.

"She had a thing for macho men, bless her. Couldn't leave well enough alone. . . May she sleep peacefully."

"How so?"

"I've said more than I should."

"Was she violent?"

"I'm not saying another word," said Mrs. Dunn.

"Okay, can you tell me where James is?"

"No, I don't . . ." Her voice trailed off. A dog barked. Then two.

"Mrs. Dunn?"

"Yes? Look, I wish to heck I could, but he's so darn elusive about all this sister stuff of his." She tucked away her irritability. "Anyway, he's back in New York. In the city somewhere. Finally putting all her papers together, once and for all."

"But you don't know where?" I said.

"No, I don't. He hardly answers his phone, anymore. He avoids me when he's overwhelmed. Maybe he stopped at her old office, The Child's Mind. And by the way, Valerie wasn't any more Catholic than we are, although she could have used some spiritual guidance, God knows."

"Does the name Sean Ducotty mean anything to you?"

"No. Father Blu-whatever, I've said enough."

"How about Hakim Vaughn? Was he violent with her?"

"Violent? If anyone was violent . . . I told you, I've said enough."

I asked, "Can I have James' cell number?"

"What? No, you may not, not unless he gives it to you," she said. "I'm not sure why you need to talk to James . . . But if you see or talk to him, ask him to call me tonight. It's been two days since I've heard from him, and I'd like to know that he's holding up okay under the strain."

"I'll do that."

"And don't expect a dime," she added, and hung up the phone.

Valerie Dunn had been a rather reclusive woman, but tracing her bank and workplace was quite easy. I stopped in at the three most proximate banks to her apartment. In the third, the bank manager acknowledged her by admitting, "Your congregation must be devastated." The miraculous perks of wearing clerical black, though I was doing less and less at the church—on Father Toll's dictate.

"It's sad," I said. "James' wife said he'd been in to close up the account."

The manager acknowledged as much. "Poor man, I'm sure you've been of great comfort to him. It's been a long haul." He offered me a seat by his desk. I declined.

"He's pretty anxious about all this," I said.

"Yes, well you can understand."

"Thank goodness for those checks." I offered a wee pious genuflect.

"Well, she loved her brother and wanted him to be secure." He caught himself, turned sullen. "What is this about? What can I do for you, Father?"

"I just thought you might have seen him in the last few days. I spoke to his wife this afternoon and she'd like to hear from him. And I've lost his phone number."

He'd turned stony-faced. "Lost his—no. No." His mouth closed, tightly. He tugged on his suit jacket. "Is that all?" His jaw shifted. A young male teller ambled up to him clutching a sheet of pink paper. He grabbed it from him. "We're done, Father." He turned to the teller, essentially dismissing me.

Once it sunk in, I veered from his desk, only to catch Sister Maryann watching me through the bank's frosted front window. She pretended not to see me and, like a shot, she was gone. Once outside, I yelled down the block to her. She waffled, enough that I knew she'd heard me, though she continued hurrying down the street. I hustled up behind her. "Sister Maryann."

She finally halted, forced to concede my presence. She turned with an embarrassed expression to face me. "I thought it was you, but I couldn't be sure."

"Out for some errands?" I asked.

"Yes. We're short on candles."

"And Candlemas but a few days away," I said.

"Yes."

"Also Groundhog Day."

It didn't loosen her up. We stood awkwardly. She rocked from one foot to the other. "I noticed your snowdrops beginning to bloom in the side garden. They're lovely."

"Yes."

"So . . ." She averted her eyes.

"Did you know, Sister, that in the Middle Ages Candlemas was the day everyone brought their candles to church to be blessed by the priest, so they'd become apotropaic? So they'd ward off evil."

"I'm sorry," she said at last.

"Sorry about what?"

"About you and Father Toll."

"He's had you checking up on me," I said.

Her eyes penitent. "Yes."

"Not to worry, Sister." I touched her shoulder.

"I'll light a candle for you."

"Thank you, Sister."

A wan smile.

"Candles," I said, releasing her from her discomfort.

"Candles, yes." And she moved on.

. . .

Next up, a trip to the Child's Mind Clinic on West 110th Street, just south of Morningside Park. It's a fairly toney neighborhood although the offices, while bright and colorful, weren't particularly posh. I was hoping for Valerie Dunn's story and maybe a little more.

Soothing music mollified the lobby. I introduced myself to the woman at the front desk, who identified herself as Angela, a silver-haired woman in her late sixties with a pleasant smile and a paisley scarf wrapped around her neck. "What can I do for you?"

"I'd like to start by offering something to *you*, to this organization. I read that much of your funding was recently cut by the administration in Washington."

She clasped her hands together in disappointment. "We're going to have to let some staff go. We're kind of a close family here."

"The behavioral and emotional needs of young children are important," I said.

"Thank you, we think so."

"This year I'd like to contribute a small portion of my monthly salary to your efforts."

Her face grew kinder still. "That's very generous, Father, but we have a few affluent donors who may step up. I'm Catholic, I know you don't make much."

"Nevertheless, I'd like to. And I have an ulterior motive. I read the short memoriam on your website about the late Valerie Dunn."

Angela looked bruised. "Oh, yes, Valerie."

"I'm sorry to bring up unhappy memories, but I'm trying to determine what happened."

Angela came from behind the reception desk. "I didn't know she was religious."

"I can't say that she was."

"But she was a member of your congregation?"

Try sticking to the truth. "No. But her boyfriend was, *is*."

"I'm not sure I understand."

"He tried to commit suicide shortly after her death," I said. "And I'm trying to pull the pieces together. He's in a vegetated state."

"Oh my." Angela's eyelids took on weight. "She didn't discuss her private life. We had no idea she had a boyfriend."

"Nothing about her private life, never, not with anyone? How about her brother, James?"

"She loved her work, loved working with her patients. We can all vouch for that. But I wouldn't call her forthcoming, not about her personal life."

"The day of her death, she had appointments?"

"Of course. What are you looking for, Father?"

"I honestly don't know. But something happened between them . . ."

"I wish I could help. But as good as she was unlocking her young clients, she was just as tightly wrapped. She seemed unhappy in her own skin. Is that cruel to say? Perhaps it was their relationship—she and the boyfriend. He must have been distraught at her death."

"Perhaps," I said. "Is there anything else, anything regarding her work or . . . I don't know?"

Angela went inward in thought. She looked up, troubled. "What's that?" I asked.

"I shouldn't conjecture about the dead," Angela said.

"But?"

"I got the feeling she was going to quit Child's Mind."

"Quit? I thought she loved her work, was good at it."

"Oh, she was, she was terrific. But I think she had doubts." I cocked my head. Angela continued. "About psychology, about her work."

"Really?"

"Well, she had a point," said Angela.

"Which was?"

"It was a silly debate over lunch."

I waited.

"She'd been reading Rank."

"Sorry." I shrugged. "I don't . . . "

"Otto Rank, the Austrian psychoanalyst, an associate of Freud. He proposed that psychology was trying to replace religious and moral ideology, but that there was danger in that because psychology places personal unhappiness back on the person. The person's the cause; he's marooned with himself, abandoned to his own guilt."

That had a familiar ring. "Interesting," I said.

"I think what bothered her most was that psychology's clinical explanation not only put the blame on the individual, but that the patient might be left with the idea that the psychoanalyst is the only one who knows, the only one who can explain it all. Like all our meaning is derived from our dealings with others, not from within. It really troubled her that she might be contributing to that model, despite her fine work.

"And occasionally, in a rare moment, she'd say something like 'I hope I still have time to be me.' I think there was something bigger tugging at her. But what do I know? We all have our demons." She looked apologetic. "Not you, of course, Father."

CHAPTER 38

Duke

The whole way back to the fire house, I played out schemes for burning through Valerie's bullshit. They all seemed lame and indecisive. I'd already let it go too far.

"Duke." Chuck Winston came out of the locker room.

"Hey Chief, what're you doing here?" I said.

"Discussions with the captain. But I gotta keep movin'. I'm sorry. Maybe we grab a coffee or a beer next week, catch up?"

"I'd like that."

"Then call me," he said.

"Will do."

He aimed his index finger at me and pulled the trigger. "Next week." He turned the corner.

The shifts were changing. The locker rooms reverberated with a drone I could hear before entering; an incoming and outgoing tide of personnel, grumbling in groups. Hakim was there, Eisler, Marjorie, Alvarez, a bunch. The air thick with innuendo about the next cuts to the roster. *Making space for the new recruits*, I heard someone say.

I kept my head down, in no mood to chit chat with anyone. Made no difference. By the time I'd reached my locker, the room had quieted, most everyone had scattered. My existence the billboard for bad news: dead man walking.

I unlatched my locker.

When Tony S and Cynthia, the new recruit, came around the corner and walked down the row of lockers laughing, I went to take a pee. Cynthia had only been there two weeks, but already Tony S had put the moves on her, and she was responding. They glanced at me as I passed and pretended not to see me, the way people do when they hope to stay far away from the impending damage.

I'd been gone five-maybe six minutes. On my return, my row had emptied out. I pulled the thermal liner off my locker shelf and there it was, a small revolver.

It wasn't the first I'd held, but its diminutive grip contoured perfectly to my hand in a way I hadn't remembered. Its stubby blue steel, cool to my touch, with so much promise. I'd shot a similar one with Hakim years before. A portable little friend.

And the donor? There wasn't a soul about. I poked around the corner. No one there either. *Who'd left it for me? Why? A mistake?* Regardless, good fortune had found me. And on the shelf in the back of the locker, a box of ammo, begging to be used.

A code, that's what you want, Val? I'll give you a fucking code that you and that skinny ass scarecrow of yours will clearly understand. You won't need a fucking interpreter or a decoding ring. I'll just wave this thing around and you'll give me some answers. Maybe I'll shoot your fucking friend where he'll do the least harm from now on. That would be justice, skinny son of a bitch. He'll see what a trespasser can expect.

On the other hand, if he's been hurting you, he'll have far worse consequences.

I imagined him cowering, pleading, apologizing, and extricating himself from her. From our lives. But if he didn't, then what?

And maybe who could blame him? Valerie was a tempter. She could have baited him as she did me. Always quoting higher principles as if that was the same as acting on them.

He might not even have known about me. She was the one, the one who grabbed hold of me, tantalized me, rubbed her spore over me, whispered the future; turned me into a fucking spineless wuss. Just so she could have control? Just so she could prove it to herself? What was she after?

All her fucking talk about the cosmos and our connection, our dedication to *the truth*. The fucking bitch had put her hook in me and reeled me in till all I wanted, all I could think of was her; I dangled at her beck and call. Once she knew she had me by the balls, she tossed me back into the East fucking River. Fucking Valerie. When I needed her the most, she was spreading her legs for another guy, expecting me to walk away like a gentleman. *Fuck that.*

My shift was about to start. I didn't give a shit. They were going to lop me off after thirty years on the force. *Fuck them.*

The restless sleep had caught up with me. My eyes itched. My brain, too. I didn't remember cutting her, but given the slut's easy disposal of me, maybe I did. I'd become disposable—as a fireman and as a man. Why not her? What did I have to lose?

The pistol slipped into my waistband, the bullets in my pocket. I snuck out of the firehouse.

. . .

I headed uptown, back to her apartment. The rush hour subway already had the stink of death, people sweating and packed one against another. Their day had just begun and already they were powerless.

I shoved my elbows right and left, making sure I took my space. I could do something. And once free of the packed car, I stormed up the station steps, through the heat to the street where I could breathe. Within two blocks, her brownstone loomed up in front of me. My heart clacking like a nail gun. I let myself into the building. Valerie was going to come back to me or pay for it.

But when I got to the top floor, slipped the key into the lock and threw open her door, she'd already left for work. *Fuck.* After all the months with her, I had no idea where that was; more of her deceitful bullshit.

I didn't know what to do with myself. I sat in the living room. I prowled. I swore aloud. The fucking fat cat came by; I kicked it away. I passed through the kitchen. On the counter was a note:

Sweet Valerie,
I'm here to share it all with you.
Thanks for making me part of your life.
Always loving you,
Jimmy

Fuck!

In the bedroom, unable to spare myself the images of her and her latest lover tumbling over each other, tasting each other, I found the bed torn apart—*again*—smelling sour of her new man. More of *Jimmy's* clothes filled the closet; he'd practically moved in.

But the most telling was a small two-tiered shrine she'd built in the corner next to the bed, her handwritten note taped to the base:

"These things must pass.
(For the incinerator)"

On it, a book I'd given her, *Dancing With Fire: A Mindful Way To Loving Relationships,* the empty urn that had carried her parent's ashes, a photo of a not-so-happy couple that—because of their eyes and mouths—hinted at being her parents. The ticket stub from our Bonnie Raitt concert, the Steely Dan t-shirt she'd appropriated from me and always wore with *nothing* else. A ring I'd never seen her wear, and another that I had; little girl trinkets, a Barbie doll and a row of candles. Her demolition shrine, suggesting *good riddance*. Dumping what she was done using. Me, a major part of that shrine. Disposable.

If I can't have her, no one will.

After that, I must have gone home. I don't remember the trip, only that—as I snaked my way home under the city—I added up my history and found a thread there: failure to complete my expectations. A steady primitive thread of being unlovable and of loss. Assuring in its sad familiarity. Illogical, but it was *mine*.

Val's promises of a better world had snapped the strand, the safety of it. I'd forever grieve for those promises. She'd betrayed me. Either that or she'd stopped believing in my intent and now I'd stopped believing hers. But I *could* complete *this* relationship the way I wanted, to *my* satisfaction. If I played it right.

At home, I *think* I played some music, wrathful, embittered music. I took out the naked photo of her and masturbated. I drank. Quite a bit. I flipped through the photos of her on my cell phone. I swore. I deleted them. *Leave no trace.*

I don't recall much else. When I woke up on my couch, the bottle of scotch was empty. The gun and shells were on the coffee table. Night had blackened my windows. Indignation still spun around me. And, of all things, guilt. A badgering guilt.

Time was off, like I'd slept for days. Even the second bottle of Johnnie Walker lacked appeal. Trinity Church chimed once. I regretted something. Something more than walking out on my shift. It lacked shape. Trinity Church chimed twice.

The phone rang. I didn't answer it. Probably the captain wondering . . .

Trinity Church chimed a third and fourth time. It was four in the morning!

My stomach roiled. My hands opened and close involuntarily, trying to wring out the dread coursing through my body. *What had I done?*

Val once told me, "You can't lie about anxiety. Got to face up to it. Only then you'll know the truth of your disorder, and begin to release it." She'd paused to reflect. "Often it's guilt, guilt of not fulfilling one's own potential."

I'd been obsessed. I'd let her manipulate me. Even when I knew better. That's why I wasn't the man for her, maybe not the man I needed to be for myself. What she said she wanted wasn't what she really needed. I'd given in to her New Age rewrite of manhood. Still, I couldn't understand how she could let a love like ours go. She'd arrived when I thought all hope was gone. She'd changed everything. She'd brought so much comfort. She was my friend.

And then she was simply done with me. I finally had to acknowledged it. I had to find a way to live on without her. I had to. I had to set myself free; return to my life as it had been, quite passable. If only I could forget her temptation. Her *willful* temptation. I had to let it go. I had to let *her* go.

All of a sudden, I was fully awake. I had to get her out of my system. Immediately. That night. Cut the cord. Let her move on, if that's what she needed. Burn her from my memory. As far from me as possible. I just wanted the truth. Even if—given the lateness of the hour—that meant I would meet Jimmy in her bed. But even as I braced for that requisite meeting, a bitter ember continued to glow in me. *Put it out once and for all. Stop being helpless.*

. . .

The platform of the #1 subway line thrummed with dis-ease. Even in the wee hours and in its shadows, I could see it on people's faces.

In their haggard eyes. The way they clutched their belongings. As if on a death march, trudging to their own execution. And when the train broke through the tunnel and screeched to a stop, I chose a mostly deserted car. Then clung to the strap all the way up to 79th Street, avoiding all contact.

The stairs to the street pulled down on me. Like quicksand. All the while I searched for a sliver of compassion; any way I could send her off in peace and salvage my virility. But blow by blow, my heart and stomach clashed. *Love her,* my heart kept advocating. *But she fucked you over.* My stomach wrenched and dripped blood. *Fuck her. Torch the motherfucker.*

Even on the street, much cooler, I loved and hated her all at the same time. My fingers missed brushing tender over her skin. My thighs longed for her. My hands craved to throw her up against a wall. Hard. And tighten around her neck as I forced her to look at me, to show *some* respect.

The unmistakable intimacy of smoke clung to the air. I turned onto her block and I could taste soot. Three temporary phosphorus lights illuminated the middle of the block. Bright yellow barricades surrounded the entrance to her building. Much of the neighborhood stood around: a middle-aged man in a woman's powder blue nightgown and Boston University tee shirt. A platinum-haired woman in her sixties in a white robe and black cycling shorts. A girl scarcely fifteen, fur coat almost to mid-thigh. An odd mixture of clothes and people and place at 4:20 in the morning. An occasional siren.

Valerie's apartment!

Next to me, the platinum woman in the white robe lit a cigarette. I asked, "Where's the woman who lived there? What happened?" Apparently, the woman didn't hear me above a siren.

Cops and an AIU guy I once met circulated through the crowd. They were looking for a sign, a sign pointing to an arsonist. Possibly someone in the crowd.

The woman kept staring at the remains of the top floor. "Somebody set fire to the place," she said at last, dragging from her cigarette. Except for her white robe and black cycling shorts, she looked ready to go to a ball.

"Where's the woman who lives there?" I pointed to the dark hull of Val's apartment.

"Dead." The woman said this so incidentally, it hardly registered as true.

"What d'ya mean?" I said.

She tapped off her cigarette ash. "Look at that." She pointed to the gutted, still-smoking apartment. "That place burned all evening, all night, up until an hour or so ago. Maybe nine-ten hours. I heard one of them say *no way she escaped*. I asked a cop ten minutes ago. He said, 'They found a finger, that's all that was left.'"

"What?"

"That's all that was left."

CHAPTER 39

Duke

What had I done?

The AIU guy made his way through the crowd which, thankfully, showed little sign of thinning despite the hour. People mesmerized by fire and reminded of its might. I used it for cover.

A finger. That's all that was left.

I ducked away from the AIU guy before he could ID me, walking off slowly. Didn't start running till I was down the block.

Light and sound ambushed me. I could see Val's first realization, her disbelief. The contradictions narrowing her pupils as she began to understand her fate. Her space becoming smaller and smaller, sealed off as the smoke and flames grew thicker, taller, stronger. Her tomb.

I'd devised it. Or my anger had. It still wasn't far off. It still burned in me. And yet . . .

No one should experience that kind of pain. Trapped and in her mental state, Val would've become awake, then hysterical, even before her body and mind started decomposing. And then the agony of being consumed alive.

All of it arranged with my expertise and set by my hand. My work—to perfection.

My sickness had jeopardized many and now it'd overcome me. Dad gone. Mom gone. My pathetic short list of women. Trying to reach *someone*. One deadfall after another. I'd become cruel. I never meant to become cruel.

Out of the ashes of those women I'd built my romance with music. *Barricaded* myself within walls of it. I couldn't remember a single face—except Valerie's.

Then again, no memory. I must have walked, must have run. *I'd rather go blind, girl, than see you walk away from me.* I hated her, I missed her. My god, I'd killed her. My best friend. My only friend. It was masterful, they'd never pin it on me. But it was sick. I was sick.

A cab blasted into me, I remember the impact. But not the pain. No sound, no sound at all. I kept running. I kept running all the way downtown because once the neighborhoods became familiar, the morning light unmasked me. My hero status now blatantly fraudulent and shameful. The way life could turn on you. I couldn't outrun it. Unlovable. Faithless. Now a killer.

As Kierkegaard said, to be alive, live in faith. The hardest thing to do. Like me, stuck between belief and faith, between vague confidence and absolute trust. *All that was left.*

With Valerie, I'd taken the leap into faith, thinking everything would be beautiful, everything exquisitely resolved. Comforting. But she'd abandoned me, left me with nothing. Worse than death, it left me with nothing to believe in.

Once inside my apartment with the gun and the bullets, I knew what I had to do. *Maybe I could be with her this way. Fool.*

I loaded the gun and placed my lips around the barrel. I glanced up at my wall of music. I pulled the trigger.

. . .

Frenzied strains of diabolical laughter and a Hammond organ ricocheted through my hospital room: Arthur Brown's tune "Fire." I was awake once more and still unseen. A large digital clock had been installed in the corner of the room, facing my bed. The block red characters read:

5:53 PM, Feb. 1

The clock and date commemorating my eight months of paralysis.

Beneath it, resting on the gurney, the priest stared at me as if expecting Arthur Brown's musical rant to kick my EEG to new heights. Nothing could kick me to new heights. His eyes scanned the encephalogram and returned to me. He put his overcoat aside and walked slowly to me. "Duke, it's time. I know you can hear me."

He looked over his shoulder to the hallway, then leaned over my bed. "Six retired Irishmen are playing poker in O'Leary's apartment when Paddy Murphy loses five hundred dollars on a single hand, clutches his chest, and drops dead at the table. Showing respect for their fallen brother, the other five continue playing standing up. Finally, Michael O'Conner looks around and asks, 'Well, me boys, someone's got to tell Paddy's wife. Who will it be?'

"They draw straws. Paul Gallagher picks the short one. They tell him to be discreet, be gentle, don't make a bad situation worse.

"'Discreet? I'm the most discreet Irishmen you'll ever meet. Discretion is me middle name. Leave it to me . . .'

"Gallagher goes over to Murphy's house and knocks on the door. Mrs. Murphy answers, and asks what he wants. Gallagher declares, 'Your husband just lost five hundred dollars, and is afraid to come home.'

"'Tell him to drop dead,' says Murphy's wife.

"'I'll go tell him.' says Gallagher."

Father Blu stepped backward and glanced at the EEG. I was surprised he had it in him, and I don't know what he saw. But it was the first time since I'd reawakened that I felt a smile, even if it didn't show.

"We're going to try something, you and I," he said. He reached to the chair in which Charli often sat, and pulled up the black and white notebook. He repeated what he'd told me before. "Charli says this isn't your handwriting. You indicated you've seen it before."

I looked at the page and thought *Valerie's idea of cleaning up was my idea of leaving a mess.* A bunch of chicken scratch. Then I flashed on her contorted face and screams as she was being consumed by the fire I'd set, so perfectly. I just wanted them all to let me die.

"Maybe it means nothing," he went on. "Maybe your girlfriend was helping you document something." It started as a statement, ended up a question. How much did he know about Valerie and me?

"Duke, I need you to look closely at this page." Again, he glanced over his shoulder to the hallway as if he'd be in trouble pushing me like that. "I'll say what I think it is. You blink once if it's *yes*, two if it's *no*. Okay?"

A note from Val! One I'd never seen. I surprised him and myself by rather quickly batting my eye. I seemed to be getting better at it.

"Wow, Duke, that's-that's excellent. Do you think this note is from Valerie Dunn?"

I blinked.

"Terrific." He skipped around. He lowered his voice. "This first one . . . " He pointed to the first entry, trying to contain himself.

10048:

He made it difficult. He tried equating the numbers to the alphabet: A-O-O-D-G. What did that mean? He tried connecting it to my wall of vinyl and CDs. Album #10048? He tried connecting it to the Book of Proverbs and to psalms by adding the numbers:

Psalm 148. By parsing the numbers: Psalm 10, Psalm 48 and so on. Obsessed with his religious forms.

He tried connecting it to a month and a year: January 2048 and January 1948.

No, no, no.

This went on for more than an hour, until I thought he was going to try to find a connection between Noah Syndergaard and Soren Kierkegaard. Each blink so exhausting, until I simply stopped replying.

About the time I wished I could scream him out of the room, Charli arrived. "What're you doing?"

"I'm trying to crack the code in this notebook," the Father said. "I think it has something to do with his music collection, maybe a note from someone—maybe Valerie Dunn before she died."

Charli looked at me, but of course she couldn't see my fatigue. "Let me see." She tugged the notebook out of his hands. She looked at the first entry. She pulled back the sleeve of my hospital gown. "There," she said pointing to the tattoo on my right arm and handed the notebook back to him. "One zero zero four eight."

"What's that mean?" he asked.

"It's a zip code," she explained. "It *used* to be. The Twin Towers. Duke was there and said he'd never forget."

Father Blu didn't hide his own restiveness. "So . . ." He held the notebook up. "You think this is about The World Trade Center and nine-eleven?"

"I think," she said taking it again and opening it to the one and only page on which there was writing, "that it's a note to or for him. See the colon?"

"Alright, then what do the rest of the notations mean?"

Charli looked at me. "Duke, do you want to continue this exercise?"

"Blink liked we agreed," said Father Blu.

Maybe they'd tie my suicide attempt to inconsolable grief. But with the mastery of an arson, who was I kidding? I was cooked. Or maybe they'd never know. So why not? I signaled *yes*.

"Okay," the Father said. "We'll start again tomorrow."

. . .

The next morning Father Blu and Charli arrived together. Apparently they'd had breakfast and had devised a more streamlined approach to decoding the book, breaking it down into smaller pieces. "This next entry," he pointed to it:

IRR/mir – 12:1-6

"Let's start by determining if you think this relates to Valerie Dunn, okay? In your opinion, did she write this? If you believe so, blink once. If not, blink twice."

I managed a blink.

"See," said Father Blu grinning at my sister. But something quickly seized him, realizing, I suppose, that my connection to Valerie was dark and probably damning.

"Okay, okay," she said full of enthusiasm. She settled on me. "Does this relate to your music collection?"

Blu shook off his uneasiness, he jumped in. "No, you can't ask it like that. He may have no idea. We've got to be precise." He showed me the page again. "I found this book tucked next to your music collection, behind that little white candle in the corner shelf. If you think it's *possible* these codes relate to your collection, blink once. Otherwise we'll move on to other ideas."

Codes. Why would she do that? But, yes, knowing Val, they could be codes. Only she had my apartment key. But how could I get the priest and my sister to reference those albums and CDs specifically? And maybe they meant nothing.

"Duke, that Jackie Greene tune, 'I'm So Gone,' was that your exit song? Did you want your sister to hear it?"

Charli put a hand on Father Blu's arm. "You said one question at a time."

He looked at her hand on his arm. He spoke to me. "You're right. Duke, was that *your* suicide note?"

It took every ounce of energy, but I batted my eye. Charli jumped.

"Okay. And you wanted your sister to hear it?"

I blinked again.

"Oh yes!" she said.

"You're doing great." Father Blu kept his eyes on me.

My sister's face was flush, I already felt drained.

"Let's go back to this first entry, could—do *you* suppose this 'IRR' relates to a song?" he asked.

They were throwing darts at several spinning targets, but who could blame them? I blinked twice.

"No?" Disappointment dragged at the priest's face.

"He's tired already," she said. "Maybe this isn't a great idea. The strain . . ."

"We're getting close to some answers," he said.

"But—"

"How bout this?" he continued. "I'm sure I can borrow a document projector somewhere and we'll throw the page onto the wall. Duke can look it over at his leisure . . ."

Leisure!

". . . and see if he sees a code. Let's give him a day to consider what it means."

She agreed and kissed me on the forehead. He smiled at me. My executioner.

When he led her out, he draped his fingers on her shoulder. The last thing I overheard him say to Charli was, "The girlfriend,

Valerie Dunn, she transferred quite a bit of money to her brother before she died."

That night a sharp squeaky sound woke me. Father Blu was moving the overhead projector into my room, with a woman; Teresa he called her. And from their brief and whispered conversation, I deduced that he was a member of an Alcoholics Anonymous group, which is where he'd borrowed the projector. He set the open notebook under the camera and it projected onto the wall. I studied it till I couldn't keep my mind on it. Anyone walking into the room might have thought my eyes were on it. I was asleep.

. . .

"Truly remarkable. Look at his encephalogram. He's been cognitive most of the night. And you notice, his eyes are *closed*. He's regained some motor control."

My eyes shot open. Dr. Kirschner and Charli jumped. "Duke," said my sister. "You're getting better."

I still lacked physical sensations. I missed my body almost as much as I missed Val's. Fucking Val.

"Can you move a finger, your head?" asked Dr. Krischner.

They watched me. I tried. I couldn't move.

"It's a little early for that," said the doctor. She spoke softly to my sister. "Don't expect anything. We're in untested waters."

"He can hear you," said Charli.

That's when Father Blu walked in. "How're we doing this morning?"

Charli met him half way and walked him to my bedside. "You were right." She hugged him. You'd have thought he was struck by lightning. His body keeled then quickly recovered, offering a polite, but compact, acknowledgement to the doctor.

"Duke, do you see a pattern?" He pointed to the wall and the projected page from the notebook.

From out of nowhere, I could, I did. I blinked.

Father Blu turned to my sister. "I think we should take him out of the hospital, to his apartment."

"Absolutely not," said Dr. Kirchner. "Any movement could set him back, maybe even dislodge the bullet and cause irreparable harm, even . . ." She didn't have to finish.

Charli's face wrenched. "Maybe we *should* wait."

Father Blu pulled Charli aside, much to the annoyance of the doctor, who kept talking. "His heart is strong. He's minimally conscious. We'll remove the EKG. We'll work on his premotor cortex."

Charli and the priest spoke quietly but animatedly in the corner. When they returned to my bedside and to Dr. Kirschner, Charli locked onto my face. "What do you want Duke? Shall we go to your apartment? You understand the danger of moving you?"

I had an attentive audience of three. Valerie's note—if that's what it was—might once and for all explain how I'd failed her. That would be worth a lot. It might explain those missing eighteen hours and my choice to destroy her. Even that would be *just*. There was so much I didn't understand.

Buried in that damn hospital bed another day, another minute, got me no closer to the truth. I could be helpless forever—suspended between life and death. More than anything I wanted movement, in some direction. Any direction. I had nothing to lose. I blinked.

"We'll rent a wheelchair and a brace," said Father Blu.

The doctor turned on Charli. "This is a mistake. We can't guarantee—"

Charli held up her hand. "It's decided."

CHAPTER 40

Father Blu

Father Toll knocked on my door and entered before I had time to consent. I looked up from my computer screen and from the bio and photo of Valerie Dunn's brother, Professor James Peter Dunn. It had added little to my fact-finding.

Father Toll's demeanor lacked the usual high superiority, though he smoothed back his hair in that way that indicated he remained satisfied with himself, as if he'd completed an unenviable task but that he was—as always—up to the demand.

"Father Toll?"

"I thought you should see this right away," he said, and crossed over to me and placed an envelope on the small table. Not the large manila envelope of photos that had been slipped under my door. My fingers went to it but its heat stopped me. "What is it?"

"It's from the Vicar. His inquiries have begun. He wants to see you."

My neck and shoulders stayed surprisingly loose, my mindset surprisingly sanguine. "Are you pleased?" I asked.

"No, why should I be pleased?" He leaned forward on my desk, looking down at me—over the computer—hands on each side of it. "You think I have it out for you, but you're mistaken. It's not personal. It's that you're not suited for this life."

I pushed back the chair and stood up, forcing him to back off. "I reflect badly on you."

"I told you it's not personal. You reflect badly on the church. You serve, but by your own rules."

"That sounds personal," I said.

"You know what I mean."

"Incompatible." I said.

"Yes, incompatible. You're not the kind to follow The Word. You think you know better than twenty-five centuries of canon and scripture."

"There seems to be so much grey area, don't you think?"

"Not at all." Father Toll, as always, casual in his intolerance.

"Questioning not so appreciated," I added.

"That works for the Jews, maybe you should convert."

I tapped the envelope. "I imagine the Vicar will have lots of questions."

"I imagine he will." Father Toll's temple pulsed, so acutely that he placed his hand to cover it, though he did so with ease. "What are you going to say to him?"

"I've already decided not to bring you or Sean Ducotty into the conversation; you've both already suffered enough."

He stood there for a moment, the incongruity of things cramping his mouth. "Thank you," he said, slightly nonplussed. He began to walk out as quickly as he'd entered.

I called after him, "You didn't need to send that woman, to take those pictures."

He stopped, his countenance already reverting to its stoic form. "What do you mean? I'm just the messenger."

"Maybe you're right," I said, "maybe the priesthood isn't for me."

"Hmmm, I'm sorry." His indifference an unavoidable, solipsistic precondition.

"But I do believe in divine intervention," I said. *Wherever it may come from.*

"That's something." He burnished his hair again. He yanked at his stole. He closed the door behind him.

For the first time in years, leaning on my intuition seemed better than the alternative.

• • •

The early morning AA meeting in the Church of the Resurrection was not one that I usually attended. But the pressure of Duke's impending showdown had me once again contemplating a drink, probably more than one. I was determined not to give in.

At that hour, a few chairs were circled in the church's basement and it was sparsely attended: besides me, a cleanly-shaven Hispanic man in his forties with trimmed Balbo facial hair read *El Diario*. A thin, balding woman in a flowered dress slept head down. A young boy, maybe fifteen or sixteen, tattoos in black, purple and red running up his legs and arms, rings piercing his nose and ears, sported a reverse Mohawk, a single shaved two-inch line down the center of his scalp. Even in the January cold, he dressed in a Lamb of God heavy metal t-shirt and cutoff baggies.

Did he know the chivalrous history of his haircut? According to Dad, my warrior ancestors had shaved their heads in dramatic ways to make their scalps more desirable to their enemies than those of the women and children in the tribe.

"Father Jamie!" Teresa, in what looked like blue-issue uniform slacks and a mismatched beige blouse, offered a lovely, if self-conscious, smile.

"Well, hi." I slipped in next to her.

She glanced at the teenager who glowered back.

"You're here early," I said.

"And you."

The boy continued to stare malevolently at her. I didn't like it.

"Don't worry," she said, seeing the boy's obvious hostility and my discomfort with it. "I brought him. I made him a deal. I let him off last night in exchange for his attendance today. I wasn't sure he'd even show up."

"Let him off?"

"I'm a dispatcher, NYPD. I was on desk when they brought him in. In the scheme of things, a minor offense but he was headed for The Tank, an all-nighter. The kid didn't stand a chance in there, not last night."

"That was kind."

She shrugged.

"How are you doing otherwise?" I asked.

"Tired. And you?"

"Tired." The old stories—Duke's, mine and Jory's—all seemed bundled. "But yielding."

A twinkle rose in her eyes. "To the present?"

"Yes."

She nodded. "Staying present is the only way to crack the cycle, but it's not easy." She leaned into me and a young Filipino woman stepped into our small circle and took a seat. "Hi," the young woman said, "I'm Ashley and I'm an alcoholic."

. . .

By noon, Duke's hospital room buzzed with activity. Two nurses scurried out. Charli had already settled Duke into his wheelchair and head brace. "You're sure you want to do this?" I asked.

He blinked and we were on our way in a rented van equipped

for wheelchairs. The driver, a turban wrapped around his head, talked nonstop. Charli and I didn't say more than five words, each of us aware that the four-mile round trip was a reckoning. Duke stared straight ahead.

At Duke's apartment, the driver laid down a metal ramp to the building's front door and helped me push Duke up it. From there, we told the driver to find a coffee shop and wait for our call. He seemed miffed, standing there until Charli and I wheeled Duke down the hallway to the rear of the building. A stink of burnt popcorn wafted from the lone nearby apartment. Only then I remembered how I'd left Duke's apartment an embattled war zone.

At the apartment door, I tugged on Charli's arm and pulled Duke's wheelchair to a stop. "In Duke's sensitive state, do you think he'll get upset if his apartment isn't as he left it?"

I didn't intend it to be humorous, but it broke the tension for her and she chuckled. "I don't think he thought he'd ever see it in *any* state again. What do you mean?"

"Well, you know how organized he is, maybe even a bit persnickety."

She kicked me—forced my eyes to follow hers to the back of her brother's head. *He could hear me.* "Right. Okay," I said. "But will he get upset?"

Just as quickly, awareness crossed her face. "I should have cleaned the blood off the wall."

"No, no. It's not that bad," I said. "There's not that much."

"Really? I guess if you say so." She readied the key in the door, so easily persuaded.

I held back her arm. "I left the apartment . . . a mess the last time I was here." I bowed my head.

"How bad?"

"Pretty bad. I broke things. I'd been drinking."

"Drinking. Again. You were drunk?" Her disillusionment undisguised.

"I'm sorry." I waited—I don't know for *what*. Dispensation? Finally, "Can he take it? Will you forgive me?"

She thought for a second, then came around to face Duke. "Duke, are you okay if Father Blu made kind of a mess of your place? Do you still want to go in?"

I'm not sure *kind of a mess* accurately described what I'd wreaked, but Duke blinked. She unlocked the door and wheeled him in.

An apocalyptic landscape stretched out before us: the empty bottle of scotch, the overturned stools, the shattered dishes. But the signed photo of Boz Scaggs and Donald Fagen had been set straight, and above it, the smoke detector hung open from the ceiling. It was the disaster I'd created . . . but different.

Duke gurgled. The first sounds we'd heard from him. I took it as a laugh. I swiveled to him and then to Charli. "Did you hear that?"

"Yeah, it sounded like a laugh." She knelt to make eye contact with her brother. "Duke, did you laugh?"

We gawked at him. He blinked.

Charli began hopping from foot to foot. She spun around. "Oh, my God! Oh, my God!" A little girl just given a pony.

Delighted and also bewildered, I questioned myself. "This isn't how I left it."

She stopped twirling. "What do you mean? *This* is pretty specific."

I scanned the room again. "No."

"Maybe you just thought—"

"No, Charli, believe me this-this is *not* how I left it."

"Maybe not, but since you and I are the only ones with keys, let's agree for now to move on." She started patting the satchel. "Where's the notebook?"

I pulled the composition book from the pouch, mystified and still craning to see what else had been moved or displaced. I handed her the notebook. "Hold it in front of Duke. You ready?"

Charli nodded. Duke blinked.

"Alright," I said. "What's the first one?"

"IRR/mir −12:1-6," read Charli. "I'm guessing he has them alphabetized in some way."

My fingers ran along the spines of the albums, then the CDs. "He seems to be coding them by artist. Is that what you were doing Duke?"

He blinked. Charli squealed in delight.

"Calm. Let's just stay calm." I ran my fingers to IRO, Iron Butterfly. The music picked up again at ISL, Isley Brothers. "There's no IRR. The space is empty." I bent toward Duke. "Should there be a CD?"

He blinked.

"A missing CD," I said aloud to no one in particular. "Let's try the next one."

Charli read it off. "CAM/des − 9:4-7+22"

At the top of the stacks, I ran my fingers along the vinyl, then the CDs. "JJ Cale and Lou Reed, Cab Calloway, Camera Obscura—CAM. Next writing is *d-e-s*?"

"Yes."

I withdrew the CD from the shelf. "Maybe a song title . . ."

"Or the name of the album. Maybe the group has more than one album," she said.

"This one is called . . ." I turned it over, "*Desire Lines*."

"That would be *d-e-s*," she said.

"Yes, yes. Next?"

"9:4-7+22"

"Ninth cut, lines four through seven."

"Plus twenty-two," Charli added. "Put it in the CD player. Do you think this might be it, Duke?" While she looked at Duke I fumbled with the player.

"Yes, you do?" I heard her say to him.

"Can you jot down the lyrics?" I said to her.

I started cut nine. We listened. We watched Duke. "Play it again," said Charli feverishly writing down the words.

"Did you get them?"

She checked the jottings on her page. "I think so. Starting with the fourth line . . . "

> *All I ever wanted was someone to rely on*
> *All I ever wanted was somewhere to call home*
> *You offer a friendship I cannot reciprocate*
> *So don't beg me, in a garden, for it not to end this way*

"Last line, line twenty-two . . ."

> *I decided to be only myself these days*

We looked at Duke. I'm sure I saw moisture in his eyes. "Duke, does this sound like a note to you?" It took a moment, but he blinked. "Let's try the next one."

It took us over an hour to find the correct musician, album, cut and compile the lyrics from each song, all but the last one which, like the first CD and song notated, was missing.

Song Number Three was HOL/lad – 5:3-8+11&12: Billie Holiday/*Lady In Satin*:

> *A kiss that is never tasted*
> *Forever and ever is wasted*
> *For all we know, we may never meet again*
> *Before you go, make this moment sweet again*
> *We won't say, goodnight until the last minute*
> *I'll hold out my hand and my heart will be in it*
> *So love me tonight, tomorrow was made for some*
> *Tomorrow may never come, for all we know*

Song Number Four was VAS/leg – 9:24-27: Tiburcio Vásquez Band/*Legendary*:

> *Mister Jimmy laughed,*
> *solution so simple he said,*
> *Dust will soon settle,*
> *if simple is 'dead'*

As I said, song Number Five was missing.

"We'd better get him back to the hospital." Charli put down her pen, her fatigue beginning to show.

She was right. But again, surveying the decimated living room and kitchen, I knew I needed to return that night; someone had come in after my drunken trashing. But who and why?

. . .

After we got Duke re-situated in the hospital, I grabbed a cab and headed back to his apartment. I stood under the decommissioned smoke detector. I questioned myself about the signed photo of Boz Scaggs and Donald Fagen.

No, I'd definitely last seen it crooked, my bout with the bottle indiscriminate in matters of *feng shui*. I hadn't righted it.

Going room to room, I looked to see if anything else had been touched or reorganized. Nothing jumped out at me. Even the other smoke detectors didn't appear to have been tampered with, until I got to the bedroom. There, as with the front room, the smoke detector was flung open without a battery.

As much as I resisted the thought, the idea that Father Toll had been there, looking for clues and ways to discredit Duke, did keep percolating in my head. How he might have gotten in, I couldn't say. Nor did I want to believe it.

On my way out, I stopped at the neighbor's door. After three or four knocks, Mrs. Rivet, Duke's neighbor, came to the door, her eye rotating around the peephole. "What is it?"

I introduced myself as Duke's priest. She talked through the door. No, she said, she hadn't seen anyone come in or out of Duke's apartment, except another fireman maybe a month ago. "I'm not the nosey type," she added.

"How do you know it was a fireman?" I asked.

"Had one of those heavy jackets," she said.

"Can you describe him?"

"Not the nosey type."

"Young? Old? Tall? Short?"

"Didn't see much through the door."

"Were you friendly with Mr. Ducotty?"

"Only in the hall from time to time. Nice enough lookin'. How is he?" She cracked open the door, a chain allowing four inches of visibility. She looked to be mid-sixties, with curlers, a young nose on a stretched face, and camouflage battle fatigues unbuttoned half-way down. "I heard he shot himself."

"Yes. Did you ever meet his girlfriend?"

"Stress?" she said.

"Probably."

"Or guilt." She waited for my reaction.

"He's in a kind of coma, but he may be coming out of it. The girlfriend?" I repeated.

"Oh, that's good. Thought he was gay."

"Why do you say that?" I asked.

"Never had any women around. Even tried to interest him."

"Oh."

"I have my ways. Not interested." She began unlatching the chain. "Would you like to come in? Have some popcorn?"

"I really have to go. Why do you say *guilt*?"

"We all have it, don't ya think? Maybe he had a lot. You sure you don't want to come in for a little Orville Redenbacher's?"

I thanked her. She jammed the door closed.

Moving down the hall, the more I thought about it, I didn't want the police involved before Charli, Duke and I could properly decipher Valerie's notes to Duke. And maybe there were additional notations that we'd missed. Calling Detective Zhōng might be met with disinterest but it might also mean Duke's apartment would be cordoned off from us; things moved around. I doubted that Detective Zhōng had made more than a perfunctory search of the apartment in the first place, given that Duke's *was* a suicide attempt. So what would be gained?

I needed someone I could trust, someone to talk to me about the situation, someone who knew Duke. So few really knew him. I wrestled with the idea of calling Captain Hoyle or Hakim Vaughn. But if a fireman had been in the apartment, who and why? Charli might have some notions, but she already thought I imagined things. Which was true, though she'd never have believed the things that I'd started accepting. Jean Stein was too remote.

I called Chuck Winston and asked him to come over. Despite the exigency in my voice, he was not nearly so motivated. He said he'd be over in the next week or so, that he had a number of things to attend to. I had no choice; I'd already asked a lot of him and decided a few more days would hardly make a difference. After all, Duke's story, like Jory's, appeared static and rooted in the past. I didn't need to be.

CHAPTER 41

Duke

Valerie's coded messages left me even more guilty, more despairing, more depressed—if that was possible. But apparently she'd wanted to reach out to me, a last-ditch effort to have me understand her love for me. Then left. *Why?* What kind of strange love is that?

The gay bar scene replayed in my head. The two guys bumping down the hallway in lust. Even other patrons found it over the top. When I said so, it wasn't exactly revelatory. But when I said so, *something* shifted. Or maybe it was just before. Or just after.

My attempts at unraveling Valerie's logic were now even more chaotic. Unresponsive to outside physical stimuli, I'd become all nerve endings inside. I was so fucked up.

I continued to study the projected image from Val's composition notebook. Her scribblings were going to follow me to my grave, a death march that would unfold endlessly for years without me taking a single step. Surrounded by hospital walls and spider-like medical devices, monitoring everything but what mattered.

More to the point, I'd murdered. I deserved it. All of it. When Father Blu discovered the truth—and it appeared to be imminent—he would rightly condemn me to a double hell for the two most heinous, unforgiveable sins I'd committed. He'd also sentence Charli to carry the burden of them for the rest of *her* days. He was either a messiah or a meddling bible-thumping moralist.

Hell, of course, had already begun, and it stretched out forever. Now all in motion, at least I would find out *why*. I focused on the code from the two missing albums:

$$IRR/mir - 12:1-6$$
$$MOT/whe - 1:2-6+11-12$$

"West Fifty-fourth Street? That's next to the Museum of Modern Art." Father Blu listened intently to the woman on the other end of the call. Her squawk spilled into my hospital room. "Yes, Teresa, thank you. You're a lifesaver."

"Who was that?" my sister asked.

"A friend in the NYPD. She found the temporary address for Valerie Dunn's brother."

"I want to go." Charli pulled her overcoat from the chair.

"I'm not sure that's wise," the Father said.

I'm going too. With all my energy, I-I-I gurgled. *I gurgled!*

"Duke?!" My sister laid her hand on my chest. "What are you trying to tell us?"

The priest began his retreat. "You should stay here. Go have some dinner." *He knew it could get ugly.*

"Is that it?" my sister asked me. "You want to go too?"

Anything that would bring some order to my tangled brain; nothing worse than half-way in and half-way out. I made another noise. I blinked.

Charli looked at Father Blu. "Why can't he go? He's up to the task, you saw that the other day."

"Let's not overdo," argued the priest.

She ran her hand into her pocketbook. "If you won't call the van, I will."

. . .

It was a small but once distinguished hotel on the West Side. Classic. From another time and place. Crenulated rows of light bulbs glowed a pale yellow across the grand marquee presiding over the entrance.

Hotel Darsett

I hadn't known what to expect, but I hadn't expected this, a place so luminous and welcoming.

We entered through the glass, brass-lined side door. Father Blu rolled me into the lobby. On my left, a newspaper stand, the size of a closet, with magazines, candies and gum. A middle-aged man with a skinny, outdated mustache and a clever aura, sat behind the glass counter, looked over his spectacles at us, nodded *hello* then went back to reading his newspaper.

To my right, along the wall, several highly polished brass doors, ostensibly for luggage and storage. A regal carpet in royal blue, red, white and gold, with a medallion in the center, spread out past the spacious front desk, through to a wide hallway, and then to a brightly lit glass-enclosed restaurant that felt stately even forty yards away.

Above us on a large coved cathedral ceiling, were hand painted blue skies and billowy white clouds, lit by retrofit bulbs along the perimeter. Possibly the closest I'd ever get to heaven, if such a place existed.

A floral bouquet tickled my nose. Roses perhaps. For a moment I could imagine an earlier life, before Valerie, even before my career as a fireman. When everything was possible, before my heart had been repeatedly shredded. The hotel's vibe brought my anxiety down a few notches.

Two gentlemen behind the front desk, dressed with a splash of British old-world charm—modified tux and boutonnière— acknowledged us. They were about to ask if they could help us when Father Blu nodded at them and bolted past, wheeling me into the elevator corridor.

"You know his room number?" Charli kept looking over her shoulder, expecting the men behind the front desk to remove us or have someone less courteous do so.

One of the two elevators opened up. An amiable, thin-lipped man in a braided mustard brown military dress hat and a matching jacket with epaulets, stepped forward welcoming us in. His brass buttons caught the light.

Once in, it was tight. Was I a convicted man going to his execution? Or a bird in a cage, watching life around me with nothing more to do, no implications? Except for the guilt. If I'd been able to speak, I would've been so ashamed of meeting James Dunn that I would never have been there; nothing I could say would ever undo the wrong I'd done.

If my sister had suffered Val's fate, and the assassin showed up at my door, I'd tear out his jugular and watch him bleed to death, eyeball to eyeball. But as that option was off the table, I became an observer at my own flagellation, so richly warranted.

Beyond that, I suppose I was hoping for some sort of clarity, something that James Dunn could tell us about Valerie that would decode the riddle of her love. What Charli and Father Blu could gain from meeting him, I didn't know, although my crime might become apparent. I just knew what I was searching for and that I had to be there.

In the elevator, Charli relaxed a bit, surveying up and around its bygone allure. "Some place, huh?" The lift operator, who reminded me of James Taylor, smiled and nodded. He closed the scissor gate, the paneled doors slid shut, and he pulled the antique bronze lever upwards. A faint bump jiggled my wheelchair and promptly smoothed out as he took us skyward.

At the top, the fifteenth floor, he opened the gates for us and we rolled out. Without so much as a word, he quietly closed the gate and disappeared into the guts of the building.

I steeled myself for Valerie's brother, his hands, his mouth, the way he moved. The start of my long, plodding penance. We rolled down the hall to the right, all the way to the end.

"You're sure you want to do this, Duke?" Father Blu looked at me, also quickly to my sister. Of the three of us, Father Blu wore the risk most outwardly, belonging I guess to his grinding examination of my sins. For all my irritation with his ordered piety and his clinging to the cross, substantial ravines had cut deeply through his face since the first time I'd seen him.

Ironically, my blank face told them nothing of how *I'd* aged, nothing of my drumming heart. I braced for the rush of shame that seeing Valerie's brother might unleash—almost certainly *would* unleash.

Charli tried to withhold her worry, but the questions had started mounting for her too—I could see the tension around her mouth.

"Do you?" The Father's eyes jerked nervously as if he was the convict walking death row. "You're sure, Duke? If so, blink." He'd spent every ounce of his being to be here and he didn't want to leave without some judgment. In that way, we were alike. "We can go home, if you've changed your mind," he repeated.

I'd earned it. All of it. My responsibility. I blinked.

Father Blu pressed the brass doorbell. It pinged, a flat uncaring sound that clashed with everything we'd seen and smelled since we'd entered the building.

He pressed it again.

My sister drew a weighty breath. We heard footsteps. Whatever it looked like, this was the portal to my remaining reality.

The door opened and the man took a surprised step backward.

"I thought you were someone else." He had a deep voice; professorial, mid-forties with glasses and disheveled reddish hair. Not at all what I expected.

"James Dunn? Professor James Dunn?" asked Father Blu. "May we come in?" Father Blu took hold of my wheelchair but the man held up his hand.

"No. Who are you?" He held very little resemblance to Valerie.

"You are James Dunn, aren't you?" repeated Father Blu.

Beyond the doorway, past the man, into the apartment, down the hall, an oval mirror reflected the dim, flickering light of the living room. It caught a fragment of me in the wheelchair: a fair representation.

"James P. Dunn?" repeated Father Blu.

"I am. What is it you want? How'd you get past the front desk?"

"Jimmy?" A husky voice came from inside the apartment. "Is it Colin Grassley?"

"No," he called back.

I thought he was going to close the door in our face. But we were such a motley crew that perhaps he needed some sort of explanation before doing so.

Father Blu said something. I refocused on the mirror. On the edge of the reflection, a candle dipped and swayed in the living room. And with the draft a tail appeared like a lazy whip, switching back and forth. A fat orange tabby cat.

A man came into the room, his shoulders reflected in the looking glass. He had dark, neatly cropped hair and wore a blue pinstriped suit. He crouched down and murmured to the cat, "Catalona."

He turned toward the mirror. His suit jacket fell open revealing a black Steely Dan t-shirt, his face haunting and familiar. He picked up the cat, his left hand missing the pinky finger. Scent memory bludgeoned then overcame me. It was Valerie!

"You're not welcome here." James Dunn began to close the door.

"I'll call security."

I couldn't cry out, but Valerie, or her male doppelganger, had already vanished from the mirror.

"Please," said Father Blu.

Neither he nor Charli had seen what I had. And what would they know; they'd never seen Valerie. Still I questioned the apparition; my mind unable to manage the truth of what I'd seen. Neither my sister nor the priest could confirm my absolution, if in fact, I had glimpsed the future.

James Dunn slammed the door. The deadbolt clicked.

The three of us remained inert, shackled by the still uncertain past and time to come, until finally Charli said, "We better get out of here."

"I'll have to come back," said Father Blu.

Our trip to the lobby was marked by the elevator's hum and little else, all of us trying to tie shreds of information together. My head spun with contradictions and images. That damn cat, Catalona, alive. Jimmy—after all my jealous thoughts—Valerie's brother. The man I'd seen within the hotel suite ever-so-briefly was either Val's *twin* brother or . . . or it was Valerie, Valerie metamorphosed.

I thought about the musical notes she'd left me, *loving* notes, notes trying to explain her torment, while my expectations had colored everything through my own refracted lens. She'd loved and wanted me, but knew I could never love her *that* way, as a man.

It might also explain the scars on her arm, self-inflicted in response to her dilemma, or as a gambit to keep me away. It might explain the large sum of money going to her brother, her savings, her life insurance. I imagined an operation like the one Val went through to be expensive; the price one pays to start a new life. The naked photos, to chronicle the metamorphosis. And the hormones, which would change her scent forever. She liked men, wanted to be with a man, as a man.

But, we *had* loved. We had loved!

Shock, relief, longing and mourning; my throat constricted then gradually surrendered. The paradoxes painful. But her secret was safe with me. My dear friend's secret.

"You okay?" asked Father Blu as he pushed me out into the celestial hotel lobby.

Charli glanced down at me. "Duke?"

I was fixed dead ahead while my mind continued, overwhelmed, in multiple directions.

"Let's just get him out of here." Charli hastened to the door and opened it.

We passed the closet magazine stand and the little man with the thin mustache. He looked at me and nodded, like St. Peter at the gate. *Not quite yet*, he seemed to say, waving goodbye, *but some-day down the road*. Father Blu wheeled me out of heaven.

CHAPTER 42

Father Blu

"Come in here. What are these?" Chief Winston had been poking around Duke's apartment and had drifted into his bedroom.

I wandered in from the kitchen. "What is what?"

He held up two CDs. "I found these under the pillow."

My neck tingled. Duke, always fastidious, bed always made, had not slept in the bed the night of his suicide attempt. "Chuck, let me see those."

The two missing CDs? On the first cover, an androgynous individual smeared in makeup and reflected in a quadrant of mirrors. The Irrepressibles, *Mirror, Mirror.* The second CD: four men in 1800's roadwork clothing, standing in front of a barn and horse buggy. Motherlode, *When I Die.*

"I need to listen to these," I said, leaving Chuck Winston to continue searching the bedroom, bathroom and closets. The CDs were Valerie's final two notes to Duke, the first and the last. I put them on and wrote down the lyrics:

IRR/mir – 12:1-6 (the twelfth cut, "In This Shirt")

I am lost in our rainbow

Now our rainbow is gone
Overcast by your shadow
As our worlds move on
In this shirt I can be you
To be near you for a while

MOT/whe – 1:2-6+11-12 (the first cut, "When I Die")
When I die I hope to be
A better man than you thought I'd be
It's been hard to make you see
What kind of man I'm tryin' to be
All I ask for you to try
To understand what it means to me
But I love you
Love you

Duke would understand, even if I didn't.

"Son of a bitch!" Chuck's voice echoed down the hallway.

"Look at these," he said when I arrived. He was kneeling in the bathroom and pulling containers out from under the sink. "There's no way." He shook his head. "No way."

Surrounding Chuck on the floor were the usual items found in a man's bathroom: toothpaste, shaving cream and blades, a bottle of Ibuprofen, even a naked photo of a woman, an almost clinical photo given the woman's self-conscious manner. *Had Duke coerced her to take the photo?*

But Winston had sectioned off a few other items that didn't look commonplace. "This one," he said holding up a metal quart container. "Take a whiff, a very small one. Careful." He unscrewed the cap.

A yellowish liquid with a disagreeable odor. "Ouff, that's awful," I said.

He quickly recapped it. "Carbon disulfide. And this . . . "

He held up a small glass bottle of white powder. "Magnesium. Combustible dust."

"What's Duke doing with this stuff?"

Chuck kept going. "And this, do you recognize this?"

"Should I?"

Then he realized. "Of course not, the can you saw was blackened and the label had been burned off. It's D-D Mixture."

"Did you see the can?" I asked.

"No, I'm just guessing."

"Okay," I said waving at the D-D Mixture. "So . . . ?"

"So these are all extremely combustible and not the kind of chemicals anyone conversant with fire would keep around the house, certainly not stashed away under a sink. And the date codes have been torn or filed off the containers. Someone didn't want the chemicals to be identified chronologically."

I felt myself falling. "Duke set those fires, didn't he?"

"No, not Duke. Not the Duke I know. He's too smart. And why would he care about the dates on the containers? No, these were planted. Didn't you say someone had been in the apartment; that's why you wanted me to come in?"

I nodded. "The neutralized smoke detectors."

"Part of the set up. No one holding these chemicals would have working smoke detectors around, too volatile. I'll bet if you look at the others in this apartment, you'll find them empty of batteries too."

"But who . . . ?" I said.

"Someone with a deep understanding of fire and firefighting, someone who could imitate what a knowledgeable firefighter might do, if *they* were trying to hide their crimes."

"A kind of reverse engineering."

"Yeah." He let go a big sigh, deciding whether to take me into his confidence. "The arson unit has been closing in for weeks. And word has been leaking out. I think these . . ." He tapped the nefarious containers. ". . . are meant to steer us away from the real pyro."

Again, he seemed to consider whether to share any more information with me. The went on. "AIU tracked down some receipts, I'll tell you that. And I'll bet these combustibles were purchased since Duke's been in the hospital. That would account for the obliterated date codes. And you remember Duke's suicide weapon, the one that was purportedly stolen from that arson-set gun shop fire, but wasn't? I think that was planted too, to give the impression that Duke had been the arsonist."

He scanned the room and nodded with assurance. "You can tell Duke he's probably off the hook." He caught himself. "Little good that'll do him now, even if he could hear you."

"Oh," I slipped the two CDs in my satchel, "he'll hear me."

. . .

A steady Valentine's Day wind blustered in from the south, an almost record setting sixty-two degrees. I decided to walk to the hospital. As usual, cynicism ate at me. Wasn't Chuck Winston's blueprint a little too neat? He was awfully sure what the exploded can of D-D Mixture looked like. Did he have a stake in the outcome of the arson investigations? Was he protecting Duke? Was he protecting himself?

I called the Darsett Hotel and was told Professor Dunn had checked out.

I called information looking for Colin Grassley's phone number and I was directed to his office phone, and a recorded greeting by a woman with an English accent: *"You've reached the offices of Colin Grassley, Psychiatrist, MD, MSW, LPCS, and CASAC substance abuse therapist, specializing in transgender counseling and preparedness. Office hours are by appointment only. General messages may be left here. If you* are a patient, please use the private, non-published phone number you were given during intake. There will be no greeting on that phone. Just leave your name and message at the beep. The doctor or staff will return your call."

I hung up. I redialed the remaining unidentified phone number from Duke's cell phone. *No greeting and a beep.*

I plugged Grassley's name into my web browser. His website repeated all his acronyms and proficiencies. An odd-looking character, thin, stringy hair, wearing a silver bolo etched with a Native American sun and the words "Two Spirit." Though I never heard of it in Mohawk culture, I understood it to mean that Two Spirit people are those blessed by their Creator to see life through the eyes of both genders. Again, Duke might make sense of these scraps, I couldn't.

But even without all the details to his story, Duke's courageous legacy had been resurrected and his sister spared additional pain. I'd come more than half way, and felt warm, and somewhat absolved— of what, I wasn't quite sure yet.

I stopped at Our Lady of Sorrows and gathered my things. I changed into a sweatshirt and jeans. I waved at Father Toll's secretary and told her I'd call with a forwarding address as soon as I got resettled. Caught unaware, she began to question what I'd said. Before she could, I asked, "Is he in?"

"Yes," she stammered, "but he doesn't want to be disturbed, he's preparing to teach catechism."

"Yes, of course, Luke 1:4, 'That you may have certainty concerning the things you have been taught.'"

She looked befuddled. "Excuse me?"

"Tell him I'll be by in the next week to thank him personally."

"Wait," she said. "I see him coming out of his office."

He sighted me and called out. I stopped and took a breath. "Father Jamie." He surveyed my jeans and sweatshirt. "I see you're leaving."

"Yes, thanks for having me in your parish. It's time for me to go."

He acknowledged my appreciation then straightaway something vaguely akin to contrition mounted his face. "I want you to know that I too began questioning who took those photos of you—not that that excuses you. I asked Father Quade to track down the lab that processed them. And he did, some small initials on a corner of the photos."

"And?"

"The lab told Father Quade they didn't know the name of the man who'd brought them in. Only that the man had waited for the photos to be processed and paid cash. The clerk remembered one other thing."

"What was that?" I said.

"The man reeked of cigar. You know anyone like that?"

A cloud lifted. "I might."

. . .

As I made my way to the hospital Teresa called, winded, on her way to the precinct. "I'm checking in. Was that information helpful? Did you find James Dunn?"

"Yes, thanks," I said.

"You sound good."

"I'm feeling good but . . ."

"But what?"

"Maybe God's out of style." I confessed, "I'm leaving the Church."

"He isn't out of style," she said, "the church is. I think it's a Hindu saying. 'We'll hide man's divinity where he can't see it: inside him. He'll search the whole world but never look inside and find what's already within.'"

I pictured Teresa's round, genial face and reddish tinged skin, the color of Madagascar passion fruit. "Would you like to have coffee sometime?"

"Why yes, Father—"

"—Jamie. From now on, just Jamie."

"Jamie. Yes, I'd like that."

. . .

With the final two CDs in my satchel I hoped to offer Duke some closure, though I guessed that I'd never completely decode what had transpired. Nor would I fully understand what had happened to me. There had been forces . . . more than one, I theorized, that had assisted me. Maybe even my brother, releasing me from long-buried mistakes and my shame with them.

And if Hoyle had those photos taken of me, it's because he wanted me to stop poking around, just like Father Toll. But for different reasons.

For Toll it was about vengeance and protecting his brother. I understood. When I drew so much attention, I became a liability.

Hoyle? I imagined that the arson investigations would offer a few more answers. Unfortunately, that still left Duke damaged.

Charli sat by his side and smiled up at me. "Father."

I unwrapped my pouch. "Let me play these."

Charli moved around Duke's bed to give me space. We brushed against each other. Her eyes widened, those spectacular gem green orbs on that pale perfect skin. For the first time I sensed an invitation. As if she saw me as a man rather than a caricature, and wanted to discover more. A fascinating invitation. But in my heart I'd already committed, at least for the time being, to another direction.

"Can I share something with you that I've learned tending to your brother?" I said.

"Sure."

"There's a difference between guilt—*it's my fault*— and remorse: *I'm sad this happened.* I think we both need to keep that in mind."

Then I played *Mirror, Mirror* and the *When I Die* CD. She and

Duke listened attentively to them—at least he appeared to. When the last song finished, his EEG had spiked several times and the genesis of a tear moistened his left eye, another good sign.

"What does it mean?" she asked.

"I don't know, but it sounds like this woman Valerie really loved him."

She looked at her brother, as if to say *you realize you've been loved*. I could only hope that affirmation had reached him.

"Was it an accident, the fire that killed her?" asked Charli.

"I don't think so," I said.

"Then who killed her? Why? Duke wouldn't do that to someone who loved him, wouldn't do that to anyone."

I wanted to say, *There's no certainty to that*. But I just shrugged. "I don't think we'll ever know. But I wanted to show Duke this, this man's face. Not sure if it will mean anything to him, but it was Valerie Dunn's therapist." I pulled out my laptop and opened it to Colin Grassley's web page. Duke just stared at it. Who knows what he thought.

Arthur Bridges, the maintenance man who'd lent us the iPod, stuck his head into the room. "How's the Duke doin'?"

As he did, and Charli welcomed him in, my cellphone pinged. "Excuse me," I said and walked out of the room and down the hall to view it: a text, from Chuck Winston:

FIRST ARSON REPORT OUT.
CHEMICALS FOUND IN DUKE'S APARTMENT
PURCHASED AFTER SUICIDE ATTEMPT.
CAPTAIN HOYLE DETAINED.
THOUGHT YOU'D WANT TO KNOW.

I'd tell Chuck Winston about the defamatory photos Hoyle had taken of me. Maybe Chuck would see the connection. I started back down the hallway, stopped and rested against a wall. Duke was free, as free as he could be under the circumstances. And, in some small way, I too had been released. I swept away the bead of moisture clouding my eyes.

Even before entering Duke's room, I heard music coming from it. Inside, Charli was in conversation with Arthur, both swaying ever so slightly to the music, Duke propped up in his bed, another inkling of a smile. "Father," she said, uncertain of my new attire, "I was wrong about your faith."

"Jamie, just Jamie," I said.

"Jamie, I was wrong about your faith. You had it all the time."

"No, you were dead-on. It wavered. I labor with strict doctrine. I need to work with ambiguity."

She surveyed me with approval. "I've never seen you out of your clerical blacks."

"Pope Francis says spirit is not the property of the hierarchy. That we need to go out to meet the people, to create and sow hope, to proclaim the faith, not from a pulpit but from our everyday life. Ergo the sweatpants."

She hung her head with a smile. Then came back up, "You're turning in/swapping out your collar?"

"The collar, yes. I think it's better for all concerned. I'm gonna find something more flexible. I'm just not sure yet what that exactly will be. But I agree with the Pope, 'I prefer a Church which is bruised, hurting and dirty because it's been out on the streets.'" *And if I'm a part of nature, I have the power—even if it's a small, positive exhale in the scheme of things—to put something positive into our shared nature, into our shared air.*

"Well, thank you." She touched Duke's arm. "My brother thanks you. The doctors think he's on his way. Maybe not a full recovery, but one in which he can function." She hesitated then embraced me. "You're terrific."

A mite uncomfortable, I patted her shoulders. "Who knew?"

She hugged a little tighter.

"What's that song?" A bit flustered, I tilted my head to the speakers.

"Stardust," said Arthur Bridges. "A classic."

And we all took a moment to listen:

> *Sometimes I wonder why I spend the lonely nights*
> *Dreaming of a song*
> *The melody haunts my reverie . . .*

"Life can only be understood backwards;
but it must be lived forwards."
Søren Kierkegaard

About the Author

PG LENGSFELDER wrote and edited his first newspaper at age seven, when he thought he was destined to be a fireman or a forest ranger. But sales of his paper reached a heady circulation of ten—at five cents a copy! He was hooked: he had readers. He's been writing ever since.

He began as a copywriter in a major New York advertising agency and co-authored the best-selling nonfiction book *FILTHY RICH* (Ten Speed Press). His first novel *BEAUTIFUL TO THE BONE* (Woodsmoke Publishing) met with critical acclaim, and he has written for numerous publications including Frontier Tales, Rocky Mountain Magazine, ArtLines magazine, and Patterns. His stories have been heard on National Public Radio and seen on CNN, Discovery Channel and other national television. He's been awarded a regional Emmy and been nominated for four others. A member of Mystery Writers of America and Rocky Mountain Fiction Writers, he lives in Colorado with his rescue dog Lakota. He believes that not everything that's real can be seen. And still, after all these years, when he can get away from his keyboard, he's happiest in nature.

Acknowledgements

As with any journey, many people have reached out to lend a hand, to push me forward or slap me upside my head to keep me on course—especially as this route took longer than I expected. Life's like that sometimes.

Thank you to my first line of cheerleaders, fellow writers Les Standiford, James W. Hall, and my writing buddy Leslie Budewitz. Your practical suggestions, insights and encouragement got me off to a good start. To my editors Peter Gelfan and Brenda Windberg, thanks as always for helping me map out a solid path. And just before crossing the finish line, Mitchell Waters at Brandt & Hochman Literary Agency offered valuable support and observations. Very much appreciated.

I'm grateful, too, to the experienced voices that kept my job-related facts on firm ground. Immeasurable thanks to Deputy Chief Trevor Richmond of the Los Angeles Fire Department, San Fernando Valley Operations; Deputy Chief John Sarracco, New Yok City Fire Department; and my dear friend Mark Evanoff, San Francisco Fire Department (retired). Also to Lynn Stadler, MA, MFT; Curtis Crane, MD, Plastic Surgery & Reconstructive Urology; Don G. Stein, PhD Neurologist; and my long-time friend Cindy Arch, who helped me wrangle the mysteries of Catholic language and hierarchy. The time each of you gave me freely will never be forgotten, and hopefully offers my readers a real view of these professions.

Finally, I cannot stress how important the following friends were to my health and my ability to complete this novel. Thank you, you will always be in my heart for your shelter from the storm:

Linda Brentano & Charlie Orth   Janet & John Lengsfelder
Sharon & Steve Eisler   Francie Martin-Olson
Tis & Bill Joseph   Rico McMahon

Song Credits